Madam by Margaret Oliphant

Margaret Oliphant Wilson was born on April 4th, 1828 to Francis W. Wilson, a clerk, and Margaret Oliphant, at Wallyford, near Musselburgh, East Lothian.

Her youth was spent in establishing a writing style and by 1849 she had her first novel published: Passages in the Life of Mrs. Margaret Maitland.

Two years later, in 1851 Caleb Field was published and also an invitation gained to contribute to Blackwood's Magazine; the beginning of a lifelong business relationship.

In May 1852, Margaret married her cousin, Frank Wilson Oliphant. Their marriage produced six children but, tragically, three died in infancy. When her husband developed signs of the dreaded consumption (tuberculosis) they moved to Florence, and then to Rome where, sadly, he died.

Margaret was naturally devastated but was also now left without support and only her income from writing to support the family. She returned to England and took up the burden of supporting her three remaining children by her literary activity.

Her incredible and prolific work rate increased both her commercial reputation and the size of her reading audience. Tragedy struck again in January 1864 when her only remaining daughter, Maggie, died.

In 1866 she settled at Windsor to be closer to her sons, who were being educated at near-by Eton School.

For more than thirty years she pursued a varied literary career but family life continued to bring problems. Cyril Francis, her eldest son, died in 1890. The younger son, Francis, who she nicknamed 'Cecco', died in 1894.

With the last of her children now lost to her, she had little further interest in life. Her health steadily and inexorably declined.

Margaret Oliphant Wilson Oliphant died at the age of 69 in Wimbledon on 20th June 1897. She is buried in Eton beside her sons.

Index of Contents

CHAPTER I

A large drawing-room in a country-house, in the perfect warmth, stillness, and good order of after-dinner, awaiting the ladies coming in; the fire perfection, reflecting itself in all the polished brass and steel and tiles of the fireplace; the atmosphere just touched with the scent of the flowers on the tables; the piano open, with candles lit upon it; some pretty work laid out upon a stand near the fire, books on another, ready for use, velvet curtains drawn. The whole softly, fully lighted, a place full of every gentle luxury and comfort in perfection—the scene prepared, waiting only the actors in it.

It is curious to look into a centre of life like this, all ready for the human affairs about to be transacted there. Tragedy or comedy, who can tell which? the clash of human wills, the encounter of hearts, or perhaps only that serene blending of kindred tastes and inclinations which makes domestic happiness. Who was coming in? A fair mother, with a flock of girls fairer still, a beautiful wife adding the last grace to the beautiful place? some fortunate man's crown of well-being and happiness, the nucleus of other happy homes to come?

A pause: the fire only crackling now and then, a little burst of flame puffing forth, the clock on the mantelpiece chiming softly. Then there entered alone a young lady about eighteen, in the simple white dinner dress of a home party; a tall, slight girl, with smooth brown hair, and eyes for the moment enlarged with anxiety and troubled meaning. She came in not as the daughter of the house in ordinary circumstances comes in, to take her pleasant place, and begin her evening occupation, whatever it may be. Her step was almost stealthy, like that of a pioneer, investigating anxiously if all was safe in a place full of danger. Her eyes, with the lids curved over them in an anxiety almost despairing, seemed to plunge into and search through and through the absolute tranquillity of this peaceful place. Then she said in a half-whisper, the intense tone of which was equal to a cry, "Mother!" Nothing stirred: the place was so warm, so perfect, so happy; while this one human creature stood on the threshold gazing—as if it had been a desert full of nothing but trouble and terror. She stood thus only for a moment, and then disappeared. It was a painful intrusion, suggestive of everything that was most alien to the sentiment of the place: when she withdrew it fell again into that soft beaming of warmth and brightness waiting for the warmer interest to come.

The doorway in which she had stood for that momentary inspection, which was deep in a solid wall, with two doors, in case any breath of cold should enter, opened into a hall, very lofty and fine, a sort of centre to the quiet house. Here the light was dimmer, the place being deserted, though it had an air of habitation, and the fire still smouldered in the huge chimney, round which chairs were standing. Sounds of voices muffled by closed doors and curtains came from the farther side where the dining-room was. The young lady shrank from this as if her noiseless motion could have been heard over the sounds of the male voices there. She hurried along to the other end of the hall, which lay in darkness with a glimmer of pale sky showing between the pillars from without. The outer doors were not yet shut. The inner glass door showed this paleness of night, with branches of trees tossing against a gray heaven full of flying clouds—the strangest weird contrast to all the warmth and luxury within. The girl shivered as she came in sight of that dreary outer world. This was the opening of the park in front of the house, a width of empty space, and beyond it the commotion of the wind, the stormy show of the coursing clouds. She went close to the door and gazed out, pressing her forehead against the glass, and searching the darkness, as she had done the light, with anxious eyes. She stood so for about five minutes, and then she breathed an impatient sigh. "What is the good?" she said to herself, half aloud.

Here something stirred near her which made her start, at first with an eager movement of hope. Then a low voice said—"No good at all, Miss Rosalind. Why should you mix yourself up with what's no concern of yours?"

Rosalind had started violently when she recognized the voice, but subdued herself while the other spoke. She answered, with quiet self-restraint: "Is it you, Russell? What are you doing here? You will make it impossible for me to do anything for you if you forget your own place!"

"I am doing what my betters are doing, Miss Rosalind—looking out for Madam, just as you are."

"How dare you say such things! I—am looking out to see what sort of night it is. It is very stormy. Go away at once. You have no right to be here!"

"I've been here longer than most folks—longer than them that has the best opinion of themselves; longer than—"

"Me perhaps," said Rosalind. "Yes, I know—you came before I was born; but you know what folly this is. Mamma," the girl said, with a certain tremor and hesitation, "will be very angry if she finds you here."

"I wish, Miss Rosalind, you'd have a little more respect for yourself. It goes against me to hear you say mamma. And your own dear mamma, that should have been lady of everything—"

"Russell, I wish you would not be such a fool! My poor little mother that died when I was born. And you to keep up a grudge like this for so many years!"

"And will, whatever you may say," cried the woman, under her breath; "and will, till I die, or till one of us—"

"Go up-stairs," said Rosalind, peremptorily, "at once! What have you to do here? I don't think you are safe in the house. If I had the power I should send you away."

"Miss Rosalind, you are as cruel as—You have no heart. Me, that nursed you, and watched over you—"

"It is too terrible a price to pay," cried the girl, stamping her foot on the floor. "Go! I will not have you here. If mamma finds you when she comes down-stairs—"

The woman laughed. "She will ask what you are doing here, Miss Rosalind. It will not be only me she'll fly out upon. What are you doing here? Who's outside that interests you so? It interests us both, that's the truth; only I am the one that knows the best."

Rosalind's white figure flew across the faint light. She grasped the shoulder of the dark shadow, almost invisible in the gloom. "Go!" she cried in her ear, pushing Russell before her; the onslaught was so sudden and vehement that the woman yielded and disappeared reluctantly, gliding away by one of the passages that led to the other part of the house. The girl stood panting and excited in the brief sudden fury of her passion, a miserable sense of failing faith and inability to explain to herself the circumstances in which she was, heightening the fervor of her indignation. Were Russell's suspicions true? Had she been in the right all along? Those who take persistently the worst view of human nature are, alas! so often in the right. And what is there more terrible than the passion of defence and apology for one whom the heart begins to doubt? The girl was young, and in her rage and pain could scarcely keep herself from those vehement tears which are the primitive attribute of passion. How calm she could have been had she been quite, quite sure! How she had laughed at Russell's prejudices in the old days when all was well. She had even excused Russell, feeling that after all it was pretty of her nurse to return continually to the image of her first mistress—Rosalind's own mother—and that in the uneducated mind the prepossession against a stepmother, the wrath with which the woman saw her own nursling supplanted, had a sort of feudal flavor which was rather agreeable than otherwise.

Rosalind had pardoned Russell as Mrs. Trevanion herself had pardoned her. So long as all was well: so long as there was nothing mysterious, nothing that baffled the spectator in the object of Russell's animadversions. But now something had fallen into life which changed it altogether. To defend those we love from undeserved accusations is so easy. And in books and plays, and every other exhibition of human nature in fiction, the accused always possesses the full confidence of those who love him. In ordinary cases they will not even hear any explanation of equivocal circumstances—they know that guilt is impossible: it is only those who do not know him who can believe anything so monstrous. Alas! this is not so in common life—the most loving and believing cannot always have that sublime faith. Sometimes doubt and fear gnaw the very souls of those who are the champions, the advocates, the warmest partisans of the accused. This terrible canker had got into Rosalind's being. She loved her stepmother with enthusiasm. She was ready to die in her defence. She would not listen to the terrible murmur in her own heart; but yet it was there. And as she stood and gazed out upon the park, upon the wild bit of stormy sky, with the black tree-tops waving wildly against it, she was miserable, as miserable as a heart of eighteen ever was. Where had Madam gone, hurrying from the dinner-table where she had smiled and talked and given no sign of trouble? She was not in her room, nor in the nursery, nor anywhere that Rosalind could think of. It was in reality a confession of despair, a sort of giving up of the cause altogether, when the girl came to spy out into the wintry world outside and look for the fugitive there.

Rosalind had resisted the impulse to do so for many an evening. She had paused by stealth in the dark window above in the corridor, and blushed for herself and fled from that spy's place. But by force of trouble and doubt and anguish her scruples had been overcome, and now she had accepted for herself this position of spy. If her fears had been verified, and she had seen her mother cross that vacant space and steal into the house, what the better would she have been? But there is in suspicion a wild curiosity, an eagerness for certainty, which grows like a fever. She had come to feel that she must know—whatever happened she must be satisfied—come what would, that would be better than the gnawing of this suspense. And she had another object too. Her father was an invalid, exacting and fretful. If his wife was not ready at his call whenever he wanted her, his displeasure was unbounded; and of late it had happened many times that his wife had not been at his call. The scenes that had followed, the reproaches, the insults even, to which the woman whom she called mother had been subjected, had made Rosalind's heart sick. If she could but see her, hasten her return, venture to call her, to bid her come quick, quick! it would be something. The girl was not philosopher enough to say to herself that Madam would not come a moment the sooner for being thus watched for. It takes a great deal of philosophy to convince an anxious woman of this in any circumstances, and Rosalind was in the pangs of a first trouble, the earliest anguish she had ever known. After she had driven Russell away, she stood with her face pressed against the glass and all her senses gone into her eyes and ears. She heard, she thought, the twitter of the twigs in the wind, the sharp sound now and then of one which broke and fell, which was like a footstep on the path; besides the louder sweep of the tree-tops in the wind, and on the other hand the muffled and faint sound of life from the dining-room, every variation in which kept her in alarm.

But it was in vain she gazed; nothing crossed the park except the sweep of the clouds driven along the sky; nothing sounded in the air except the wind, the trees, and sometimes the opening of a distant door or clap of a gate; until the dining-room became more audible, a sound of chairs pushed back and voices rising, warning the watcher. She flew like an arrow through the hall, and burst into the still sanctuary of domestic warmth and tranquillity as if she had been a hunted creature escaping from a fatal pursuit with her enemies at her heels. Her hands were like ice, her slight figure shivering with cold, yet her heart beating so that she could scarcely draw her breath. All this must disappear before the gentlemen came in. It was Rosalind's first experience in that strange art which comes naturally to a woman, of obliterating herself and her own sensations; but how was she to still her pulse, to restore her color, to bring warmth to her chilled heart? She felt sure that her misery, her anguish of suspense, her appalling doubts and terrors, must be written in her face; but it was not so. The emergency brought back a rush of the warm blood tingling to her fingers' ends. Oh never, never, through her, must the mother she loved be betrayed! That brave impulse brought color to her cheek and strength to her heart. She made one or two of those minute changes in the room which a woman always finds occasion for, drawing the card-table into a position more exactly like that which her father approved, giving an easier angle to his chair, with a touch moving that of Madam into position as if it had been risen from that moment. Then Rosalind took up the delicate work that lay on the table, and when the gentlemen entered was seated on a low seat within the circle of the shaded lamp, warm in the glow of the genial fireside, her pretty head bent a little over her pretty industry, her hands busy. She who had been the image of anxiety and unrest a moment before was now the culminating-point of all the soft domestic tranquillity, luxury, boundless content and peace, of which this silent room was the home. She looked up with a smile to greet them as they came in. The brave girl had recovered her sweet looks, her color, and air of youthful composure and self-possession, by sheer force of will, and strain of the crisis in which she stood to maintain the honor of the family at every hazard. She had been able to do that, but she could not yet for the moment trust herself to speak.

CHAPTER II

The gentlemen who came into the drawing-room at Highcourt were four in number: the master of the house, his brother, the doctor, and a young man fresh from the university, who was a visitor. Mr. Trevanion was an invalid; he had been a tall man, of what is called aristocratic appearance; a man with fine, clearly cut features, holding his head high, with an air "as if all the world belonged to him." These fine features were contracted by an expression of fastidious discontent and dissatisfaction, which is not unusually associated with such universal proprietorship, and illness had taken the flesh from his bones, and drawn the ivory skin tightly over the high nose and tall, narrow forehead. His lips were thin and querulous, his shoulders stooping, his person as thin and angular as human form could be. When he had warmed his ghostly hands at the fire, and seated himself in his accustomed chair, he cast a look round him as if seeking some subject of complaint. His eyes were blue, very cold, deficient in color, and looked out from amid the puckers of his eyelids with the most unquestionable meaning. They seemed to demand something to object to, and this want is one which is always supplied. The search was but momentary, so that he scarcely seemed to have entered the room before he asked, "Where is your mother?" in a high-pitched, querulous voice.

Mr. John Trevanion had followed his brother to the fire, and stood now with his back to the blaze looking at Rosalind. His name was not in reality John, but something much more ornamental and refined; but society had availed itself of its well-known propensity in a more judicious manner than usual, and rechristened him with the short and manly monosyllable which suited his character. He was a man who had been a great deal about the world, and had discovered of how little importance was a Trevanion of Highcourt, and yet how it simplified life to possess a well-known name. One of these discoveries without the other is not improving to the character, but taken together the result is mellowing and happy. He was very tolerant, very considerate, a man who judged no one, yet formed very shrewd opinions of his own, upon which he was apt to act, even while putting forth every excuse and acknowledging every extenuating circumstance. He looked at Rosalind with a certain veiled anxiety in his eyes, attending her answer with solicitude; but to all appearance he was only spreading himself out as an Englishman loves to do before the clear glowing fire. Dr. Beaton had gone as far away as possible from that brilliant centre. He was stout, and disapproved, he said, "on principle," of the habit of gathering round the fireside. "Let the room be properly warmed," he was in the habit of saying, "but don't let us bask in the heat like the dogues," for the doctor was Scotch, and betrayed now and then in a pronunciation, and always in accent, his northern origin. He had seated himself on the other side of the card-table, ready for the invariable game. Young Roland Hamerton, the Christchurch man, immediately gravitated towards Rosalind, who, to tell the truth, could not have given less attention to him had he been one of the above-mentioned "dogues."

"Where is your mother?" Mr. Trevanion said, looking round for matter of offence.

"Oh!" said Rosalind, with a quick drawing of her breath; "mamma has gone for a moment to the nursery—I suppose." She drew breath again before the last two words, thus separating them from what had gone before—a little artifice which Uncle John perceived, but no one else.

"Now this is a strange thing," said Mr. Trevanion, "that in my own house, and in my failing state of health, I cannot secure my own wife's attention at the one moment in the day when she is indispensable to me. The nursery! What is there to do in the nursery? Is not Russell there? If the woman is not fit to be trusted, let her be discharged at once and some one else got."

"Oh! it is not that there is any doubt about Russell, papa, only one likes to see for one's self."

"Then why can't she send you to see for yourself. This is treatment I am not accustomed to. Oh, what do I say? Not accustomed to it! Of course I am accustomed to be neglected by everybody. A brat of a child that never ailed anything in its life is to be watched over, while I, a dying man, must take my chance. I have put up with it for years, always hoping that at last—But the worm will turn, you know; the most patient will break down. If I am to wait night after night for the one amusement, the one little pleasure, such as it is—Night after night! I appeal to you, doctor, whether Mrs. Trevanion has been ready once in the last fortnight. The only thing that I ask of her—the sole paltry little complaisance—"

He spoke very quickly, allowing no possibility of interruption, till his voice, if we may use such a word, overran itself and died away for want of breath.

"My dear sir," said the doctor, taking up the cards, "we are just enough for our rubber; and, as I have often remarked, though I bow to the superiority of the ladies in most things, whist, in my opinion, is altogether a masculine game. Will you cut for the deal?"

But by this time Mr. Trevanion had recovered his breath. "It is what I will not put up with," he said; "everybody in this house relies upon my good-nature. I am always the souffre-douleur. When a man is too easy he is taken advantage of on all hands. Where is your mother? Oh, I mean your stepmother, Rosalind; her blood is not in your veins, thank Heaven! You are a good child; I have no reason to find fault with you. Where is she? The nursery? I don't believe anything about the nursery. She is with some of her low friends; yes, she has low friends. Hold your tongue, John; am I or am I not the person that knows best about my own wife? Where is your mistress? Where is Madam? Don't stand there looking like a stuck pig, but speak!"

This was addressed to an unlucky footman who had come in prowling on one of the anonymous errands of domestic service—to see if the fire wanted looking to—if there were any coffee-cups unremoved—perhaps on a mission of curiosity, too. Mr. Trevanion was the terror of the house. The man turned pale and lost his self-command. "I—I don't know, sir. I—I think, sir, as Madam—I—I'll send Mr. Dorrington, sir," the unfortunate said.

John Trevanion gave his niece an imperative look, saying low, "Go and tell her." Rosalind rose trembling and put down her work. The footman had fled, and young Hamerton, hurrying to open the door to her (which was never shut) got in her way and brought upon himself a glance of wrath which made him tremble. He retreated with a chill running through him, wondering if the Trevanion temper was in her too, while the master of the house resumed. However well understood such explosions of family disturbance may be, they are always embarrassing and uncomfortable to visitors, and young Hamerton was not used to them and did not know what to make of himself. He withdrew to the darker end of the room, where it opened into a very dimly lighted conservatory, while the doctor shuffled the cards, letting them drop audibly through his fingers, and now and then attempting to divert the flood of rising rage by a remark. "Bless me," he said, "I wish I had been dealing in earnest; what a bonnie thing for a trump card!" and, "A little farther from the fire, Mr. Trevanion, you are getting overheated; come, sir, the young fellow will take a hand to begin with, and after the first round another player can cut in." These running interruptions, however, were of little service; Mr. Trevanion's admirable good-nature which was always imposed upon; his long-suffering which everybody knew; the advantage the household took of him; the special sins of his wife for whom he had done everything—"Everything!" he cried; "I took her without a penny or a friend, and this is how she repays me"—afforded endless scope. It was nothing to him in his passion that he disclosed what had been the secrets of his life; and, indeed, by this time, after the perpetual self-revelation of these fits of passion there were few secrets left to keep. His ivory countenance reddened, his thin hands gesticulated, he leaned forward in his chair, drawing up the sharp angles of his knees, as he harangued about himself and his virtues and wrongs. His brother stood and listened, gazing blankly before him as if he heard nothing. The doctor sat behind, dropping the cards from one hand to another with a little rustling sound, and interposing little sentences of soothing and gentle remonstrance, while the young man, ashamed to be thus forced into the confidence of the family, edged step by step farther away into the conservatory till he got to the end, where was nothing but a transparent wall of glass between him and the agitations of the stormy night.

Rosalind stole out into the hall with a beating heart. Her father's sharp voice still echoed in her ears, and she had an angry and ashamed consciousness that the footman who had hurried from the room before her, and perhaps other servants, excited by the crisis, were watching her and commenting upon the indecision with which she stood, not knowing what to do. "Go and tell her." How easy it was to say so! Oh, if she but knew where to go, how to find her, how to save her not only from domestic strife but from the gnawing worm of suspicion and doubt which Rosalind felt in her own heart! What was she to do? Should she go up-stairs again and look through all the rooms, though she knew it would be in vain? To disarm her father's rage, to smooth over this moment of misery and put things back on their old footing, the girl would have done anything; but as the moments passed she became more and more aware that this was not nearly all that was wanted, that even she herself, loving Mrs. Trevanion with all her heart, required more. Her judgment cried out for more. She wanted explanation; a reason for these strange disappearances. Why should she choose that time of all others when her absence must be so much remarked; and where, oh, where did she go? Rosalind stood with a sort of stupefied sense of incapacity in the hall. She would not go back. She could not pretend to make a search which she knew to be useless. She could not rush to the door again and watch there, with the risk of being followed and found at that post, and thus betray her suspicion that her mother was out of the house. She went and stood by one of the pillars and leaned against it, clasping her hands upon her heart and trying to calm herself and to find some expedient. Could she say that little Jack was ill, that something had happened? in the confusion of her mind she almost lost the boundary between falsehood and truth; but then the doctor would be sent to see what was the matter, and everything would be worse instead of better. She stood thus against the pillar and did not move, trying to think, in a whirl of painful imaginations and self-questionings, feeling every moment an hour. Oh, if she could but take it upon herself, and bear the weight, whatever it might be; but she was helpless and could do nothing save wait there, hidden, trembling, full of misery, till something should happen to set her free.

Young Hamerton in the conservatory naturally had none of these fears. He thought that old Trevanion was (as indeed everybody knew) an old tyrant, a selfish, ill-tempered egoist, caring for nothing but his own indulgences. How he did treat that poor woman, to be sure! a woman far too good for him whether it was true or not that he had married her without a penny. He remembered vaguely that he had never heard who Madam Trevanion was before her marriage. But what of that? He knew what she was: a woman still full of grace and charm, though she was no longer in her first youth. And what a life that old curmudgeon, that selfish old skeleton, with all his fantastical complaints, led her! When a young man has the sort of chivalrous admiration for an elder woman which Roland Hamerton felt for the mistress of this house, he becomes sharp to see the curious subjection, the cruelty of circumstances, the domestic oppressions which encircle so many. And Madam Trevanion was more badly off, more deeply tried, than any other woman, far or near. She was full of spirit and intelligence, and interest in the higher matters of life; yet she was bound to this fretful master, who would not let her out of his sight, who cared for nothing better than a society newspaper, and who demanded absolute devotion, and the submission of all his wife's wishes and faculties to his. Poor lady! no wonder if she were glad to escape now and then for a moment, to get out of hearing of his sharp voice, which went through your ears like a skewer.

While these thoughts went through young Hamerton's mind he had gradually made his way through the conservatory, in which there was but one dim lamp burning, to the farther part, which projected out some way with a rounded end into the lawn which immediately surrounded the house. He was much startled, as he looked cautiously forth, without being aware that he was looking, to see something moving, like a repetition of the waving branches and clouds above close to him upon the edge of a path which led through the park. At first it was but movement and no more, indistinguishable among the shadows. But he was excited by what he had been hearing, and his attention was aroused. After a time he could make out two figures more or less distinct, a man he thought and a woman, but both so dark that it was only when by moments they appeared out of the tree-shadows, with which they were confused, against the lighter color of the gravel that he could make them out. They parted while he looked on; the man disappeared among the trees; the other, he could see her against the faint lightness of the distance, stood looking after the retreating figure; and then turned and came towards the house. Young Hamerton's heart leaped up in his breast. What did it mean? Did he recognize the pose of the figure, the carriage of the head, the fine movement, so dignified yet so free? He seized hold on himself, so to speak, and put a violent stop to his own thoughts. She! madness! as soon would he suppose that the queen could do wrong. It must be her maid, perhaps some woman who had got the trick of her walk and air through constant association: but she—

Just then, while Hamerton retired somewhat sick at heart, and seated himself near the door of the conservatory to recover, cursing as he did so the sharp, scolding tones of Mr. Trevanion going on with his grievances, Rosalind, standing against the pillar, was startled by something like a step or faint stir outside, and then the sound, which would have been inaudible to faculties less keen and highly strung, of the handle of the glass door. It was turned almost noiselessly and some one came in. Some one. Whom? With a shiver which convulsed her, Rosalind watched: this dark figure might be any one—her mother's maid, perhaps, even Russell, gone out to pry and spy as was her way. Rosalind had to clutch the pillar fast as she watched from behind while the new-comer took a shawl from her head, and, sighing, arranged with her hands her head-dress and hair. Whatever had happened to her she was not happy. She sighed as she set in order the lace upon her head. Alas! the sight of that lace was enough, the dim light was enough: no one else in the house moved like that. It was the mother, the wife, the mistress of Highcourt, Madam Trevanion, whom all the country looked up to for miles and miles around. Rosalind could not speak. She detached her arms from the pillar and followed like a white ghost as her stepmother moved towards the drawing-room. In the night and dark, in the stormy wind amid all those black trees, where had she been?

CHAPTER III

"I married her without a penny," Mr. Trevanion was saying. "I was a fool for my pains. If you think you will purchase attention and submission in that way you are making a confounded mistake. Set a beggar on horseback, that's how it ends. A duke's daughter couldn't stand more by her own way; no, nor look more like a lady," he added with a sort of pride in his property; "that must be allowed her. I married her without a penny; and this is how she serves me. If she had brought a duchy in her apron, or the best blood in England, like Rosalind's mother, my first poor wife, whom I regret every day of my life—O-h-h!—so you have condescended, Madam, to come at last."

She was a tall woman, with a figure full of dignity and grace. If it was true that nobody knew who she was, it was at least true also, as even her husband allowed, that she might have been a princess so far as her bearing and manners went. She was dressed in soft black satin which did not rustle or assert itself, but hung in long sweeping folds, here and there broken in outline by feathery touches of lace. Her dark hair was still perfect in color and texture. Indeed, she was still under forty, and the prime of her beauty scarcely impaired. There was a little fitful color on her cheek, though she was usually pale, and her eyes had a kind of feverish, suspicious brightness like sentinels on the watch for danger signals. Yet she came in without hurry, with a smile from one to another of the group of gentlemen, none of whom showed, whatever they may have felt, any emotion. John Trevanion, still blank and quiet against the firelight; the doctor, though he lifted his eyes momentarily, still dropping through his hands, back and forwards, the sliding, smooth surfaces of the cards. From the dimness in the background Hamerton's young face shone out with a sort of Medusa look of horror and pain, but he was so far out of the group that he attracted no notice. Mrs. Trevanion made no immediate reply to her husband. She advanced into the room, Rosalind following her like a shadow. "I am sorry," she said calmly, "to be late: have you not begun your rubber? I knew there were enough without me."

"There's never enough without you," her husband answered roughly; "you know that as well as I do. If there were twice enough, what has that to do with it? You know my play, which is just the one thing you do know. If a man can't have his wife to make up his game, what is the use of a wife at all? And this is not the first time, Madam; by Jove, not the first time by a dozen. Can't you take another time for your nap, or your nursery, or whatever it is? I don't believe a word of the nursery. It is something you don't choose to have known, it is some of your low—"

"Rosalind, your father has no footstool," said Mrs. Trevanion. She maintained her calm unmoved. "There are some fresh cards, doctor, in the little cabinet."

"And how the devil," cried the invalid, in his sharp tones, "can I have my footstool, or clean cards, or anything I want when you are away—systematically away? I believe you do it on purpose to set up a right—to put me out in every way, that goes without saying, that everybody knows, is the object of your life."

Still she did not utter a word of apology, but stooped and found the footstool, which she placed at her husband's feet. "This is the one that suits you best," she said. "Come, John, if I am the culprit, let us lose no more time."

Mr. Trevanion kicked the footstool away. "D'ye think I am going to be smoothed down so easily?" he cried. "Oh, yes, as soon as Madam pleases, that is the time for everything. I shall not play. You can amuse yourselves if you please, gentlemen, at Mrs. Trevanion's leisure, when she can find time to pay a little attention to her guests. Give me those newspapers, Rosalind. Oh, play, play! by all means play! don't let me interrupt your amusement. A little more neglect, what does that matter? I hope I am used to—Heaven above! they are not cut up. What is that rascal Dorrington about? What is the use of a pack of idle servants? never looked after as they ought to be; encouraged, indeed, to neglect and ill-use the master that feeds them. What can you expect? With a mistress who is shut up half her time, or out of the way or—What's that? what's that?"

It was a singular thing enough, and this sudden exclamation called all eyes to it. Mrs. Trevanion, who had risen when her husband kicked his footstool in her face, and, turning round, had taken a few steps across the room, stopped with a slight start, which perhaps betrayed some alarm in her, and looked back. The train of her dress was sweeping over the hearthrug, and there in the full light, twisted into her lace, and clinging to her dress, was a long, straggling, thorny branch, all wet with the damp of night. Involuntarily they were all gazing—John Trevanion looking down gravely at this strange piece of evidence which was close to his feet; the doctor, with the cards in his hand, half risen from his seat stooping across the table to see; while Rosalind, throwing herself down, had already begun to detach it with hands that trembled.

"Oh, mamma!" cried the girl, with a laugh which sounded wild, "how careless, how horrid of Jane! Here is a thorn that caught in your dress the last time you wore it; and she has folded it up in your train, and never noticed. Papa is right, the servants are—"

"Hold your tongue, Rose," said Mr. Trevanion, with an angry chuckle of satisfaction; "let alone! So, Madam, this is why we have to wait for everything; this is why the place is left to itself; and I—I—the master and owner, neglected. Good heavens above! while the lady of the house wanders in the woods in a November night. With whom, Madam? With whom?" he raised himself like a skeleton, his fiery eyes blazing out of their sockets. "With whom, I ask you? Here, gentlemen, you are witnesses; this is more serious than I thought. I knew my wishes were disregarded, that my convenience was set at naught, that the very comforts that are essential to my life were neglected, but I did not think I was betrayed. With whom, Madam? Answer! I demand his name."

"Reginald," said John Trevanion, "for God's sake don't let us have another scene. You may think what you please, but we know all that is nonsense. Neglected! Why she makes herself your slave. If the other is as true as that! Doctor, can't you put a stop to it? He'll kill himself—and her."

"Her! oh, she's strong enough," cried the invalid. "I have had my suspicions before, but I have never uttered them. Ah, Madam! you thought you were too clever for me. A sick man, unable to stir out of the house, the very person, of course, to be deceived. But the sick man has his defenders. Providence is on his side. You throw dust in the eyes of these men; but I know you; I know what I took you from; I've known all along what you were capable of. Who was it? Heaven above! down, down on your knees, and tell me his name."

Mrs. Trevanion was perfectly calm, too calm, perhaps, for the unconsciousness of innocence; and she was also deadly pale. "So far as the evidence goes," she said quietly, "I do not deny it. It has not been folded up in my train, my kind Rosalind. I have been out of doors; though the night, as you see, is not tempting; and what then?"

She turned round upon them with a faint smile, and took the branch out of Rosalind's hand. "You see it is all wet," she said, "there is no deception in it. I have been out in the park, on the edge of the woods. Look, I did not stop even to change my shoes, they are wet too. And what then?"

"One thing," cried the doctor, "that you must change them directly, before another word is said. This comes in my department, at least. We don't want to have you laid up with congestion of the lungs. Miss Rosalind, take your mamma away, and make her, as we say in Scotland, change her feet."

"Let her go altogether, if she pleases," said the invalid; "I want to see no more of her. In the park, in the woods—do you hear her, gentlemen? What does a woman want in the woods in a winter night? Let her have congestion of the lungs, it will save disgrace to the family. For, mark my words, I will follow this out. I will trace it to the foundation. Night after night she has done it. Oh, you think I don't know? She has done it again and again. She has been shameless; she has outraged the very house where—Do you hear, woman? Who is it? My God! a groom, or some low fellow—"

The doctor grasped his arm with a hand that thrilled with indignation as well as professional zeal, while John Trevanion started forward with a sudden flush and menace—

"If you don't respect your wife, for God's sake think of the girl—your own child! If it were not for their sakes I should not spend another night under this roof—"

"Spend your night where you please," said the infuriated husband, struggling against the doctor's attempt to draw him back into his chair. "If I respect her? No, I don't respect her. I respect nobody that ill-uses me. Get out of the way, Rosalind! I tell you I'll turn out that woman. I'll disgrace her. I'll show what she's made of. She's thrown dust in all your eyes, but never in mine. No, Madam, never in mine; you've forgotten, I suppose, what you were when I took you and married you, like a fool—but I've never forgotten; and now to break out at your age? Who do you suppose can care for you at your age? It is for what he can get, the villain, that he comes over an old hag like you. Oh, women, women! that's what women are. Turn out on a winter's night to philander in the woods with some one, some—"

He stopped, incapable of more, and fell back in his chair, and glared and foamed insults with his bloodless lips which he had not breath to speak.

Mrs. Trevanion stood perfectly still while all this was going on. Her face showed by its sudden contraction when the grosser accusations told, but otherwise she made no movement. She held the long, dangling branch in her hand, and looked at it with a sort of half-smile. It was so small a matter to produce so much—and yet it was not a small matter. Was it the hand of fate! Was it Providence, as he said, that was on his side! But she did not say another word in self-defence. It was evident that it was her habit to stand thus, and let the storm beat. Her calm was the resignation of long usage, the sense that it was beyond remedy, that the only thing she could do was to endure. And yet the accusations of this evening were new, and there was something new in the contemplative way in which she regarded this piece of evidence which had convicted her. Hitherto the worst accusations that had rained upon her had been without evidence, without possibility—and everybody had been aware that it was so. Now there was something new. When she had borne vituperation almost as violent for her neglect, for her indifference, sometimes for her cruelty, the wrong had been too clear for any doubt. But now: never before had there even been anything to explain. But the bramble was a thing that demanded explanation. Even John Trevanion, the just and kind, had shown a gleam of surprise when he caught sight of it. The good doctor, who was entirely on her side, had given her a startled look. Rosalind, her child, had put forth a hesitating plea—a little lie for her. All this went to her heart with a wringing of pain, as if her very heart had been crushed with some sudden pressure. But the habit of endurance was unbroken even by these secret and novel pangs. She did not even meet the eyes directed to her with any attempt at self-defence. But yet the position was novel; and standing still in her old panoply of patience, she felt it to be so, and that former expedients were inadequate to the occasion. For the first time it would have better become her to speak. But what? She had nothing to say.

The scene ended as such scenes almost invariably ended here—in an attack of those spasms which were wearing Mr. Trevanion's life away. The first symptoms changed in a moment the aspect of his wife. She put down the guilty bramble and betook herself at once to her oft-repeated, well-understood duty. The room was cleared of all the spectators, even Rosalind was sent away. It was an experience with which the house was well acquainted. Mrs. Trevanion's maid came noiselessly and swift at the sound of a bell, with everything that was needed; and the wife, so angrily vituperated and insulted, became in a moment the devoted nurse, with nothing in her mind save the care of the patient who lay helpless in her hands. The doctor sat by with his finger on the fluttering pulse—while she, now fanning, now bathing his forehead, following every variation and indication of the attack, fulfilled her arduous duties. It did not seem to cross her mind that anything had passed which could slacken her vigilance or make her reluctant to fulfil those all-absorbing duties; neither when the patient began to moan did there seem any consciousness in him that the circumstances were anyhow changed. He began to scold in broken terms almost before he had recovered consciousness, demanding to know why he was there, what they were doing to him, what was the occasion of the appliances they had been using. "I'm all right," he stammered, before he could speak, pushing away the fan she was using. "You want to kill me. Don't let her kill me, doctor; take that confounded thing away. I'm—I'm—all right; I—I want to get to bed. You are keeping me out of bed, on purpose—to kill me!" he cried with a new outburst. "That is all right; he'll do now," said the doctor, cheerfully. "Wait a moment, and we'll get you to bed—" The peaceful room had changed in the most curious way while all these rapid changes had gone on. The very home of tranquillity at first, then a stage of dramatic incident and passion, now a scene in which feeble life was struggling with the grip of death at its throat. Presently all this commotion and movement was over, and the palpitations of human existence swept away, leaving, indeed, a little disorder in the surroundings; a cushion thrown about, a corner of the carpet turned up, a tray with water-bottles and essences on the table: but nothing more to mark the struggle, the conflicts which had been, the suffering and misery. Yes; one thing more: the long trail of bramble on another table, which was the most fatal symbol of all.

When everything was quiet young Hamerton, with a pale face, came out of the conservatory. He had again retreated there when Mrs. Trevanion came in, and the husband had begun to rage. It pained him to be a party to it; to listen to all the abuse poured upon her was intolerable. But what was more intolerable still was to remember what he had seen. That woman, standing so pale and calm, replying nothing, bearing every insult with a nobleness which would have become a saint. But, oh heavens! was it her he had seen—her—under shelter of the night? The young man was generous and innocent, and his heart was sick with this miserable knowledge. He was in her secret. God help her! Surely she had excuse enough; but what is to become of life or womanhood when such a woman requires an excuse at all?

CHAPTER IV

The hall was dimly lighted, the fire dying out in the great fireplace, everything shadowy, cold, without cheer or comfort. Mr. Trevanion had been conveyed to his room between the doctor and his valet, his wife following, as usual, in the same order and fashion as was habitual, without any appearance of change. Rosalind, who was buried in a great chair, nothing visible but the whiteness of her dress in the imperfect light, and John Trevanion, who stood before the fire there as he had done in the drawing-room, with his head a little bent, and an air of great seriousness and concern, watched the little procession without a word as it went across the hall. These attacks were too habitual to cause much alarm; and the outburst of passion which preceded was, unfortunately, common enough also. The house was not a happy house in which this volcano was ready to burst forth at any moment, and the usual family subterfuges to conceal the family skeleton had become of late years quite impossible, as increasing weakness and self-indulgence had removed all restraints of self-control from the master of the house. They were all prepared for the outbreak at any moment, no matter who was present. But yet there were things involved which conveyed a special sting to-night. When the little train had passed, the two spectators in the hall remained for some time quite silent, with a heaviness and oppression upon them which, perhaps, the depressing circumstances around, the want of light and warmth and brightness, increased. They did not, as on ordinary occasions, return to the drawing-room. For some time they said nothing to each other. By intervals a servant flitted across the hall, from one room to another, or the opening of a door roused these watchers for a moment; but presently everything fell back into stillness and the chill of the gathering night.

"Rosalind, I think you should go to bed—"

"Oh, Uncle John, how can I go to bed? How can any one in this house rest or sleep?"

"My dear, I admit that the circumstances are not very cheerful. Still, you are more or less accustomed to them; and we shall sleep all the same, no doubt, just as we should sleep if we were all to be executed to-morrow."

"Should we? but not if some one else, some one we loved—was to be—executed, as you say."

"Perhaps that makes a little difference: while the condemned man sleeps, I suppose his mother or his sister, poor wretches, are wakeful enough. But there is nothing of that kind in our way, my little Rose. Come! it is no worse than usual: go to bed."

"It is worse than usual. There has never before—oh!" the girl cried, clasping her hands together with a vehement gesture. Her misery was too much for her: and then another sentiment came in and closed her mouth. Uncle John was very tender and kind, but was he not on the other side?

"My dear," he said gently, "I think it will be best not to discuss the question. If there is something new in it, it will develop soon enough. God forbid! I am little disposed, Rosalind, to think that there is anything new."

She did not make any reply. Her heart was sore with doubt and suspicion; the more strange these sentiments, all the more do they scorch and sting. In the whirl which they introduced into her mind she had been trying in vain to get any ground to stand upon. There might have been explanations; but then how easy to give them, and settle the question. It is terrible, in youth, to be thrown into such a conflict of mind, and all the more to one who has never been used to think out anything alone, who has shared with another every thought that arose in her, and received on everything the interchanged ideas of a mind more experienced, wiser, than her own. She was thus suddenly cut off from her anchors, and felt herself drifting on wild currents unknown to her, giddy, as if buffeted by wind and tide—though seated there within the steadfast walls of an old house which had gone through all extremities of human emotion, and never quivered, through hundreds of troublous years.

"I think," said John Trevanion, after a pause, "that it would be good for you to have a little change. Home, of course, is the best place for a girl. Still, it is a great strain upon young nerves. I wonder we none of us have ever thought of it before. Your aunt Sophy would be glad to have you, and I could take you there on my way. I really think, Rosalind, this would be the best thing you could do. Winter is closing in, and in present circumstances it is almost impossible to have visitors at Highcourt. Even young Hamerton, how much he is in the way; though he is next to nobody, a young fellow! Come! you must not stay here to wear your nerves to fiddlestrings. I must take you away."

She looked up at him with an earnest glance which he was very conscious of, but did not choose to meet. "Why at this moment above all others?" she said.

"Why? that goes without saying, Rosalind. Your father, to my mind, has never been so bad; and your—I mean Madam—"

"You mean my mother, Uncle John. Well! is she not my mother? I have never known any other. Poor dear little mamma was younger than I am. I never knew her. She is an angel in heaven, and she cannot be jealous of any one on earth. So you think that because papa has never been so ill, and my mother never had so much to bear, it would be the right thing for me, the eldest, the one that can be of most use, to go away?"

"She has her own children, Rosalind."

"Yes, to be sure. Rex, who is at school, and knows about as much of what she needs as the dogs do; and little Sophy, who is barely nine. You must think very little of Rosalind, uncle, if you think these children can make up for me."

"I think a great deal of Rosalind; but we must be reasonable. I thought a woman's own children, however little worth they may be in themselves, were more to her than any one else's. Perhaps I am wrong, but that's in all the copybooks."

"You want to make me believe," said Rosalind, with passion, "that I am nobody's child, that I have no right to love or any home in all the world!"

"My dear! this is madness, Rose. There is your father: and I hope even I count for something; you are the only child I shall ever love. And your aunt Sophy, for whom, in fact, I am pleading, gives you a sort of adoration."

She got up hastily out of the great gloomy house of a chair and came into the dim centre of light in which he stood, and clasped his arm with her hands. "Uncle John," she said, speaking very fast and almost inarticulately, "I am very fond of you. You have always been so good and kind; but I am her, and she is me. Don't you understand? I have always been with her since I was a child. Nobody but me has seen her cry and break down. I know her all through and through. I think her thoughts, not my own. There are no secrets between us. She does not require even to speak, I know what she means without that. There are no secrets between her and me—"

"No secrets," he said; "no secrets! Rosalind, are you so very sure of that—now?"

Her hands dropped from his arm: she went back and hid herself, as if trying to escape from him and herself in the depths of the great chair; and then there burst from her bosom, in spite of her, a sob—suppressed, restrained, yet irrestrainable—the heaving of a bosom filled to overflowing with unaccustomed misery and pain.

John Trevanion did not take advantage of this piteous involuntary confession. He paused a little, being himself somewhat overcome. "My dear little girl," he said at last, "I am talking of no terrible separation. People who are the most devoted to each other, lovers even, have to quit each other occasionally, and pay a little attention to other ties. Come! you need not take this so tragically. Sophy is always longing for you. Your father's sister, and a woman alone in the world; don't you think she has a claim too?"

Rosalind had got herself in check again while he was speaking. "You mean a great deal more than that," she said.

Once more he was silent. He knew very well that he meant a great deal more than that. He meant that his niece should be taken away from the woman who was not her mother, a woman of whom he himself had no manner of doubt, yet who, perhaps—how could any one tell?—was getting weary of her thankless task, and looking forward to the freedom to come. John Trevanion's mind was not much more at rest than that of Rosalind. He had never been supposed to be a partisan of his brother's wife, but perhaps his abstention from all enthusiasm on this subject was out of too much, not too little feeling. He had been prejudiced against her at first; but his very prejudice had produced a warm revulsion of feeling in her favor, when he saw how she maintained her soul, as she went over the worse than red-hot ploughshares of her long ordeal. It would have injured, not helped her with her husband, had he taken her part; and therefore he had refrained with so much steadiness and gravity, that to Rosalind he had always counted as on the other side. But in his heart he had never been otherwise than on the side of the brave woman who, whether her motives had been good or bad in accepting that place, had nevertheless been the most heroic of wives, the tenderest of mothers. It gave him a tender pleasure to be challenged and defied by the generous impetuosity of Rosalind, all in arms for the mother of her soul. But—there was a but, terrible though it was to acknowledge it—he had recognized, as soon as he arrived on this visit, before any indication of suspicion had been given, that there was some subtle change in Madam Trevanion—something furtive in her eye, a watchfulness, a standing on her guard, which had never been there before. It revolted and horrified him to doubt his sister-in-law; he declared to himself with anxious earnestness that he did not, never would or could doubt her; and yet, in the same breath, with that terrible indulgence which comes with experience, began in an under-current of thought to represent to himself her terrible provocations, the excuses she would have, the temptations to which she might be subject. A man gets his imagination polluted by the world even when he least wishes it. In the upper-current of his soul he believed in her with faith unbounded; but underneath was a little warping eddy, a slimy under-draught which brought up silently the apologies, the reasons, the excuses for her. And if, by any impossibility, it should be so, then was it not essential that Rosalind, too pure to imagine, too young to know any evil or what it meant, or how it could be, should be withdrawn? But he was no more happy than Rosalind was, in the conflict of painful thoughts.

"Yes; I mean more than that," he resumed, after an interval. "I mean that this house, at present, is not a comfortable place. You must see now that even you cannot help Mrs. Trevanion much in what she has to go through. I feel myself entirely de trop. No sympathy I could show her would counter-balance the pain she must feel in having always present another witness of your father's abuse—"

"Sympathy!" said Rosalind, with surprise. "I never knew you had any sympathy. I have always considered you as on the other side."

"Does she think so?" he asked quickly, with a sharp sound of pain in his voice; then recollected himself in another moment. "Ah, well," he said, "that's natural, I suppose; the husband's family are on his side—yes, yes, no doubt she has thought so: the more right am I in my feeling that my presence just now must be very distasteful. And even you, Rosalind; think what she must feel to have all that dirt thrown at her in your presence. Do you think the privilege of having a good cry, as you say, when you are alone together, makes up to her for the knowledge that you are hearing every sort of accusation hurled at her head? I believe in my heart," he added hurriedly, with a fictitious fervor, "that it would be the greatest relief possible to her to have the house to herself, and see us all, you included, go away."

Rosalind did not make any reply. She gazed at him from her dark corner with dilated eyes, but he did not see the trouble of her look, nor divine the sudden stimulus his words had given to the whirl of her miserable thoughts. She said to herself that her mother would know, whoever doubted her, that Rosalind never would doubt; and at the same time there came a wondering horror of a question whether indeed her mother would be glad to be rid of her, to have her out of the way, to keep her at least unconscious of the other thing, the secret, perhaps the wrong, that was taking place in those dark evening hours? Might it be, as Uncle John said, better to fly, to turn her back upon any revelation, to refuse to know what it was. The anguish of this conflict of thought tore her unaccustomed heart in twain. And then she tried to realize what the house would be without her, with that profound yet perfectly innocent self-importance of youth which is at once so futile and so touching. So sometimes a young creature dying will imagine, with far more poignant regret than for any suffering of her own, the blank of the empty room, the empty chair, the melancholy vacancy in the house, when she or he has gone hence and is no more. Rosalind saw the great house vacant of herself with a feeling that was almost more than she could bear. When her mother came out of the sick-room, to whom would she go for the repose, the soothing of perfect sympathy—upon whom would she lean when her burden was more than she could bear? When Sophy's lessons were over, where would the child go? Who would write to Rex, and keep upon the schoolboy the essential bond of home? Who would play with the babies in the nursery when their mother was too much occupied to see them? Mamma would have nobody but Russell, who hated her, and her own maid Jane, who was like her shadow, and all the indifferent servants who cared about little but their own comfort. As she represented all these details of the picture to herself, she burst forth all at once into the silence with a vehement "No, no!" John Trevanion had fallen into thought, and the sound of her voice made him start. "No, no!" she cried, "do you think, Uncle John, I am of so little use? Everybody, even papa, would want me. Sometimes he will bid me sit down, that I am something to look at, something not quite so aggravating as all the rest. Is not that something for one's father to say? And what would the children do without me, and Duckworth, who cannot always see mamma about the dinner? No, no, I am of use here, and it is my place. Another time I can go to Aunt Sophy—later on, when papa is—better—when things are going smoothly," she said, with a quiver in her voice, holding back. And just then the distant door of Mr. Trevanion's room opened and closed, and the doctor appeared, holding back the heavy curtains that screened away every draught from the outer world.

CHAPTER V

"Well," said Dr. Beaton, rubbing his hands as he came forward, "at last we are tolerably comfortable. I have got him to bed without much more difficulty than usual, and I hope he will have a good night. But how cold it is here! I suppose, however careful you may be, it is impossible to keep draughts out of an apartment that communicates with the open air. If you will take my advice, Miss Rosalind, you will get to your warm room, and to bed, while your uncle and I adjourn to the smoking-room, where there are creature comforts—"

The doctor was always cheerful. He laughed as if all the incidents of the evening had been the most pleasant in the world.

"Is papa better, doctor?"

"Is Mrs. Trevanion with my brother?"

These two questions were asked together. The doctor answered them both with a "Yes—yes—where would she be but with him? My dear sir, you are a visitor, you are not used to our ways. All that is just nothing. He cannot do without her. We know better, Miss Rosalind; we take it all very easy. Come, come, there is nothing to be disturbed about. I will have you on my hands if you don't mind. My dear young lady, go to bed."

"I have been proposing that she should go to her aunt for a week or two for a little change."

"The very best thing she could do. This is the worst time of the year for Highcourt. So much vegetation is bad in November. Yes—change by all means. But not," said the doctor, with a little change of countenance, "too long, and not too far away."

"Do you think," said Rosalind, "that mamma will not want me to-night? then I will go as you say. But if you think there is any chance that she will want me—"

"She will not leave the patient again. Good-night, Miss Rosalind, sleep sound and get back your roses—or shall I send you something to make you sleep? No? Well, youth will do it, which is best."

She took her candle, and went wearily up the great staircase, pausing, a white figure in the gloom, to wave her hand to Uncle John before she disappeared in the gallery above. The two men stood and watched her without a word. A tender reverence and pity for her youth was in both their minds. There was almost an oppression of self-restraint upon them till she was out of sight and hearing. Then John Trevanion turned to his companion:

"I gather by what you say that you think my brother worse to-night."

"Not worse to-night; but only going the downhill road, and now and then at his own will and pleasure putting on a spurt. The nearer you get to the bottom the greater is the velocity. Sometimes the rate is terrifying at the last."

"And you think, accordingly, that if she goes away it must not be too far; she must be within reach of a hasty summons?"

Dr. Beaton nodded his head several times in succession. "I may be mistaken," he said, "there is a vitality that fairly surprises me; but that is in any other case what I should say."

"Have these outbursts of temper much to do with it? Are they accelerating the end?"

"That's the most puzzling question you could ask. How is a poor medical man, snatching his bit of knowledge as he can find it, to say yea or nay? Oh yes, they have to do with it; everything has to do with it either as cause or effect? If it were not perhaps for the temper, there would be less danger with the heart; and if it were not for the weak heart, there would be less temper. Do ye see? Body and soul are so jumbled together, it is ill to tell which is which. But between them the chances grow less and less. And you will see, by to-night's experience, it's not very easy to put on the drag."

"And yet Mrs. Trevanion is nursing him, you say, as if nothing had happened."

The doctor gave a strange laugh. "A sick man is a queer study," he said, "and especially an excitable person with no self-control and all nerves and temper, like—if you will excuse me for saying so—your brother. Now that he needs her he is very capable of putting all this behind him. He will just ignore it, and cast himself upon her for everything, till he thinks he can do without her again. Ah! it is quite a wonderful mystery, the mind of a sick and selfish man."

"I was thinking rather of her," said John Trevanion.

"Oh! her?" said the doctor, waving his hand; "that's simple. There's nothing complicated in that. She is the first to accept that grand reason as conclusive, just that he has need of her. There's a wonderful philosophy in some women. When they come to a certain pitch they will bear anything. And she is one of that kind. She will put it out of her mind as I would put a smouldering bombshell out of this hall. At least," said the doctor, with that laugh which was so inappropriate, "I hope I would do it, I hope I would not just run away. The thing with women is that they cannot run away."

"These are strange subjects to discuss with—pardon me—a stranger; but you are not a stranger—they can have no secrets from you. Doctor, tell me, is the scene to-night a usual one? Was there nothing particular in it?"

John Trevanion fixed very serious eyes—eyes that held the person they looked on fast, and would permit no escape—on the doctor's face. The other shifted about uneasily from one foot to the other, and did his utmost to avoid that penetrating look.

"Oh, usual enough, usual enough; but there might be certain special circumstances," he said.

"You mean that Mrs. Trevanion—"

"Well, if you will take my opinion, she had probably been to see the coachman's wife, who is far from well, poor body; I should say that was it. It is across a bit of the park, far enough to account for everything."

"But why then not give so simple a reason?"

"Ah! there you beat me; how can I tell? The way in which a thing presents itself to a woman's mind is not like what would occur to you and me."

"Is the coachman's wife so great a favorite? Has she been ill long, and is it necessary to go to see her every night?"

"Mr. Trevanion," said the doctor, "you are well acquainted with the nature of evidence. I cannot answer all these questions. There is no one near Highcourt, as you are aware, that does not look up to Madam; a visit from her is better than physic. She has little time, poor lady, for such kindness. With all that's exacted from her, I cannot tell, for my part, what other moment she can call her own."

John Trevanion would not permit the doctor to escape. He held him still with his keen eyes. "Doctor," he said, "I think I am as much concerned as you are to prove her in the right, whatever happens; but it seems to me you are a special pleader—making your theory to fit the circumstances, ingenious rather than certain."

"Mr. John Trevanion," said the doctor, solemnly, "there is one thing I am certain of, that yon poor lady by your brother's bedside is a good woman, and that the life he leads her is just a hell on earth."

After this there was a pause. The two men stood no longer looking at each other: they escaped from the scrutiny of each other, which they had hitherto kept up, both somewhat agitated and shaken in the solicitude and trouble of the house.

"I believe all that," said John Trevanion at last. "I believe every word. Still—But yet—"

Dr. Beaton made no reply. Perhaps these monosyllables were echoing through his brain too. He had known her for years, and formed his opinion of her on the foundation of long and intimate knowledge. But still—and yet: could a few weeks, a few days, undo the experience of years? It was no crime to walk across the park at night, in the brief interval which the gentlemen spent over their wine after dinner. Why should not Madam Trevanion take the air at that hour if she pleased? Still he made no answer to that breath of doubt.

The conversation was interrupted by the servants who came to close doors and windows, and perform the general shutting-up for the night. Neither of the gentlemen was sorry for this interruption. They separated to make that inevitable change in their dress which the smoking-room demands, with a certain satisfaction in getting rid of the subject, if even for a moment. But when Dr. Beaton reached, through the dim passages from which all life had retired, that one centre of light and fellowship, the sight of young Hamerton in his evening coat, with a pale and disturbed countenance, brought back to him the subject he had been so glad to drop. Hamerton had forgotten his dress-coat, and even that smoking-suit which was the joy of his heart. He had been a prisoner in the drawing-room, or rather in the conservatory, while that terrible scene went on. Never in his harmless life had he touched the borders of tragedy before, and he was entirely unmanned. The doctor found him sitting nervously on the edge of a chair, peering into the fire, his face haggard, his eyes vacant and bloodshot. "I say, doctor," he said, making a grasp at his arm, "I want to tell you; I was in there all the time. What could I do? I couldn't get out with the others. I had been in the conservatory before—and I saw—Good gracious, you don't think I wanted to see! I thought it was better to keep quiet than to show that I had been there all the time."

"You ought to have gone away with the others," said the doctor, "but there is no great harm done; except to your nerves; you look quite shaken. He was very bad. When a man lets himself go on every occasion, and does and says exactly what he has a mind to, that's what it ends in at the last. It is, perhaps, as well that a young fellow like you should know."

"Oh, hang it," said young Hamerton, "that is not the worst. I never was fond of old Trevanion. It don't matter so much about him."

"You mean that to hear a man bullying his wife like that makes you wish to kill him, eh? Well, that's a virtuous sentiment; but she's been long used to it. Let us hope she is like the eels and doesn't mind—"

"It's not that," said the youth again. John Trevanion was in no hurry to appear, and the young man's secret scorched him. He looked round suspiciously to make sure there was no one within sight or hearing. "Doctor," he said, "you are Madam's friend. You take her side?"

Dr. Beaton, who was a man of experience, looked at the agitation of his companion with a good deal of curiosity and some alarm. "If she had a side, yes, to the last of my strength."

"Then I don't mind telling you. When he began to swear—What an old brute he is!"

"Yes? when he began to swear—"

"I thought they mightn't like it, don't you know? We're old friends at home, but still I have never been very much at Highcourt; so I thought they mightn't like to have me there. And I thought I'd just slip out of the way into the conservatory, never thinking how I was to get back. I went right in to the end part where there was no light. You can see out into the park. I never thought of that. I was not thinking anything: when I saw—"

"Get it out, for Heaven's sake! You had no right to be there. What did you see? Some of the maids about—"

"Doctor, I must get it off my mind. I saw Madam Trevanion parting with—a man. I can't help it, I must get it out. I saw her as plainly as I see you."

The doctor was very much disturbed and pale, but he burst into a laugh. "In a dark night like this! You saw her maid I don't doubt, or a kitchen girl with her sweetheart. At night all the cats are gray. And you think it is a fine thing to tell a cock-and-bull story like this—you, a visitor in the house?"

"Doctor, you do me a great deal of injustice." The young man's heart heaved with agitation and pain. "Don't you see it is because I feel I was a sort of eavesdropper against my will, that I must tell you? Do you think Madam Trevanion could be mistaken for a maid? I saw her—part from him and come straight up to the house—and then, in another moment, she came into the room, and I—I saw all that happened there."

"For an unwilling witness, Mr. Hamerton, you seem to have seen a great deal," said the doctor, with a gleam of fury in his eyes.

"So I was—unwilling, most unwilling: you said yourself my nerves were shaken. I'd rather than a thousand pounds I hadn't seen her. But what am I to do? If there was any trial or anything, would they call me as a witness? That's what I want to ask. In that case I'll go off to America or Japan or somewhere. They sha'n't get a word against her out of me."

The moral shock which Dr. Beaton had received was great, and yet he scarcely felt it to be a surprise. He sat for some moments in silence, pondering how to reply. The end of his consideration was that he turned round upon the inquirer with a laugh. "A trial," he said, "about what? Because Mr. Trevanion is nasty to his wife, and says things to her a man should be ashamed to say? Women can't try their husbands for being brutes, more's the pity! and she is used to it; or because (if it was her at all) she spoke to somebody she met—a groom most likely—and gave him his orders! No, no, my young friend, there will be no trial. But for all that," he added, somewhat fiercely, "I would advise you to hold your tongue on the subject now that you have relieved your mind. The Trevanions are kittle customers when their blood's up. I would hold my tongue for the future if I were you."

And then John Trevanion came in, cloudy and thoughtful, in his smoking-coat, with a candle in his hand.

CHAPTER VI

Reginald Trevanion of Highcourt had made at thirty a marriage which was altogether suitable, and everything that the marriage of a young squire of good family and considerable wealth ought to be, with a young lady from a neighboring county with a pretty face and a pretty fortune, and connections of the most unexceptionable kind. He was not himself an amiable person even as a young man, but no one had ever asserted that his temper or his selfishness or his uneasy ways had contributed to bring about the catastrophe which soon overwhelmed the young household. A few years passed with certain futile attempts at an heir which came to nothing; and it was thought that the disappointment in respect to Rosalind, who obstinately insisted upon turning out a girl, notwithstanding her poor young mother's remorseful distress and her father's refusal to believe that Providence could have played him so cruel a trick, had something to do with the gradual fading away of young Madam Trevanion. She died when Rosalind was but a few weeks old, and her husband, whom all the neighborhood credited with a broken heart, disappeared shortly after into that vague world known in a country district as "Abroad;" where healing, it is to be supposed, or at least forgetfulness, is to be found for every sorrow. Nothing was known of him for a year or two. His brother, John Trevanion, was then a youth at college, and, as Highcourt was shut up during its master's absence, disposed of his vacation among other branches of the family, and never appeared; while Sophy, the only sister, who had married long before, was also lost to the district. And thus all means of following the widower in his wanderings were lost to his neighbors. When Mr. Trevanion returned, three years after his first wife's death, the first intimation that he had married again was the appearance of the second Madam Trevanion by his side in the carriage. The servants, indeed, had been prepared by a letter, received just in time to enable them to open hurriedly the shut-up rooms, and make ready for a lady; but that was all. Of course, as everybody allowed, there was nothing surprising in the fact. It is to be expected that a young widower, especially if heartbroken, will marry again; the only curious thing was that no public intimation of the event should have preceded the arrival of the pair. There had been nothing in the papers, no intimation "At the British Embassy—," no hint that an English gentleman from one of the Midland counties was about to bring home a charming wife. And, as a matter of fact, nobody had been able to make out who Mrs. Trevanion was. Her husband and she had met abroad. That was all that was ever known. For a time the researches of the parties interested were very active, and all sorts of leading questions were put to the new wife. But she was of force superior to the country ladies, and baffled them all. And the calm of ordinary existence closed over Highcourt, and the questions in course of time were forgot. Madam Trevanion was not at all of the class of her predecessor. She was not pretty like that gentle creature. Even those who admired her least owned that she was striking, and many thought her handsome, and some beautiful. She was tall; her hair and her eyes were dark; she had the wonderful grace of bearing and movement which is associated with the highest class, but no more belongs to it exclusively than any other grace or gift. Between Madam Trevanion and the Duchess of Newbury, who was herself a duke's daughter, and one of the greatest ladies in England, no chance spectator would have hesitated for a moment as to which was the highest; and yet nobody knew who she was. It was thought by some persons that she showed at first a certain hesitation about common details of life which proved that she had not been born in the purple. But, if so, all that was over before she had been a year at Highcourt, and her manners were pronounced by the best judges to be perfect. She was not shy of society as a novice would have been, nor was her husband diffident in taking her about, as a proud man who has married beneath him so generally is. They accepted all their invitations like people who were perfectly assured of their own standing, and they saw more company at Highcourt than that venerable mansion had seen before for generations. And there was nothing to which society could take exception in the new wife. She had little Rosalind brought home at once, and was henceforth as devoted as any young mother could be to the lovely little plaything of a three-years-old child. Then she did her duty by the family as it becomes a wife to do. The first was a son, as fine a boy as was ever born to a good estate, a Trevanion all over, though he had his mother's eyes—a boy that never ailed anything, as robust as a young lion. Five or six others followed, of whom two died; but these were ordinary incidents of life which establish a family in the esteem and sympathy of its neighbors. The Trevanions had fulfilled all that was needed to be entirely and fully received into the regard of the county when they "buried," as people say, their two children. Four remained, the first-born, young Reginald, and his next sister, who were at the beginning of this history fourteen and nine respectively, and the two little ones of five and seven, who were also, to fulfil all requirements, girl and boy.

But of all these Rosalind had remained, if that may be said of a step-child when a woman has a family of her own, the favorite, the mother's constant companion, everything that an eldest girl could be. Neither the one nor the other ever betrayed a consciousness that they were not mother and daughter. Mr. Trevanion himself, when in his capricious, irritable way he permitted any fondness to appear, preferred Reginald, who was his heir and personal representative. But Rosalind was always by her mother's side. But for Russell, the nurse, and one or two other injudicious persons, she would probably never have found out that Madam was not her mother; but the discovery had done good rather than harm, by inspiring the natural affection with a passionate individual attachment in which there were all those elements of choice and independent election which are the charm of friendship. Mrs. Trevanion was Rosalind's example, her heroine, the perfect type of woman to her eyes. And, indeed, she was a woman who impressed the general mind with something of this character. There are many good women who do not do so, who look commonplace enough in their life, and are only known in their full excellence from some revelation afterwards of heroism unknown. But Mrs. Trevanion carried her diploma in her eyes. The tenderness in them was like sunshine to everybody about her who was in trouble. She never was harsh, never intolerant, judged nobody—which in a woman so full of feeling and with so high a standard of moral excellence was extraordinary. This was what gave so great a charm to her manners. A well-bred woman, even of an inferior type, will not allow a humble member of society to feel himself or herself de trop; but there are many ways of doing this, and the ostentatious way of showing exaggerated attention to an unlucky stranger is as painful to a delicate mind as neglect. But this was a danger which Mrs. Trevanion avoided. No one could tell what the rank was of the guests in her drawing-room, whether it was the duchess or the governess that was receiving her attentions. They were all alike gentlewomen in this gracious house. The poor, who are always the hardest judges of a new claimant of their favor, and who in this case were much set on finding out that a woman who came from "abroad" could be no lady, gave in more reluctantly, yet yielded too like their betters—with the exception of Russell and the family in the village to which she belonged. These were the only enemies, so far as any one was aware, whom Madam possessed, and they were enemies of a visionary kind, in no open hostility, receiving her favors like the rest, and kept in check by the general state of public opinion. Still, if there was anything to be found out about the lady of Highcourt, these were the only hostile bystanders desirous of the opportunity of doing her harm.

But everything had fallen into perfect peace outside the house for years. Now and then, at long intervals, it might indeed be remarked in the course of a genealogical conversation such as many people love, that it was not known who Mrs. Trevanion the second had been. "His first wife was a Miss Warren, one of the Warrens of Warrenpoint. The present one—well, I don't know who she was; they married abroad." But that was all that now was ever said. It would be added probably that she was very handsome, or very nice, or quite comme il faut, and so her defect of parentage was condoned.

Everything was harmonious, friendly, and comfortable outside. The county could not resist her fine manners, her looks, her quiet assumption of the place that belonged to her. But within doors Mrs. Trevanion soon came to know that no very peaceful life was to be expected. There were people who said that she had not the look of a happy woman even when she first came home. In repose her face was rather sad than otherwise at all times. Mr. Trevanion was still in the hot fit of a bridegroom's enthusiasm when he brought her home, but even then he was the most troublesome, the most exacting, the most fidgety of bridegrooms. Her patience with all his demands was boundless. She would change her dress half a dozen times in an evening to please him. She would start off with him on a sudden wild expedition at half an hour's notice, without a word or even look of annoyance. And when the exuberance of love wore off, and the exactions continued, with no longer caresses and sweet words, but blame and reproach and that continual fault-finding which it is so hard to put up with amiably, Mrs. Trevanion still endured everything, consented to everything, with a patience that would not be shaken. It was now nearly ten years since the heart-disease which had brought him nearly to death's door first showed itself. He had rheumatic fever, and then afterwards, as is so usual, this terrible legacy which that complaint leaves behind it. From that moment, of course, the patience which had been so sweetly exercised before became a religious duty. It was known in the house that nothing must cross or agitate or annoy Mr. Trevanion. But, indeed, it was not necessary that anything should annoy him; he was his own chief annoyance, his own agitator. He would flame up in sudden wrath at nothing at all, and turn the house upside down, and send everybody but his wife flying, with vituperations which scarcely the basest criminal could have deserved. And his wife, who never abandoned him, became the chief object of these passionate assaults. He accused her of every imaginable fault. He began to talk of all she owed him, to declare that he married her when she had nothing, that he had taken her out of the depths, that she owed everything to him; he denounced her as ungrateful, base, trying to injure his health under pretence of nursing him, that she might get the power into her own hands. But she would find out her mistake, he said; she would learn, when he was gone, the difference between having a husband to protect her and nobody. To all these wild accusations and comments the little circle round Mrs. Trevanion had become familiar and indifferent. "Pegging away at Madam, as usual," Mr. Dorrington, the butler, said. "Lord, I'd let him peg! I'd leave him to himself and see how he likes it," replied the cook and housekeeper. No one had put the slightest faith in the objurgations of the master. To Rosalind they were the mere extravagances of that mad temper which she had been acquainted with all her life. What her father said about his wife was about as reasonable as his outburst of certainty that England was going to the devil when the village boys broke down one of the young trees. She did not judge papa for such a statement. She cried a little at his vehemence, which did himself so much harm, and laughed a little secretly, with a heavy sense of guilt, at his extravagance and exaggerations. Poor papa! it was not his fault, it was because he was so ill. He was too weak and ailing to be able to restrain himself as other people did. But he did not mean it—how could he mean it? To say that mamma wanted to break his neck if she did not put his pillow as he liked it, to accuse her of a systematic attempt to starve him if his luncheon was two minutes late or his soup not exactly to his taste—all that was folly. And no doubt it was also folly, all that about raising her from nothing and taking her without a penny. Rosalind, though very much disturbed when she was present at one of these scenes, yet permitted herself to laugh at it when it was over or she had got away. Poor papa! and then when he had raged himself into a fit of those heart-spasms he was so ill; how sad to see him suffering so terribly, gasping for breath! Poor papa! to think that he did so much to bring it on himself was only a pity the more.

Thus things had gone on for years. When Dr. Beaton came to live in the house there had been a temporary amendment. The presence of a stranger, perhaps, had been a check upon the patient; and perhaps the novelty of a continual and thoroughly instructed watcher—who knew how to follow the symptoms of the malady, and foresaw an outburst before it came—did something for him; and certainly there had been an amendment. But by and by familiarity did away with these advantages. Dr. Beaton exhausted all the resources of his science, and Mr. Trevanion ceased to be upon his guard with a man whom he saw every day. Thus the house lived in a forced submission to the feverish vagaries of its head; and he himself sat and railed at everybody, pleased with nothing, claiming every thought and every hour, but never contented with the service done him. And greater and greater became the force of his grievances against his wife and his sense of having done everything for her; how he had stood by her when nobody else would look at her, how he had lifted her out of some vague humiliation and abandonment, how she owed him everything, yet treated him with brutal carelessness, and sought his death, were the most favorite accusations on his lips. Mrs. Trevanion listened with a countenance that rarely showed any traces of emotion. She had shrunk a little at first from these painful accusations; but soon had come to listen to them with absolute calm. She had borne them like a saint, like a philosopher; and yet within the last month everybody saw there had been a change.

CHAPTER VII

When Mrs. Trevanion came to Highcourt, she brought with her a maid who had, during all the sixteen years of her married life, remained with her without the slightest breach of fidelity or devotion. Jane was, the household thought, somewhat like her mistress, a resemblance in all likelihood founded upon the constant attendance of the one upon the other, and the absorbing admiration, rising almost to a kind of worship, with which Jane regarded her lady. After all, it was only in figure and movement, not in face, that the resemblance existed. Jane was tall like Mrs. Trevanion. She had caught something of that fine poise of the head, something of the grace, which distinguished her mistress; but whereas Mrs. Trevanion was beautiful, Jane was a plain woman, with somewhat small eyes, a wide mouth, and features that were not worth considering. She was of a constant paleness and she was marked with smallpox, neither of which are embellishing. Still, if you happened to walk behind her along one of the long passages, dressed in one of Madam's old gowns, it was quite possible that you might take her for Madam. And Jane was not a common lady's maid. She was entirely devoted to her mistress, not only to her service, but to her person, living like her shadow—always in her rooms, always with her, sharing in everything she did, even in the nursing of Mr. Trevanion, who tolerated her presence as he tolerated that of no one else. Jane sat, indeed, with the upper servants at their luxurious and comfortable table, but she did not live with them. She had nothing to do with their amusements, their constant commentary upon the family. One or two butlers in succession—for before Mr. Trevanion gave up all active interference in the house there had been a great many changes in butlers—had done their best to make themselves agreeable to Jane; but though she was always civil, she was cold, they said, as any fish, and no progress was possible. Mrs. Jennings, the cook and housekeeper, instinctively mistrusted the quiet woman. She was a deal too much with her lady that astute person said. That was deserting her own side: for do not the masters form one faction and the servants another? The struggle of life may be conducted on more or less honorable terms, but still a servant who does not belong to his own sphere is unnatural, just as a master is who throws himself into the atmosphere of the servants' hall. The domestics felt sure that such a particular union between the mistress and the maid could not exist in the ordinary course of affairs, and that it must mean something which was not altogether right. Jane never came, save for her meals, to the housekeeper's room. She was always up-stairs, in case, she said, that she should be wanted. Why should she be wanted more than any other person in her position? When now and then Mrs. Trevanion, wearied out with watching and suffering, hurried to her room to rest, or to bathe her aching forehead, or perhaps even to lighten the oppression of her heart by a few tears, Jane was always there to soothe and tend and sympathize. The other servants knew as well as Jane how much Madam had to put up with, but yet they thought it very peculiar that a servant should be so much in her mistress's confidence. There was a mystery in it. It had been suspected at first that Jane was a poor relation of Madam's; and the others expected jealously that this woman would be set over their heads, and themselves humiliated under her sway. But this never took place, and the household changed as most households change, and one set of maids and men succeeded each other without any change in Jane. There remained a tradition in the house that she was a sort of traitor in the camp, a servant who was not of her own faction, but on the master's side; but this was all that survived of the original prejudice, and no one now expected to be put under the domination of Jane, or regarded her with the angry suspicion of the beginning, or supposed her to be Madam's relation. Jane, like Madam, had become an institution, and the present generation of servants did not inquire too closely into matters of history.

This was true of all save one. But there was one person in the house who was as much an institution as Jane, or even as Jane's mistress, with whom nobody interfered, and whom it was impossible to think of as dethroned or put aside from her supreme place. Russell was in the nursery what Madam herself was in Highcourt. In that limited but influential domain she was the mistress, and feared nobody. She had been the chosen of the first Mrs. Trevanion, and the nurse of Rosalind, with whom she had gone to her Aunt Sophy's during Mr. Trevanion's widowhood, and in charge of whom she had returned to Highcourt when he married. Russell knew very well that the estates were entailed and that Rosalind could not be the heir, but yet she resented the second marriage as if it had been a wrong done at once to herself and her charge. If Jane was of Madam's faction, Russell was of a faction most strenuously and sternly antagonistic to Madam. The prejudice which had risen up against the lady who came from abroad, and whom nobody knew, and which had died away in the course of time, lived and survived in this woman with all the force of the first day. She had been on the watch all these years to find out something to the discredit of her mistress, and no doubt the sentiment had been strengthened by the existence of Jane, who was a sort of rival power in her own sphere, and lessened her own importance by being as considerable a person as herself. Russell had watched these two women with a hostile vigilance which never slackened. She was in her own department the most admirable and trustworthy of servants, and when she received Mrs. Trevanion's babies into her charge, carried nothing of her prejudice against their mother into her treatment of them. If not as dear to her as her first charge, Rosalind, they were still her children, Trevanions, quite separated in her mind from the idea of their mother. Perhaps the influence of Russell accounted for certain small griefs which Madam had to bear as one of the consequences of her constant attendance on her husband, the indifference to her of her little children in their earlier years. But she said to herself with a wonderful philosophy that she could expect no less; that absorbed as she was in her husband's sick-room all day, it was not to be expected that the chance moments she could give to the nursery would secure the easily diverted regard of the babies, to whom their nurse was the principal figure in earth and heaven. And that nurse was so good, so careful, so devoted, that it would have been selfishness indeed to have deprived the children of her care because of a personal grievance of this kind. "Why should Russell dislike me so much?" she would say sometimes to Rosalind, who tried to deny the charge, and Jane, who shook her head and could not explain. "Oh, dear mamma, it is only her temper. She does not mean it," Rosalind would say. And Madam, who had so much to suffer from temper in another quarter, did not reject the explanation. "Temper explains a great many things," she said, "but even that does not quite explain. She is so good to the children and hates their mother. I feel I have a foe in the house so long as she is here." Rosalind had a certain love for her nurse, notwithstanding her disapproval of her, and she looked up with some alarm. "Do you mean to send her away?"

"Miss Rosalind," said Jane, "my lady is right. It is a foe and nothing less, a real enemy she has in that woman; if she would send Russell away I'd be very glad for one."

"You need not fear, my love," Madam said. "Hush, Jane, if she is my foe, you are my partisan. I will never send Russell away, Rosalind; but when the children are grown up, if I live to see it, or if she would be so kind as to marry, and go off in a happy way, or even if when you are married she preferred to go with you—I think I should draw my breath more freely. It is painful to be under a hostile eye."

"The nurse's eye, mamma, and you the mistress of the house!"

"It does not matter, my dear. I have always had a sympathy for Haman, who could not enjoy his grandeur for thinking of that Jew in the gate that was always looking at him so cynically. It gets unendurable sometimes. You must have a very high opinion of yourself to get over the low view taken of you by that sceptic sitting in the gate. But now I must go to your father," Mrs. Trevanion said. She had come up-stairs with a headache, and had sat down by the open window to get a little air, though the air was intensely cold and damp. It was a refreshment, after the closeness of the room in which the invalid sat with an unvarying temperature and every draught shut out. Rosalind stood behind her mother's chair with her hands upon Mrs. Trevanion's shoulders, and the tired woman leaned back upon the girl's young bosom so full of life. "But you will catch cold at the window, my Rose! No, it does me good, I want a little air, but it is too cold for you. And now I must go back to your father," she said, rising. She stooped and kissed the cheek of the girl she loved, and went away with a smile to her martyrdom. These moments of withdrawal from her heavy duties were the consolations of her life.

"Miss Rosalind," said Jane, "that you should love your old nurse I don't say a word against it—but if ever there is a time when a blow can be struck at my lady that woman will do it. She will never let the little ones be here when their mamma can see them. They're having their sleep, or they're out walking, or they're at their lessons; and Miss Sophy the same. And if ever she can do us an ill turn—"

"How could she do you an ill turn? That is, Jane, I beg your pardon, she might, perhaps, be nasty to you—but, mamma! What blow, as you call it, can be struck at mamma?"

"Oh, how can I tell?" said Jane; "I never was clever; there's things happening every day that no one can foresee; and when a woman is always watching to spy out any crevice, you never can tell, Miss Rosalind, in this world of trouble, what may happen unforeseen."

This speech made no great impression on Rosalind's mind at the time, but it recurred to her after, and gave her more trouble than any wickedness of Russell's had power to do. In the meantime, leaving Jane, she went to the nursery, and with the preoccupation of youth carried with her the same subject, heedless and unthinking what conclusions Russell, whose faculties were always alert on this question, might draw.

"Russell," she said, after a moment, "why are you always so disagreeable to mamma?"

"Miss Rosalind, I do hate to hear you call her mamma. Why don't you say 'my stepmother,' as any other young lady would in your place?"

"Because she is not my stepmother," said the girl, with a slight stamp on the floor. "Just look at little Johnny, taking in all you say with his big eyes. She is all the mother I have ever known, and I love her better than any one in the world."

"And just for that I can't bear it," cried the woman. "What would your own dear mamma say?"

"If she were as jealous and ill-tempered as you I should not mind what she said," said the girl. "Don't think, if you continue like this, you will ever have any sympathy from me."

"Oh, Miss Rosalind, what you are saying is as bad as swearing; worse, it's blasphemy; and the time will come when you'll remember and be sorry. No, though you think I'm a brute, I sha'n't say anything before the children. But the time will come—"

"What a pity you are not on the stage, Russell! You would make a fine Meg Merrilies, or something of that kind; the old woman that is always cursing somebody and prophesying trouble. That is just what you are suited for. I will come and see you your first night."

"Me! on the stage!" cried Russell, with a sense of outraged dignity which words cannot express. Such an insult had never been offered to her before. Rosalind went out of the room quickly, angry but laughing when she had given this blow. She wanted to administer a stinging chastisement, and she had done so. Her own cleverness in discovering what would hit hardest pleased her. She began to sing, out of wrathful indignation and pleasure, as she went down-stairs.

"Me! on the stage!" Russell repeated to herself. A respectable upper servant in a great house could not have had a more degrading suggestion made to her. She could have cried as she sat there gnashing her teeth. And this too was all on account of Madam, the strange woman who had taken her first mistress's place even in the heart of her own child. Perhaps if Rosalind had treated her stepmother as a stepmother ought to be treated, Russell would have been less antagonistic; but Mrs. Trevanion altogether was obnoxious to her. She had come from abroad; she had brought her own maid with her, who was entirely unsociable, and never told anything; who was a stranger, a foreigner perhaps, for anything that was known of her, and yet was Russell's equal, or more, by right of Madam's favor, though Russell had been in the house for years. What subtle antipathy there might be besides these tangible reasons for hating them, Russell did not know. She only knew that from the first moment she had set eyes upon her master's new wife she had detested her. There was something about her that was not like other women. There must be a secret. When had it ever been known that a maid gave up everything—the chat, the game at cards, the summer stroll in the park, even the elegant civilities of a handsome butler—for the love of her mistress? It was unnatural; no one had ever heard of such a thing. What could it be but a secret between these women which held them together, which it was their interest to conceal from the world? But the time would come, Russell said to herself. If she watched night and day she should find it out; if she waited for years and years the time and opportunity would come at last.

CHAPTER VIII

This conversation, or series of conversations, took place shortly before the time at which this history begins, and it was very soon after that the strange course of circumstances commenced which was of so much importance in the future life of the Trevanions of Highcourt. When the precise moment was at which the attention of Rosalind was roused and her curiosity excited, she herself could not have told. It was not until Madam Trevanion had fallen for some time into the singular habit of disappearing after dinner, nobody knew where. It had been very usual with her to run up to the nursery when she left the dining-room, to see if the children were asleep. Mr. Trevanion, when he was at all well, liked to sit, if not over his wine, for he was abstemious by force of necessity, yet at the table, talking with whomsoever might be his guest. Though his life was so little adapted to the habits of hospitality, he liked to have some one with whom he could sit and talk after dinner, and who would make up his rubber when he went into the drawing-room. He had been tolerably well, for him, during the autumn, and there had been a succession of three-days' visitors, all men, succeeding each other, and all chosen on purpose to serve Mr. Trevanion's after-dinner talk and his evening rubber. And it was a moment in which the women of the household felt themselves free. As for Rosalind, she would establish herself between the lamp and the fire and read a novel, which was one of her favorite pastimes; while Mrs. Trevanion, relieved from the constant strain of attendance, would run up-stairs, "to look at the children," as she said. Perhaps she did not always look long at the children, but this served as the pretext for a moment of much-needed rest, Rosalind had vaguely perceived a sort of excitement about her for some time—a furtive look, an anxiety to get away from the table as early as possible. While she sat there she would change color, as was not at all her habit, for ordinarily she was pale. Now flushes and pallor contended with each other. When she spoke there was a little catch as of haste and breathlessness in her voice, and when she made the usual little signal to Rosalind her hand would tremble, and the smile was very uncertain on her lip. Nor did she stop to say anything, but hurried up-stairs like one who has not a moment to lose. And it happened on several occasions that Mr. Trevanion and the guest and the doctor were in the drawing-room, however long they sat, before Madam had returned. For some time Rosalind took no notice of this. She did not indeed remark it. It had never occurred to her to watch or to inspect her stepmother's conduct. Hitherto she had been convinced that it was right always. She read her novel in her fireside corner, and never discovered that there was any break in the usual routine. When the first painful light burst upon her she could not tell. It was first a word from Russell, then the sight of Jane gazing out very anxiously upon the night, when it rained, from a large staircase window, and then the aspect of affairs altogether. Mr. Trevanion began to remark very querulously on his wife's absence. Where was she? What did she mean by always being out of the way just when he wanted her? and much more of the same kind. And when Madam came in she looked flushed and hurried, and brought with her a whole atmosphere of fresh out-door air from the damp and somewhat chilly night. It was the fragrance and sensation of this fresh air which roused Rosalind the most. It startled her with a sense of something that was new, something that she did not understand. The thought occurred to her next morning when she first opened her eyes, the first thing that came into her mind. That sudden gush of fresh air, how did it come? It was not from the nursery that one could bring an atmosphere like that.

And thus other days and other evenings passed. There was something new altogether in Mrs. Trevanion's face, a sort of awakening, but not to happiness. When they drove out she was very silent, and her eyes were watchful as though looking for something. They went far before the carriage, before the rapid horses, with a watchful look. For whom could she be looking? Rosalind ventured one day to put the question. "For whom—could I be looking? I am looking for no one," Mrs. Trevanion said, with a sudden rush of color to her face; and whereas she had been leaning forward in the carriage, she suddenly leaned back and took no more notice, scarcely speaking again till they returned home. Such caprice was not like Madam. She did everything as usual, fulfilled all her duties, paid her calls, and was quite as lively and interested as usual in the neighbors whom she visited, entering into their talk almost more than was her habit. But when she returned to the society of her own family she was not as usual.

Sometimes there was a pathetic tone in her voice, and she would excuse herself in a way which brought the tears to Rosalind's eyes.

"My dear," she would say, "I fear I am bad company at present. I have a great deal to think of."

"You are always the best of company," Rosalind would say in the enthusiasm of her affection, and Mrs. Trevanion looked at her with a tender gratitude which broke the girl's heart.

"When I want people to hear the best that can be said of me, I will send them to you, Rosalind," she said. "Oh, what a blessing of God that you should be the one to think most well of me! God send it may always be so!" she added, with a voice full of feeling so deep and anxious that the girl did not know what to think.

"How can you speak so, mamma? Think well! Why, you are my mother; there is nobody but you," she said.

"Do you know, Rosalind," said Mrs. Trevanion, "that the children who are my very own will not take me for granted like you."

"And am not I your very own? Whom have I but you?" Rosalind said.

Mrs. Trevanion turned and kissed her, though it was in the public road. Rosalind felt that her cheek was wet. What was the meaning of it? They had always been mother and daughter in the fullest sense of the word, unconsciously, without any remark, the one claiming nothing, the other not saying a word of her devotion. It was already a painful novelty that it should be mentioned between them how much they loved each other, for natural love like this has no need of words.

And then sometimes Madam would be severe.

"Mamma," said little Sophy on one of these drives, "there is somebody new living in the village—a gentleman—well, perhaps not a gentleman. Russell says nobody knows who he is. And he gets up in the middle of the day, and goes out at night."

"I should not think it could be any concern of yours who was living in the village," Mrs. Trevanion said, far more hastily and hotly than her wont.

"Oh, but mamma, it is so seldom any one comes; and he lives at the Red Lion; and it is too late for sketching, so he can't be an artist; and, mamma, Russell says—"

"I will not have Russell fill your head with the gossip of the village," said Madam, with a flush of anger. "You are too much disposed to talk about your neighbors. Tell Russell I desire you to have nothing to do with the village news—"

"Oh, but mamma, it isn't village news, it's a stranger. Everybody wants to find out about a stranger; and he is so—"

Mrs. Trevanion gave a slight stamp of impatience and anger. "You have still less to do with strangers. Let me hear no more about this," she said. She did not recover from the thrill of irritation during the whole course of the drive. Sophy, who was unused to such vehemence, retired into sulkiness and tears, while Rosalind, wounded a little to see that her mother was fallible, looked on, surprised. She who was never put out! And then again Madam Trevanion came down from her eminence and made a sort of excuse which troubled her young adorer almost more than the fact. "I am afraid I am growing irritable. I have so much to think of," she said.

What was it she had to think of now above other times? Mr. Trevanion, for him, was well. They had people staying in the house who amused him; and John Trevanion was coming, Uncle John, whom everybody liked. And the children were all well; and nothing wrong, so far as any one was aware, in the business matters which Mrs. Trevanion bore the weight of to serve her husband; the farms were all let, there was nothing out of gear anywhere. What had she to think of? Rosalind was greatly, painfully puzzled by this repeated statement. And by degrees her perplexity grew. It got into the air, and seemed to infect all the members of the household. The servants acquired a watchful air. The footman who came in to take away the teacups looked terribly conscious that Madam was late. There was a general watchfulness about. You could not cross the hall, or go up-stairs, or go through a corridor from one part of the house to another, without meeting a servant who would murmur an apology, as if his or her appearance was an accident, but who were all far too wide awake and on the alert to have come there accidentally. Anxiety of this kind, or even curiosity, is cumulative, and communicates itself imperceptibly with greater and greater force as it goes on. And in the midst of the general drama a curious side-scene was going on always between the two great antagonists in the household—Russell and Jane. They kept up a watch, each on her side. The one could not open her door or appear upon the upper stairs without a corresponding click of the door of the other; a stealthy inspection behind a pillar, or out of a corner, to see what was going on; and both of them had expeditions of their own which would not bear explanation, both in the house and without. In this point Jane had a great advantage over her adversary. She could go out almost when she pleased, while Russell was restrained by the children, whom she could not leave. But Russell had other privileges that made up for this. She had nursery-maids under her orders; she had spies about in all sorts of places; her relations lived in the village. Every piece of news, every guess and suspicion, was brought to her. And she had a great faculty for joining her bits of information together. By and by Russell began to wear a triumphant look, and Jane a jaded and worn one; they betrayed in their faces the fact that whatever their secret struggle was, one was getting the better of the other. Jane gave Rosalind pathetic looks, as if asking whether she might confide in her, while Russell uttered hints and innuendoes, ending, indeed, as has been seen, in intimations more positive. When she spoke so to Rosalind it may be supposed that she was not silent to the rest of the house; or that she failed, with the boldness of her kind, to set forth and explain the motives of her mistress. For some time before the incident of the bramble, every one in the house had come to be fully aware that Madam went out every evening, however cold, wet, and miserable it might be. John Trevanion acquired the knowledge he could not tell how; he thought it was from that atmosphere of fresh air which unawares she brought with her on those occasions when she was late, when the gentlemen had reached the drawing-room before she came in. This was not always the case. Sometimes they found her there, seated in her usual place, calm enough, save for a searching disquiet in her eyes, which seemed to meet them as they came in, asking what they divined or knew. They all knew—that is to say, all but Mr. Trevanion himself, whose vituperations required no particular occasion, and ran on much the same whatever happened, and the temporary three-days' guest, who at the special moment referred to was young Hamerton. Sometimes incidents would occur which had no evident bearing upon this curious secret which everybody knew, but yet nevertheless disturbed the brooding air with a possibility of explosion. On one occasion little Sophy was the occasion of a thrill in this electrical atmosphere which nobody quite understood. The child had come in to dessert, and was standing by her father's side, consuming all the sweetmeats she could get.

"Oh, mamma!" Sophy said suddenly and loudly, addressing her mother across the table; "you know that gentleman at the Red Lion I told you about?"

"What gentleman at the Red Lion?" said her father, who had a keen ear for gossip.

"Do not encourage her, Reginald," said Madam from the other end of the table; "I cannot let her bring the village stories here."

"Let us hear about the gentleman from the Red Lion," he said; "perhaps it is something amusing. I never am allowed to hear what is going on. Come, Sophy, what's about him? We all want to know."

"Oh, but mamma will be so cross if I tell you! She will not let me say a word. When I told her before she stamped her foot—"

"Ha, Madam!" said the husband, "we've caught you. I thought you were one that never lost your temper. But Sophy knows better. Come, what of this gentleman—"

"I think, Rosalind, we had better go," said Mrs. Trevanion, rising. "I do not wish the child to bring tales out of the village. Sophy!" The mother looked at her with eyes of command. But the little girl felt herself the heroine of the occasion, and perfectly secure, held in her father's arm.

"Oh, it is only that nobody knows him!" she said in her shrill little voice; "and he gets up in the middle of the day, and never goes out till night. Russell knows all about him. Russell says he is here for no good. He is like a man in a story-book, with such big eyes. Oh! Russell says she would know him anywhere, and I think so should I—"

Mrs. Trevanion stood listening till all was said. Her face was perfectly without color, her eyes blazing upon the malicious child with a strange passion. What she was doing was the most foolish thing a woman could do. Her anger succeeded by so strange a calm, the intense seriousness with which she regarded what after all was nothing more than a childish disobedience, gave the most exaggerated importance to the incident. Why should she take it so seriously, everybody asked? What was it to her? And who could hinder the people who were looking on, and knew that Madam was herself involved in something unexplainable, something entirely new to all her habits, from receiving this new actor into their minds as somehow connected with it, somehow appropriated by her? When the child stopped, her mother interfered again with the same exaggeration of feeling, her very voice thrilling the tranquillity of the room as she called Sophy to follow her. "Don't beat her," Mr. Trevanion called out, with a chuckling laugh. "Sophy, if they whip you, come back to me. Nobody shall whip you for answering your father. Come and tell me all you hear about the gentleman, and never mind what Madam may say."

Sophy was frightened, however, there could be no doubt, as she followed her mother. She began to cry as she crept through the hall. Mrs. Trevanion held her head high; there was a red spot on each of her cheeks. She paused for a moment and looked at Rosalind, as if she would have spoken; then hurried away, taking no notice of the half-alarmed, half-remorseful child, who stood and gazed after her, at once relieved and disappointed. "Am I to get off?" Sophy whispered, pulling at Rosalind's dress. And then she burst into a sudden wail of crying: "Oh, Rosalind, mamma has never said good-night!"

"You do not deserve it, after having disobeyed her," said Rosalind. And with her young mind all confused and miserable, she went to the drawing-room to her favorite seat between the fire and the lamp; but though her novel was very interesting, she did not read it that night.

CHAPTER IX

Next day, as they drove out in the usual afternoon hour while Mr. Trevanion took his nap after luncheon, a little incident happened which was nothing, yet gave Rosalind, who was alone with her stepmother in the carriage, a curious sensation. A little way out of the village, on the side of the road, she suddenly perceived a man standing, apparently waiting till they should pass. Madam had been very silent ever since they left home, so much more silent than it was her habit to be that Rosalind feared she had done something to incur Mrs. Trevanion's displeasure. Instead of the animated conversations they used to have, and the close consultations that were habitual between them, they sat by each other silent, scarcely exchanging a word in a mile. Rosalind was not herself a great talker, but when she was with this other and better self, she flowed forth in lively observation and remark, which was not talk, but the involuntary natural utterance which came as easily as her breath. This day, however, she had very little to say, and Madam nothing. They leaned back, each in her corner, with a blank between them, which Rosalind now and then tried to break with a wistful question as to whether mamma was cold, whether she did not find the air too keen, if she would like the carriage closed, etc., receiving a smile and a brief reply, but no more. They had fallen into silence almost absolute as they passed through the village, and it was when they emerged once more into the still country road that the incident which has been referred to took place. Some time before they came up to him, Rosalind remarked the man standing under one of the hedgerow trees, close against it, looking towards them, as if waiting for the carriage to pass. Though she was not eager for the tales of the village like Sophy, Rosalind had a country girl's easily roused curiosity in respect to a stranger. She knew at once by the outline of him, before she could make out even what class he belonged to, that this was some one she had never seen before. As the carriage approached rapidly she grew more and more certain. He was a young man, a gentleman—at least his dress and attitude were like those of a gentleman; he was slim and straight, not like the country louts. As he turned his head towards the carriage, Rosalind thought she had never seen a more remarkable face. He was very pale; his features were large and fine, and his pallor and thinness were made more conspicuous by a pair of very large, dreamy, uncertain dark eyes. These eyes were looking so intently towards the carriage that Rosalind had almost made up her mind that there was to be some demand upon their sympathy, some petition or appeal. She could not help being stirred with all the impetuosity of her nature, frank and warm-hearted and generous, towards this poor gentleman. He looked as if he had been ill, as if he meant to throw himself upon their bounty, as if—The horses sped on with easy speed as she sat up in the carriage and prepared herself for whatever might happen. It is needless to say that nothing happened as far as the bystander was concerned. He looked intently at them, but did no more. Rosalind was so absorbed in a newly awakened interest that she thought of nothing else, till suddenly, turning round to her companion, she met—not her stepmother's sympathetic countenance, but the blackness of a veil in which Mrs. Trevanion had suddenly enveloped herself. "That must surely be the gentleman Sophy was talking of," she said. Madam gave a slight shiver in her furs. "It is very cold," she said; "it has grown much colder since we came out."

"Shall I tell Robert to close the carriage, mother?"

"Oh, no, it is unnecessary. You can tell him to go home by the Wildwood gate. I should not have come out if I had known it was so cold."

"I hope you have not taken cold, mamma. To me the air seems quite soft. I suppose," Rosalind said, in that occasional obtuseness which belongs to innocence, "you did not notice, as you put down your veil just then, that gentleman on the road? I think he must be the gentleman Sophy talked about—very pale, with large eyes. I think he must have been ill. I feel quite interested in him too."

"No, I did not observe—"

"I wish you had noticed him, mamma. I should know him again anywhere; it is quite a remarkable face. What can he want in the village? I think you should make the doctor call, or send papa's card. If he should be ill—"

"Rosalind, you know how much I dislike village gossip. A stranger in the inn can be nothing to us. There is Dr. Smith if he wants anything," said Madam, hurriedly, almost under her breath. And she shivered again, and drew her furred mantle more closely round her. Though it was November, the air was soft and scarcely cold at all, Rosalind thought in her young hardiness; but then Mrs. Trevanion, shut up so much in an overheated room, naturally was more sensitive to cold.

This was in the afternoon; and on the same evening there occurred the incident of the bramble, and all the misery that followed, concluding in Mr. Trevanion's attack, and the sudden gloom and terror thrown upon the house. Rosalind had no recollection of so trifling a matter in the excitement and trouble that followed. She saw her stepmother again only in the gray of the winter morning, when waking suddenly, with that sense of some one watching her which penetrates the profoundest sleep, she found Mrs. Trevanion seated by her bedside, extremely pale, with dark lines under her eyes, and the air of exhaustion which is given by a sleepless night.

"I came to tell you, dear, that your father, at last, is getting a little sleep," she said.

"Oh, mamma—But you have had no sleep—you have been up all night!"

"That does not much matter. I came to say also, Rosalind, that I fear my being so late last night and his impatience had a great deal to do with bringing on the attack. It might be almost considered my fault."

"Oh, mamma! we all know," cried Rosalind, inexpressibly touched by the air with which she spoke, "how much you have had to bear."

"No more than what was my duty. A woman when she marries accepts all the results. She may not know what there will be to bear, but whatever it is it is all involved in the engagement. She has no right to shrink—"

There was a gravity, almost solemnity, in Madam's voice and look which awed the girl. She seemed to be making a sort of formal and serious explanation. Rosalind had seen her give way under her husband's cruelty and exactions. She had seen her throw herself upon the bed and weep, though there had never been a complaint in words to blame the father to the child. This was one point in which, and in which alone, the fact that Rosalind was his daughter, and not hers, had been apparent. Now there was no accusation, but something like a statement, formal and solemn, which was explained by the exhaustion and calm as of despair that was in her face.

"That has been my feeling all through," she said. "I wish you to understand it, Rosalind. If Reginald were at home—well, he is a boy, and I could not explain to him as I can to you. I want you to understand me; I have had more to bear, a great deal more, than I expected. But I have always said to myself it was in the day's work. You may perhaps be tempted to think, looking back, that I have had, even though he has been so dependent upon me, an irritating influence. Sometimes I have myself thought so, and that some one else—But if you will put one thing to another," she added, going on in the passionless, melancholy argument, "you will perceive that the advantage to him of my knowledge of all his ways counter-balances any harm that might arise from that; and then there is always the doubt whether any one else would not have been equally irritating after a time."

"Mother," cried Rosalind, who had raised herself in her bed and was gazing anxiously into the pale and worn-out face which was turned half away from her, not looking at her; "mother! why do you say all this to me? Do I want you to explain yourself, I who know that you have been the best, the kindest—"

Mrs. Trevanion did not look at her, but put up her hand to stop this interruption.

"I am saying this because I think your father is very ill, Rosalind."

"Worse, mamma?"

"I have myself thought that he was growing much weaker. We flattered ourselves, you know, that to be so long without an attack was a great gain; but I have felt he was growing weaker, and I see now that Dr. Beaton agrees with me. And to have been the means of bringing on this seizure when he was so little able to bear it—"

"Oh, mamma! how can you suppose that any one would ever blame—"

"I am my own judge, Rosalind. No, you would not blame me, not now at least, when you are entirely under my influence. I think, however, that had it not been this it would have been something else. Any trifling matter would have been enough. Nothing that we could have done would have staved it off much longer. That is my conviction. I have worked out the question, oh, a hundred times within myself. Would it be better to go away, and acknowledge that I could not—I was doing as much harm as good—"

Rosalind here seized upon Mrs. Trevanion's arm, clasping it with her hands, with a cry of "Go away! leave us, mother!" in absolute astonishment and dismay.

"And so withdraw the irritation. But then with the irritation I should have deprived him of a great deal of help. And there was always the certainty that no other could do so much, and that any other would soon become an irritation too. I have argued the whole thing out again and again. And I think I am right, Rosalind. No one else could have been at his disposal night and day like his wife. And if no one but his wife could have annoyed him so much, the one must be taken with the other."

"You frighten me, mamma; is it so very serious? And you have done nothing—nothing?"

Here Mrs. Trevanion for the first time turned and looked into Rosalind's face.

"Yes," she said. There was a faint smile upon her lips, so faint that it deepened rather than lightened the gravity of her look. She shook her head and looked tenderly at Rosalind with this smile. "Ah, my dear," she said, "you would willingly make the best of it; but I have done something. Not, indeed, what he thinks, what perhaps other people think, but something I ought not to have done." A deep sigh followed, a long breath drawn from the inmost recesses of her breast to relieve some pain or pressure there. "Something," she continued, "that I cannot help, that, alas! I don't want to do; although I think it is my duty, too."

And then she was silent, sitting absorbed in her own thoughts by Rosalind's bed. The chilly winter morning had come in fully as she talked till now the room was full of cold daylight, ungenial, unkindly, with no pleasure in it. Rosalind in her eager youth, impatient of trouble, and feeling that something must be done or said to make an end of all misery, that it was not possible there could be no remedy, held her mother's hand between hers, and cried and kissed it and asked a hundred questions. But Madam sat scarcely moving, her mind absorbed in a labyrinth from which she saw no way of escape. There seemed no remedy either for the ills that were apparent or those which nobody knew.

"You ought at least to be resting," the girl said at last; "you ought to get a little sleep. I will get up and go to his room and bring you word if he stirs."

"He will not stir for some time. No, I am not going to bed. After I have bathed my face Jane will get me a cup of tea, and I shall go down again. No, I could not sleep. I am better within call, so that if he wants me—But I could not resist the temptation of coming in to speak to you, Rosalind. I don't know why—just an impulse. We ought not to do things by impulse, you know, but alas! some of us always do. You will remember, however, if necessary. Somehow," she said, with a pathetic smile, her lips quivering as she turned to the girl's eager embrace, "you seem more my own child, Rosalind, more my champion, my defender, than those who are more mine."

"Nothing can be more yours, mother, all the more that we chose each other. We were not merely compelled to be mother and child."

"Perhaps there is something in that," said Mrs. Trevanion.

"And the others are so young; only I of all your children am old enough to understand you," cried Rosalind, throwing herself into her stepmother's arms. They held each other for a moment closely in that embrace which is above words, which is the supreme expression of human emotion and sympathy, resorted to when all words fail, and yet which explains nothing, which leaves the one as far as ever from understanding the other, from divining what is behind the veil of individuality which separates husband from wife and mother from child. Then Mrs. Trevanion rose and put Rosalind softly back upon her pillow and covered her up with maternal care as if she had been a child. "I must not have you catch cold," she said, with a smile which was her usual motherly smile with no deeper meaning in it. "Now go to sleep, my love, for another hour."

In her own room Madam exchanged a few words with Jane, who had also been up all night, and who was waiting for her with the tea which is a tired watcher's solace. "You must do all for me to-day, Jane," she said; "I cannot leave Mr. Trevanion; I will not, which is more. I have been, alas! partly the means of bringing on this attack."

"Oh, Madam, how many attacks have there been before without any cause!"

"That is a little consolation to me; still, it is my fault. Tell him how unsafe it is to be here, how curious the village people are, and that I implore him, for my sake, if he thinks anything of that, and for God's sake, to go away. What can we do more? Tell him what we have both told him a hundred times, Jane!"

"I will do what I can, Madam; but he pays no attention to me, as you know."

"Nor to any one," said Madam, with a sigh. "I have thought sometimes of telling Dr. Beaton everything; he is a kind man, he would know how to forgive. But, alas! how could I tell if it would do good or harm?"

"Harm! only harm! He would never endure it," the other said.

Again Mrs. Trevanion sighed; how deep, deep down was the oppression which those long breaths attempted to relieve. "Oh," she said, "how happy they are that never stray beyond the limits of nature! Would not poverty, hard work, any privation, have been better for all of us?"

"Sixteen years ago, Madam," Jane said.

CHAPTER X

Mr. Trevanion's attack wore off by degrees, and by and by he resumed his old habits, appearing once more at dinner, talking as of old after that meal, coming into the drawing-room for his rubber afterwards. Everything returned into the usual routine. But there were a few divergences from the former habits of the house. The invalid was never visible except in the evening, and there was a gradual increase of precaution, a gradual limitation of what he was permitted or attempted to do, which denoted advancing weakness. John Trevanion remained, which was another sign. He had made all his arrangements to go, and then after a conversation with the doctor departed from them suddenly, and announced that if it did not interfere with any of Madam's arrangements he would stay till Christmas, none of his engagements being pressing. Other guests came rarely, and only when the invalid burst forth into a plaint that he never saw any one, that the sight of the same faces day by day was enough to kill a man. "And every one longer than the other," he cried. "There is John like a death's head, and the doctor like a grinning waxwork, and Madam—why, she is the worst of all. Since I interfered with her little amusements, going out in the dark like one of her own housemaids, by Jove, Madam has been like a whipped child. She that had always an argument ready, she has taken up the submissive rôle at last. It's a new development. Eh? don't you think so? Did you ever see Madam in the rôle of Griselda before? I never did, I can tell you. It is a change! It won't last long, you think, John? Well, let us get the good of it while we can. It is something quite novel to me."

"I said nothing on the subject," said John, "and indeed I think it would be better taste to avoid personal observations."

"Especially in the presence of the person, eh? That's not my way. I say the worst I have to say to your face, so you need not fear what is said behind your back—Madam knows it. She is so honest; she likes honesty. A woman that has set herself to thwart and cross her husband for how many—sixteen years, she can't be in much doubt as to his opinion of her, eh? What! will nothing make you speak?"

"It is time for this tonic, Reginald. Dr. Beaton is very anxious that you should not neglect it."

"Is that all you have got to say? That is brilliant, certainly; quinine, when I want a little amusement. Bitter things are better than sweet, I suppose you think. In that case I should be a robust fox-hunter instead of an invalid, as I am—for I have had little else all my life."

"I think you have done pretty well in your life, Reginald. What you have wanted you have got. That does not happen to all of us. Except health, which is a great deduction, of course."

"What I have wanted! I wanted an heir and a family like other men, and I got a poor little wife who died at nineteen, and a useless slip of a girl. Then my second venture—perhaps you think my second venture was very successful—a fine robust wife, and a mischievous brat like Rex, always in scrapes at school, besides that little spiteful minx Sophy, who would spite her own mother if she could, and the two imps in the nursery. What good are they to me? The boy will succeed me, of course, and keep you out. I had quite as lief you had it, John. You are my own brother, after all, and that boy is more his mother's than mine. He has those eyes of hers. Lord! what a fool a young fellow is! To imagine I should have given up so much when I ought to have known better, and taken so many burdens on my shoulders for the sake of a pair of fine eyes. They are fine eyes still, but I know the meaning of them now."

"This is simply brutal, Reginald," said his brother, in high indignation. He got up to go away, but a sign from Mrs. Trevanion, behind her husband's back, made him pause.

"Brutal, is it? which means true. Give me some of that eau-de-Cologne. Can't you be quick about it? You take half an hour to cross the room. I've always meant to tell you about that second marriage of mine. I was a fool, and she was—Shall I tell him all about it, Madam? when we met, and how you led me on. By Jove! I have a great mind to publish the whole business, and let everybody know who you are and what you are—or, rather, were when I married you."

"I wish you would do so, Reginald. The mystery has never been my doing. It would be for my happiness if you would tell John."

The sick man looked round upon her with a chuckling malice. "She would like to expose herself in order to punish me," he said. "But I sha'n't do it; you may dismiss that from your mind. I don't wish the country to know that my wife was—" Then he ended with a laugh which was so insulting that John Trevanion involuntarily clinched his fist and made a step forward; then recollected himself, and fell back with a suppressed exclamation.

"It is quite natural you should take her part, Jack. She's a fine woman still of her years, though a good bit older than you would think. How old were you, Madam, when I married you? Oh, old enough for a great deal to have happened—eight-and-twenty or thereabouts—just on the edge of being passée then, the more fool I! Jove! what a fool I was, thrusting my head into the bag. I don't excuse myself. I posed myself in those days as a fellow that had seen life, and wasn't to be taken in. But you were too many for me. Never trust to a woman, John, especially a woman that has a history and that sort of thing. You are never up to their tricks. However knowing you may be, take my word for it, they know a thing or two more than you."

"If you mean to do nothing but insult your wife, Reginald—"

"John, for Heaven's sake! What does it matter? You will think no worse of me for what he says, and no better. Let him talk!" cried Madam, under her breath.

"What is she saying to you—that I am getting weak in my mind and don't know what I am saying? Ah! that's clever. I have always expected something of the sort. Look here, Madam! sit down at once and write to Charley Blake, do you hear? Charley—not the old fellow. Ask him to come here from Saturday to Monday, I want to have a talk with him. You are not fond of Charley Blake. And tell him to bring all his tools with him. He will know"—with a significant laugh—"what I mean."

She went to the writing-table without a word, and wrote the note. "Will you look at it, Reginald, to see if it is what you wish."

The patient snarled at her with his laugh. "I can trust you," he said, "and you shall see when Blake comes."

"What do you want with Blake, Reginald? Why should you trouble yourself with business in your present state of health? You must have done all that is necessary long ago, I wish you would keep quiet and give yourself a chance."

"A chance! that's Beaton's opinion, I suppose—that I have more than a chance. That's why you all gather round me like a set of crows, ready to pounce upon the carcass. And Madam, Madam here, can scarcely hold herself in, thinking how soon she will be free." He pushed back his chair, and gazed from one to another with fiery eyes which seemed ready to burst from their sockets. "A chance! that's all I've got, is it? You needn't wait for it, John; there's not a penny for you."

"Reginald, what the doctor says is that you must be calm, that nothing must be done to bring on those spasms that shake you so. Never mind what John says; he does not know."

"Oh, you!" cried the sick man; "you—you've motive enough. It's freedom to you. I don't tell you to scheme for it, I know that's past praying for. Nobody can doubt it's worth your while—a good settlement, and freedom to dance on my grave as soon as you like, as soon as you have got me into it. But John has got no motive," he said again, with a sort of garrulous pathos; "he'll gain nothing. He'll rather lose something perhaps, for he couldn't have the run of the house if it were yours, as he has done all his life. Yours!" the sick man added, with concentrated wrath and scorn; "it shall never be yours; I shall see to that. Where is the note to Charley—Charley Blake? John, take charge of it for me; see that it's put in the post. She has the bag in her hands, and how can I tell whether she will let it go? She was a great deal too ready to write it, eh? don't you think, knowing it was against herself?"

After this cheerful morning's talk, which was the ordinary kind of conversation that went on in Mr. Trevanion's room, from which John Trevanion could escape and did very shortly, but Madam could not and did not, the heavy day went on, little varied. Mrs. Trevanion appeared at lunch with a sufficiently tranquil countenance, and entered into the ordinary talk of a family party with a composure or philosophy which was a daily miracle to the rest. She checked little Sophy's impertinences and attended to the small pair of young ones like a mother embarrassed with no cares less ignoble. There was an air of great gravity about her, but not more than the critical condition of her husband's health made natural. And the vicar, who came in to lunch to ask after the squire, saw nothing in Madam's manner that was not most natural and seemly. He told his wife afterwards that she took it beautifully; "Very serious, you know, very anxious, but resigned and calm." Mrs. Vicar was of opinion that were she Mrs. Trevanion she would be more than resigned, for everybody knew that Madam had "a great deal to put up with." But from her own aspect no one could have told the continual flood of insult to which she was exposed, the secret anxiety that was gnawing at her heart. In the evening, before dinner, she met her brother-in-law by accident before the great fireplace in the hall. She was sitting there, thrown down in one of the deep chairs, like a worn-out creature. It was rare to see her there, though it was the common resort of the household, and so much, in spite of himself, had John Trevanion been moved by the sense of mystery about, and by his brother's vituperations, that his first glance was one of suspicion. But his approach took her by surprise. Her face was hidden in her hands, and there was an air of abandon in her attitude and figure as if she had thrown herself, like a wounded animal, before the fire. She uncovered her face, and, he thought, furtively, hastily dried her eyes as she turned to see who was coming. Pity was strong in his heart, notwithstanding his suspicion, he came forward and looked down upon her kindly. "I am very glad," he said, "to see that you are able to get a moment to yourself."

"Yes," she said, "Reginald seems more comfortable to-night."

"Grace," said John Trevanion, "it is beyond human patience. You ought not to have all this to bear."

"Oh, nothing is beyond human patience," she said, looking up at him suddenly with a smile. "Never mind, I can bear it very well. After all, there is no novelty in it to wound me. I have been bearing the same sort of thing for many years."

"And you have borne it without a murmur. You are a very wonderful woman, or—"

"What do you mean? Do you think me a bad one? It would not be wonderful after all you have heard. But I am not a bad woman, John. I am not without blame; who is? But I am not what he says. This is mere weakness to defend myself; but when one has been beaten down all day long by one perpetual flood like a hailstorm—What was that? I thought I heard Reginald's voice."

"It was nothing; some of the servants. I am very sorry for you, Grace. If anything can be done to ease you—"

"Nothing can be done. I think talking does him good; and what is the use of a man's wife if not to hear everything he has to say? It diverts the evil from others, and I hope from himself too. Yes, I do think so; it is an unpleasant way of working it out, and yet I think, like the modes they adopt in surgery sometimes, it relieves the system. So let him talk," she went on with a sigh. "It will be hard, though, if I am to lose the support of your good opinion, John."

To this he made no direct answer, but asked, hurriedly, "What do you suppose he wants with Charley Blake? Charley specially, not his father, whom I have more faith in?"

"Something about his will, I suppose. Oh, perhaps not anything of consequence. He tries to scare me, threatening something—but it is not for that that I am afraid."

"We shall be able to do you justice in that point. Of what are you afraid?"

She rose with a sudden impulse and stood by him in the firelight, almost as tall as he, and with a certain force of indignation in her which gave her an air of command and almost grandeur beside the man who suspected and hesitated. "Nothing!" she said, as if she flung all apprehension from her. John, whose heart had been turned from her, felt himself melting against his will. She repeated after a time, more gently, "I know that if passion can suggest anything it will be done. And he will not have time to reconsider, to let his better nature—" (here she paused, and in spite of herself a faint smile, in which there was some bitterness, passed over her face) "his better nature speak," she said, slowly; "therefore I am prepared for everything and fear nothing."

"This sounds not like courage, but despair."

"And so it is. Is it wonderful that it should be despair rather than courage after all these years? I am sure there is something wrong. Listen; don't you hear it? That is certainly Reginald's voice."

"No, no, you are excited. What could it be? He wants something, perhaps, and he always calls loudly for whatever he wants. It is seldom I can see you for a moment. I want to tell you that I will see Blake and find out from him—"

"I must go to Reginald, John."

She was interrupted before she had crossed the hall by the sudden appearance of Russell, who pushed through the curtain which hung over the passage leading to Mr. Trevanion's room, muffling herself in it in her awkwardness. The woman was scared and trembling. "Where's Madam, Madam?" she said. "She's wanted; oh, she's wanted badly! He's got a fit again."

Mrs. Trevanion flew past the trembling woman like a shadow. "It is your doing," she said, with a voice that rung into Russell's heart. The intruder was entirely unhinged. "I never saw him in one before. It's dreadful; oh, it's dreadful! Doctor! doctor! oh, where's the doctor?" she cried, losing all command of herself, and shrieking forth the name in a way which startled the house. The servants came running from all sides; the children, terror-stricken, half by the cry, half by the sound of Russell's voice, so familiar to them, appeared, a succession of little wistful faces, upon the stair, while the doctor himself pushed through, startled, but with all his wits about him. "How has it happened? You've been carrying your ill-tempered chatter to him. I'll have you tried for manslaughter," the doctor said.

CHAPTER XI

Rosalind Trevanion was a girl who had never had a lover—at least, such was her own conviction. She even resented the fact a little, thinking it wonderful that when all the girls in novels possessed such interests she had none. To attain to the mature age of eighteen, in a wealthy and well-known house where there were many visitors, and where she had all the advantages that a good position can give, without ever having received that sign of approbation which is conveyed by a declaration of love, was very strange in the point of view of fiction. And as she had few friends of her own age at hand to consult with, and an absorbing attachment and friendship for an older woman to fill up the void, novels were her chief informants as to the ordinary events of youthful life. It is an unfortunate peculiarity of these works that their almost exclusive devotion to one subject is too likely to confuse the ideas of young women in this particular. In old-fashioned English fiction, and in the latest American variety of the art, no girl who respected herself could be satisfied with less than half a dozen proposals: which is a circumstance likely to rouse painful questionings in the hearts of our young contemporaries. Here was a girl not unconscious that she was what is generally known as "a nice girl," with everything favorable in her circumstances; and yet she had not as yet either accepted or refused anybody! It was curious. Young Hamerton, who had been staying at Highcourt at the uncomfortable moment already described, was indeed prone to seek her society, and unfolded himself rashly to her in talk, with that indescribable fatuity which young men occasionally show in presence of girls, moved perhaps by the too great readiness of the kind to laugh at their jokes and accept their lead. Rosalind, protected by her knowledge of minds more mature, looked upon Hamerton with a kind of admiring horror, to think how wonderful it was that a man should be a man, and superior to all women, and have an education such as women of ambition admired and envied, and yet be such a —. She did not say fool, being very courteous, and unused to strong language. She only said such a —; and naturally could no more take him into consideration as a lover than if he had been one of the footmen. It was not beyond her consciousness either, perhaps, that Charley Blake, the son and partner of the family lawyer, whom business often brought to Highcourt, contemplated her often with his bold black eyes in a marked and unmistakable way. But that was a piece of presumption which Miss Trevanion thought of as a princess royal might regard the sighs of a courtier. Rosalind had the eclectic and varying political views held by young women of intelligence in the present time. She smiled at the old Toryism about her. She chose her men and her measures from both parties, and gave her favorites a hot but somewhat fluctuating support. She felt very sure that of all things in the world she was not an aristocrat, endeavoring to shut the gates of any exclusive world against success (which she called genius); therefore it could not be this thoroughly old-world feeling which prompted her disdain of Charley Blake. She was of opinion that a poor man of genius struggling upward towards fame was the sublimest sight on earth, and that to help in such a struggle was a far finer thing for a woman to do than to marry a duke or a prince. But no such person had ever come in her way, nor any one else so gifted, so delightful, so brilliant, and so tender as to merit the name of a lover. She was a little surprised, but referred the question to statistics, and said to herself that because of the surplus of women those sort of things did not happen nowadays: though, indeed, this was a theory somewhat invalidated by the fact that most of the young ladies in the county were married or about to be so. The position altogether did not convey any sense of humiliation to Rosalind. It gave her rather a sense of superiority, as of one who lifts her head in native worth superior to the poor appreciation of the crowd. How the sense of being overlooked should carry with it this sense of superiority is for the philosopher to say.

These thoughts belonged to the lighter and happier portion of her life, and were at present subdued by very sombre reflections. When she walked out in the morning after these events there was, however, a certain sense of emancipation in her mind. Her father had again been very ill—so ill that during the whole night the house had been on the alert, and scarcely any one had ventured to go to bed. Rosalind had spent half the night in the hall with her uncle, expecting every moment a summons to the sick-room, to what everybody believed to be the deatbed of the sufferer; and there had crept through the house a whisper, how originating no one could tell, that it was after an interview with Russell that the fit had come on, and that she had carried him some information about Madam which had almost killed him. Nobody had any doubt that it was to Madam that Russell's report referred, and there were many wonderings and questions in the background, where the servants congregated, as to what it was. That Madam went out of nights; that she met some one in the park, and there had long and agitated interviews; that Jane knew all about it, more than any one, and could ruin her mistress if she chose to speak; but that Russell too had found out a deal, and that it had come to master's ears through her; and full time it did, for who ever heard of goings-on like this in a gentleman's house?—this is what was said among the servants. In superior regions nothing was said at all. Rosalind and her uncle kept together, as getting a vague comfort in the universal dreariness from being together. Now and then John Trevanion stole to the door of his brother's room, which stood open to give all the air possible, to see or hear how things were going. One time when he did so his face was working with emotion.

"Rosalind," he said, in the whisper which they spoke in, though had they spoken as loudly as their voices would permit no sound could have reached the sick-room; "Rosalind, I think that woman is sublime. She knows that the first thing he will do will be to harm and shame her, and yet there she is, doing everything for him. I don't know if she is a sinner or not, but she is sublime—"

"Who are you speaking of as that woman?—of MY MOTHER, Uncle John?" cried Rosalind, expanding and growing out of her soft girlhood into a sort of indignant guardian angel. He shook his head impatiently and sat down; and nothing more was said between them till the middle of the night, when Dr. Beaton coming in told them the worst was over, and for the moment the sick man would "pull through." "But I'll have that nurse in confinement. I'll send her to the asylum. It is just manslaughter," he said. Russell, very pale and frightened, was at her door when Rosalind went up-stairs.

"The doctor says he will have you tried for manslaughter," Rosalind said, as she passed her. "No, I will not say good-night. You have all but killed papa."

"It is not I that have killed him," said Russell; "it's those that do what they didn't ought to."

Rosalind, in her excitement, stamped her foot upon the floor.

"He says you shall be sent to the asylum; and I say you shall be sent away from here. You are a bad woman. Perhaps now you will kill the children to complete your work. We are none of us safe so long as you are here."

At this Russell gave a bitter cry and threw up her hands to heaven.

"The children," she cried, "that I love like my own—that I give my heart's blood for—not safe! Oh, Miss Rosalind! God forgive you!—you, that I have loved the best of all!"

"How should I forgive you?" cried Rosalind, relentless. "I will never forgive you. Hate me if you please, but never dare to say you love me. Love!—you don't know what it is. You should go away to-night if it were I who had the power and not mamma."

"She has the power yet. She will not have it long," the woman cried, in her terror and passion. And she shut herself up in her room, which communicated with the children's, and flung herself on the floor in a panic which was perhaps as tragical as any of the other sensations of this confused and miserable house.

And yet when Rosalind went out next morning she was able to withdraw herself, in a way inconceivable to any one who has not been young and full of imaginations, from the miseries and terrors of the night. Mr. Trevanion was much exhausted, but living, and in his worn-out, feeble state required constant care and nursing, without being well enough to repay that nursing with abuse, as was his wont. Rosalind, with no one to turn to for companionship, went out and escaped. She got clear of that small, yet so important, world, tingling with emotion, with death and life in the balance, and everything that is most painful in life, and escaped altogether, as if she had possessed those wings of a dove for which we all long, into another large and free and open world, in which there was a wide, delightful air which blew in her face, and every kind of curiosity and interest and hope. How it was she fell to thinking of the curious fact that she had not, and had never had, a lover, at such a moment, who can tell? Perhaps because it occurred to her at first that it would be well to have something, somebody, to escape to and take comfort in, when she was so full of trouble, without knowing that the wide atmosphere and fresh sky and bare trees, that discharged, whenever the breath of the wind touched them, a sharp little shower of rain-drops, were enough at her age to woo her out of the misery which was not altogether personal, though she was so wound up in the lives of all the sufferers. She escaped. That thought about the lover, which was intended to be pathetic, beguiled her into a faint laugh under her breath; for indeed it was amusing, if even only ruefully amusing, to be so unlike the rest of the young world. That opened to her, as it were, the gate; and then her imagination ran on, like the lawless, sweet young rover it was, to all kinds of things amusing and wonderful. Those whose life is all to come, what a playground they have to fly into when the outside is unharmonious! how to fill up all those years; what to do in the time that is endless, that will never be done; how to meet those strange events, those new persons, those delights and wonders that are all waiting round the next and the next corner! If she had thought of it she would have been ashamed of herself for this very amusement, but fortunately she did not think of it, and so let herself go, like the child she was. She took her intended walk through the park, and then, as the morning was bright, after lingering at the gate a little, went out into the road, and turned to the village without any particular intention, because it was near and the red roofs shone in the light. It was a fresh, bright morning, such as sometimes breaks the dulness of November. The sky was as blue as summer, with wandering white cloudlets, and not a sign of any harm, though there had been torrents of rain the night before. Indeed, no doubt it was the pouring down of those torrents which had cleared away the tinge of darkness from the clouds, which were as innocent and filmy and light as if it had been June. Everything was glistening and gleaming with wet, but that only made the country more bright, and as Rosalind looked along the road, the sight of the red village with its smoke rising ethereal into air so pure that it was a happiness to gaze into its limpid, invisible depths, or rather heights, ending in heavens, was enough to cheer any young soul. She went on, with a little sense of adventure, for though she often went to the village, it was rare to this girl to have the privilege of being absolutely alone. The fresh air, the glistening hedgerows, the village roofs, in all the shining of the sunshine, pleased her so much that she did not see till she was close to it a break in the road, where the water which had submerged the low fields on either side had broken across the higher ground, finding a sort of channel in a slight hollow of the road. The sight of a laborer plashing through it, with but little thought, though it came up to the top of his rough boots, arrested Rosalind all at once. What was she to do? Her boots, though with the amount of high heel which only a most independent mind can escape from, were clearly quite unequal to this crossing. She could not but laugh to herself at the small matter which stopped progress, and stood on the edge of it measuring the distance with her eye, and calculating probabilities with a smiling face, amused by the difficulty. While she stood thus she heard a voice behind her calling to the laborer in front. "Hi!" some one said; "Hallo, you there! help me to lift this log over the water, that the lady may cross." The person appealed to turned round, and so did Rosalind. And then she felt that here was indeed an adventure. Behind her, stooping over some large logs of wood on the side of the pathway, was the man who had looked so intently at the carriage the other day when she passed with her stepmother. Before she saw his face she was sure, with a little jump of her heart, that it was the same man. He was dressed in dark tweed clothes, somewhat rough, which might have been the garb of a gentleman or of a gamekeeper, and did not fit him well, which was more like the latter than the former. She could see, as he stooped, his cheek and throat reddened as with the unusual exertion.

"Oh, please do not take the trouble," she cried; "it is of no consequence. I have nothing to do in the village."

"It is no trouble," he said; and in a minute or two the logs were rolled across the side path so that she could pass. The man who had been called upon to help was one of the farm-laborers whom she knew. She thanked him cheerfully by name, and turned to the stranger, who stood with his hat off, his pale face, which she remembered to have been so pale that she thought him ill, now covered with a brilliant flush which made his eyes shine. Rosalind was startled by the beauty of the face, but it was not like that of the men she was accustomed to see. Something feminine, something delicate and weak, was in it.

"You are very kind to take so much trouble; but I am afraid you have over-exerted yourself," she cried.

This made the young man blush more deeply still.

"I am not very strong," he said half indignantly, "but not so weak as that." There was a tone of petulance in the reply; and then he added, "Whatever trouble it might be is more than repaid," with a somewhat elaborate bow.

What did it mean? The face was refined and full of expression, but then probably he was not a gentleman, Rosalind thought, and did not understand. She said hurriedly again, "I am very much obliged to you," and went on, a little troubled by the event. She heard him make a few steps after her. Was he going to follow? In her surprise it was almost on her lips to call back William from the farm.

"I beg your pardon," said the stranger, "but may I take the liberty of asking how is Mr. Trevanion? I heard he was worse last night."

Rosalind turned round, half reassured.

"Oh, do you know papa?" she said. "He has been very ill all night, but he is better, though terribly exhausted. He has had some sleep this morning."

She was elevated upon the log, which she had begun to cross, and thus looked down upon the stranger. If he knew her father, that made all the difference; and surely the face was one with which she was not unfamiliar.

"I do not know Mr. Trevanion, only one hears of him constantly in the village. I am glad he is better."

He hesitated, as if he too was about to mount the log.

"Oh, thank you," said Rosalind, hurrying on.

CHAPTER XII

"To whom were you talking, Rosalind?"

"To—nobody, Uncle John!" she said, in her surprise at the sudden question which came over her shoulder, and, turning round, waited till he joined her. She had changed her mind and come back after she had crossed the water upon the impromptu bridge, with a half apprehension that her new acquaintance intended to accompany her to the village, and had, to tell the truth, walked rather quickly to the park gates.

"But I met the man—a young fellow—whose appearance I don't know."

"Oh! I don't know who it was either; a gentleman; at least, I suppose he was a gentleman."

"And yet you doubt. What cause had you to doubt?"

"Well, Uncle John, his voice was nice enough, and what he said. The only thing was, he paid me a sort of a—compliment."

"What was that?" said John Trevanion, quickly.

"Oh, nothing," said Rosalind, inconsistently. "When I said I was sorry he had taken the trouble, he said, 'Oh, if it was any trouble it was repaid.' Nothing at all! Only a gentleman would not have said that to a girl who was—alone."

"That is true; but it was not very much after all. Fashions change. A few generations ago it would have been the right thing." Then he dropped the subject as a matter without importance, and drew his niece's arm within his own. "Rosie," he said, "I am afraid we shall have to face the future, you and I. What are we to do?"

"Are things so very bad, Uncle John?" she cried, and the tears came welling up into her eyes as she raised them to his face.

"Very bad, I fear. This last attack has done him a great deal of harm, more than any of the others; perhaps, because, as the doctor says, the pace is quicker as he gets near the end, perhaps because he is still as angry as ever, though he is not able to give it vent. I wonder if such fury may not have some adequate cause."

"Oh, Uncle John!" Rosalind cried; she clasped her hands upon his arm, looking up at him through her tears. He knew what was the meaning in her tone, though it was a meaning very hard to put into words. A child cannot say of her father when he is dying that his fury has often been without any adequate cause.

"I know," he said, "and I acknowledge that no one could have a more devoted nurse. But whether there have not been concealments, clandestine acts, things he has a right to find fault with—"

"Even I," said Rosalind, hastily, "and I have nothing to hide—even I have had to make secrets from papa."

"That is the penalty, of course, of a temper so passionate. But she should not have let you do so, Rosalind."

"It was not she. You think everything is her fault; oh, how mistaken you are! My mother and I," cried the girl, impetuously, "have no secrets from each other."

John Trevanion looked into the young, ingenuous countenance with anxiety: "Then, Rosalind," he said, "where is it that she goes? Why does she go out at that hour of all others, in the dark? Whom does she meet? If you know all this, I think there cannot be another word to say; for nothing that is not innocent would be intrusted to you."

Rosalind was silent. She ceased to look at him, and even withdrew her clasping hands from his arm.

"You have nothing to say? There it is: she has no secrets from you, and yet you can throw no light on this one secret. I have always had a great admiration and respect for your stepmother, Rosalind."

"I wish you would not call her my stepmother! It hurts me. What other mother have I ever known?"

"My dear, your love for her is a defence in itself. But, Rosalind, forgive me, there is some complication here. If she will not explain, what are we to do? A mystery is always a sign of something wrong; at least, it must be taken for something wrong if it remains unexplained. I am, I hope, without passion or prejudice. She might have confided in me—"

"If there was anything to confide," Rosalind said under her breath. But he went on.

"And now your father has sent for his lawyer—to do something, to change something. I can't tell what he means to do, but it will be trouble in any case. And you, Rosalind—I said so before, you—must not stay here."

"If you mean that I am to leave my mother, Uncle John—"

"Hush! not your mother. My dear, you must allow others to judge for you here. Had you been her child it would have been different: but we must take thought for your best interests. Who is that driving in at the gate? Why, it is Blake already. I wonder if a second summons has been sent. He was not expected till to-morrow. This looks worse and worse, Rosalind."

"Uncle John, if you will let me, I will run in another way. I—don't wish to meet Mr. Blake."

"Hallo, Rosalind! you don't mean to say that Charley Blake has ever presumed—Ah! this comes of not having a mother's care."

"It is nothing of the kind," she cried, drawing her hand violently from his arm. "He hates her because she never would—Oh, how can you be so cruel, so prejudiced, so unjust?" In her vehemence Rosalind pushed him away from her with a force which made his steady, middle-aged figure almost swerve, and darted across the park away from him just in time to make it evident to Mr. Blake, driving his dog-cart quickly to make up to the group in advance, that it was to avoid him Miss Trevanion had fled.

"How is he?" was the eager question he put as he came up to John Trevanion. "I hope I am not too late."

"For what? If it is my brother you mean, I hear he is a little better," said John, coldly.

"Then I suppose it is only one of his attacks," the new-comer said, with a slight tone of disappointment; not that he had any interest in the death of Mr. Trevanion, but that the fall from the excitement of a great crisis to the level of the ordinary is always disagreeable. "I thought from the telegram this morning there was no time to lose."

"Who sent you the telegram this morning?"

"Madam Trevanion, of course," said the young man.

This reply took John Trevanion so much by surprise that he went on without a word.

She knew very well what Blake's visit portended to herself. But what a strange, philosophical stoic was this woman, who did not hesitate herself to summon, to hasten, lest he should lose the moment in which she could still be injured, the executioner of her fate. A sort of awe came over John. He begun to blame himself for his miserable doubts of such a woman. There was something in this silent impassioned performance of everything demanded from her that impressed the imagination. After a few minutes' slow pacing along, restraining his horse, Blake threw the reins to his groom, and, jumping down, walked on by John Trevanion's side.

"I suppose there is no such alarming hurry, then," he said. "Of course you know what's up now?"

"If you mean what are my brother's intentions, I know nothing about them," John said.

"No more do I. I can't think what he's got in his mind; though we have been very confidential over it all." Mr. Blake elder was an old-fashioned and polite old gentleman, but his son belonged to another world, and pushed his way by means of a good deal of assurance and no regard to any one's feelings. "It would be a great assistance to me," he said, "if he's going to tamper with that will again, to know how the land lies. What is wrong? There must have been, by all I hear, a great flare-up."

"Will you remember, Blake, that you are speaking of my brother's affairs? We are not in the habit of having flares-up here."

"I mean no offence," said the other. "It's a lie, then, that is flying about the country."

"What is flying about the country? If it is about a flare-up you may be sure it is a lie."

"I don't stand upon the word," said Blake. "I thought I might speak frankly to you. Rumors are flying everywhere—that Mr. Trevanion is out of one fit into another—dying of it—and that Madam—"

"What of Madam?" said John Trevanion, firmly.

"I have myself the greatest respect for Mrs. Trevanion," said the lawyer, making a sudden pause.

"You would be a bold man if you expressed any other sentiment here; but rumor has not the same reverential and perfectly just feeling, I suppose. What has it ventured to say of my sister?"

John Trevanion, with all his gravity, was very impulsive; and the sense that her secret, whatever it was, had been betrayed, bound him at once to her defence. He had probably never called her his sister before.

"Of course it is all talk," said Blake. "I dare say the story means nothing; but knowing as I do so much about the state of affairs generally—a lawyer, you know, like a doctor, and people used to say a clergyman—"

"Is bound to hold his tongue, is he not?" John Trevanion said.

"Oh, as for that, a member of the family is not like a stranger. I took it for granted you would naturally be on the injured husband's side."

"Mr. Blake," said John, "you make assumptions which would be intolerable even to a stranger, and to a brother and friend, understanding the whole matter, I hope, a little better than you do, they are not less so, but more. Look here; a lawyer has this advantage, that he is sometimes able to calm the disordered fancy of a sick man, and put things in a better light. Take care what you do. Don't let the last act of his life be an injustice if you can help it. Your father—if your father were here—"

"Would inspire Mr. John Trevanion with more confidence," said the other, with a suppressed sneer. "It is unfortunate, but that is not your brother's opinion. He has preferred the younger man, as some do."

"I hope you will justify his choice," said John Trevanion, gravely. "It is a great responsibility. To make serious changes in a moment of passion is always dangerous—and, remember, my brother will in all probability have no time to repent."

"The responsibility will be Mr. Trevanion's, not mine," said Blake. "You should warn him, not me. His brother must have more constant access to him than even his family lawyer, and is in a better position. I am here to execute his wishes; that is all that I have to do with it."

John Trevanion bowed without a word. It was true enough. The elder Blake would perhaps have been of still less use in stemming the passionate tide of the sick man's fury, but at least he would have struggled against it. They walked up to the house almost without exchanging another word. In the hall they were met by Madam Trevanion, upon whom the constant watching had begun to tell. Her eyes were red, and there were deep lines under them. All the lines of her face were drawn and haggard. She met the new-comer with an anxious welcome, as if he had been a messenger of good and not of evil.

"I am very glad you have come, Mr. Blake. Thank you for being so prompt. My husband perhaps, after he has seen you, will be calmer and able to rest. Will you come to his room at once?"

If he had been about to secure her a fortune she could not have been more anxious to introduce him. She came back to the hall after she had led him to Mr. Trevanion's room.

"I am restless," she said; "I cannot be still. Do you know, for the first time he has sent me away. He will not have me with him. Before, whatever he might have against me was forgotten when he needed me. God grant that this interview he is so anxious for may compose him and put things on their old footing."

Perhaps it was only her agitation and distress, but as she spoke the tears came and choked her voice. John Trevanion came up to her, and laying his hands upon her shoulders gazed into her face.

"Grace," he said, "is it possible that you can be sincere?"

"Sincere!" she cried, looking at him with a strange incomprehension. She had no room in her mind for metaphysical questions, and she was impatient of them at such a crisis of fate.

"Yes, sincere. You know that man has come for some evil purpose. Whatever they say or do together it will be to your hurt, you know; and yet you hasten his coming, and tell him you are glad when he arrives—"

"And you think it must be false? No, it is not false, John," she said, with a faint smile. "So long as he does it and gets it off his mind, what is it to me? Do you know that he is perhaps dying? I have nursed him and been the only one that he would have near him for years. Do you think I care what happens after? But I cannot bear to be put out of my own place now."

"Your own place! to bear all his caprices and abuse!"

"My own place, by my husband's bedside," she said with tears. "When he has done whatever he wants to do his mind will be relieved. And I can do more for him than any one. He shortens his own life when he sends me away."

CHAPTER XIII

The house was in a curious commotion up-stairs. The nursery apartments were at the end of a passage, but on the same level with those of Mrs. Trevanion, in which Jane, Madam's attendant and anxious maid, was watching—coming out now and then to listen, or standing within the shelter of the half-closed door. Mrs. Trevanion's room opened into the gallery to which the great staircase led, and from which you could look down into the hall. The nursery was at the end of a long passage, and, when the door was open, commanded also a view of the gallery. There many an evening when there was fine company at Highcourt had the children pressed to see the beautiful ladies coming out in their jewels and finery, dressed for dinner. The spectacle now was not so imposing, but Russell, seated near the door, watched it with concentrated interest. She was waiting too to see what would happen, with excitement indescribable and some terror and sense of guilt. Sometimes Jane would do nothing more than open her mistress's door, and wait within for any sound or sight that might be possible. Sometimes she would step out with a furtive, noiseless step upon the gallery, and cast a quick look round and below into the hall, then return again noiselessly. Russell watched all these evidences of an anxiety as intense as her own with a sense of relief and encouragement. Jane was as eager as she was, watching over her mistress. Why was she thus watching? If Madam had been blameless, was it likely that any one would be on the alert like this? Russell herself was very sure of her facts. She had collected them with the care which hatred takes to verify its accusations; and yet cold doubts would trouble her, and she was relieved to see her opponent, the devoted adherent of the woman whose well-being was at stake, in a state of so much perturbation and anxiety. It was another proof, more potent than any of the rest. The passage which led to Russell's domain was badly lighted, and she could not be seen as she sat there at her post like a spy. She watched with an intense passion which concentrated all her thoughts. When she heard the faint little jar of the door she brightened involuntarily. The figure of Jane—slim, dark, noiseless—standing out upon the gallery was comfort to her very soul. The children were playing near. Sophy, perched up at the table, was cutting out pictures from a number of illustrated papers and pasting them into a book, an occupation which absorbed her. The two younger children were on the floor, where they went on with their play, babbling to each other, conscious of nothing else. It had begun to rain, and they were kept indoors perforce. A more peaceful scene could not be. The fire, surrounded by the high nursery fender, burned warmly and brightly. In the background, at a window which looked out upon the park, the nursery-maid—a still figure, like a piece of still life but for the measured movement of her hand—sat sewing. The little ones interchanged their eager little volleys of talk. They were "pretending to be" some of the actors in the bigger drama of life that went on over their heads. But their little performance was only Comedy, and it was Tragedy incarnate, with hands trembling too much to knit the little sock which she held, with dry lips parted with excitement, eyes feverish and shining, and an impassioned sense of power, of panic, and of guilt, that sat close to them in her cap and apron at the open door.

When Rosalind's figure flitted across the vacant scene, which was like the stage of a theatre to Russell, her first impulse was to start up and secure this visitor from the still more important field of battle below, so as to procure the last intelligence how things were going; and it was with a deepened sense of hostility, despite, and excitement that she now saw her approached by the rival watcher. Jane arrested the young lady on her way to her room, and they had an anxious conversation, during which first one and then both approached the railing of the gallery and looked over. It was all that the woman could do to restrain herself. What were they looking at? What was going on? It is seldom that any ordinary human creature has the consciousness of having set such tremendous forces in motion. It might involve ruin to her mistress, death to her master. The children whom she loved might be orphaned by her hand. But she was not conscious of anything deeper than a latent, and not painful, though exciting, thrill of guilt, and she was very conscious of the exultation of feeling herself an important party in all that was going on. What had she done? Nothing but her duty. She had warned a man who was being deceived; she had exposed a woman who had always kept so fair an appearance, but whom she, more clear-sighted than any one, had suspected from the first. Was she not right in every point, doing her duty to Mr. Trevanion and the house that had sheltered her so long? Was not she indeed the benefactor of the house, preserving it from shame and injury? So she said to herself, justifying her own actions with an excitement which betrayed a doubt; and in the meantime awaiting the result with passionate eagerness, incapable of a thought that did not turn round this centre—What was to happen? Was there an earthquake, a terrible explosion, about to burst forth? The stillness was ominous and dreadful to the watching woman who had put all these powers in motion. She feared yet longed for the first sound of the coming outburst; and yet all the while had a savage exultation in her heart in the thought of having been able to bring the whole world about her to such a crisis of fate.

Jane in the meantime had stopped Rosalind, who was breathless with her run across the park. The woman was much agitated and trembling. "Miss Rosalind," she said, with pale lips, "is there something wrong? I see Madam in the hall; she is not with master, and he so ill. Oh! what is wrong—what is wrong?"

"I don't know, Jane; nothing, I hope. Papa is perhaps asleep, and there is some one—Mr. Blake—come to see him. My mother is waiting till he is gone."

"Oh! that is perhaps why she is there," said Jane, with relief; then she caught the girl timidly by the arm. "You will forgive me, Miss Rosalind; she has enemies—there are some who would leave nothing undone to harm her."

"To harm mamma!" said Rosalind, holding her head high; "you forget yourself, Jane. Who would harm her in this house?"

Jane gave the girl a look which was full of gratitude, yet of miserable apprehension. "You will always be true to her, Miss Rosalind," she said; "and oh, you have reason, for she has been a good mother to you."

Rosalind looked at the woman somewhat sternly, for she was proud in her way. "If I did not know how fond you are of mamma," she said, "I should be angry. Does any one ever talk so of mother and daughter? That is all a matter of course; both that she is the best mother in the world, and that I am part of herself."

Upon this Jane did what an Englishwoman is very slow to do. She got hold of Rosalind's hand, and made a struggle to kiss it, with tears. "Oh, Miss Rosalind, God bless you! I'd rather hear that than have a fortune left me," she cried. "And my poor lady will want it all; she will want it all!"

"Don't be silly, Jane. My mother wants nothing but that we should have a little sense. What can any one do against her, unless it is you and the rest annoying her by foolish anxiety about nothing. Indeed, papa is very ill, and there is reason enough to be anxious," the girl added, after a pause.

In the meantime Madam Trevanion sat alone in the hall below. She received Blake, when he arrived, as we have seen, and she had a brief conversation with her brother-in-law, which agitated her a little. But when he left her, himself much agitated and not knowing what to think, she sat down again and waited, alone and unoccupied; a thing that scarcely ever in her full life happened to her. She, too, felt the stillness before the tempest. It repeated itself in her mind in a strange, fatal calm, a sort of cessation of all emotion. She had said to John Trevanion that she did not care what came after; and she did not; yet the sense that something was being done which would seriously affect her future life, even though she was not susceptible of much feeling on the subject, made the moment impressive. Calm and strong, indeed, must the nerves be of one who can wait outside the closed door of a room in which her fate is being decided, without a thrill. But a sort of false tranquillity—or was it perhaps the calmest of all moods, the stillness of despair?—came on her as she waited. There is a despair which is passion, and raves; but there is a different kind of despair, not called forth by any great practical danger, but by a sense of the impossibilities of life, the powerlessness of human thought or action, which is very still and says little. The Byronic desperation is very different from that which comes into the heart of a woman when she stands still amid the irreconcilable forces of existence and feels herself helpless amid contending wills, circumstances, powers, which she can neither harmonize nor overcome. The situation in which she stood was impossible. She saw no way out of it. The sharp sting of her present uselessness, and the sense that she had been for the first time turned away from her husband's bedside, had given a momentary poignancy to her emotions which roused her, but as that died away she sat and looked her position in the face with a calm that was appalling. This was what she had come to at the end of seventeen years—that her position was impossible. She did not know how to turn or what step to take. On either side of her was a mind that did not comprehend and a heart that did not feel for her. She could neither touch nor convince the beings upon whom her very existence depended. Andromeda, waiting for the monster to devour her, had at least the danger approaching but from one quarter, and, on the other, always the possibility of a Perseus in shining armor to cleave the skies. But Madam had on either side of her an insatiable fate, and no help, she thought, on earth or in heaven. For there comes a moment in the experience of all who have felt very deeply, when Heaven, too, seems to fail. Praying long, with no visible reply, drains out the heart. There seems nothing more left to say even to God, no new argument to employ with him, who all the while knows better than he can be told. And there she was, still, silent in her soul as well as with her lips, waiting, with almost a sense of ease in the thought that there was nothing more to be done, not even a prayer to be said, her heart, her thoughts, her wishes, all standing arrested as before an impenetrable wall which stopped all effort. And how still the house was! All the doors closed, the sounds of the household lost in the distance of long passages and shut doors and curtains; nothing to disturb the stillness before the tempest should burst. She was not aware of the anxious looks of her maid, now and then peering over the balustrade of the gallery above, for Jane's furtive footstep made no sound upon the thick carpet. Through the glass door she saw the clear blue of the sky, radiant in the wintry sunshine, but still, as wintry brightness is, without the flickers of light and shadow. And thus the morning hours went on.

A long time, it seemed a lifetime, passed before her repose was disturbed. It had gradually got to be like an habitual state, and she was startled to be called back from it. The heavy curtain was lifted, and first Mr. Blake, then Dr. Beaton, came forth. The first looked extremely grave and disturbed, as he came out with a case of papers which he had brought with him in his hand. He looked at Mrs. Trevanion with a curious, deprecating air, like that of a man who has injured another unwillingly. They had never been friends, and Madam had shown her sentiments very distinctly as to those overtures of admiration which the young lawyer had taken upon himself to make to Rosalind. The politeness he showed to her on ordinary occasions was the politeness of hostility. But now he looked at her alarmed, as if he could not support her glance, and would fain have avoided the sight of her altogether. Dr. Beaton, on the other hand, came forward briskly.

"I have just been called in to our patient," he said, "and you are very much wanted, Mrs. Trevanion."

"Does he want me?" she said.

"I think so—certainly. You are necessary to him; I understand your delicacy in being absent while Mr. Blake—"

"Do not deceive yourself, doctor; it was not my delicacy."

"Come, please," said the doctor, almost impatiently; "come at once."

Blake stood looking after them till both disappeared behind the curtain, then drew a long breath, as if relieved by her departure. "I wonder if she has any suspicion," he said to himself. Then he made a long pause and walked about the hall, and considered the pictures with the eye of a man who might have to look over the inventory of them for sale. Then he added to himself, "What an old devil!" half aloud. Of whom it was that he uttered this sentiment no one could tell, but it came from the bottom of his heart.

Madam did not leave the sick-chamber again that day. She did not appear at luncheon, for which perhaps the rest were thankful, as she was herself. How to look her in the face, with this mingled doubt of her and respect for her, nobody knew. Rosalind alone was disappointed. The doctor took everything into his own hands. He was now the master of the situation, and ruled everybody. "She is the best woman I ever knew," he said, with fervor. "I would rather trust her with a case than any Sister in the land. I said to her that I thought she would do better to stay. Mr. Trevanion was very glad to get her back."

CHAPTER XIV

As so often happens when all is prepared and ready for the catastrophe, the stroke of fate was averted. That night proved better than the last, and then there passed two or three quiet days. It was even possible, the doctor thought, that the alarm might be a false one, and the patient go on, if tranquil and undisturbed, until, in the course of nature, another crisis prepared itself or external commotion accelerated nature. He had received his wife back after her few hours' banishment with a sort of chuckling satisfaction, and though even his reduced and enfeebled state did not make him incapable of offence, the insulting remarks he addressed to her were no more than his ordinary method. Madam said nothing of them; she seemed, strangely enough, glad to return to her martyrdom. It was better, it appeared, than the sensation of being sent away. She was with him, without rest or intermission, the whole day and a great portion of the night. The two or three hours allowed her for repose were in the middle of the night, and she never stirred abroad nor tasted the fresh air through this period of confinement. The drives which had been her daily refreshment were stopped, along with every other possibility of freedom. In the meantime there appeared something like a fresh development of confidence and dependence upon her, which wrung the heart of the enemy in her stronghold, and made Russell think her work had been all in vain. Mr. Trevanion could not, it was said, bear his wife out of his sight.

It is a mistake when a dying person thus keeps all his world waiting. The sympathetic faculties are worn out. The household in general felt a slight sensation of resentment towards the sick man who had cheated them into so much interest. It was not as if he had been a man whom his dependents loved, and he had defrauded them of that profound and serious interest with which the last steps of any human creature—unless in a hospital or other agglomeration of humanity, where individual characteristics are abolished—are accompanied. The servants, who had with a little awe attended the coming of death, were half disappointed, half disgusted by the delay. Even John Trevanion, who had made up his mind very seriously and somewhat against his own convictions to wait "till all was over," had a sensation of annoyance: he might go on for weeks, perhaps for months, all the winter—"thank God!" they said, mechanically; but John could not help thinking how inconvenient it would be to come back—to hang on all the winter, never able to go anywhere. It would have been so much more considerate to get it over at once, but Reginald was never one who considered other people's convenience. Dr. Beaton, who had no desire to leave Highcourt, and who, besides, had a doctor's satisfaction in a successful fight with disease, took it much more pleasantly. He rubbed his hands and expressed his hopes of "pulling" his patient through, with much unnecessary cordiality. "Let us but stave off all trouble till spring, and there is no saying what may happen," he said, jauntily. "The summer will be all in his favor, and before next winter we may get him away." The younger members of the family took this for granted. Reginald, who had been sent for from school, begged his mother another time to be sure there was some real need for it before summoning a fellow home in the middle of the half; and Rosalind entirely recovered her spirits. The cloud that had hung over the house seemed about to melt away. Nobody was aware of the agitating conferences which Jane held with her mistress in the few moments when they saw each other; or the miserable anxiety which contended in Madam's mind with her evident and necessary duties. She had buried her troubles too long in her own bosom to exhibit them now. And thus the days passed slowly away; the patient had not yet been allowed to leave his bed, and, indeed, was in a state of alarming feebleness, but that was all.

Rosalind was left very much to herself during these days. She had now no longer any one to go out with. Sometimes, indeed, her uncle would propose a walk, but that at the most occupied but a small part of the day, and all her usual occupations had been suspended in the general excitement. She took to wandering about the park, where she could stray alone as much as pleased her, fearing no intrusion. A week or ten days after the visit of Mr. Blake, she was walking near the lake which was the pride of

Highcourt. In summer the banks of this piece of water were a mass of flowering shrubs, and on the little artificial island in the middle was a little equally artificial cottage, the creation of Rosalind's grandmother, where still the children in summer would often go to have tea. One or two boats lay at a little landing-place for the purpose of transporting visitors, and it was one of the pleasures of the neighborhood, when the family were absent, to visit the Bijou, as it was called. At one end of the little lake was a road leading from the village, to which the public of the place had a right. It was perhaps out of weariness with the monotony of her lonely walks that Rosalind directed her steps that way on an afternoon when all was cold and clear, an orange-red sunset preparing in the west, and indications of frost in the air. The lake caught the reflection of the sunset blaze and was all barred with crimson and gold, with the steely blue of its surface coming in around and intensifying every tint. Rosalind walked slowly round the margin of the water, and thought of the happy afternoons when the children and their mother had been rowed across, she herself and Rex taking the control of the boat. The water looked tempting, with its bars of color, and the little red roof of the Bijou blazed in the slanting light. She played with the boats at the landing-place, pushing one into the water with a half fancy to push forth into the lake, until it had got almost too far off to be pulled back again, and gave her some trouble, standing on the edge of the tiny pier with an oar in her hand, to bring it back to its little anchorage. She was standing thus, her figure relieved against the still, shining surface of the water, when she heard a footstep behind her, and thinking it the man who had charge of the cottage and the boats, called to him without turning round, "Come here, Dunmore; I have loosed this boat and I can't get it back—"

The footstep advanced with a certain hesitation. Then an unfamiliar voice said, "I am not Dunmore—but if you will allow me to help you—"

She started and turned round. It was the same stranger whom she had already twice seen on the road. "Oh! pray don't let me trouble you. Dunmore will be here directly," she said.

This did not, however, prevent the young man from rendering the necessary assistance. He got into one of the nearer boats, and stretching out from the bow of it, secured the stray pinnace. It was not a dangerous act, nor even one that gave the passer-by much trouble, but Rosalind, partly out of a sense that she had been ungracious, partly, perhaps—who can tell—out of the utter monotony of all around her, thanked him with eagerness. "I am sorry to give you trouble," she said again.

"It is no trouble, it is a pleasure." Was he going to be so sensible, so judicious, as to go away after this? He seemed to intend so. He put on his hat after bowing to her, and turned away, but then there seemed to be an after-thought which struck him. He turned back again, took off his hat again, and said: "I beg your pardon, but may I ask for Mr. Trevanion? The village news is so uncertain."

"My father is still very ill," said Rosalind, "but it is thought there is now some hope."

"That is good news indeed," the stranger said. Certainly he had a most interesting face. It could not be possible that a man with such a countenance was "not a gentleman," that most damning of all sentences. His face was refined and delicate; his eyes large, liquid, full of meaning, which was increased by the air of weakness which made them larger and brighter than eyes in ordinary circumstances. And certainly it was kind of him to be glad.

"Oh, yes, you told me before you knew my father," Rosalind said.

"I cannot claim to know Mr. Trevanion; but I do know a member of the family very well, and I have heard of him all my life."

Rosalind was no more afraid of a young man than of an old woman, and she thought she had been unjust to this stranger, who, after all, notwithstanding his rough dress, had nothing about him to find fault with. She said, "Yes; perhaps my Uncle John? In any case I am much obliged to you, both for helping me and for your interest in papa."

"May I sometimes ask how he is? The villagers are so vague."

"Oh, certainly," said Rosalind; "they have a bulletin at the lodge, or if you care to come so far as Highcourt, you will always have the last report."

"You are very kind, I will not come to the house. But I know that you often walk in the park. If I may ask you when we—chance to meet?"

This suggestion startled Rosalind. It awoke in her again that vague alarm—not, perhaps, a gentleman. But when she looked at the eyes which were searching hers with so sensitive a perception of every shade of expression, she became confused and did not know what to think. He was so quickly sensible of every change that he saw he had taken a wrong step. He ought to have gone further, and perceived what the wrong step was, but she thought he was puzzled and did not discover this instinctively, as a gentleman would have done. She withdrew a step or two involuntarily. "Oh, no," she said with gentle dignity, "I do not always walk the same way; but you may be sure of seeing the bulletin at the lodge." And with this she made him a courtesy and walked away, not hurrying, to show any alarm, but taking a path which was quite out of the way of the public, and where he could not follow. Rosalind felt a little thrill of agitation in her as she went home. Who could he be, and what did he do here, and why did he throw himself in her way? If she had been a girl of a vulgarly romantic imagination, she would no doubt have jumped at the idea of a secret adoration which had brought him to the poor little village for her sake, for the chance of a passing encounter. But Rosalind was not of this turn of imagination, and that undefined doubt which wavered in her mind did a great deal to damp the wings of any such fancy. What he had said was almost equal to asking her to meet him in the park. She blushed all over at the thought—at the curious impossibility of it, the want of knowledge. It did not seem an insult to her, but such an incomprehensible ignorance in him that she was ashamed of it; that he should have been capable of such a mistake. Not a gentleman! Oh, surely he could never, never—And yet the testimony of those fine, refined features—the mouth so delicate and sensitive, the eyes so eloquent—was of such a different kind. And was it Uncle John he knew? But Uncle John had passed him on the road and had not known him. It was very strange altogether. She could not banish the beautiful, pleading eyes out of her mind. How they looked at her! They were almost a child's eyes in their uncertainty and wistfulness, reading her face to see how far to go. And altogether he had the air of extreme youth, almost as young as herself, which, of course, in a man is boyhood. For what is a man of twenty? ten years, and more, younger and less experienced than a woman of that sober age. There was a sort of yearning of pity in her heart towards him, just tempered by that doubt. Poor boy! how badly he must have been brought up—how sadly ignorant not to know that a gentleman—And then she began to remember Lord Lytton's novels, some of which she had read. There would have been nothing out of place in them had such a youth so addressed a lady. He was, indeed, not at all unlike a young man in Lord Lytton. He interested her very much, and filled her mind as she went lightly home. Who could he be, and why so anxious about her father's health? or was that merely a reason for addressing her—a way, perhaps he thought, of securing her acquaintance, making up some sort of private understanding between them. Had not

Rosalind heard somewhere that a boy was opt to select a much older woman as the object of his first admiration? Perhaps that might furnish an explanation for it, for he must be very young, not more than a boy.

When she got home her first step into the house was enough to drive every thought of this description out of her mind. She was aware of the change before she could ask—before she saw even a servant of whom to inquire. The hall, all the rooms, were vacant. She could find nobody, until, coming back after an ineffectual search, she met Jane coming away from the sick-room, carrying various things that had been used there. Jane shook her head in answer to Rosalind's question. "Oh, very bad again—worse than ever. No one can tell what has brought it on. Another attack, worse than any he has had. I think, Miss Rosalind," Jane said, drawing close with a tremulous shrill whisper, "it was that dreadful woman that had got in again the moment my poor lady's back was turned."

"What dreadful woman?"

"Oh, Russell, Miss Rosalind. My poor lady came out of the room for five minutes—I don't think it was five minutes. She was faint with fatigue; and all at once we heard a cry. Oh, it was not master, it was that woman. There she was, lying at the room door in hysterics, or whatever you call them. And the spasms came on again directly. I pushed her out of my lady's way; she may be lying there yet, for anything I know. This time he will never get better, Miss Rosalind," Jane said.

"Oh, do not say so—do not say so," the girl cried. He had not been a kind father nor a generous master. But such was the awe of it, and the quivering sympathy of human nature, that even the woman wept as Rosalind threw herself upon her shoulder. The house was full of the atmosphere of death.

CHAPTER XV

Russell meant no harm to her master. In the curious confusion which one passionate feeling brings into an undisciplined mind, she had even something that might be called affection for Mr. Trevanion, as the victim of the woman she hated. Something that she called regard for him was the justification in her own mind of her furious antipathy to his wife. And after all her excitement and suspense, to be compelled to witness what seemed to her the triumph of Madam, the quieting down of all suspicions, and her return, as more than ever indispensable, to the bedside of her husband, drove the woman almost to madness. How she lived through the week and executed her various duties, as in ordinary times, she did not know. The children suffered more or less, but not so much as might be supposed. For to Russell's perverted perception the children were hers more than their mother's, and she loved them in her way, while she hated Mrs. Trevanion. Indeed, the absorption of Madam in the sick-room left them very much in Russell's influence, and, on the surface, more evidently attached to her than to the mother of whom they saw so little. If they suffered from the excitement that disturbed her temper, as well as other things, it was in a very modified degree, and they were indulged and caressed by moments, as much as they were hustled and scolded at others. The nursery-maids, indeed, found Russell unbearable, and communicated to each other their intention to complain as soon as Madam could be supposed able to listen to them; if not, to give notice at once. But they did not tell for very much in the house, and the nurse concealed successfully enough from all but them the devouring excitement which was in her. It was the afternoon hour, when nature is at its lowest, and when excitement and suspense are least supportable, that Russell found her next opportunity. She had gone down-stairs, seeking she knew not what—looking for something new—a little relief to the strain of suspense, when she suddenly saw the door of the sick-room open and Mrs. Trevanion come out. She did not stop to ask herself what she was to gain by risking an outbreak of fury from her master, and of blame and reproach from every side, by intruding upon the invalid. The temptation was too strong to be resisted. She opened the door without leaving herself time to think, and went in.

Then terror seized her. Mr. Trevanion was propped up in his bed, a pair of fiery, twinkling eyes, full of the suspicion and curiosity that were natural to him, peering out of the skeleton head, which was ghastly with illness and emaciation. Nothing escaped the fierce vitality of those eyes. He saw the movement of the door, the sudden apparition of the excited face, at first so eager and curious, then blanched with terror. He was himself comparatively at ease, in a moment of vacancy in which there was neither present suffering enough to occupy him, nor anything else to amuse his restless soul. "Hallo!" he cried, as soon as he saw her; "come in—come in. You have got something more to tell me? Faithful woman—faithful to your master! Come in; there is just time before Madam comes back to hear what you have to say."

"I beg your pardon, sir," said the valet, who had taken Madam's place, "but the doctor's orders is—"

"What do I care for the doctor's orders? Get out of the way and let Russell in. Here, woman, you have got news for me. A faithful servant, who won't conceal from her master what he ought to know. Out, Jenkins, and let the woman come in."

He raised himself up higher in his bed; the keen angles of his knees seemed to rise to his chin. He waved impatiently his skeleton hands. The valet made wild signs at the intruder. "Can't you go away? You'll kill him!" he cried in a hoarse whisper. "Come in—come in!" shrieked the skeleton in the bed, in all the excitement of opposition. Then it was that Russell, terrified, helpless, distracted, gave that cry which echoed through all the house, and brought Dr. Beaton rushing from one side and Mrs. Trevanion from the other. The woman had fallen at the door of the room in hysterics, as Jane said, a seizure for which all the attendants, absorbed in a more immediate danger, felt the highest contempt. She was pushed out of the way, to be succored by the maids, who had been brought by the cry into the adjacent passage, in high excitement to know what was going on. But Russell could not throw any light upon what had happened even when she came to herself. She could only sob and cry, with starts of nervous panic. She had done nothing, and yet what had she done? She had not said a word to him, and yet—It was soon understood throughout all the house that Mr. Trevanion had another of his attacks, and that Dr. Beaton did not think he could ever rally again.

The room where the patient lay was very large and open. It had once been the billiard-room of the house, and had been prepared for him when it was found no longer expedient that he should go up and down even the easy, luxuriously carpeted stairs of Highcourt. There was one large window filling almost one side of the room, without curtains or even blind, and which was now thrown open to admit the air fully. The door, too, was open, and the draught of fresh, cold, wintry air blowing through made it more like a hillside than a room in a sheltered house. Notwithstanding this, Mrs. Trevanion stood by the bed, waving a large fan, to get more air into the panting and struggling lungs. On the other side of the bed the doctor stood, with the bony wrist of the patient in his warm, living grasp. It seemed to be Death in person with whom these anxious ministrants were struggling, rather than a dying man. Other figures flitted about in the background, Jane bringing, with noiseless understanding, according to the signs the doctor made to her, the things he wanted—now a spoonful of stimulant, now water to moisten his lips. Dead silence reigned in the room; the wind blew through, fluttering a bit of paper on the table; the slight beat of the fan kept a vibration in the air. Into this terrible scene Rosalind stole trembling, and after her her uncle; they shivered with the chill blast which swept over the others unnoticed, and still more with the sight of the gasping and struggle. Rosalind, unused to suffering, hid her face in her hands. She could do nothing. Jane, who knew what was wanted, was of more use than she. She stood timidly at the foot of the bed, now looking up for a moment at what she could see of her dying father, now at the figure of his wife against the light, never intermitting for a moment her dreadful, monotonous exercise. Mr. Trevanion was seated almost upright in the midst of his pillows, laboring in that last terrible struggle for breath, for death, not for life.

He had cried out at first in broken gasps for "The woman—the woman! She's got something—to tell me. Something more—to tell me. I'll hear it—I'll he-ar it—I'll know—everything!" he now shrieked, waving his skeleton arms to keep them away, and struggling to rise. But these efforts soon gave way to the helplessness of nature. His cries soon sank into a hoarse moaning, his struggles to an occasional wave with his arms towards the door, an appeal with his eyes to the doctor, who stood over him inexorable. Every agitating movement had dropped before Rosalind came in into the one grand effort for breath. That was all that was left him in this world to struggle for. A man of so many passions, who had got everything he had set his heart on in life: a little breath now, which the November breeze, the winnowing of the air by the great fan, every aid that could be used, could not bring to his panting lungs. Who can describe the moment when nurses and watchers, and children and lovers stand thus awed and silent, seeing the struggle turn into a fight for death—not against it: feeling their own hearts turn, and their prayers, to that which hitherto they have been resisting with all that love and skill and patience can do? Nature is strong at such a time. Few remember that the central figure has been an unkind husband, a careless father; they remember only that he is going away from them into darkness unfathomable, which they can never penetrate till they follow; that he is theirs, but soon will be theirs no more.

Then there occurred a little pause; for the first moment Dr. Beaton, with a lifted finger and eyes suddenly turned upon the others, was about to say, "All is over," when a faintly renewed throb of the dying pulse under his finger contradicted him. There was a dead calm for a few moments, and then a faint rally. The feverish, eager eyes, starting out of their sockets, seemed to calm, and glance with something like a dim perception at John Trevanion and Rosalind, who approached. Rosalind, entirely overcome by emotion and the terrible excitement of witnessing such an event, dropped down on her knees by the bedside, where with a slight flickering of the eyelids her father's look seemed to follow her. But in the act that look was arrested by the form of his wife, standing always in the same position, waving the fan, sending wafts of air to him, the last and only thing he now wanted. His eyes steadied then with a certain meaning in them—a last gleam which gradually strengthened. He looked at her fixedly, with what in a person less exhausted would have been a wave of the hand towards her. Then there was a faint movement of the lips. "John!" was it perhaps? or "Look!" Then the words became more audible. "She's—good nurse—faithful—Air!—stands—hours—but—" Then the look softened a little, the voice grew stronger; "I'm—almost—sorry—" it said.

For what—for what? In the intense stillness every feeble syllable was heard. Only a minute or two more was left to make amends for the cruelty of a life. The spectators held their breath. As for the wife, whose life perhaps hung upon these syllables as much as his did, she never moved or spoke, but went on fanning, fanning, supplying to him these last billows of air for which he labored. Suddenly a change came over the dying face, the eyes with all their old eagerness turned to the doctor, asking pitifully—was it for help in the last miserable strain of nature, this terrible effort to die?

Mrs. Trevanion seemed turned into stone. She stood and fanned after all need was over, solemnly winnowing the cold, penetrating air, which was touched with the additional chill of night, in waves towards the still lips which had done with that medium of life. To see her standing there, as if she had fainted or become unconscious, yet stood at her post still exercising that strange mechanical office, was the most terrible of all. The doctor came round and took her by the arm, and took the fan out of her hand.

"There's no more need for that," he cried in a broken voice; "no more need. Let us hope he is gone to fuller air than ours."

She was so strained and stupefied that she scarcely seemed to understand this. "Hush!" she said, pulling it from his hands, "I tell you it does him good." She had recovered the fan again and begun to put it in motion, when her eyes suddenly opened wide and fixed upon the dead face. She looked round upon them all with a great solemnity, yet surprise. "My husband is dead!" she said.

"Grace," said John Trevanion, "come away. You have done everything up to the last moment. Come, now, and rest for the sake of the living. He needs you no more."

He was himself very much moved. That which had been so long looked for, so often delayed, came now with all the force of a surprise. Rosalind, in an agony of tears, with her face hidden in the coverlid; Madam standing there, tearless, solemn, with alas, he feared, still worse before her than anything she divined; the young fatherless children outside, the boy at school, the troubles to be gone through, all rushed upon John Trevanion as he stood there. In a moment he who had been the object of all thought had abdicated or been dethroned, and even his brother thought of him no more. "For the sake of the living," he repeated, taking his sister-in-law by the arm. The touch of her was like death; she was cold, frozen where she stood—penetrated by the wintry chill and by the passing of that chiller presence which had gone by her—but she did not resist. She suffered him to lead her away. She sank into a chair in the hall, as if she had no longer any power of her own. There she sat for a little while unmoving, and then cried out suddenly, "For the living!—for which of the living? It would be better for the living if you would bury me with him, he and I in one grave."

Her voice was almost harsh in this sudden cry. What was it—a lie, or the truth? That a woman who had been so outraged and tormented should wish to be buried with her husband seemed to John Trevanion a thing impossible; and yet there was no falsehood in her face. He did not know what to think or say. After a moment he went away and left her alone with her—what?—her grief, her widowhood, her mourning—or was it only a physical frame that could bear no more, the failure of nature, altogether exhausted and worn out?

CHAPTER XVI

"The mother might have managed better, Rosie—why wasn't I sent for? I'm the eldest and the heir, and I ought to have been here. Poor old papa—he would miss me, I know. He was fond of me because I was the biggest. He used to tell me things, I ought to have been sent for. Why didn't she send for me, Rosalind?"

"I have told you before, Rex. We did not know. When I went out in the afternoon he was better and all going well; and when I came back—I had only been in the park—he was dying. Oh, you should be rather glad you were not there. He took no notice of any one, and death is terrible. I never understood what it was—"

Reginald was silent for a little. He was sufficiently awestricken even now by the sensation of the closed shutters and darkened house. "That may be," he said, in a softened voice, "but though you did not know, she would know, Rosie. Do you think she wanted me not to be there? Russell says—"

"Don't speak to me of that woman, Rex. She killed my father—"

"Oh, come, Rosie, don't talk nonsense, you know. How could she kill him? She wanted to tell him something that apparently he ought to have known. It was that that killed him," said the boy, with decision.

They were sitting together in one of the dark rooms; Reginald in the restless state of querulous and petulant unhappiness into which enforced seclusion, darkness, and the cessation of all active occupation warp natural sorrow in the mind of a young creature full of life and movement; Rosalind in the partially soothed exhaustion of strong but simple natural feeling. When she spoke of her father the tears came; but yet already this great event was over, and her mind was besieged, by moments, with thoughts of the new life to come. There were many things to think of. Would everything go on as before under the familiar roof, or would there be some change? And as for herself, what was to be done with her? Would they try to take her from the side of her mother and send her away among strangers? Mrs. Trevanion had retired after her husband's death to take the rest she wanted so much. For twenty-four hours no one had seen her, and Jane had not allowed even Rosalind to disturb the perfect quiet. Since then she had appeared again, but very silent and self-absorbed. She was not less affectionate to Rosalind, but seemed further away from her, as if something great and terrible divided them. When even the children were taken to their mother they were frightened and chilled by the dark room and the cap which she had put on over her beautiful hair, and were glad when the visit was over and they could escape to their nursery, where there was light, and many things to play with. Sometimes children are the most sympathetic of all living creatures; but when it is not so, they can be the most hard-hearted. In this case they were impatient of the quiet, and for a long time past had been little accustomed to be with their mother. When she took the two little ones into her arms, they resigned themselves with looks half of fright at each other, but were very glad, after they had hugged her, to slip down and steal away. Sophy, who was too old for that, paced about and turned over everything. "Are those what are called widow's caps, mamma? Shall you always wear them all your life, like old Widow Harvey, or will it only be just for a little while?" In this way Sophy made herself a comfort to her mother. The poor lady would turn her face to the wall and weep, when they hurried away, pleased to get free of her. And when Reginald came home, he had, after the first burst of childish tears, taken something of the high tone of the head of the house, resentful of not having been called in time, and disposed to resist the authority of Uncle John, who was only a younger brother. Madam had not got much comfort from her children, and between her and Rosalind there was a distance which wrung the girl's heart, but which she did not know how to surmount.

"Don't you know," Reginald said, "that there was something that Russell had to tell him? She will not tell me what it was; but if it was her duty to tell him, how could it be her fault?"

"As soon as mamma is well enough to think of anything, Russell must go away."

"You are so prejudiced, Rosalind. It does not matter to me; it is a long time since I had anything to do with her," said the boy, who was so conscious of being the heir. "But for the sake of the little ones I shall object to that."

"You!" cried Rosalind, with amazement.

"You must remember," said the boy, "that things are changed now. The mother, of course, will have it all in her hands (I suppose) for a time. But it is I who am the head. And when she knows that I object—"

"Reginald," his sister cried; "oh, how dare you speak so? What have you to do with it?—a boy at school."

A flush came over his face. He was half ashamed of himself, yet uplifted by his new honors. "I may be at school—and not—very old; but I am Trevanion of Highcourt now. I am the head of the family, whatever Uncle John may say."

Rosalind looked at her young brother for some time without saying anything, with an air of surprise. She said at last with a sigh, "You are very disappointing, Rex. I think most people are. One looks for something so different. I thought you would be sorry for mamma and think of her above everything, but it is of yourself you are thinking. Trevanion of Highcourt! I thought people had the decency to wait at least until—Papa is in the house still," she added, with an overflow of tears.

At this Reginald, who was not without heart, felt a sudden constriction in his throat, and his eyes filled too. "I didn't mean," he said, faltering, "to forget papa." Then, after a pause, he added, "Mamma, after all, won't be so very much cut up, Rosie. He—bullied her awfully. I wouldn't say a word, but he did, you know. And so I thought, perhaps, she might get over it—easier—"

To this argument what could Rosalind reply? It was not a moment to say it, yet it was true. She was confused between the claims of veracity and that most natural superstition of the heart which is wounded by any censure of the dead. She cried a little; she could not make any reply. Mrs. Trevanion did not show any sign of taking it easily. The occupation of her life was gone. That which had filled all her time and thoughts had been removed entirely from her. If love had survived in her through all that selfishness and cruelty could do to destroy it, such miracles have been known. At all events, the change was one to which it was hard to adapt herself, and the difficulty, the pain, the disruption of all her habits, even, perhaps, the unaccustomed thrill of freedom, had such a confusing and painful effect upon her as produced all the appearances of grief. This was what Rosalind felt, wondering within herself whether, after all she had borne, her mother would in reality "get over it easier," as Reginald said—a suggestion which plunged her into fresh fields of unaccustomed thought when Reginald left her to make a half-clandestine visit to the stables; for neither grief nor decorum could quench in the boy's heart the natural need of something to do. Rosalind longed to go and throw herself at her mother's feet, and claim her old place as closest counsellor and confidante. But then she paused, feeling that there was a natural barrier between them. If it should prove true that her father's death was a relief to his oppressed and insulted wife, that was a secret which never, never could be breathed in Rosalind's ear. It seemed to the girl, in the absoluteness of her youth, as if this must always stand between them, a bar to their intercourse, which once had no barrier, no subjects that might not be freely discussed. When she came to think of it, she remembered that her father never had been touched upon as a subject of discussion between them; but that, indeed, was only natural. For Rosalind had known no other phase of fatherhood, and had grown up to believe that this was the natural development. When men were strong and well, no doubt they were more genial; but sick and suffering, what so natural as that wives and daughters, and more especially wives, should be subject to all their caprices? These were the conditions under which life had appeared to her from her earliest consciousness, and she had never learned to criticise them. She had been indignant at times and taken violently Mrs. Trevanion's side; but with the principle of the life Rosalind had never quarrelled. She had known nothing else. Now, however, in the light of these revelations, and the penetration of ordinary light into the conditions of her own existence, she had begun to understand better. But the awakening had been very painful. Life itself had stopped short and its thread was broken. She could not tell in what way it was to be pieced together again.

Nothing could be more profoundly serious than the aspect of Uncle John as he went and came. It is not cheerful work at any time to make all the dismal arrangements, to provide for the clearing away of a life with all its remains, and make room for the new on the top of the old. But something more than this was in John Trevanion's face. He was one of the executors of his brother's will; he and old Mr. Blake, the lawyer, who had come over to Highcourt, and held what seemed a very agitating consultation in the library, from which the old lawyer came forth "looking as if he had been crying," Sophy had reported to her sister. "Do gentlemen ever cry?" that inquisitive young person had added. Mr. Blake would see none of the family, would not take luncheon, or pause for a moment after he had completed his business, but kept his dog-cart standing at the door, and hurried off as soon as ever the conference was over, which seemed to make John Trevanion's countenance still more solemn. As Reginald went out, Uncle John came into the room in which Rosalind was sitting. There was about him, too, a little querulousness, produced by the darkened windows and the atmosphere of the shut-up house.

"Where is that boy?" he said, with a little impatience. "Couldn't you keep him with you for once in a way, Rosalind? There is no keeping him still or out of mischief. I did hope that you could have exercised a little influence over him—at this moment at least."

"I wish I knew what to do, Uncle John. Unless I amuse him I cannot do anything; and how am I to amuse him just now?"

"My dear," said Uncle John, in the causeless irritation of the moment, "a woman must learn to do that whether it is possible or not. Better that you should exert yourself a little than that he should drift among the grooms, and amuse himself in that way. If this was a time to philosophize, I might say that's why women in general have such hard lives, for we always expect the girls to keep the boys out of mischief, without asking how they are to do it." When he had said this, he came and threw himself down wearily in a chair close to the little table at which Rosalind was sitting. "Rosie," he said, in a changed voice, "we have got a terrible business before us. I don't know how we are to get out of it. My heart fails me when I think—"

Here his voice stopped, and he threw himself forward upon the table, leaning his elbow on it, and covering his face with his hand.

"You mean—Wednesday, Uncle John?" She put out her hand and slid it into his, which rested on the table, or rather placed it, small and white, upon the brown, clinched hand, with the veins standing out upon it, with which he had almost struck the table. Wednesday was the day appointed for the funeral, to which, as a matter of course, half the county was coming. She pressed her uncle's hand softly with hers. There was a faint movement of surprise in her mind that he, so strong, so capable of everything that had to be done, should feel it so.

He gave a groan. "Of what comes after," he said, "I can't tell you what a terrible thing we have to do. God help that poor woman! God forgive her if she has done wrong, for she has a cruel punishment to bear."

"Mamma?" cried Rosalind, with blanched lips.

He made no distinct reply, but sat there silent, with a sort of despair in the pose of every limb. "God knows what we are all to do," he said, "for it will affect us all. You, poor child, you will have to judge for yourself. I don't mean to say or suggest anything. You will have to show what mettle is in you, Rosalind; you as well as the rest."

"What is this terrible thing?" said Rosalind. "Oh, Uncle John, can't you tell me? You make me wretched; I fancy I don't know what."

John Trevanion raised himself from the table. His face was quite colorless. "Nothing that you can fear will be so bad as the reality," he said. "I cannot tell you now. It would be wrong to say anything till she knows; but I am as weak as a child, Rosie. I want your hand to help me; poor little thing, there is not much strength in it. That hour with old Blake this morning has been too much both for him and me."

"Is it something in the will?" cried Rosalind, almost in a whisper. He gave a little nod of assent, and got up and began to pace about the room, as if he had lost power to control himself.

"Charley Blake will not show. He is ashamed of his share in it; but I suppose he could do nothing. It has made him ill, the father says. There's something—in Dante, is it?—about men being possessed by an evil spirit after their real soul is gone. I wonder if that is true. It would almost be a sort of relief to believe—"

"Uncle John, you are not speaking of my father?"

"Don't ask any questions, Rosalind. Haven't I told you I can't answer you? The fact is, I am distracted with one thing and another, all the business coming upon me, and I can't tell what I am saying. Where is that boy?"

"I think he has gone to the stables, Uncle John. It is hard upon him, being always used to the open air. He doesn't know what to do. There is nothing to amuse him."

"Oh, to be sure, it is necessary that his young lordship should be amused," cried John, with something like a snarl of disgust. "Can't you manage to keep him in the house at least, with your feminine influence that we hear so much of? Better anywhere than among those grooms, hearing tales, perhaps—Rosie, forgive me," he cried, coming up to her suddenly, stooping over her and kissing her, "if I snap and snarl even at you, my dear; but I am altogether distracted, and don't know what I am saying or doing. Only, for God's sake, dance or sing, or play cards, or anything, it does not matter what you do, it will be a pious office; only keep him in-doors, where he will hear no gossip; that would be the last aggravation; or go and take him out for a walk, it will be better for you both to get into the fresh air."

CHAPTER XVII

Thus a whole week of darkness and depression passed away.

Mr. Trevanion was a great personage in the county. It was fit that all honor should be done him. All the greatest persons in the neighborhood had to be convened to conduct him in due state to his other dwelling among the marbles of the mausoleum which his fathers had built. It had been necessary to arrange a day that would suit everybody, so that nothing should be subtracted from this concluding grandeur; and accordingly Highcourt remained, so to speak, in its suit of sables, with blinds drawn down and shutters closed, as if darkness had veiled this part of the earth. And, indeed, as it was the end of November, the face of the sky was dim with clouds, and heavy mists gathered over the trees, adding a deeper gloom to the shut-up house within. Life seemed to be congealed in the silent rooms, except when broken by such an outburst of impassioned feeling as that which John Trevanion had betrayed to Rosalind. Perhaps this relieved him a little, but it put a burden of vague misery upon her which her youth was quite unequal to bear. She awaited the funeral with feverish excitement, and a terror to which she could give no form.

The servants in a house are the only gainers on such an occasion: they derive a kind of pleasure from such a crisis of family fate. Blinds are not necessarily drawn down in the housekeeper's room, and the servants' hall is exempt from those heavier decorums which add a gloom above-stairs; and there is a great deal to talk about in the tragedy that is past and in the new arrangements that are to come, while all the details of a grand funeral give more gratification to the humbler members of the family, whose hearts are little affected, than they can be expected to do to those more immediately concerned. There was a stir of sombre pleasure throughout the house in preparation for the great ceremony which was being talked of over all the county: though Dorrington and his subordinates bore countenances more solemn than it is possible to portray, even that solemnity was part of the gloomy festival, and the current of life below was quickened by the many comers and goers whose office it was to provide everything that could show "respect" to the dead. Undertakers are not cheerful persons to think of, but they brought with them a great deal of commotion which was far from disagreeable, much eating and drinking, and additional activity everywhere. New mourning liveries, dresses for the maids, a flutter of newness and general acquisition lightened the bustle that was attendant upon the greater event. Why should some score of people mourn because one man of bad temper, seen perhaps once or twice a day by the majority, by some never seen at all, had been removed from the midst of them? It was not possible; and as everything that is out of the way is more or less a pleasure to unembarrassed minds, there was a thrill of subdued satisfaction, excitement, and general complacency, forming an unfit yet not unnatural background to the gloom and anxiety above. The family assembled at their sombre meals, where there was little conversation kept up, and then dispersed to their rooms, to such occupations as they could find, conversation seeming impossible. In any case a party at table must either be cheerful—which could not be looked for—or be silent, for such conversation as is natural while still the father lies dead in the house is not to be maintained by a mixed company around a common meal.

The doctor, who, of course, was one of the party, did his best to introduce a little variety into the monotonous meetings, but John Trevanion's sombre countenance at the foot of the table was enough to have silenced any man, even had not the silence of Mrs. Trevanion and the tendency of Rosalind to sudden tears been enough to keep him in check. Dr. Beaton, however, was Reginald's only comfort. They kept up a running talk, which perhaps even to the others was grateful, as covering the general gloom. Reginald had been much subdued by hearing that he was to return to school as soon as the funeral was over. He had found very little sympathy with his claims anywhere, and he was very glad to fall back upon the doctor. Indeed, if Highcourt was to be so dull as this, Rex could not but think school was far better. "Of course, I never meant," he said to his sister, "to give up school—a fellow can't do that. It looks as if he had been sent away. And now there's those tiresome examinations for everything, even the Guards."

"We shall be very dull for a long time," said Rosalind. "How could it be possible otherwise? But you will cheer us up when you come home for the holidays; and, oh, Rex, you must always stand by mamma!"

"By mamma!" Rex said, with some surprise. "Why, she will be very well off—better off than any of us." He had not any chivalrous feeling about his mother. Such a feeling we all think should spring up spontaneously in a boy's bosom, especially if he has seen his mother ill-used and oppressed; but, as a matter of fact, this assumption is by no means to be depended on. A boy is at least as likely to copy a father who rails against women, and against the one woman in particular who is his wife, as to follow a vague general rule, which he has never seen put in practice, of respect and tender reverence for woman. Reginald had known his mother as the doer of everything, the endurer of everything. He had never heard that she had any weakness to be considered, and had never contemplated the idea that she should be put upon a pedestal and worshipped; and if he did not hit by insight of nature upon some happy medium between the two, it was not, perhaps, his fault. In the meantime, at all events, no sentiment on the subject inspired his boyish bosom.

Mrs. Trevanion, as these days went on, resumed gradually her former habits, so far as was possible in view of the fact that all her married life had been devoted to her husband's service, and that she had dropped one by one every pursuit that separated her from him. The day before the funeral she came into the little morning-room in which Rosalind was sitting, and drew a chair to the fire. "I had almost forgotten the existence of this room," she said. "So many things have dropped away from me. I forget what I used to do. What used I to do, Rosalind, before—"

She looked up with a pitiful smile. And, indeed, it seemed to both of them as if they had not sat quietly together, undisturbed, for years.

"You have always done—everything for everybody—as long as I can remember," said Rosalind, with tender enthusiasm.

She shook her head. "I don't think it has come to much use. I have been thinking over my life, over and over, these few days. It has not been very successful, Rosalind. Something has always spoiled my best efforts, I wonder if other people feel the same? Not you, my dear, you know nothing about it; you must not answer with your protestations. Looking back, I can see how it has always failed somehow. It is a curious thing to stand still, so living as I am, and look back upon my life, and sum it up as if it were past."

"It is because a chapter of it is past," said Rosalind. "Oh, mamma, I do not wonder! And you have stood at your post till the last moment; no wonder you feel as if everything were over."

"Yes, I stood at my post: but perhaps another kind of woman would have soothed him when I irritated him. Your father—was not kind to me, Rosalind—"

The girl rose and put her arms round Mrs. Trevanion's neck and kissed her. "No, mother," she said.

"He was not kind. And yet, now that he has gone out of my life I feel as if nothing were left. People will think me a hypocrite. They will say I am glad to be free. But it is not so, Rosalind, remember: man and wife, even when they wound each other every day, cannot be nothing to each other. My occupation is gone; I feel like a wreck cast upon the shore."

"Mother! how can you say that when we are all here, your children, who can do nothing without you?"

"My children—which children?" she said, with a wildness in her eyes as if she did not know what she was saying; and then she returned to her metaphor, like one thinking aloud; "like a wreck—that perhaps a fierce, high sea may seize again, a high tide, and drag out upon the waves once more. I wonder if I could beat and buffet those waves again as I used to do, and fight for my life—"

"Oh, mother, how could that ever be?—there is no sea here."

"No, no sea—one gets figurative when one is in great trouble—what your father used to call theatrical, Rosalind. He said very sharp things—oh, things that cut like a knife. But I was not without fault any more than he; there is one matter in which I have not kept faith with him. I should like to tell you, to see what you think. I did not quite keep faith with him. I made him a promise, and—I did not keep it. He had some reason, though he did not know it, in all the angry things he said."

Rosalind did not know what to reply; her heart beat high with expectation. She took her stepmother's hand between hers, and waited, her very ears tingling, for the next word.

"I have had no success in that," Mrs. Trevanion said, in the same dreary way, "in that no more than the rest. I have not done well with anything; except," she said, looking up with a faint smile and brightening of her countenance, "you, Rosalind, my own dear, who are none of mine."

"I am all of yours, mother," cried the girl; "don't disown me, for I shall always claim you—always! You are all the mother I have ever known."

Then they held each other close for a moment, clinging one to the other. Could grief have appeared more natural? The wife and daughter, in their deep mourning, comforting each other, taking a little courage from their union—yet how many strange, unknown elements were involved. But Mrs. Trevanion said no more of the confidence she had seemed on the point of giving. She rose shortly after and went away, saying she was restless and could not do anything, or even stay still in one place. "I walk about my room and frighten Jane, but that is all I can do."

"Stay here, mamma, with me, and walk about, or do what you please. I understand you better than Jane."

Mrs. Trevanion shook her head; but whether it was to contradict that last assertion or merely because she could not remain, it was impossible to say. "To-morrow," she said, "will be the end, and, perhaps, the beginning. I feel as if all would be over to-morrow. After that, Rosalind—"

She went away with the words on her lips. "After to-morrow." And to Rosalind, too, it seemed as if her powers of endurance were nearly ended, and to-morrow would fill up the sum. But then, what was that further mysterious trouble which Uncle John feared?

Mrs. Trevanion appeared again to dinner, which was a very brief meal, but retired immediately; and the house was full of preparation for to-morrow—every one having, or seeming to have, something to do.

Rosalind was left alone. She could not go and sit in the great, vacant drawing-room, all dimly lighted, and looking as if some party of the dead might be gathered about the vacant hearth; or in the hall, where now and then some one of the busy, nameless train of to-morrow's ceremony would steal past. And it was too early to go to bed. She wrapped herself in a great shawl, and, opening the glass door, stole out into the night. The sweeping of the chill night air, the rustle of the trees, the stars twinkling overhead, gave more companionship than the silence and gloom within. She stood outside on the broad steps, leaning against one of the pillars, till she got chilled through and through, and began to think, with a kind of pleasure, of the glow of the fire.

But as she turned to go in a great and terrible shock awaited her. She had just come away from the pillar, which altogether obliterated her slight, dark figure in its shadow and gave her a sort of invisibility, when the glass door opened at a touch, and some one else came out. They met face to face in the darkness. Rosalind uttered a stifled cry; the other only by a pant of quickened breathing acknowledged the alarm. She was gliding past noiselessly, when Rosalind, with sudden courage, caught her by the cloak in which she was wrapped from head to foot. "Oh, not to-night, oh, not to-night!" she said, with a voice of anguish; "for God's sake, mother, mother, not to-night!"

There was a pause, and no reply but the quick breathing, as if the passer-by had some hope of concealing herself. But then Madam spoke, in a low, hurried tone—"I must go; I must! but not for any pleasure of mine!"

Rosalind clung to her cloak with a kind of desperation. "Another time," she said, "but not, oh, not to-night!"

"Let me go. God bless my dear! I cannot help it. I do only what I must. Rosalind, let me go," she said.

And next moment the dark figure glided swiftly, mysteriously, among the bushes towards the park. Rosalind came in with despair in her heart. It seemed to her that nothing more was left to expect, or hope for. Her mother, the mistress of this sad house, the wife of the dead who still lay there awaiting his burial. At no other moment perhaps would the discovery have come upon her with such a pang; and yet at any moment what could it be but misery? Jane was watching furtively on the stairs to see that her mistress's exit had been unnoticed. She was in the secret, the confidante, the—But Rosalind's young soul knew no words; her heart seemed to die within her. She could do or hope no more.

CHAPTER XVIII

All was dark; the stars twinkling ineffectually in the sky, so far off, like spectators merely, or distant sentinels, not helpers; the trees in all their winter nakedness rustling overhead, interrupting the vision of these watchers; the grass soaked with rain and the heavy breath of winter, slipping below the hurrying feet. There was no sound, but only a sense of movement in the night as she passed. The most eager gaze could scarcely have made out what it was—a shadow, the flitting of a cloud, a thrill of motion among the dark shrubs and bushes, as if a faint breeze had got up suddenly and was blowing by. At that hour there was very little chance of meeting anybody in these damp and melancholy glades, but the passenger avoided all open spaces until she had got to some distance from the house. Even then, as she hurried across, her muffled figure was quite unrecognizable. It was enough to raise a popular belief that the park was haunted, but no more. She went on till she came to a thick copse about half-way between the house and the village. Then another figure made a step out of the thick cover to receive her, and the two together withdrew entirely into its shade.

What was said there, what passed, no one, even though skirting the copse closely, could have told. The whisperers, hidden in its shade, were not without an alarm from time to time; for the path to the village was not far off, and sometimes a messenger from the house would pass at a distance, whistling to keep his courage up, or talking loudly if there were two, for the place was supposed to be ghostly. On this occasion the faint movement among the bare branches would stop, and all be as still as death. Then a faint thrill of sound, of human breathing, returned. The conversation was rapid. "At last!" the other said; "do you know I have waited here for hours these last nights?"

"You knew it was impossible. How could I leave the house in such circumstances? Even now I have outraged decency by coming. I have gone against nature—"

"Not for the first time," was the answer, with a faint laugh.

"If so, you should be the last to reproach me, for it was for you."

"Ah, for me! that is one way of putting it. Like all those spurious sacrifices, if one examined a little deeper. You have had the best of it, anyhow."

"All this," she said, with a tone of despair, "has been said so often before. It was not for this you insisted on my coming. What is it? Tell me quickly, and let me go before I am found out. Found out! I am found out already. I dare not ask myself what they think."

"Whatever they think you may be sure it is not the truth. Nobody could guess at the truth. It is too unnatural, that I should be lurking here in wretchedness, and you—"

"But you are comfortable," she said quickly. "Jane told me—"

"Comfortable according to Jane's ideas, which are different from mine. What I want is to know what you are going to do; what is to become of me? Will you do me justice now, at last?"

"Oh, Edmund, what justice have you made possible? What can I do but implore you to go? Are not you in danger every day?"

"Less here than anywhere; though I understand there have been inquiries made; the constable in the village shows a degree of interest—"

"Edmund," she cried, seizing him by the arm, "for God's sake, go!"

"And not bring shame upon you, Madam? Why should I mind? If I have gone wrong, whose fault is it? You must take that responsibility one time or other. And now that you are free—"

"I cannot defy the law," she said, with a miserable moan. "I can't deliver you from what you have done. God knows, though it had been to choose between you and everything else, I would have done you justice, as you say, as soon as it was possible. But to what use now? It would only direct attention to you—bring the—" She shuddered, and said no more.

"The police, you mean," he replied, with a careless laugh. "And no great harm either, except to you; for of course all my antecedents would be published. But there are such things as disguises, and I am clever at a make-up. You might receive me, and no one would be the wiser. The cost of a new outfit, a new name—you might choose me a nice one. Of all places in the world, a gentleman's house in the country is the last where they would look for me. And then if there was any danger you could swear I was—"

"Oh, Edmund, Edmund, spare me! I cannot do this—to live in a deception under my children's eyes."

"Your children's eyes!" he said, and laughed. The keen derision of his tone went to her very heart.

"I am used to hear everything said to me that can be said to a woman," she said quickly, "and if there was anything wanting you make it up. I have had full measure, heaped up and running over. But there is no time for argument now. All that might have been possible in other circumstances; now there is no safety for you but in getting away. You know this, surely, as well as I do. The anxiety you have kept me in it is impossible to tell. I have been calmer since he is gone: it matters less. But for your own sake—"

The other voice said, with a change of tone, "I am lost anyhow. I shall do nothing for my own sake—"

"Oh, Edmund, Edmund, do not break my heart—at your age! If you will only set your mind to better ways, everything can be put right again. As soon as I know you are safe I will take it all in hand. I have not been able hitherto, and now I am afraid to direct observation upon you. But only go away; let me know you are safe: and you have my promise I will pay anything, whatever they ask."

"Misprision of felony! They won't do that; they know better. If there is any paying," he said, with his careless laugh, "it had much better be to me."

"You shall be provided," she said breathlessly, "if you will only think of your own safety and go away."

"Are you sure, then, of having come into your fortune? Has the old fellow shown so much confidence in you? All the better for me. Your generosity in that way will always be fully appreciated. But I would not trouble about Liverpool; they're used to such losses. It does them no harm, only makes up for the salaries they ought to pay their clerks, and don't."

"Don't speak so lightly, Edmund. You cannot feel it. To make up to those you have—injured—"

"Robbed, if you like, but not injured. That's quite another matter. I don't care a straw for this part of the business. But money," he said, "money is always welcome here."

A sigh which was almost a moan forced itself from her breast. "You shall have what you want," she said. "But, Edmund, for God's sake, if you care either for yourself or me, go away!"

"You would do a great deal better to introduce me here. It would be safer than Spain. And leave it to me to make my way. A good name—you can take one out of the first novel that turns up—and a few good suits of clothes. I might be a long-lost relative come to console you in your distress. That would suit me admirably. I much prefer it to going away. You should see how well I would fill the post of comforter—"

"Don't!" she cried; "don't!" holding out her hands in an appeal for mercy.

"Why," he said, "it is far the most feasible way, and the safest, if you would but think. Who would look for an absconded clerk at Highcourt, in the midst of family mourning and all the rest of it? And I have views of my own—Come, think it over. In former times I allow it would have been impossible, but now you are free."

"I will not," she said, suddenly raising her head. "I have done much, but there are some things that are too much. Understand me, I will not. In no conceivable circumstances, whatever may happen. Rather will I leave you to your fate."

"What!" he said, "and bring shame and ruin on yourself?"

"I do not care. I am desperate. Much, much would I do to make up for my neglect of you, if you can call it neglect; but not this. Listen! I will not do it. It is not to be mentioned again. I will make any sacrifice, except of truth—except of truth!"

"Of truth!" he said, with a sneer; but then was silent, evidently convinced by her tone. He added, after a time, "It is all your fault. What was to be expected? I have never had a chance. It is just that you should bear the brunt, for it is your fault."

"I acknowledge it," she said; "I have failed in everything; and whatever I can do to atone I will do. Edmund, oh, listen! Go away. You are not safe here. You risk everything, even my power to help you. You must go, you must go," she added, seizing him firmly by the arm in her vehemence; "there is no alternative. You shall have money, but go, go! Promise me that you will go."

"If you use force—" he said, freeing himself roughly from her grasp.

"Force! what force have I against you? It is you who force me to come here and risk everything. If I am discovered, God help me! on the eve of my husband's funeral, how am I to have the means of doing anything for you? You will understand that. You shall have the money; but promise me to go."

"You are very vehement," he said. Then, after another pause, "That is strong, I allow. Bring me the money to-morrow night, and we shall see."

"I will send Jane."

"I don't want Jane. Bring it yourself, or there is not another word to be said."

Mrs. Trevanion got back, as she thought, unseen to the house. There was nobody in the hall when she opened noiselessly the glass door, and flung down the cloak she had worn among the wraps that were always there. She went up-stairs with her usual stately step; but when she had safely reached the shelter of her own room, she fell into the arms of the anxious Jane, who had been waiting in miserable suspense, fearing discovery in every sound. She did not faint. Nerves strong and highly braced to all conclusions, and a brain yet more vigorous, still kept her vitality unimpaired, and no merciful cloud came over her mind to soften what she had to bear—there are some to whom unconsciousness is a thing never accorded, scarcely even in sleep. But for a moment she lay upon the shoulder of her faithful servant, getting some strength from the contact of heart with heart. Jane knew everything; she required no explanation. She held her mistress close, supporting her in arms that had never failed her, giving the strength of two to the one who was in deadly peril. After a time Mrs. Trevanion roused herself. She sat down shivering in the chair which Jane placed for her before the fire. Warmth has a soothing effect upon misery. There was a sort of restoration in it, and possibility of calm. She told all that had passed to the faithful woman who had stood by her in all the passages of her life—her confidante, her go-between: other and worse names, if worse can be, had been ere now expended upon Jane.

"Once more," Madam said, with a long sigh, "once more; and then it is to be over, or so he says, at least. On the night of my husband's funeral day; on the night before—What could any one think of me, if it were known? And how can I tell that it is not known?"

"Oh, dear Madam, let us hope for the best," said Jane. "Besides, who has any right to find fault now? Whatever you choose to do, you have a right to do it. The only one that had any right to complain—"

"And the only one," said Mrs. Trevanion, with sudden energy, "who had no right to complain." Then she sank back again into her chair. "I care nothing for other people," she said; "it is myself. I feel the misery of it in myself. This night, of all others, to expose myself—and to-morrow. I think my punishment is more than any woman should have to bear."

"Oh, Madam, do not think of it as a punishment."

"As what, then—a duty? But one implies the other. God help us! If I could but hope that after this all would be over, at least for the time. I have always been afraid of to-morrow; I cannot tell why. Not because of the grave and the ceremony; but with a kind of dread as if there were something in it unforeseen, something new. Perhaps it is this last meeting which has been weighing upon me—this last meeting, which will be a parting, too, perhaps forever—"

She paused for a moment, and then burst forth into tears. "I ought to be thankful. That is the only thing to be desired. But when I think of all that might have been, and of what is—of my life all gone between the one who has been my tyrant, and the other—the other against whom I have sinned. And that one has died in anger, and the other—oh, the other!"

It was to Jane's faithful bosom that she turned again to stifle the sobs which would not be restrained. Jane stood supporting her, weeping silently, patting with pathetic helplessness her mistress's shoulder. "Oh, Madam," she said, "who can tell? his heart may be touched at the last."

CHAPTER XIX

Next day there was a great concourse of people at Highcourt, disturbing the echoes which had lain so silent during that week of gloom. Carriages with the finest blazons, quartered and coronetted; men of the greatest importance, peers, and those commoners who hold their heads higher than any recent peers—M.P.'s; the lord-lieutenant and his deputy, everything that was noted and eminent in those parts. The procession was endless, sweeping through the park towards the fine old thirteenth-century church which made the village notable, and in which the Trevanion chantry, though a century later in date, was the finest part; though the dark opening in the vault, canopied over with fine sculptured work, and all that pious art could do to make the last resting-place beautiful, opened black as any common grave for the passage of the departed. There was an unusual band of clergy gathered in their white robes to do honor to the man who had given half of them their livings, and all the villagers, and various visitors from the neighboring town, shopkeepers who had rejoiced in his patronage, and small gentry to whom Madam had given brevet rank by occasional notice. Before the procession approached, a little group of ladies, in crape from head to foot and closely veiled, were led in by the curate reverently through a side door. A murmur ran through the gathering crowd that it was Madam herself who walked first, with her head bowed, not seeing or desiring the curate's anxiously offered arm. The village had heard a rumor of trouble at the great house, and something about Madam, which had made the elders shake their heads, and remind each other that she was a foreigner and not of these parts, which accounted for anything that might be wrong; while the strangers, who had also heard that there was a something, craned their necks to see her through the old ironwork of the chancel-screen, behind which the ladies were introduced. Many people paused in the midst of the service, and dropped their prayer-books to gaze again, and wonder what she was thinking now, if she had indeed, as people said, been guilty. How must she feel when she heard the deep tones of the priest, and the organ pealing out its Amens. Blessed are the dead that die in the Lord. Had he forgiven her before he died? Was she broken down with remorse and shame, or was she rejoicing in her heart, behind her crape veil, in her freedom? It must not be supposed, because of this general curiosity, that Madam Trevanion had lost her place in the world, or would not have the cards of the county showered upon her, with inquiries after her health from all quarters; but only that there was "a something" which gave piquancy, such as does not usually belong to such a melancholy ceremonial, to the great function of the day. The most of the audience, in fact, sympathized entirely with Madam, and made remarks as to the character of the man so imposingly ushered into the realm of the dead, which did not fit in well with the funeral service. There were many who scoffed at the hymn which was sung by the choirs of the adjacent parishes, all in the late Mr. Trevanion's gift, and which was very, perhaps unduly, favorable to the "dear saint" thus tenderly dismissed. He had not been a dear saint; perhaps, in such a case, the well-known deprecation of trop de zèle is specially appropriate. It made the scoffer blaspheme to hear so many beautiful qualities attributed to Mr. Trevanion. But perhaps it is best to err on the side of kindness. It was, at all events, a grand funeral. No man could have desired more.

The third lady who accompanied Mrs. Trevanion and her daughter was the Aunt Sophy to whom there had been some question of sending Rosalind. She was the only surviving sister of Mr. Trevanion, Mrs. Lennox, a wealthy widow, without any children, to whom the Highcourt family were especially dear. She was the softest and most good-natured person who had ever borne the name of Trevanion. It was supposed to be from her mother, whom the Trevanions in general had worried into her grave at a very early age, that Aunt Sophy got a character so unlike the rest of the family. But worrying had not been successful in the daughter's case; or perhaps it was her early escape by her marriage that saved her. She was so apt to agree with the last person who spoke, that her opinion was not prized as it might have been by her connections generally; but everybody was confident in her kindness. She had arrived only the morning of the funeral, having come from the sickbed of a friend whom she was nursing, and to whom she considered it very necessary that she should get back; but it was quite possible that, being persuaded her sister-in-law or Rosalind had more need of her, she might remain at Highcourt, notwithstanding that it was so indispensable that she should leave that afternoon, for the rest of the year.

The shutters had been all opened, the blinds raised, the windows let in the light, the great doors stood wide when they came back. The house was no longer the house of the dead, but the house of the living. In Mr. Trevanion's room, that chamber of state, the curtains were all pulled down already, the furniture turned topsy-turvy, the housemaids in possession. In proportion as the solemnity of the former mood had been, so was the anxiety now to clear away everything that belonged to death. The children, in their black frocks, came to meet their mother, half reluctant, half eager. The incident of papa's death was worn out to them long ago, and they were anxious to be released, and to see something new. Here Aunt Sophy was of the greatest assistance. She cried over them, and smiled, and admired their new dresses, and cried again, and bade them be good and not spoil their clothes, and be a comfort to their dear mamma. The ladies kept together in the little morning-room till everybody was gone. It was very quiet there, out of the bustle; and they had been told that there was no need for their presence in the library where the gentlemen were, John Trevanion with the Messrs. Blake. There was no need, indeed, for any formal reading of the will. There could be little uncertainty about a man's will whose estates were entailed, and who had a young family to provide for. Nobody had any doubt that he would deal justly with his children, and the will was quite safe in the hands of the executors. Refreshments were taken to them in the library, and the ladies shared the children's simple dinner. It was all very serious, very quiet, but there could be no doubt that the weight and oppression were partially withdrawn.

The short afternoon had begun to darken, and Aunt Sophy had already asked if it were not nearly time for tea, when Dorrington, the butler, knocked at the door, and with a very solemn countenance delivered "Mr. John Trevanion's compliments, and would Madam be so good as step into the library for a few minutes?"

The few minutes were Dorrington's addition. The look of the gentlemen seated at the table close together, like criminals awaiting execution, and fearing that every moment would bring the headsman, had alarmed Dorrington. He was favorable to his mistress on the whole; and he thought this summons meant something. So unconsciously he softened his message. A few minutes had a reassuring sound. They all looked up at him as the message was given.

"They will want to consult you about something," said Aunt Sophy; "you have managed everything for so long. He said only a few minutes. Make haste, dear, and we will wait for you for tea."

"Shall I go with you, mamma?" said Rosalind, rising and following to the door.

Mrs. Trevanion hesitated for a moment. "Why should I be so foolish?" she said, with a faint smile. "I would say yes, come; but that it is too silly."

"I will come, mamma."

"No; it is absolute folly. As if I were a novice! Make your aunt comfortable, dear, and don't let her wait for me." She was going away when something in Rosalind's face attracted her notice. The girl's eyes were intent upon her with a pity and terror in them that was indescribable. Mrs. Trevanion made a step back again and kissed her. "You must not be frightened, Rosalind. There can be nothing bad enough for that; but don't let your aunt wait," she said; and closing the door quickly behind her, she left the peaceful protection of the women with whom she was safe, and went to meet her fate.

The library was naturally a dark room, heavy with books, with solemn curtains and sad-colored furniture. The three large windows were like shaded lines of vertical light in the breadth of the gloom. On the table some candles had been lighted, and flared with a sort of wild waving when the door was opened. Lighted up by them, against the dark background, were the pale faces of John Trevanion and old Mr. Blake. Both had a look of agitation, and even alarm, as if they were afraid of her. Behind them, only half visible, was the doctor, leaning against a corner of the mantelpiece, with his face hidden by his hand. John Trevanion rose without a word, and placed a chair for his sister-in-law close to where they sat. He drew nearer to his colleague when he sat down again, as if for protection, which, however, Mr. Blake, a most respectable, unheroic person, with his countenance like ashes, and looking as if he had seen a ghost, was very little qualified to give.

"My dear Grace," said John, clearing his voice, which trembled, "we have taken the liberty to ask you to come here, instead of going to you."

"I am very glad to come if you want me, John," she said, simply, with a frankness and ease which confused them more and more.

"Because," he went on, clearing his throat again, endeavoring to control his voice, "because we have something—very painful to say."

"Very painful; more painful than anything I ever had to do with in all my life," Mr. Blake added, in a husky voice.

She looked from one to another, questioning their faces, though neither of them would meet her eyes. The bitterness of death had passed from Mrs. Trevanion's mind. The presentiment that had hung so heavily about her had blown away like a cloud. Sitting by the fire in the innocent company of Sophy, with Rosalind by her, the darkness had seemed to roll together and pass away. But when she looked from one of these men to the other, it came back and enveloped her like a shroud. She said "Yes?" quickly, her breath failing, and looked at them, who could not meet her eyes.

"It is so," said John. "We must not mince our words. Whatever may have passed between you two, whatever he may have heard or found out, we can say nothing less than that it is most unjust and cruel."

"Savage, barbarous! I should never have thought it, I should have refused to do it," his colleague cried, in his high-pitched voice.

"But we have no alternative. We must carry his will out, and we are bound to let you know without delay."

"This delay is already too much," she said hurriedly. "Is it something in my husband's will? Why try to frighten me? Tell me at once."

"God knows we are not trying to frighten you. Nothing so terrible could occur to your mind, or any one's, Grace," said John Trevanion, with a nervous quivering of his voice. "The executioner used to ask pardon of those he was about to—I think I am going to give you your sentence of death."

"Then I give you—my pardon—freely. What is it? Do not torture me any longer," she said.

He thrust away his chair from the table, and covered his face with his hands. "Tell her, Blake; I cannot," he cried.

Then there ensued a silence like death; no one seemed to breathe; when suddenly the high-pitched, shrill voice of the old lawyer came out like something visible, mingled with the flaring of the candles and the darkness all around.

"I will spare you the legal language," said Mr. Blake. "It is this. The children are all provided for, as is natural and fit, but with this proviso—that their mother shall be at once and entirely separated from them. If Mrs. Trevanion remains with them, or takes any one of them to be with her, they are totally disinherited, and their money is left to various hospitals and charities. Either Mrs. Trevanion must leave them at once, and give up all communication with them, or they lose everything. That is in brief what we have to say."

She sat listening without changing her position, with a dimness of confusion and amaze coming over her clear gaze. The intimation was so bewildering, so astounding, that her faculties failed to grasp it. Then she said, "To leave them—my children? To be separated from my children?" with a shrill tone of inquiry, rising into a sort of breathless cry.

John Trevanion took his hands from his face, and looked at her with a look which brought more certainty than words. The old lawyer clasped his hands upon the papers before him, without lifting his eyes, and mournfully nodded again and again his gray head. But she waited for an answer. She could not let herself believe it. "It is not that? My head is going round. I don't understand the meaning of words. It is not that?"

And then she rose up suddenly to her feet, clasping her hands together, and cried out, "My God!" The men rose too, as with one impulse; and John Trevanion called out loudly to the doctor, who hurried to her. She put them away with a motion of her hands. "The doctor? What can the doctor do for me?" she cried, with the scorn of despair. "Go, go, go! I need no support." The men had come close to her on either side, with that confused idea that the victim must faint or fall, or sustain some physical convulsion, which men naturally entertain in respect to a woman. She made a motion, as if to keep them away, with her arms, and stood there in the midst, her pale face, with the white surroundings of her distinctive dress, clearly defined against the other dusk and troubled countenances. They thought the moments of suspense endless, but to her they were imperceptible. Not all the wisest counsellors in the world could have helped her in that effort of desperation which her lonely soul was making to understand. There was so much that no one knew but herself. Her mind went through all the details of a history unthought of. She had to put together and follow the thread of events, and gather up a hundred indications which now came all flashing about her like marsh-lights, leading her swift thoughts here and there, through the hitherto undivined workings of her husband's mind, and ripening of fate. Thus it was that she came slowly to perceive what it meant, and all that it meant, which nature, even when perceiving the sense of the words, had refused to believe. When she spoke they all started with a sort of panic and individual alarm, as if something might be coming which would be too terrible to listen to. But what she said had a strange composure, which was a relief, yet almost a horror, to them. "Will you tell me," she asked, "exactly what it is, again?"

Old Mr. Blake sat down again at the table, fumbled for his spectacles, unfolded his papers. Meanwhile she stood and waited, with the others behind her, and listened without moving while he read, this time in its legal phraseology, the terrible sentence. She drew a long breath when it was over. This time there was no amaze or confusion. The words were like fire in her brain.

"Now I begin to understand. I suppose," she said, "that there is nothing but public resistance, and perhaps bringing it before a court of law, that could annul that? Oh, do not fear. I will not try; but is that the only way?"

The old lawyer shook his head. "Not even that. He had the right; and though he has used it as no man should have used it, still, it is done, and cannot be undone."

"Then there is no help for me," she said. She was perfectly quiet, without a tear or sob or struggle. "No help for me," she repeated, with a wan little smile about her mouth. "After seventeen years! He had the right, do you say? Oh, how strange a right! when I have been his wife for seventeen years." Then she added, "Is it stipulated when I am to go? Is there any time given to prepare? And have you told my boy?"

"Not a word has been said, Grace—to any one," John Trevanion said.

"Ah, I did not think of that. What is he to be told? A boy of that age. He will think his mother is—John, God help me! what will you say to my boy?"

"God help us all!" cried the strong man, entirely overcome. "Grace, I do not know."

"The others are too young," she said; "and Rosalind—Rosalind will trust me; but Rex—it will be better to tell him the simple truth, that it is his father's will; and perhaps when he is a man he will understand." She said this with a steady voice, like some queen making her last dispositions in full health and force before her execution—living, yet dying. Then there ensued another silence, which no one ventured to break, during which the doomed woman went back into her separate world of thought. She recovered herself after a moment, and, looking round, with once more that faint smile, asked, "Is there anything else I ought to hear?"

"There is this, Mrs. Trevanion," said old Blake. "One thing is just among so much—What was settled on you is untouched. You have a right to—"

She threw her head high with an indignant motion, and turned away; but after she had made a few steps towards the door, paused and came back. "Look," she said, "you gentlemen; here is something that is beyond you, which a woman has to bear. I must accept this humiliation, too. I cannot dig, and to beg I am ashamed." She looked at them with a bitter dew in her eyes, not tears. "I must take his money and be thankful. God help me!" she said.

CHAPTER XX

Mrs. Trevanion appeared at dinner as usual, coming into the drawing-room at the last moment, to the great surprise of the gentlemen, who stared and started as if at a ghost as she came in, their concealed alarm and astonishment forming a strange contrast to the absolute calm of Mrs. Lennox, the slight boyish impatience of Reginald at being kept waiting for dinner, and the evident relief of Rosalind, who had been questioning them all with anxious eyes. Madam was very pale; but she smiled and made a brief apology. She took old Mr. Blake's arm to go in to dinner, who, though he was a man who had seen a great deal in his life, shook "like as a leaf," he said afterwards; but her arm was as steady as a rock, and supported him. The doctor said to her under his breath as they sat down, "You are doing too much. Remember, endurance is not boundless." "Is it not?" she said aloud, looking at him with a smile. He was a man of composed and robust mind, but he ate no dinner that day. The dinner was indeed a farce for most of the company. Aunt Sophy, indeed, though with a shake of her head, and a sighing remark now and then, took full advantage of her meal, and Reginald cleared off everything that was set before him with the facility of his age; but the others made such attempts as they could to deceive the calm but keen penetration of Dorrington, who saw through all their pretences, and having served many meals in many houses after a funeral, knew that "something" must be "up," more than Mr. Trevanion's death, to account for the absence of appetite. There was not much conversation either. Aunt Sophy, indeed, to the relief of every one, took the position of spokeswoman. "I would not have troubled to come down-stairs this evening, Grace," she said. "You always did too much. I am sure all the watching and nursing you have had would have killed ten ordinary people; but she never spared herself, did she, doctor? Well, it is a satisfaction now. You must feel that you neglected nothing, and that everything that could be thought of was done—everything! I am sure you and I, John, can bear witness to that, that a more devoted nurse no man ever had. Poor Reginald," she added, putting her handkerchief to her eyes, "if he did not always seem so grateful as he ought, you may be sure, dear, it was his illness that was to blame, not his heart." No one dared to make any reply to this, till Madam herself said, after a pause, her voice sounding distinct through a hushed atmosphere of attention, "All that is over and forgotten; there is no blame."

"Yes, my dear," said innocent Sophy; "that is a most natural and beautiful sentiment for you. But John and I can never forget how patient you were. A king could not have been better taken care of."

"Everybody," said the doctor, with fervor, "knows that. I have never known such nursing;" and in the satisfaction of saying this he managed to dispose of the chicken on his plate. His very consumption of it was to Madam's credit. He could not have swallowed a morsel, but for having had the opportunity for this ascription of praise.

"And if I were you," said Mrs. Lennox, "I would not worry myself about taking up everything so soon again. I am sure you must want a thorough rest. I wish, indeed, you would just make up your mind to come home with me, for a change would do you good. I said to poor dear Maria Heathcote, when I left her this morning, 'My dear, you may expect me confidently to-night; unless my poor dear sister-in-law wants me. But dear Grace has, of course, the first claim upon me,' I said. And if I were you I would not try my strength too much. You should have stayed in your room to-night, and have had a tray with something light and trifling. You don't eat a morsel," Aunt Sophy said, with true regret. "And Rosalind and I would have come up-stairs and sat with you. I have more experience than you have in trouble," added the good lady with a sigh (who, indeed, "had buried two dear husbands," as she said), "and that has always been my experience. You must not do too much at first. To-morrow is always a new day."

"To-morrow," Mrs. Trevanion said, "there will be many things to think of." She lingered on the word a little, with a tremulousness which all the men felt as if it had been a knife going into their hearts. Her voice got more steady as she went on. "You must go back to school on Monday, Rex," she said; "that will be best. You must not lose any time now, but be a man as soon as you can, for all our sakes."

"Oh, as for being a man," said Reginald, "that doesn't just depend on age, mother. My tutor would rather have me for his captain than Smith, who is nineteen. He said so. It depends upon a fellow's character."

"That is what I think too," she said, with a smile upon her boy. "And, Sophy, if you will take Rosalind and your godchild instead of me, I think it will do them good. I—you may suppose I have a great many things to think of."

"Leave them, dear, till you are stronger, that is my advice; and I know more about trouble than you do," Mrs. Lennox said.

Mrs. Trevanion gave a glance around her. There was a faint smile upon her face. The three gentlemen sitting by did not know even that she looked at them, but they felt each like a culprit, guilty and responsible. Her eyes seemed to appeal speechlessly to earth and heaven, yet with an almost humorous consciousness of good Mrs. Lennox's superiority in experience. "I should like Rosalind and Sophy to go with you for a change," she said, quietly. "The little ones will be best at home. Russell is not good for Sophy, Rosalind; but for the little ones it does not matter so much. She is very kind and careful of them. That covers a multitude of sins. I think, for their sakes, she may stay."

"I would not keep her, mamma. She is dangerous; she is wicked."

"What do you mean by that, Rose? Russell! I should as soon think of mamma going as of Russell going," cried Rex. "She says mamma hates her, but I say—"

"I wonder," said Mrs. Trevanion, "that you do not find yourself above nursery gossip, Rex, at your age. Never mind, it is a matter to be talked of afterwards. You are not going away immediately, John?"

"Not as long as—" He paused and looked at her wistfully, with eyes that said a thousand things. "As long as I can be of use," he said.

"As long as—I think I know what you mean," Mrs. Trevanion said.

The conversation was full of these sous-entendus. Except Mrs. Lennox and Rex, there was a sense of mystery and uncertainty in all the party. Rosalind followed every speaker with her eyes, inquiring what they could mean. Mrs. Trevanion was the most composed of the company, though meanings were found afterwards in every word she said. The servants had gone from the room while the latter part of this conversation went on. After a little while she rose, and all of them with her. She called Reginald, who followed reluctantly, feeling that he was much too important a person to retire with the ladies. As she went out, leaning upon his arm, she waved her hand to the other gentlemen. "Good-night," she said. "I don't think I am equal to the drawing-room to-night."

"What do you want with me, mother? It isn't right, it isn't, indeed, to call me away like a child. I'm not a child; and I ought to be there to hear what they are going to settle. Don't you see, mamma, it's my concern?"

"You can go back presently, Rex; yes, my boy, it is your concern. I want you to think so, dear. And the little ones are your concern. Being the head of a house means a great deal. It means thinking of everything, taking care of the brothers and sisters, not only being a person of importance, Rex—"

"I know, I know. If this is all you wanted to say—"

"Almost all. That you must think of your duties, dear. It is unfortunate for you, oh, very unfortunate, to be left so young; but your Uncle John will be your true friend."

"Well, that don't matter much. Oh, I dare say he will be good enough. Then you know, mammy," said the boy condescendingly, giving her a hurried kiss, and eager to get away, "when there's anything very hard I can come and talk it over with you."

She did not make any reply, but kissed him, holding his reluctant form close to her. He did not like to be hugged, and he wanted to be back among the men. "One moment," she said. "Promise me you will be very good to the little ones, Rex."

"Why, of course, mother," said the boy; "you didn't think I would beat them, did you? Good-night."

"Good-bye, my own boy." He had darted from her almost before she could withdraw her arm. She paused a moment to draw breath, and then followed to the door of the drawing-room, where the other ladies were gone. "I think, Sophy," she said, "I will take your advice and go to my room; and you must arrange with Rosalind to take her home with you, and Sophy too."

"That I will, with all my heart; and I don't despair of getting you to come. Good-night, dear. Should you like me to come and sit with you a little when you have got to bed?"

"Not to-night," said Mrs. Trevanion. "I am tired out. Good-night, Rosalind. God bless you, my darling!" She held the girl in her arms, and drew her towards the door. "I can give you no explanation about last night, and you will hear other things. Think of me as kindly as you can, my own, that are none of mine," she said, bending over her with her eyes full of tears.

"Mother," said the girl, flinging herself into Mrs. Trevanion's arms with enthusiasm, "you can do no wrong."

"God bless you, my own dear!"

This parting seemed sufficiently justified by the circumstances. The funeral day! Could it be otherwise than that their nerves were highly strung, and words of love and mutual support, which might have seemed exaggerated at other times, should now have seemed natural? Rosalind, with her heart bursting, went back to her aunt's side, and sat down and listened to her placid talk. She would rather have been with her suffering mother, but for that worn-out woman there was nothing so good as rest.

Mrs. Trevanion went back to the nursery, where her little children were fast asleep in their cots, and Sophy preparing for bed. Sophy was still grumbling over the fact that she had not been allowed to go down to dessert. "Why shouldn't I go down?" she cried, sitting on the floor, taking off her shoes. "Oh, here's mamma! What difference could it have made? Grown-up people are nasty and cruel. I should not have done any harm going down-stairs. Reggie is dining down-stairs. He is always the one that is petted, because he is a boy, though he is only five years older than me."

"Hush, Miss Sophy. It was your mamma's doing, and mammas are always right."

"You don't think so, Russell. Oh, I don't want to kiss you, mamma. It was so unkind, and Reggie going on Monday; and I have not been down to dessert—not for a week."

"But I must kiss you, Sophy," the mother said. "You are going away with your aunt and Rosalind, on a visit. Is not that better than coming down to dessert?"

"Oh, mamma!" The child jumped up with one shoe on, and threw herself against her mother's breast. "Oh, I am so glad. Aunt Sophy lets us do whatever we please." She gave a careless kiss in response to Mrs. Trevanion's embrace. "I should like to stay there forever," Sophy said.

There was a smile on the mother's face as she withdrew it, as there had been a smile of strange wonder and wistfulness when she took leave of Rex. The little ones were asleep. She went and stood for a moment between the two white cots. Then all was done; and the hour had come to which, without knowing what awaited her, she had looked with so much terror on the previous night.

A dark night, with sudden blasts of rain, and a sighing wind which moaned about the house, and gave notes of warning of the dreary wintry weather to come. As Mrs. Lennox and Rosalind sat silent over the fire, there suddenly seemed to come in and pervade the luxurious house a blast, as if the night had entered bodily, a great draught of fresh, cold, odorous, rainy air, charged with the breath of the wet fields and earth. And then there was the muffled sound as of a closed door. "What is that?" said Aunt Sophy, pricking up her ears, "It cannot be visitors come so late, and on such a day as this."

"It sounds like some one going out," Rosalind said, with a shiver, thinking on what she had seen last night. "Perhaps," she added eagerly, after a moment, with a great sense of relief, "Mr. Blake going away."

"It will be that, of course, though I did not hear wheels; and what a dismal night for his drive, poor old gentleman. That wind always makes me wretched. It moans and groans like a human creature. But it is very odd, Rosalind, that we did not hear any wheels."

"The wind drowns other sounds," Rosalind said.

"That must be so, I suppose. Still, I hope he doesn't think of walking, Rosalind; an old man of that age."

And then once more all fell into silence in the great luxurious house. Outside the wind blew in the faces of the wayfarers. The rain drenched them in sudden gusts, the paths were slippery and wet, the trees discharged sharp volleys of collected rain as the blasts blew. To struggle across the park was no easy matter in the face of the blinding sleet and capricious wind; and you could not hear your voice under the trees for the din that was going on overhead.

CHAPTER XXI

Rosalind spent a very restless night. She could not sleep, and the rain coming down in torrents irritated her with its ceaseless pattering. She thought, she could not tell why, of the poor people who were out in it—travellers, wayfarers, poor vagrants, such as she had seen about the country roads. What would the miserable creatures do in such a dismal night? As she lay awake in the darkness she pictured them to herself, drenched and cold, dragging along the muddy ways. No one in whom she was interested was likely to be reduced to such misery, but she thought of them, she could not tell why. She had knocked at Mrs. Trevanion's door as she came up-stairs, longing to go in to say another word, to give her a kiss in her weariness. Rosalind had an ache and terrible question in her heart which she had never been able to get rid of, notwithstanding the closeness of the intercourse on the funeral day and the exuberant profession of faith to which she had given vent: "You can do no wrong." Her heart had cried out this protestation of faith, but in her mind there had been a terrible drawing back, like that of the wave which has dashed brilliantly upon a stony beach only to groan and turn back again, carrying everything with it. Through all this sleepless night she lay balancing between these two sensations—the enthusiasm and the doubt. Her mother! It seemed a sort of blasphemy to judge or question that highest of all human authorities—that type and impersonation of all that was best. And yet it would force itself upon her, in spite of all her holding back. Where was she going that night? Supposing the former events nothing, what, oh, what was the new-made widow going to do on the eve of her husband's funeral out in the park, all disguised and concealed in the dusk? The more Rosalind denied her doubts expression the more bitterly did that picture force itself upon her—the veiled, muffled figure, the watching accomplice, and the door so stealthily opened. Without practice and knowledge and experience, who could have done all that? If Rosalind herself wanted to steal out quietly, a hundred hinderances started up in her way. If she tried anything of the kind she knew very well that every individual whom she wished to avoid would meet her and find her out. It is so with the innocent, but with those who are used to concealment, not so. These were the things that said themselves in her mind without any consent of hers as she labored through the night. And when the first faint sounds of waking began to be audible, a distant door opening, an indication that some one was stirring, Rosalind got up too, unable to bear it any longer. She sprang out of bed and wrapped herself in her dressing-gown, resolved to go to her mother's room and disperse all those ghosts of night. How often had she run there in childish troubles and shaken them off! That last court of appeal had never been closed to her. A kiss, a touch of the soft hand upon her head, a comforting word, had charmed away every spectre again and again. Perhaps Rosalind thought she would have the courage to speak all out, perhaps to have her doubts set at rest forever; but even if she had not courage for that, the mere sight of Mrs. Trevanion was enough to dispel all prejudices, to make an end of all doubts. It was quite dark in the passages as she flitted across the large opening of the stairs. Down-stairs in the great hall there was a spark of light, where a housemaid, kneeling within the great chimney, was lighting the fire. There was a certain relief even in this, in the feeling of a new day and life begun again. Rosalind glided like a ghost, in her warm dressing-gown, to Mrs. Trevanion's door. She knocked softly, but there was no reply. Little wonder, at this hour of the morning; no doubt the mother was asleep. Rosalind opened the door.

There is a kind of horror of which it is difficult to give any description in the sensations of one who goes into a room expecting to find a sleeper in the safety and calm of natural repose and finds it empty, cold, and vacant. The shock is extraordinary. The certainty that the inhabitant must be there is so profound, and in a moment is replaced by an uncertainty which nothing can equal—a wild dread that fears it knows not what, but always the worst that can be feared. Rosalind went in with the soft yet confident step of a child, who knows that the mother will wake at a touch, almost at a look, and turn with a smile and a kiss to listen, whatever the story that is brought to her may be. Fuller confidence never was. She did not even look before going straight to the bedside. She had, indeed, knelt down there before she found out. Then she sprang to her feet again with the cry of one who had touched death unawares. It was like death to her, the touch of the cold, smooth linen, all folded as it had been in preparation for the inmate—who was to sleep there no more. She looked round the room as if asking an answer from every corner. "Mother, where are you? Mother! Where are you, mother?" she cried, with a wild voice of astonishment and dismay.

There was no light in the room; a faint paleness to show the window, a silence that was terrible, an atmosphere as of death itself. Rosalind flew, half frantic, into the dressing-room adjoining, which for some time past had been occupied by Jane. There a night-light which had been left burning flickered feebly, on the point of extinction. The faint light showed the same vacancy—the bed spread in cold order, everything empty, still. Rosalind felt her senses giving way. Her impulse was to rush out through the house, calling, asking, Where were they? Death seemed to be in the place—death more mysterious and more terrible than that with which she had been made familiar. After a pause she left the room and hurried breathless to that occupied by her uncle. How different there was the atmosphere, charged with human breath, warm with occupation. She burst in, too terrified for thought.

"Uncle John!" she cried, "Uncle John!" taking him by the shoulder.

It was not easy to wake him out of his deep sleep. At last he sat up in his bed, half awake, and looked at her with consternation.

"Rosalind! what is the matter?" he cried.

"Mamma is not in her room—where is she, where is she?" the girl demanded, standing over him like a ghost in the dark.

"Your mother is not—I—I suppose she's tired, like all the rest of us," he said, with a sleepy desire to escape this premature awakening. "Why, it's dark still, Rosalind. Go back to bed, my dear. Your mother—"

"Listen, Uncle John. Mamma is not in her room. No one has slept there to-night; it is all empty; my mother is gone, is gone! Where has she gone?" the girl cried, wildly. "She has not been there all night."

"Good God!" John Trevanion cried. He was entirely roused now. "Rosalind, you must be making some mistake."

"There is no mistake. I thought perhaps you might know something. No one has slept there to-night. Oh, Uncle John, Uncle John, where is my mother? Let us go and find her before everybody knows."

"Rosalind, leave me, and I will get up. I can tell you nothing—yes, I can tell you something; but I never thought it would be like this. It is your father who has sent her away."

"Papa!" the girl cried; "oh, Uncle John, stop before you have taken everything away from me; neither father nor mother!—you take everything from me!" she said, with a cry of despair.

"Go away," he said, "and get dressed, Rosalind, and then we can see whether there is anything to be done."

An hour later they stood together by the half-kindled fire in the hall. John Trevanion had gone through the empty rooms with his niece, who was distracted, not knowing what she did. By this time a pale and gray daylight, which looked like cold and misery made visible, had diffused itself through the great house. That chill visibleness, showing all the arrangements of the room prepared for rest and slumber, where nobody had slept, had something terrible in it that struck them both with awe. There was no letter, no sign to be found of leave-taking. When they opened the wardrobe and drawers, a few dresses and necessaries were found to be gone, and it appeared that Jane had sent two small boxes to the village which she had represented to be old clothes, "colored things," for which her mistress would now have no need. It was to Rosalind like a blow in the dark, a buffet from some ghostly hand, additional to her other pain, when she found it was these "colored things" and not the prepared, newly made mourning which her stepmother had taken with her. This seemed a cutting off from them, an entire abandonment, which made her misery deeper; but naturally John Trevanion did not think of that. He told her the story of the will while they stood together in the hall. But he could think of nothing to do, nor could he give any hope that this terrible event was a thing to be undone or concealed. "It must have happened," he said, "sooner or later; and though it is a shock—a great shock—"

"Oh, Uncle John, it is—there was never anything so terrible. How can you use ordinary words? A shock! If the wind had blown down a tree it would be a shock. Don't you see, it is the house that has been blown down? we have nothing—nothing to shelter us, we children. My mother and my father! We are orphans, and far, far worse than orphans. We having nothing left but shame—nothing but shame!"

"Rosalind, it is worse for the others than for you. You, at least, are clear of it; she is not your mother."

"She is all the mother I have ever known," Rosalind cried for the hundredth time. "And," she added, with quivering lips, "I am the daughter of the man who on his death-bed has brought shame upon his own, and disgraced the wife that was like an angel to him. If the other could be got over, that can never be got over. He did it, and he cannot undo it. And she is wicked too. She should not have yielded like that; she should have resisted—she should have refused; she should not have gone away."

"Had she done so it would have been our duty to insist upon it," said John Trevanion, sadly. "We had no alternative. You will find when you think it over that this sudden going is for the best."

"Oh, that is so easy to say when it is not your heart that is wrung, but some one else's; and how can it ever be," cried Rosalind, with a dismal logic which many have employed before her, "that what is all wrong from beginning to end can be for the best?"

This was the beginning of a day more miserable than words can describe. They made no attempt to conceal the calamity; it was impossible to conceal it. The first astounded and terror-stricken housemaid who entered the room spread it over the house like wildfire. Madam had gone away. Madam had not slept in her bed all night. When Rosalind, who could not rest, made one of her many aimless journeys up-stairs, she heard a wail from the nurseries, and Russell, rushing out, suddenly confronted her. The woman was pale with excitement; and there was a mixture of compunction and triumph and horror in her eyes.

"What does this mean, Miss Rosalind? Tell me, for God's sake!" she cried.

It did Rosalind a little good in her misery to find herself in front of an actor in this catastrophe; one who was guilty and could be made to suffer. "It means," she cried, with sudden rage, "that you must leave my mother's children at once—this very moment! My uncle will give you your wages, whatever you want, but you shall not stay here, not an hour."

"My wages!" the woman cried, with a sort of scream; "do I care for wages? Leave my babies, as I have brought up? Oh, never, never! You may say what you please, you that were always unnatural, that held for her instead of your own flesh and blood. You are cruel, cruel; but I won't stand it—I won't. There's more to be consulted, Miss Rosalind, than you."

"I would be more cruel if I could—I would strike you," cried the impassioned girl, clinching her small hands, "if it were not a shame for a lady to do it—you, who have taken away mother from me and made me hate and despise my own father, oh, God forgive me! And it is your doing, you miserable woman. Let me never see you again. To see you is like death to me. Go away—go away!"

"And yet I was better than a mother to you once," said Russell, who had cried out and put her hand to her heart as if she had received a blow. Her heart was tender to her nursling, though pitiless otherwise. "I saved your life," she cried, beginning to weep; "I took you when your true mother died. You would have loved me but for that woman—that—"

Rosalind stamped her foot passionately upon the floor; she was transported by misery and wrath. "Do not dare to speak to me! Go away—go out of the house. Uncle John," she cried, hurrying to the balustrade and looking down into the hall where he stood, too wretched to observe what was going on, "will you come and turn this woman away?"

He came slowly up-stairs at this call, with his hands in his pockets, every line of his figure expressing despondency and dismay. It was only when he came in sight of Russell, flushed, crying, and injured, yet defiant too, that he understood what Rosalind meant by the appeal. "Yes, it will be well that you should go," he said. "You have made mischief that never can be mended. No one in this house will ever forgive you. The best thing you can do is to go—"

"The mischief was not my making," cried Russell. "It's not them that tells but them that goes wrong that are to blame. And the children—there's the children to think of—who will take care of them like me? I'd die sooner than leave the children. They're the same as my flesh and blood. They have been in my hands since ever they were born," the woman cried with passion. "Oh, Mr. Trevanion, you that have always been known for a kind gentleman, let me stay with the children! Their mother, she can desert them, but I can't; it will break my heart."

"You had better go," said John Trevanion, with lowering brows. At this moment Reginald appeared on the scene from another direction, pulling on his jacket in great hurry and excitement. "What does it all mean?" the boy cried, full of agitation. "Oh, if it's only Russell! They told me some story about—Why are you bullying Russell, Uncle John?"

"Oh, Mr. Reginald, you'll speak for me. You are my own boy, and you are the real master. Don't let them break my heart," cried Russell, holding out her imploring hands.

"Oh, if it's only Russell," the boy cried, relieved; "but they said—they told me—"

Another door opened as he spoke, and Aunt Sophy, dishevelled, the gray locks falling about her shoulders, a dressing-gown huddled about her ample figure, appeared suddenly. "For God's sake, speak low! What does it all mean? Don't expose everything to the servants, whatever it is," she cried.

CHAPTER XXII

Presently they all assembled in the hall—a miserable party. The door of the breakfast-room stood open, but no one went near it. They stood in a knot, all huddled together, speaking almost in whispers. Considering that everybody in the house now knew that Madam had never been in bed at all, that she must have left Highcourt secretly in the middle of the night, no precaution could have been more foolish. But Mrs. Lennox had not realized this; and her anxiety to silence scandal was extreme. She stood quite close to her brother, questioning him. "But what do you mean? How could Reginald do it? What did he imagine? And, oh! couldn't you put a stop to it, for the sake of the family, John?"

Young Reginald stood on the other side, confused between anger and ignorance, incapacity to understand and a desire to blame some one. "What does she mean by it?" he said. "What did father mean by it? Was it just to make us all as wretched as possible—as if things weren't bad enough before?" It was impossible to convey to either of them any real understanding of the case. "But how could he part the children from their mother?" said Aunt Sophy. "She is their mother, their mother; not their stepmother. You forget, John; she's Rosalind's stepmother. Rosalind might have been made my ward; that would have been natural; but the others are her own. How could he separate her from her own? She ought not to have left them! Oh, how could she leave them?" the bewildered woman cried.

"If she had not done it the children would have been destitute, Sophy. It was my business to make her do it, unless she had been willing to ruin the children."

"Not me," cried Reginald, loudly. "He could not have taken anything from me. She might have stuck to me, and I should have taken care of her. What had she to be frightened about? I suppose," he added after a pause, "there would have been plenty—to keep all the children too—"

"Highcourt is not such a very large estate, Rex. Lowdean and the rest are unentailed. You would have been much impoverished too."

"Oh!" Reginald cried, with an angry frown; but then he turned to another side of the question, and continued vehemently, "Why on earth, when she knew papa was so cranky and had it all in his power, why did she aggravate him? I think they must all have been mad together, and just tried how to spite us most!" cried the boy, with a rush of passionate tears to his eyes. The house was miserable altogether. He wanted his breakfast, and he had no heart to eat it. He could not bear the solemn spying of the servants. Dorrington, in particular, would come to the door of the breakfast-room and look in with an expression of mysterious sympathy for which Reginald would have liked to kill him. "I wish I had never come away from school at all. I wish I were not going back. I wish I were anywhere out of this," he cried. But he did not suggest again that his mother should have "stuck to" him. He wanted to know why somebody did not interfere; why this thing and the other was permitted to be done. "Some one could have stopped it if they had tried," Reginald said; and that was Aunt Sophy's opinion too.

The conclusion of all was that Mrs. Lennox left Highcourt with the children and Rosalind as soon as their preparations could be made, by way of covering as well as possible the extraordinary revolution in the house. It was the only expedient any of these distracted people could think of to throw a little illusion over Mrs. Trevanion's abrupt departure. Of course they were all aware everything must be known. What is there that is not known? And to think that a large houseful of servants would keep silent on such a piece of family history was past all expectation. No doubt it was already known through the village and spreading over the neighborhood. "Madam" had been caught meeting some man in the park when her husband was ill, poor gentleman! And now, the very day of the funeral, she was off with the fellow, and left all her children, and everything turned upside down. The older people all knew exactly what would be said, and they knew that public opinion would think the worst, that no explanations would be allowed, that the vulgarest, grossest interpretation would be so much easier than anything else, so ready, so indisputable—she had gone away with her lover. Mrs. Lennox herself could not help thinking so in the depths of her mind, though on the surface she entertained other vague and less assured ideas.

What else could explain it? Everybody knew the force of passion, the way in which women will forsake everything, even their children, even their homes—that was comprehensible, though so dreadful. But nothing else was comprehensible. Aunt Sophy, in the depth of her heart, though she was herself an innocent woman, was not sure that John was not inventing, to shield his sister-in-law, that incredible statement about the will. She felt that she herself would say anything for the same purpose—she would not mind what it was—anything rather than that Grace, a woman they had all thought so much of, had "gone wrong" in such a dreadful way. Nevertheless it was far more comprehensible that she had "gone wrong" than any other explanation could be. Though she had been a woman upon whom no breath of scandal had ever come, a woman who overawed evil speakers, and was above all possibility of reproach, yet it was always possible that she might have "gone wrong." Against such hazards there could be no defence. But Mrs. Lennox was very willing to do anything to cover up the family trouble. She even went the length of speaking somewhat loudly to her own maid, in the hearing of some of the servants of the house, about Mrs. Trevanion's "early start." "We shall catch her up on the way," Mrs. Lennox said. "I don't wonder, do you, Morris, that she went by that early train? Poor dear! I remember when I lost my first dear husband I couldn't bear the sight of the house and the churchyard where he was lying. But we shall catch her up," the kind-hearted hypocrite said, drying her eyes. As if the housemaids were to be taken in so easily! as if they did not know far more than Mrs. Lennox did, who thus lent herself to a falsehood! When the children came down, dressed in their black frocks, with eyes wide open and full of eager curiosity, Mrs. Lennox was daunted by the cynical air with which Sophy, her namesake and godchild, regarded her. "You needn't say anything to me about catching up mamma, for I know better," the child said, vindictively. "She likes somebody else better than us, and she has just gone away."

"Rosalind," Mrs. Lennox cried, in dismay, "I hope that woman is not coming with us, that horrible woman that puts such things into the children's heads. I hope you have sent Russell away."

But when the little ones were all packed in the carriage with their aunt, who could not endure to see any one cry, there was a burst of simultaneous weeping. "I neber love nobody but Nana. I do to nobody but Nana," little Johnny shouted. His little sister said nothing, but her small mouth quivered, and the piteous aspect of her face, struggling against a passion of restrained grief, was the most painful of all. Sophy, however, continued defiant. "You may send her away, but me and Reginald will have her back again," she said. Aunt Sophy could scarcely have been more frightened had she taken a collection of bombshells with her into the carriage. The absence of mamma was little to the children, who had been so much separated from her by their father's long illness; but Russell, the "Nana" of their baby affections, had a closer hold.

With these rebellious companions, and with all the misery of the family tragedy overshadowing her, Rosalind made the journey more sadly than any of the party. At times it seemed impossible for her to believe that all the miseries that had happened were real. Was it not rather a dream from which she might awaken, and find everything as of old? To think that she should be leaving her home, feeling almost a fugitive, hastily, furtively, in order to cover the flight of one who had been her type of excellence all her life: to think that father and mother were both gone from her—gone out of her existence, painfully, miserably; not to be dwelt upon with tender grief, such as others had the privilege of enduring, but with bitter anguish and shame. The wails of the children as they grew tired with the journey, the necessity of taking the responsibility of them upon herself, hushing the cries of the little ones for "Nana," silencing Sophy, who was disposed to be impertinent, keeping the weight of the party from the too susceptible shoulders of the aunt, made a complication and interruption of her thoughts which Rosalind was too inexperienced to feel as an alleviation, and which made a fantastic mixture of tragedy and burlesque in her mind. She had to think of the small matters of the journey, and to satisfy

Aunt Sophy's fears as to the impossibility of getting the other train at the junction, and the risk of losing the luggage, and to persuade her that Johnny's restlessness, his refusal to be comforted by the anxious nursery-maid, and wailing appeals for Russell, would wear off by and by as baby-heartbreaks do. "But I have known a child fret itself to death," Mrs. Lennox cried. "I have heard of instances in which they would not be comforted, Rosalind; and what should we do if the child was to pine, and perhaps to die?" Rosalind, so young, so little experienced, was overwhelmed by this suggestion. She took Johnny upon her own lap, and attempted to soothe him, with a sense that she might turn out a kind of murderer if the child did not mend. It was consolatory to feel that, warmly wrapped, and supported against her young bosom, Johnny got sleepy, and moaned himself into oblivion of his troubles. But this was not so pleasant when they came to the junction, and Rosalind had to stumble out of the carriage somehow, and hurry to the waiting train with poor little Johnny's long legs thrust out from her draperies. It was at this moment, as she got out, that she saw a face in the crowd which gave her a singular thrill in the midst of her trouble. The wintry afternoon was falling into darkness, the vast, noisy place was swarming with life and tumult. She had to walk a little slower than the rest on account of her burden, which she did not venture to give into other arms, in case the child should wake. It was the face of the young man whom she had met in the park—the stranger, so unlike anybody else, about whom she had been so uncomfortably uncertain whether he was or not—But what did that matter? If he had been a prince of the blood or the lowest adventurer, what was it to Rosalind? Her mind was full of other things, and no man in the world had a right to waylay her, to follow her, to trace her movements. It made her hot and red with personal feeling in the midst of all the trouble that surrounded her. He had no right—no right; and yet the noblest lover who ever haunted his lady's window to see her shadow on the blind had no right; and perhaps, if put into vulgar words, Romeo had no right to scale that wall, and Juliet on her balcony was a forward young woman. There are things which are not to be defended by any rule, which youth excuses, nay, justifies; and to see a pair of sympathetic eyes directed towards her through the crowd—eyes that found her out amid all that multitude—touched Rosalind's heart. Somehow they made her trouble, and even the weight of her little brother, who was heavy, more easy to bear. She was weak and worn out, and this it was, perhaps, which made her so easily moved. But the startled sensation with which she heard a voice at her side, somewhat too low and too close, saying, "Will you let me carry the child for you, Miss Trevanion?" whirled the softer sensation away into eddies of suspicion and dark thrills of alarm and doubt. "Oh, no, no!" she cried, instinctively hurrying on.

"I ask nothing but to relieve you," he said.

"Oh, thanks! I am much obliged to you, but it is impossible. It would wake him," she said hurriedly, not looking up.

"You think me presumptuous, Miss Trevanion, and so I am; but it is terrible to see you so burdened and not be able to help."

This made her burden so much the more that Rosalind quickened her steps, and stumbled and almost fell. "Oh, please," she said, "go away. You may mean to be kind. Oh, please go away."

The nursery-maid, who came back at Mrs. Lennox's orders to help Rosalind, saw nothing particular to remark, except that the young lady was flushed and disturbed. But to hurry along a crowded platform with a child in your arms was enough to account for that. The maid could very well appreciate such a drawback to movement. She succeeded, with the skill of her profession, in taking the child into her own arms, and repeated Mrs. Lennox's entreaties to make haste. But Rosalind required no solicitation in this respect. She made a dart forward, and was in the carriage in a moment, where she threw herself into a seat and hid her face in her hands.

"I knew it would be too much for you," said Aunt Sophy, soothingly. "Oh, Thirza is used to it. I pity nurses with all my heart; but they are used to it. But you, my poor darling, in such a crowd! Did you think we should miss the train? I know what that is—to hurry along, and yet be sure you will miss it. Here, Thirza, here; we are all right; and after all there is plenty of time." After a pause Aunt Sophy said, "I wonder who that is looking so intently into this carriage. Such a remarkable face! But I hope he does not mean to get in here; we are quite full here. Rosalind, you look like nothing at all in that corner, in your black dress. He will think the seat is vacant and come in if you don't make a little more appearance. Rosalind—Good gracious, I believe she has fainted!"

"No, Aunt Sophy." Rosalind raised her head and uncovered her pale face. She knew that she should see that intruder looking at her. He seemed to be examining the carriages, looking for a place, and as she took her hands from her face their eyes met. There was that unconscious communication between them which betrays those who recognize each other, whether they make any sign or not. Aunt Sophy gave a wondering cry.

"Why, you know him! and yet he does not take his hat off. Who is it, Rosalind?"

"I have seen him—in the village—"

"Oh, I know," cried little Sophy, pushing forward. "It is the gentleman. I have seen him often. He lived at the Red Lion. Don't you remember, Rosalind, the gentleman that mamma wouldn't let me—"

"Oh, Sophy, be quiet!" cried the girl. What poignant memories awoke with the words!

"But how strange he looks," cried Sophy. "His hat down over his eyes, and I believe he has got a beard or something—"

"You must not run on like that. I dare say it is quite a different person," said Aunt Sophy. "What made me notice him is that he has eyes exactly like little Johnny's eyes."

It was one of Aunt Sophy's weaknesses that she was always finding out likenesses; but Rosalind's mind was disturbed by another form of her original difficulty about the stranger. It might be forgiven him that he hung about her path, and even followed at a distance; it was excusable that he should ask if he could help her with the child; but having thus ventured to accost her, and having established a sort of acquaintance by being useful to her, why, when their eyes met, did he make no sign of recognition? No, he could not be a gentleman! Then Rosalind awoke with horror to find that on the very first day after all the calamities that had befallen her family she was able to discuss such a question with herself.

CHAPTER XXIII

John Trevanion remained in the empty house. It had seemed that morning as if nothing could be more miserable: but it was more miserable now, when every cheerful element had gone out of it, and not even the distant sound of a child's voice, or Rosalind's dress, with its faint sweep of sound, was to be heard in the vacancy. After he had seen them off he walked home through the village with a very heavy heart. In front of the little inn there was an unusual stir: a number of rustic people gathered about the front of the house, surrounding two men of an aspect not at all rustic, who were evidently questioning the slow but eager rural witnesses. "It must ha' been last night as he went," said one. "I don't know when he went," said another, "but he never come in to his supper, I'll take my oath o' that." They all looked somewhat eagerly towards John, who felt himself compelled to interfere, much as he disliked doing so. "What is the matter?" he asked, and then from half a dozen eager mouths the story rushed out. "A gentleman" had been living at the Red Lion for some time back. Nobody, it appeared, could make out what he wanted there; everybody (they now said) suspected him from the first. He would lie in bed all morning, and then get up towards afternoon. Nothing more was necessary to demonstrate his immorality, the guilt of the man. He went out trapesing in the woods at night, but he wasn't no poacher, for he never seemed to handle a gun nor know aught about it. He would turn white when anybody came in and tried a trigger, or to see if the ball was drawn. No, he wasn't no poacher: but he did always be in the woods o' night, which meant no good, the rustics thought. There were whisperings aside, and glances, as this description was given, which were not lost upon John, but his attention was occupied in the first place by the strangers, who came forward and announced that they were detectives in search of an offender, a clerk in a merchant's office, who had absconded, having squandered a considerable sum of his master's money. "But this is an impossible sort of place for such a culprit to have taken refuge in," John said, astounded. The chief of the two officers stepped out in front of the other, and asked if he might say a few words to the gentleman, then went on accompanying John, as he mechanically continued his way, repressing all appearance of the extraordinary commotion thus produced in his mind.

"You see, sir," said the man, "it's thought that the young fellow had what you may call a previous connection here."

"Ah! was he perhaps related to some one in the village? I never heard his name." (The name was Everard, and quite unknown to the neighborhood.)

"No, Mr. Trevanion," said the other, significantly, "not in the village."

"Where, then—what do you mean? What could the previous connection that brought him here be?"

The man took a pocket-book from his pocket, and produced a crumpled envelope. "You may have seen this writing before, sir," he said.

John took it with a thrill of pain and alarm, recognizing the paper, the stamp of "Highcourt," torn but decipherable on the seal, and feeling himself driven to one conclusion which he would fain have pushed from him; but when he had smoothed it out, with a hand which trembled in spite of himself, he suddenly cried out, with a start of overwhelming surprise and relief, "Why, it is my brother's hand!"

"Your brother's?" cried the officer, with a blank look. "You mean, sir, the gentleman that was buried yesterday?"

"My brother, Mr. Trevanion, of Highcourt. I do not know how he can have been connected with the person you seek. It must have been some accidental link. I have already told you I never heard the name."

The man was as much confused and startled as John himself. "If that's so," he said, "you have put us off the track, and I don't know now what to do. We had heard," he added, with a sidelong look of vigilant observation, "that there was a lady in the case."

"I know nothing about any lady," said John Trevanion, briefly.

"There's no trusting to village stories, sir. We were told that a lady had disappeared, and that it was more than probable—"

"As you say, village stories are entirely untrustworthy," said John. "I can throw no light on the subject, except that the address on the envelope (Everard, is it?) is in my brother's hand. He might, of course, have a hundred correspondents unknown to me, but I certainly never heard of this one. I suppose there is no more I can do for you, for I am anxious to get back to Highcourt. You have heard, no doubt, that the family is in deep mourning and sorrow."

"I am very sorry, sir," said the official, "and distressed to have interrupted you at such a moment, but it is our duty to leave no stone unturned." Then he lingered for a moment. "I suppose, then," he said, "there is no truth in the story about the lady—"

John turned upon him with a short laugh. "You don't expect me, I hope, to answer for all the village stories about ladies," he said, waving his hand as he went on. "I have told you all I know."

He quickened his pace and his companion fell back. But the officer was not satisfied, and John Trevanion went on, with his mind in a dark and hopeless confusion, not knowing what extraordinary addition of perplexity was added to the question by this new piece of evidence, but feeling vaguely that it increased the darkness all around him. He had not in any way associated the stranger whom he had met on the road with his sister-in-law. He had thought it likely enough that the young man, perhaps of pretensions too humble to get admittance at Highcourt, had lingered about in foolish youthful adoration of Rosalind, which, however presumptuous it might be, was natural enough. To hear now that the young man who had presumed to do Miss Trevanion a service was a criminal in hiding made his blood boil. But his brother's handwriting threw everything into confusion. How did this connect with the rest, what light did it throw upon the imbroglio, in what way could it be connected with the disappearance of Madam? All these things surged about him vaguely as he walked, but he could make nothing coherent, no rational whole out of them. The park and the trees lay in a heavy mist. The day was not cold, but stifling, with a low sky, and heavy vapors in the air, everything around wet, sodden, dreary. Never had the long stretches of turf and distant glades of trees seemed to him so lonely, so deserted and forsaken. There was not a movement to be seen, nobody coming by that public pathway which had been so great a grievance to the Trevanions for generations back. John, though he shared the family feeling in this respect, would have gladly now seen a village procession moving along the contested path. The house seemed to him to lie in a cold enclosure of mist and damp, abandoned by everybody, a spot on which there was a curse. But this, of course, was merely fanciful; and he shook off the feeling. There was pain enough involved in its recent history without the aid of imagination.

There was plenty to do, however. Mr. Trevanion's papers had to be put in order, his personal affairs wound up; and it was almost better to have no interruption in this duty, and so get over it as quickly as possible. There is something dreadful under all circumstances in fulfilling this office. To examine into the innermost recesses in which a man has kept his treasures, his most intimate possessions, the records, perhaps, of his affections and ambitions; to open his desk, to pull out his drawers, to turn over the letters which, perhaps, to him were sacred, never to be revealed to any eye but his own, is an office from which it is natural to shrink. The investigator feels himself a spy, taking advantage of the pathetic helplessness of the dead, their powerlessness to protect themselves. John Trevanion sat down in the library with the sense of intrusion strong upon him, yet with a certain painful curiosity too. He was afraid of discovering something. At every new harmless paper which he opened he drew a long breath of relief. The papers of recent times were few—they were chiefly on the subject of money, the investments which had been made, appeals for funds sent to him for the needs of the estate, for repairs and improvements, which it was evident Mr. Trevanion had been slow to yield to. It seemed from the letters addressed to him that most of his business had been managed through his wife, which was a fact his brother was aware of; but somehow the constant reference to her, and the evident position assigned to her as in reality the active agency in the whole, added a curious and bewildering pang to the confusion in which all this had closed. It seemed beyond belief that this woman, who had stood by her husband so faithfully, his nurse, his adviser, his agent, his eyes and ears, should be now a sort of fugitive, under the dead man's ban, separated from all she cared for in the world. John stopped in the middle of a bundle of letters to ask himself whether he had ever known a similar case. There was nothing like it in the law reports, nothing even in those causes célèbres which include so many wonders. A woman with everything in her hands, her husband's business as well as his health, and the governance of her great household, suddenly turned away from it without reason given or any explanation—surely the man must have been mad—surely he must have been mad! It was the only solution that seemed possible. But then there arose before the thinker's troubled vision those scenes which had preceded his brother's death—the bramble upon her dress, the wet feet which she had avowed, with—was it a certain bravado? And again, that still more dreadful moment in the park, on the eve of her husband's funeral, when he had himself seen her meet and talk with some one who was invisible in the shadow of the copse. He had seen it, there could be no question on the subject. What did it mean? He got up, feeling the moisture rise to his forehead in the conflict of his feelings; he could not sit still and go for the hundredth time over this question. What did it mean?

While he was walking up and down the library, unable to settle to any examination of those calm business papers in which no agitation was, a letter was brought to him. It bore the stamp of a post-town at a short distance, and he turned it over listlessly enough, until it occurred to him that the writing was that of his sister-in-law. Madam wrote as many women write; there was nothing remarkable about her hand. John Trevanion opened the letter with excitement. It was as follows:

"DEAR BROTHER JOHN,—You may not wish me to call you so now, but I have always felt towards you so, and it still seems a link to those I have left behind to have one relationship which I may claim. There seems no reason why I should not write to you, or why I should conceal from you where I am. You will not seek to bring me back; I am safe enough in your hands. I am going out of England, but if you want to communicate with me on any subject, the bankers will always know where I am. It is, as I said, an additional humiliation in my great distress that I must take the provision my husband has made, and cannot fling it back to you indignantly as a younger woman might. I am old enough to know, and bitterly acknowledge, that I cannot hope to maintain myself; and I have others dependent on me. This necessity will always make it easy enough to find me, but I do not fear that you will wish to seek me out or bring me back.

"I desire you to know that I understand my husband's will better than any one else, and perhaps, knowing his nature, blame him less than you will be disposed to do. When he married me I was very forlorn and miserable. I had a story, which is the saddest thing that can be said of a woman. He was generous to me then in every particular but one, but that one was very important. I had to make a sacrifice, an unjustifiable sacrifice, and a promise which was unnatural. Herein lies my fault. I have not kept that promise; I could not; it was more than flesh and blood was capable of; and I deceived him. I was always aware that if he discovered it he might, and probably would, take summary vengeance. Now he has discovered it, and he has done without ruth what he promised me to do if I broke my word to him. I deserve it, you see, though not in the way the vulgar will suppose. To them I cannot explain, and circumstances, alas, make it impossible for me to be explicit even with you. But perhaps, even in writing so much, you may be delivered from some suspicions of me which, if I read you right, you will be glad to find are not justified.

"Farewell, dear John; if we ever should meet in this world—if I should ever be cleared—I cannot tell—most likely not—my children will grow up without knowing me; but I dare not think on that subject, much less say anything. God bless them! Be as much a father to them as you can, and let my Rosalind have the letter I enclose; it will do her no harm: anyhow, she would not believe harm of me, even though she saw what looked like harm. Pity me a little, John. I have taken my doom quietly because I have no hope—neither in what I leave nor in what I go to is there any hope.

GRACE TREVANION."

This letter forced tears, such as a man is very slow to shed, to John Trevanion's eyes; but there was in reality no explanation in it, no light upon the family catastrophe, or the confusion of misery and perplexity she had left behind.

CHAPTER XXIV

"Have you ever noticed in your walks, doctor, a young fellow?—you couldn't but remark him—a sort of primo tenore, big eyed, pale faced—"

"All pulmonary," said Dr. Beaton. "I know the man you mean. He has been hanging about for a month, more or less, with no visible object. To tell the truth—"

John Trevanion raised his hand instinctively. "I find," he said, interrupting with a hurried precaution, "that he has been in hiding for some offence, and men have come after him here because of an envelope with the Highcourt stamp—"

Here Dr. Beaton began, with a face of regret, yet satisfaction, to nod his head, with that offensive air of "I knew it all the time," which is more exasperating than any other form of remark.

"The Highcourt stamp," continued Trevanion, peremptorily, "and a direction written in my poor brother's hand."

"In your brother's hand!"

"I thought I should surprise you," John said, with a grim satisfaction. "I suppose it is according to the rules of the profession that so much time should have been let slip. I am very glad of it, for my part. Whatever Reginald can have had to do with the fellow—something accidental, no doubt—it would have been disagreeable to have his name mixed up—I saw the man myself trying to make himself agreeable to Rosalind."

"To Miss Trevanion?" cried the doctor, with evident dismay. "Why, I thought—"

"Oh, it was a very simple matter," said John, interrupting again. "He laid down some planks for her to cross the floods. And the recompense she gave him was to doubt whether he was a gentleman, because he had paid her a compliment—which I must say struck me as a very modest attempt at a compliment."

"It was a tremendous piece of presumption," said the doctor, with Scotch warmth. "I don't doubt Miss Rosalind's instinct was right, and that he was no gentleman. He had not the air of it, in my opinion—a limp, hollow-eyed, phthisical subject."

"But consumption does not spare even the cream of society, doctor. It appears he must have had warning of the coming danger, for he seems to have got away."

"I thought as much!" said Dr. Beaton. "I never expected to see more of him after—Oh, I thought as much!"

John Trevanion eyed the doctor with a look that was almost threatening, but he said nothing more. Dr. Beaton, too, was on the eve of departure; his occupation was gone, and his tête-à-tête with John Trevanion not very agreeable to either of them. But the parting was friendly on all sides. "The doctor do express himself very nicely," Dorrington said, when he joined the company in the housekeeper's room, after having solemnly served the two gentlemen at dinner, "about his stay having been agreeable and all that—just what a gentleman ought to say. There are medical men of all kinds, just as there are persons of all sorts in domestic service; and the doctor, he's one of the right sort."

"And a comfort, whatever ailed one, to know there was a doctor in the house, and as you'd be right done by," the housekeeper said, which was the general view in the servants' hall. These regions were, as may be supposed, deeply agitated. Russell, one of the most important among them, had been sent forth weeping and vituperating, and the sudden departure of the family had left the household free to make every commentary, possible and impossible. Needless to say that Madam's disappearance had but one explanation among them. In all circles the question would have been so decided by the majority; in the servants' hall there was unanimity; no one was bold enough to make a different suggestion, and had it been made it would have been laughed to scorn. There were various stories told about her supposed lover, and several different suppositions current. Gentlemen of different appearances had been seen about the park by different spectators, and men in careful disguises had even been admitted into the house, some were certain. That new man who came to wind the clocks! Why should a new man have been sent? And he had white hands, altogether unlike the hands of one who worked for his living. The young man who had lived at the Red Lion was not left out of the suspicions of the house, but he had not so important a place there as he had in the mind, for example, of Dr. Beaton, who had, with grief and pain, but now not without a certain satisfaction, concluded upon his identity. The buzz and talk, and the whirl of suppositions and real or imaginary evidence, made a sort of reverberation through the house. Now and then, when doors were open and the household off their guard, which, occurred not unfrequently in the extraordinary calm and leisure, the sounds of the eager voices were heard even as far as the library, in which John Trevanion sat with his papers, and sometimes elicited from him a furious message full of bitterness and wrath. "Can't you keep your subordinates quiet and your doors shut," he said to Dorrington, "instead of leaving them to disturb me with their infernal clatter and gossip?" "I will see to it, sir," said Dorrington, with dignity; "but as for what goes on in the servants' 'all, I 'ear it only as you 'ear it yourself, sir." John bade the over-fine butler to go to—a personage who need not be named, to whom very fine persons go; and went on with his papers with a consciousness of all that was being said, the flutter of endless talk which before now must have blown abroad over all the country, and the false conclusions that would be formed. He could not publish her letter in the same way—her letter, which said so much yet so little, which did not, alas, explain anything. She had accepted the burden, fully knowing what it was, not deceiving herself as to anything that was to follow; but in such a case the first sufferer is scarcely so much to be pitied as the succeeding victims, who have all the misery of seeing the martyr misconstrued and their own faith laughed at. There were times indeed when John Trevanion was not himself sure that he had any faith, and felt himself incapable of striving any longer with the weight of probability against her which she had never attempted to remove or explain.

He went through all the late Mr. Trevanion's papers without finding any light on the subject of his connection with Everard, or which could explain the fact of his letter to that person. Several letters from his bankers referred indeed to the payment of money at Liverpool, which was where the offender had lived, but this was too faint a light to be calculated upon. As the days went on, order came to a certain degree out of the confusion in John Trevanion's mind. To be suddenly turned out of the easy existence of a London bachelor about town, with his cosey chambers and luxurious club, and made to assume the head and charge of a family so tragically abandoned, was an extraordinary effort for any man. It was a thing, could he have known it beforehand, which would have made him fly to the uttermost parts of the earth to avoid such a charge; but to have no choice simplifies matters, and the mind habituates itself instinctively to what it is compelled to do. He decided, after much thought, that it was better the family should not return to Highcourt. In the changed circumstances, and deprived of maternal care and protection as they were, no woman about them more experienced than Rosalind, their return could not be otherwise than painful and embarrassing. He decided that they should remain with their aunt, having absolute confidence in her delighted acceptance of their guardianship. Sophy, indeed, was quite incapable of such a charge, but they had Rosalind, and they had the ordinary traditions by which such families are guided. They would, he thought, come to no harm. Mrs. Lennox lived in the neighborhood of Clifton, far enough off to avoid any great or general knowledge of the family tragedy. The majority of the servants were consequently dismissed, and Highcourt, with its windows all closed and its chimneys all but smokeless, fell back into silence, and stood amid its park and fine trees, a habitation of the dead.

It was not until he had done this that John Trevanion carried her stepmother's letter to Rosalind. He had a very agitating interview with her on the day of his arrival at the Limes, which was the suburban appellation of Sophy's house. He had to bear the artillery of anxious looks during dinner, and to avoid as he could his sister's questions, which were not over wise, as to what he had heard, and what he thought, and what people were saying; and it was not till the evening, when the children were disposed of, and Sophy herself had retired, that Rosalind, putting her hand within his arm, drew him to the small library, in which Mrs. Lennox allowed the gentlemen to "make themselves comfortable," as she said, tolerating tobacco. "I know you have something to say to me, Uncle John—something that you could not say before—them all."

"Little to say, but something to give you, Rosalind." She recognized her stepmother's handwriting in a moment, though it was, as we have said, little remarkable, and with a cry of agitated pleasure threw herself upon it. It was a bulky letter, not like that which he had himself received, but when it was opened was found to contain a long and particular code of directions about the children, and only a small accompanying note. This Rosalind read with an eagerness which made her cheeks glow.

"My Rosalind, I am sometimes glad to think now that you are not mine, and never can have it said to you that your mother is not—as other mothers are. Sophy and little Amy are not so fortunate. You must make it up to them, my darling, by being everything to them—better than I could have been. And when people see what you are they will forget me.

"That is not to say, my dearest, that you are to give up your faith in me. For the moment all is darkness—perhaps will always be darkness, all my life. There are cases that may occur in which I shall be able to tell you everything, but what would that matter so long as your father's prohibition stands? My heart grows sick when I think that in no case—But we will not dwell upon that. My own (though you are not my own), remember me, love me. I am no more unworthy of it than other women are. I have written down all I can think of about the children. You will no doubt have dismissed Russell, but after a time I almost think she should be taken back, for she loves the children. She always hated me, but she loves them. If you can persuade yourself to do it, take her back. Love is too precious to be lost. I am going away from you all very quietly, not permitting myself to reflect. When you think of me, believe that I am doing all I can to live—to live long enough to see my children again. My darling, my own child, I will not say good-bye to you, but only God bless you; and till we meet again,

"Your true

MOTHER AND FRIEND."

"My true mother," Rosalind said, with the tears in her eyes, "my dearest friend! Oh, Uncle John, was there ever any such misery before? Was it ever so with any woman? Were children ever made wretched like this, and forced to suffer? And why should it fall to our share?"

John Trevanion shook his head, pondering over the letter, and over the long, perfectly calm, most minute, and detailed instructions which accompanied it. There was nothing left out or forgotten in these instructions. She must have spent the night in putting down every little detail, the smallest as well as the greatest. The writing of the letter to Rosalind showed a little trembling; a tear had fallen on it at one spot; but the longer paper showed nothing of the kind. It was as clear and steady as the many manuscripts from the same hand which he had looked over among his brother's papers; statements of financial operations, of farming, of improvements. She had put down all the necessary precautions to be taken for her children in the same way, noting all their peculiarities, for the guidance of the young sister who was hereafter to have the charge of them. This document filled the man with the utmost wonder. Rosalind took it a great deal more easily. To her it was natural that her mother should give these instructions; they were of the highest importance to herself in her novel position, and she understood perfectly that Madam would be aware of the need of them, and that to make some provision for that need would be one of the first things to occur to her. But John Trevanion contemplated the paper from a very different point of view. That a woman so outraged and insulted as (if she were innocent) she must feel herself to be, should pause on the eve of her departure from everything dear to her, from honor and consideration, her home and her place among her peers, to write about Johnny's tendency to croup and Amy's readiness to catch cold, was to him more marvellous than almost anything that had gone before. He lingered over it, reading mechanically all those simple directions. A woman at peace, he thought, might have done it, one who knew no trouble more profound than a child's cough or chilblains. But this woman—in the moment of her anguish—before she disappeared into the darkness of the distant world! "I do not understand it at all," he said as he put it down.

"Oh," cried Rosalind, "who could understand it? I think papa must have been mad. Are not bad wills sometimes broken, Uncle John?"

"Not such a will as this. He had a right to leave his money as he pleased."

"But if we were all to join—if we were to show the mistake, the dreadful mistake, he had made—"

"What mistake? You could prove that your stepmother was no common woman, Rosalind. A thing like this is astounding to me. I don't know how she could do it. You might prove that she had the power to make fools of you and me. But you could prove nothing more, my dear. Your father knew something more than we know. It might be no mistake; he might have very good reason. Even this letter, though it makes you cry, explains nothing, Rosalind."

"I want nothing explained," cried the girl. "Do you think I have any doubt of her? I could not bear that she should explain—as if I did not know what she is! But, Uncle John, let us all go together to the judge that can do it, and tell him everything, and get him to break the will."

"The judge who can do that is not to be found in Westminster, Rosalind. It must be one that sees into the heart. I believe in her too—without any reason—but to take it to law would only be to make our domestic misery a little better known."

Rosalind looked at him with large eyes full of light and excitement. She felt strong enough to defy the world. "Do you mean to say that, whatever happens, though we could prove what we know of her, that she is the best—the best woman in the world—"

"Were she as pure as ice, as chaste as snow, there is nothing to be done. Your father does not say, because of this or that. What he says is absolute. If she continue with the children, or in communication with them, they lose everything."

"Then let us lose everything," cried Rosalind in her excitement; "rather be poor and work for our bread, than lose our mother."

John Trevanion shook his head. "She has already chosen," he said.

CHAPTER XXV

Russell left Highcourt in such wild commotion of mind and temper, such rage, grief, compunction, and pain, that she was incapable of any real perception of what had happened, and did not realise, until the damp air blowing in her face as she hurried across the park, sobbing and crying aloud, and scarcely able to keep herself from screaming, brought back her scattered faculties, either what it was that she had been instrumental in doing, or what she had brought upon herself. She did not now understand what it was that had happened to Madam, though she had a kind of vindictive joy, mingled with that sinking of the heart which those not altogether hardened to human suffering feel in regarding a catastrophe brought about by their means, in the thought that she had brought illimitable, irremediable harm to her mistress, whom she had always hated. She had done this whatever might come of it, and even in the thrill of her nerves that owned a human horror of this calamity, there was a fierce exhilaration of success in having triumphed over her enemy. But perhaps she had never wished, never thought, of so complete a triumph. The desire of revenge, which springs so naturally in the undisciplined mind, and is so hot and reckless in its efforts to harm its object, has most generally no fixed intention, but only a vague wish to injure, or, rather, punish; for Russell, to her own consciousness, was inspired by the highest moral sentiment, and meant only to bring retribution on the wicked and to open the eyes of a man who was deceived. She did not understand what had really occurred, but the fact that she had ruined her mistress was at the same time terrible and delightful to her. She did not mean so much as that; but no doubt Madam had been found out more wicked than was supposed, and her heart swelled with pride and a gratified sense of importance even while she trembled. But the consequences to herself were such as she had never foreseen, and for the moment overwhelmed her altogether. She wept hysterically as she hurried to the village, stumbling over the inequalities of the path, wild with sorrow and anger. She had meant to remain in Madam's service, though she had done all she could to destroy her. She thought nothing less than that life would go on without much visible alteration, and that she herself, because there was nobody like her, would necessarily remain with the children to whom her care was indispensable. She had brought them all up from their birth. She had devoted herself to them, and felt her right in them almost greater than their mother's. "My children," she said, as the butler said "my plate," and the housemaid "my grates and carpets." She spent her whole life with them, whereas it is only a part of hers that the most devoted mother can give. The woman, though she was cruel and hard-hearted in one particular, was in this as tender and sensitive as the most gentle and feminine of women. She loved the children with passion. The idea that they could be torn away from her had never entered her mind. What would they do without her? The two little ones were delicate: they required constant care; without her own attention she felt sure they never could be "reared:" and to be driven from them at a moment's notice, without time to say good-bye! Sobs came from her breast, convulsive and hysterical, as she rushed along. "Oh, my children!" she cried, under her breath, as if it were she who had been robbed, and who refused to be comforted. She passed some one on the way, who stopped astonished, to look after her, but whom she could scarcely see through the mist of her tears, and at last, with a great effort, subduing the passionate sounds that had been bursting from her, she hurried through the nearest corner of the village to her mother's house, and there, flinging herself down upon a chair, gave herself up to all the violence of that half-artificial, half-involuntary transport known as hysterics. Her mother was old, and beyond such violent emotions; but though greatly astonished, she was not unacquainted with the manifestation. She got up from the big chair in which she was seated, tottering a little, and hurried to her daughter, getting hold of and smoothing out her clinched fingers. "Dear, dear, now, what be the matter?" she said, soothingly; "Sarah, Sarah, come and look to your poor sister. What's come to her, what's come to her, the poor dear? Lord bless us, but she do look bad. Fetch a drop of brandy, quick; that's the best thing to bring her round."

When Russell had been made to swallow the brandy, and had exhausted herself and brought her mother and sister into accord with her partial frenzy, she permitted herself to be brought round. She sat up wildly while still in their hands, and stared about her as if she did not know where she was. Then she seized her mother by the arm; "I have been sent away," she said.

"Sent away. She's off of her head still, poor dear! Sent away, when they can't move hand nor foot without you!"

"That's not so now, mother. It's all true. I've been all the same as turned out of the house, and by her as I nursed and thought of most of all; her as was like my very own; Miss Rosalind! Oh!" and Russell showed inclination to "go off" again, which the assistants resisted by promptly taking possession of her two arms, and opening the hands which she would have clinched if she could.

"There now, deary; there now! don't you excite yourself. You're among them that wishes you well here."

"Oh, I know that, mother. But Miss Rosalind, she's as good as taken me by the shoulders and put me out of the house, and took my children from me as I've brought up; and what am I to do without my babies? Oh, oh! I wish I had never been born."

"I hope you've got your wages and board wages, and something over to make up? You ought to have that," said the sister, who was a woman of good sense. Russell, indeed, had sufficient command of herself to nod in assent.

"And your character safe?" said the old woman. "I will say that for you, deary, that you have always been respectable. And whatever it is that's happened, so long as it's nothing again your character, you'll get another place fast enough. I don't hold with staying too long in one family. You'd just like to stick there forever."

"Oh, don't speak to me about new places. My children as I've brought up! It has nothing to do with me; it's all because I told master of Madam's goings-on. And he's been and put her away in his will—and right too. And Miss Rosalind, that always was unnatural, that took to that woman more than to her aunt, or me, or any one, she jumps up to defend Madam, and 'go out of the house, woman!' and stamping with her foot, and going on like a fury. And my little Master Johnny, that would never go to nobody but me! Oh, mother, I'll die of it, I'll die of it—my children that I've brought up!"

"I've told you all," said the old woman, "never you meddle with the quality. It can't come to no good." She had given up her ministrations, seeing that her patient had come round, and retired calmly to her chair. "Madam's goings-on was no concern of yours. You ought to have known that. When a poor person puts herself in the way of a rich person, it's always her as goes to the wall."

Of these maxims the mother delivered herself deliberately as she sat twirling her thumbs. The sister, who was the mistress of the cottage, showed a little more sympathy.

"As long as you've got your board wages," she said, "and a somethin' to make up. Mother's right enough, but I'll allow as it's hard to do. They're all turned topsy-turvy at the Red Lion about Madam's young man—him as all this business was about."

"What's about him?" cried Russell, for the first time with real energy raising her head.

"It turns out as he's robbed his masters in Liverpool," said Sarah, with the perfect coolness of a rustic spectator; "just what was to be expected; and the detectives is after him. He was here yesterday, I'll take my oath, but now he's gone, and there's none can find him. There's a reward of—"

"I'll find him," cried Russell, springing to her feet. "I'll track him. I'm good for nothing now in a common way. I cannot rest, I cannot settle to needlework or that sort." She was fastening her cloak as she spoke, and tying on her bonnet. "I've heaps of mending to do, for I never had a moment's time to think of myself, but only of them that have showed no more gratitude—My heart's broke, that's what it is—I can't settle down; but here's one thing I'm just in a humor to do—I'll track him out."

"Lord, Lizzie! what are you thinking of it? You don't know no more than Adam what way they're gone, or aught about him."

"And if you'll take my advice, deary," said the old woman, "you'll neither make nor meddle with the quality. Right or wrong, it's always the poor folk as go to the wall."

"I'll track him, that's what I'll do. I'm just in the humor for that," cried Russell, savagely. "Don't stop me. What do I care for a bit of money to prove as I'm right. I'll go and I'll find them. Providence will put me on the right way. Providence'll help me to find all that villainy out."

"But, Lizzie! stop and have a bit to eat at least. Don't go off like that, without even a cup of tea—"

"Oh, don't speak to me about cups of tea!" Russell rushed at her mother and dabbed a hurried kiss upon her old cheek. She waved her hand to her sister, who stood open-mouthed, wondering at her, and finally rushed out in an excitement and energy which contrasted strangely with her previous prostration. The two rustic spectators stood gazing after her with consternation. "She was always one as had no patience," said the mother at last. "And without a bit of dinner or a glass of beer, or anything," said Sarah. After that they returned to their occupations and closed the cottage door.

Russell rushed forth to the railway station, which was at least a mile from the village. She was transported out of herself with excitement, misery, a sense of wrong, a sense of remorse—all the conflicting passions which the crisis had brought. To prove to herself that her suspicions were justified about Madam was in reality as strong a motive in her mind as the fierce desire of revenge upon her mistress, which drove her nearly frantic; and she had that wild confidence in chance, and indifference to reason, which are at once the strength and weakness of the uneducated. She would get on the track somehow; she would find them somehow; Madam's young man, and Madam herself. She would give him up to justice, and shame the woman for whose sake she had been driven forth. And, as it happened, Russell, taking her ticket for London, found herself in the same carriage with the man who had come in search of the stranger at the Red Lion, and acquired an amount of information and communicated a degree of zeal which stimulated the search on both sides. When they parted in town she was provided with an address to which to telegraph instantly on finding any trace of the fugitives, and flung herself upon the great unknown world of London with a faith and a virulence which were equally violent. She did not know where to go nor what to do; she had very little acquaintance with London. The Trevanions had a town house in a street near Berkeley Square, and all that she knew was the immediate neighborhood of that dignified centre—of all places in the world least likely to shelter the fugitives. She went there, however, in her helplessness, and carried consternation to the bosom of the charwoman in charge, who took in the strange intelligence vaguely, and gaped and hoped as it wasn't true. "So many things is said, and few of 'em ever comes true," this philosophical observer said. "But I've come out of the middle of it, and I know it's true, every word," she almost shrieked in her excitement. The charwoman was a little hard of hearing. "We'll hope as it'll all turn out lies—they mostly does," she said. This was but one of many rebuffs the woman met with. She had spent more than a week wandering about London, growing haggard and thin; her respectable clothes growing shabby, her eyes wild—the want of proper sleep and proper food making a hollow-eyed spectre of the once smooth and dignified upper servant—when she was unexpectedly rewarded for all her pangs and exertions by meeting Jane one morning, sharply and suddenly, turning round a corner. The two women paused by a mutual impulse, and then one cried, "What are you doing here?" and the other, grasping her firmly by the arm, "I've caught you at last."

"Caught me! Were you looking for me? What do you want? Has anything happened to the children?" Jane cried, beginning to tremble.

"The children! how dare you take their names in your mouth, you as is helping to ruin and shame them? I'll not let you go now I've got you; oh, don't think it! I'll stick to you till I get a policeman."

"A policeman to me!" cried poor Jane, who, not knowing what mysterious powers the law might have, trembled more and more. "I've done nothing," she said.

"But them as you are with has done a deal," cried Russell. "Where is that young man? Oh, I know—I know what he's been and done. I have took an oath on my Bible that I'll track him out. If I'm to be driven from my place and my dear children for Madam's sake, she shall just pay for it, I can tell you. You thought I'd put up with it and do nothing, but a worm will turn. I've got it in my power to publish her shame, and I'll do it. I know a deal more than I knew when I told master of her goings-on. But now I've got you I'll stick to you, and them as you're with, and I'll have my revenge," Russell cried, her wild eyes flaming, her haggard cheeks flushing; "I'll have my revenge. Ah!"

She paused here with a cry of consternation, alarm, dismay, for there stepped out of a shop hard by, Madam herself, and laid a hand suddenly upon her arm.

"Russell," she said, "I am sorry they have sent you away. I know you love the children." At this a convulsive movement passed across her face, which sent through the trembling, awe-stricken woman a sympathetic shudder. They were one in this deprivation, though they were enemies. "You have always hated me, I do not know why: but you love the children. I would not have removed you from them. I have written to Miss Rosalind to bid her have you back when—when she is calmer. And you that have done me so much harm, what do you want with me?" said Madam, looking with the pathetic smile which threw such a strange light upon her utterly pale face, upon this ignorant pursuer.

"I've come—I've come"—she gasped, and then stood trembling, unable to articulate, holding herself up by the grasp she had taken with such different intentions of Jane's arm, and gazing with her hollow eyes with a sort of fascination upon the lady whom at last she had hunted down.

"I think she is fainting," Madam said. "Whatever she wants, she has outdone her strength." There was a compassion in the tone, which, in Russell's weakened state, went through and through her. Her mistress took her gently by the other arm, and led her into the shop she had just left. Here they brought her wine and something to eat, of which she had the greatest need. "My poor woman," said Madam, "your search for me was vain, for Mr. John Trevanion knows where to find me at any moment. You have done me all the harm one woman could do another; what could you desire more? But I forgive you for my children's sake. Go back, and Rosalind will take you again, because you love them; and take care of my darlings, Russell," she said, with that ineffable smile of anguish; "say no ill to them of their mother."

"Oh, Madam, kill me!" Russell cried.

That was the last that was seen in England of Madam Trevanion. The woman, overcome with passion, remorse, and long fasting and misery, fainted outright at her mistress's feet. And when she came to herself the lady and her maid were both gone, and were seen by her no more.

CHAPTER XXVI

There is nothing more strange in all the experiences of humanity than the manner in which a great convulsion either in nature or in human history ceases after a while to affect the world. Grass grows and flowers wave over the soil which an earthquake has rent asunder; and the lives of men are similarly torn in twain without leaving a much more permanent result. The people whom we see one year crushed by some great blow, when the next has come have begun to pursue their usual course again. This means no infidelity of nature, no forgetting; but only the inevitable progress by which the world keeps going. There is no trouble, however terrible, that does not yield to the touch of time.

Some two years after these events Rosalind Trevanion felt herself, almost against her will, emerging out of the great shadow which had overwhelmed her life. She had been for a time swallowed up in the needs of the family, all her powers demanded for the rearrangement of life on its new basis, and everything less urgent banished from her. But by degrees the most unnatural arrangements fall into the calm of habit, the most unlooked-for duties become things of every day. Long before the period at which this history resumes, it had ceased to be wonderful to any one that Rosalind should take her place as head of the desolated house. She assumed unconsciously that position of sister-mother which is one of the most touching and beautiful that exist, with the ease which necessity brings—not asking how she could do it, but doing it; as did the bystanders who criticise every course of action and dictate what can and what cannot be done, but who all accepted her in her new duties with a composure which soon made everybody forget how strange, how unlikely, to the girl those duties were. The disappearance of the mother, the breaking-up of the house, was no doubt a nine-days' wonder, and gave occasion in the immediate district for endless discussions; but the wonder died out as every wonder dies out. Outside of the county it was but vaguely known, and to those who professed to tell the details with authority there was but a dull response; natural sentiment at a distance being all against the possibility that anything so extraordinary and odious could be true. "You may depend upon it, a woman who was going to behave so at the end must have shown signs of it from the beginning," people said, and the propagation of the rumor was thus seriously discouraged. Mrs. Lennox, though she was not wise, had enough of good sense and good feeling not to tell even to her most intimate friends the circumstances of her sister-in-law's disappearance; and this not so much for Madam's sake as for that of her brother, whose extraordinary will appeared to her simple understanding so great a shame and scandal that she kept it secret for Reginald's sake. Indeed, all she did in the matter was for Reginald's sake. She did not entertain the confidence in Madam with which Rosalind and John enshrined the fugitive. To Rosalind, Mrs. Lennox said little on the subject, with a respect for the girl's innocence which persons of superior age and experience are not always restrained by; but that John, a man who knew the world, should go on as he did, was a thing which exasperated his sister. How he could persuade himself of Mrs. Trevanion's innocence was a thing she could not explain. Why, what could it be? she asked herself, angrily. Everybody knows that the wisest of men or women are capable of going wrong for one cause; but what other could account for the flight of a woman, of a mother from her children, the entire disappearance of her out of all the scenes of her former life? When her brother told her that there was no help for it, that in the interests of her children Madam was compelled to go away, Aunt Sophy said "Stuff!" What was a woman good for if she could not find some means of eluding such a monstrous stipulation? "Do you think I would have minded him? I should have disguised myself, hidden about, done anything rather than desert my family," she cried; and when it was suggested to her that Madam was too honorable, too proud, too high-minded to deceive, Sophy said nothing but "Stuff!" again. "Do you think anything in the world would make me abandon my children—if I had any?" she cried. But though she was angry with John and impatient of Rosalind, she kept the secret. And after a time all audible comments on the subject died away. "There is something mysterious about the matter," people said; "I believe Mrs. Trevanion is still living." And then it began to be believed that she was ill and obliged to travel for her health, which was the best suggestion that could have been made.

And Rosalind gradually, but nevertheless fully, came out of the shadow of that blighting cloud. What is there in human misery which can permanently crush a heart under twenty? Nothing, at least save the last and most intolerable of personal losses, and even then only in the case of a passionate, undisciplined soul or a feeble body. Youth will overcome everything if it has justice and fresh air and occupation. And Rosalind made her way out of all the ways of gloom and misery to the sky and sunshine. Her memory had, indeed, an indelible scar upon it at that place. She could not turn back and think of the extraordinary mystery and anguish of that terrible moment without a convulsion of the heart, and sense that all the foundations of the earth had been shaken. But happily, at her age, there is not much need of turning back upon the past. She shivered when the momentary recollection crossed her mind, but could always throw it off and come back to the present, to the future, which are always so much more congenial.

This great catastrophe, which made a sort of chasm between her and her former life, had given a certain maturity to Rosalind. At twenty she had already much of the dignity, the self-possession, the seriousness of a more advanced age. She had something of the air of a young married woman, a young mother, developed by the early experiences of life. The mere freshness of girlhood, even when it is most exquisite, has a less perfect charm than this; and the fact that Rosalind was still a girl, notwithstanding the sweet and noble gravity of her responsible position, added to her an exceptional charm. She was supposed by most people to be five years at least older than she was: and she was the mother of her brothers and sisters, at once more and less than a mother; perhaps less anxious, perhaps more indulgent, not old enough to perceive with the same clearness or from the same point of view, seeing from the level of the children more than perhaps a mother can. To see her with her little brother in her lap was the most lovely of pictures. Something more exquisite even than maternity was in this virgin-motherhood. She was a better type of the second mother than any wife. This made a sort of halo around the young creature who had so many responsibilities. But yet in her heart Rosalind was only a girl; the other half of her had not progressed beyond where it was before that great crisis. There was within her a sort of decisive consciousness of the apparent maturity which she had thus acquired, and she only such a child—a girl at heart.

In this profound girlish soul of hers, which was her very self, while the other was more or less the product of circumstances, it still occurred to Rosalind now and then to wonder how it was that she had never had a lover. Even this was meant in a manner of her own. Miss Trevanion of Highcourt had not been without suitors; men who had admired her beauty or her position. But these were not at all what she meant by a lover. She meant what an imaginative girl means when such a thought crosses her mind. She meant Romeo, or perhaps Hamlet—had love been restored to the possibilities of that noblest of all disenchanted souls—or even such a symbol as Sir Kenneth. She wondered whether it would ever be hers to find wandering about the world the other part of her, him who would understand every thought and feeling, him to whom it would be needless to speak or to explain, who would know; him for whom mighty love would cleave in twain the burden of a single pain and part it, giving half to him. The world, she thought, could not hold together as it did under the heavens, had it ceased to be possible that men and women should meet each other so. But such a meeting had never occurred yet in Rosalind's experience, and seeing how common it was, how invariable an occurrence in the experience of all maidens of poetry and fiction, the failure occasioned her always a little surprise. Had she never seen any one, met about the world any form, in which she could embody such a possibility? She did not put this question to herself plainly, but there was in her imagination a sort of involuntary answer to it, or rather the ghost of an answer, which would sometimes make itself known, from without, she thought, more than from within—as if a face had suddenly looked at her, or a whisper been breathed in her ear. She did not give any name to this vision or endeavor to identify it.

But imagination is obstinate and not to be quenched, and in inadvertent moments she half acknowledged to herself that it had a being and a name. Who or what he was, indeed, she could not tell; but sometimes in her imagination the remembered tone of a voice would thrill her ears, or a pair of eyes would look into hers. This recollection or imagination would flash upon her at the most inappropriate moments; sometimes when she was busy with her semi-maternal cares, or full of household occupation which left her thoughts free—moments when she was without defence. Indeed, temptation would come upon her in this respect from the most innocent quarter, from her little brother, who looked up at her with eyes that were like the eyes of her dream. Was that why he had become her darling, her favorite, among the children? Oh, no; it was because he was the youngest, the baby, the one to whom a mother was most of all wanting. Aunt Sophy, indeed, who was so fond of finding out likenesses, had said—And there was a certain truth in it. Johnny's eyes were very large and dark, shining out of the paleness of his little face; he was a delicate child; or perhaps only a pale-faced child looking delicate, for there never was anything the matter with him. His eyes were very large for a child, appearing so, perhaps, because he was himself so little; a child of fine organization, with the most delicate, pure complexion, and blue veins showing distinctly through the delicate tissue of his skin. Rosalind felt a sort of dreamy bliss come over her when Johnny fixed his great, soft eyes upon her, looking up with a child's devout attention. She loved the child dearly, was not that enough? And then there was the suggestion. Likenesses are very curious; they are so arbitrary, no one can tell how they come; there was a likeness, she admitted to herself; and then wondered—half wishing it, half angry with herself for the idea—whether perhaps it was the likeness to her little brother which had impressed the face of a stranger so deeply upon her dreams.

Who was he? Where did he come from? Where, all this long time, for these many months, had he gone? If it was because of her he had come to the village, how strange that he should never have appeared again! It was impossible it could have been for her; yet, if not for her, for whom could he have come? She asked herself these questions so often that her vision gradually lost identity and became a tradition, an abstraction, the true lover after whom she had been wondering. She endowed him with all the qualities which girls most dearly prize. She talked to him upon every subject under heaven. In all possible emergencies that arose to her fancy he came and stood by her and helped her. No real man is ever so noble, so tender, so generous as such an ideal man can be. And Rosalind forgot altogether that she had asked herself whether it was certain that he was a gentleman, the original of this shadowy figure which had got into her imagination she scarcely could tell how.

CHAPTER XXVII

Mrs. Lennox's house was not a great country-house like Highcourt. It was within a mile of Clifton, a pretty house, set in pretty grounds, with a few fields about it, and space enough to permit of a sufficient but modest establishment; horses and dogs, and pets in any number to satisfy the children. Reginald, indeed, when he came home for the holidays, somewhat scoffed at the limited household, and declared that there was scarcely room to breathe. For the young master of Highcourt everything was small and shabby, but as his holidays were broken by visits to the houses of his schoolfellows, where young Mr.

Trevanion of Highcourt had many things in his favor, and as he thus managed to get as much shooting and hunting and other delights as a schoolboy can indulge in, he was, on the whole, gracious enough to Aunt Sophy and Rosalind, and their limited ways. The extraordinary changes that followed his father's death had produced a curious effect upon the boy; there had been, indeed, a moment of impulse in which he had declared his intention of standing by his mother, but a fuller understanding of all that was involved had summarily checked this. The youthful imagination, when roused by the thought of wealth and importance, is as insatiable in these points as it is when inflamed by the thirst for pleasure, and it is, perhaps, more difficult to give up or consent to modify greatness which you have never had, but have hoped for, than to give up an actual possession. Reginald had felt this importance as his father's heir so much, that the idea of depriving himself of it for the sake of his mother brought a sudden damp and chill all over his energies. He was silent when he heard what a sacrifice was necessary, even though it was a sacrifice in imagination only, the reality being unknown to him. And from that moment the thing remarkable in him was that he had never mentioned his mother's name.

With the other children this effect had at the end of the year been almost equally attained, but by degrees; they had ceased to refer to her as they had ceased to refer to their father. Both parents seemed to have died together to these little ones. The one, like the other, faded as the dead do out of their personal sphere, and ceased to have any place in their life. They said Rosalind now, when they used to say mamma. But with Reginald the effect was different—young though he was, in his schoolboy sphere he had a certain knowledge of the world. He knew that it was something intolerable when a fellow's family was in everybody's mouth, and his mother was discussed and talked of, and there was a sort of half-fury against her in his mind for subjecting him to this. The pangs which a proud boy feels in such circumstances are difficult to fathom, for their force is aggravated by the fact that he never betrays them. The result was that he never mentioned her, never asked a question, put on a mien of steel when anything was said which so much as suggested her existence, and from the moment of his departure from Highcourt ignored altogether the name and possibility of a mother. He was angry with the very name.

Sophy was the only one who caused a little embarrassment now and then by her recollections of the past life of Highcourt and the household there. But Sophy was not favorable to her mother, which is a strange thing to say, and had no lingering tenderness to smother; she even went so far now and then as to launch a jibe at Rosalind on the subject of mamma. As for the little ones, they already remembered her no more. The Elms, which was the suburban title of Mrs. Lennox's small domain, became the natural centre of their little lives, and they forgot the greater and more spacious house in which they were born. And now that the second year was nearly accomplished since the catastrophe happened, natural gayety and consolation had come back. Rosalind went out to such festivities as offered. She spent a few weeks in London, and saw a little of society. The cloud had rolled away from her young horizon, leaving only a dimness and mist of softened tears. And the Elms was, in its way, a little centre of society. Aunt Sophy was very hospitable. She liked the pleasant commotion of life around her, and she was pleased to feel the stir of existence which the presence of a girl brings to such a house. Rosalind was not a beauty so remarkable as to draw admirers and suitors from every quarter of the compass. These are rare in life, though we are grateful to meet so many of them in novels; but she was extremely pleasant to look upon, fair and sweet as so many English girls are, with a face full of feeling, and enough of understanding and poetry to give it something of an ideal charm. And though it was, as we have said, the wonder of her life that she had never, like young ladies in novels, had a lover, yet she was not without admiration nor without suitors, quite enough to maintain her self-respect and position in the world.

One of these was the young Hamerton who was a visitor at Highcourt at the opening of this history. He was the son of another county family of the Highcourt neighborhood; not the eldest son, indeed, but still not altogether to be ranked among the detrimentals, since he was to have his mother's money, a very respectable fortune. And he was by way of being a barrister, although not so unthoughtful of the claims of others as to compete for briefs with men who had more occasion for them. He had come to Clifton for the hunting, not, perhaps, without a consciousness of Rosalind's vicinity. He had not shown at all during the troubles at Highcourt or for some time after, being too much disturbed and alarmed by his own discovery to approach the sorrowful family. But by degrees this feeling wore off, and a girl who was under Mrs. Lennox's wing, and who, after all, was not "really the daughter" of the erring woman, would have been most unjustly treated had she been allowed to suffer in consequence of the mystery attached to Madam Trevanion and her disappearance from the world. Mrs. Lennox had known Roland Hamerton's father as well as Rosalind knew himself. The families had grown up together, calling each other by their Christian names, on that preliminary brother-and-sister footing which is so apt with opportunity to grow into something closer. And Roland had always thought Rosalind the prettiest girl about. When he got over the shock of the Highcourt mystery his heart had come back to her with a bound. And if he came to Clifton for the hunting instead of to any other centre, it was with a pleasant recollection that the Elms was within walking distance, and that there he was always likely to find agreeable occupation for "off" days. On such occasions, and even on days which were not "off" days, he would come, sometimes to luncheon, sometimes in the afternoon, with the very frequent consequence of sending off a message to Clifton for "his things," and staying all night. He was adopted, in short, as a sort of son or nephew of the house.

It is undeniable that a visitor of this sort (or even more than one) is an addition to the cheerfulness of a house in the country. It may, perhaps, be dangerous to his own peace of mind, or even, if he is frivolous, to the comfort of a daughter of the same, but so long as he is on these easy terms, with no definite understanding one way or the other, he is a pleasant addition. The least amiable of men is obliging and pleasant in such circumstances. He is on his promotion. His raison d'être is his power of making himself agreeable. When he comes to have a definite position as an accepted lover, everything is changed again, and he may be as much in the way as he once was handy and desirable; but in his first stage he is always an addition, especially when the household is chiefly composed of women. Hamerton fell into this pleasant place with even more ease than usual. He was already so familiar with them all, that everything was natural in the arrangement. And Mrs. Lennox, there was no doubt, wished the young man well. It would not be a brilliant match, but it would be "quite satisfactory." Had young Lord Elmore come a-wooing instead of Roland, that would have been, no doubt, more exciting. But Lord Elmore paid his homage in another direction, and his antecedents were not quite so good as Hamerton's, who was one of those young men who have never given their parents an anxiety—a qualification which, it is needless to say, was dear above every other to Aunt Sophy's heart.

He was seated with them in the drawing-room at the Elms on an afternoon of November. It had been a day pleasant enough for the time of year, but not for hunting men—a clear frosty day, with ice in all the ditches, and the ground hard and resounding; a day when it is delightful to walk, though not to ride. Rosalind had met him strolling towards the house when she was out for her afternoon walk. Perhaps he was not so sorry for himself as he professed to the ladies. "I shall bore you to death," he said; "I shall always be coming, for I see now we are in for a ten days' frost, which is the most dolorous prospect—at least, it would be if I had not the Elms to fall back upon." He made this prognostication of evil with a beaming face.

"You seem on the whole to take it cheerfully," Mrs. Lennox said.

"Yes, with the Elms to fall back upon; I should not take it cheerfully otherwise."

"But you were here on Saturday, Roland, when the meet was at Barley Wood, and everybody was out," cried little Sophy. "I don't think you are half a hunting man. I shouldn't miss a day if it were me; nor Reginald wouldn't," she added, with much indifference to grammar.

"It is all the fault of the Elms," the young man said, with a laugh.

"I don't know what you find at the Elms. Reginald says we are so dull here. I think so too—nothing but women; and you that have got two or three clubs and can go where you like."

"You shall go to the clubs, Sophy, instead of me."

"That is what I should like," said Miss Sophy. "Everybody says men are cleverer than women, and I am very fond of good talk. I like to hear you talk of horses and things; and of betting a pot on Bucephalus—"

"Sophy! where did you hear such language? You must be sent back to the nursery," cried Mrs. Lennox, "if you go on like that."

"Well," said Sophy, "Reginald had a lot on Bucephalus: he told me so. He says it's dreadful fun. You are kept in such a state till the last moment, not knowing which is to win. Sometimes the favorite is simply nowhere, and if you happen to have drawn a dark horse—"

"Sophy! I can't allow such language."

"And the favorite has been cooked, don't you know, or come to grief in the stable," cried Sophy, breathless, determined to have it out, "then you win a pot of money! It was Reginald told me all that. I don't know myself, more's the pity; and because I am a girl I don't suppose I shall ever know," the little reprobate said, regretfully.

"Dear me, I never thought those things were permitted at Eton," said Mrs. Lennox. "I always thought boys were safe there. Afterwards, one knows, not a moment can be calculated upon. That is what is so nice about you, Roland; you never went into anything of that kind. I wish so much, if you are here at Christmas, you would give Reginald a little advice."

"I don't much believe in advice, Mrs. Lennox. Besides, I'm not so immaculate as you think me; I've had in my day a pot on something or other, as Sophy says—"

"Sophy must not say those sort of things," said her aunt. "Rosalind, give us some tea. It is quite cold enough to make the fire most agreeable and the tea a great comfort. And if you have betted you have seen the folly of it, and you could advise him all the better. That is always the worst with boys when they have women to deal with. They think we know nothing. Whether it is because we have not education, or because we have not votes, or what, I can't tell. But Reginald for one does not pay the least attention. He thinks he knows ever so much better than I do. And John is abroad; he doesn't care very much for John either. He calls him an old fogy; he says the present generation knows better than the last. Did you ever hear such impertinence? And he is only seventeen. I like two lumps of sugar, Rosalind. But I thought at Eton they ought to be safe."

"I suppose you are going home for Christmas, Roland? Shall you all be at home? Alice and her baby, and every one of you?" Rosalind breathed softly a little sigh. "I don't like Christmas," she said; "it is all very well so long as you are quite young, but when you begin to get scattered and broken up—"

"My dear, I am far from being quite young, and I hope I have been scattered as much as anybody, and had every sort of thing to put up with, but I never grow too old or too dull for Christmas."

"Ah, Aunt Sophy, you! But then you are not like anybody else; you take things so sweetly, even Rex and his impertinence."

"Christmas is pleasant enough," said young Hamerton. "We are not so much scattered but that we can all get back, and I like it well enough. But," he added, "if one was wanted elsewhere, or could be of use, I am not such a fanatic for home but that I could cut it once in a way, if there was anything, don't you know, Mrs. Lennox, that one would call a duty; like licking a young cub into shape, or helping a—people you are fond of." He blushed and laughed, in the genial, confusing glow of the fire, and cast a glance at Rosalind to see whether she noted his offer, and understood the motive of it. "People one is fond of;" did she think that meant Aunt Sophy? There was a pleasant mingling of obscurity and light even when the cheerful flame leaped up and illuminated the room: something in its leaping and uncertainty made a delightful shelter. You might almost stare at the people you were fond of without being betrayed as the cold daylight betrays you; and as for the heat which he felt suffuse his countenance, that was altogether unmarked in the genial glow of the cheerful fire.

CHAPTER XXVIII

In an easy house, where punctuality is not rampant, the hour before dinner is pleasant to young people. The lady of the house is gone to dress. If she is beginning to feel the weight of years, she perhaps likes a nap before dinner, and in any case she will change her dress in a leisurely manner and likes to have plenty of time; and the children have been carried off to the nursery that their toilet may be attended to, and no hurried call afterwards interfere with the tying of their sashes. The young lady of the house is not moved by either of these motives. Five minutes is enough for her, she thinks and says, and the room is so cosey and the half light so pleasant, and it is the hour for confidences. If she has another girl with her, they will drift into beginnings of the most intimate narrative, which must be finished in their own rooms after everybody has gone to bed; and if it is not a girl, but the other kind of companion, those confidences are perhaps even more exciting. Rosalind knew what Roland Hamerton wanted, vaguely: she was, on the surface, not displeased with his devotions. She had no intention of coming to so very decided a step as marriage, nor did she for a moment contemplate him as the lover whose absence surprised her. But he was nice enough. She liked well enough to talk to him. They were like brother and sister, she would have said. "Roland—why, I have known him all my life," she would have exclaimed indignantly to any one who had blamed her for "encouraging" this poor young man. Indeed, Rosalind was so little perfect that she had already on several occasions defended herself in this way, and had not the slightest intention of accepting Roland, and yet allowed him to persuade her to linger and talk after Aunt Sophy had gone up-stairs. This was quite unjustifiable, and a more high-minded young woman would not have done it. But poor Rosalind, though her life had been crossed by a strain of tragedy and though her feelings were very deep and her experiences much out of the common, and her mind capable and ready to respond to very high claims, was yet not the ideal of a high-minded girl. It is to be hoped that she was unacquainted with flirtation and above it, but yet she did not dislike—so long as she could skilfully keep him from anything definite in the way of a proposal, anything that should be compromising and uncomfortable to sit and listen to—the vague adoration which was implied in Hamerton's talk, and to feel that the poor young fellow was laying himself out to please her. It did please her, and it amused her—which was more. It was sport to her, though it might be death to him. She did not believe that there was anything sufficiently serious in young Hamerton's feelings or in his character to involve anything like death, and she judged with some justice that he preferred the happiness of the moment, even if it inspired him with false hopes, to the collapse of all those hopes which a more conscientious treatment would have brought about. Accordingly, Rosalind lingered in the pleasant twilight. She sent her aunt's butler, Saunders, away when he appeared to light the lamps.

"Not yet, Saunders," she said, "we like the firelight," in a manner which made Roland's heart jump. It seemed to that deceived young man that nothing but a flattering response of sentiment in her mind would have made Rosalind, like himself, enjoy the firelight. "That was very sweet of you," he said.

"What was sweet of me?" The undeserved praise awakened a compunction in her. "There is nothing good in saying what is true. I do like talking by this light. Summer evenings are different, they are always a little sad; but the fire is cheerful, and it makes people confidential."

"If I could think you wanted me to be confidential, Rosalind!"

"Oh, I do; everybody! I like to talk about not only the outside, but what people are really thinking of. One hears so much of the outside: all the runs you have had, and how Captain Thornton jumps, and Miss Plympton keeps the lead."

"If you imagine that I admire Miss Plympton—"

"I never thought anything of the kind. Why shouldn't you admire her? Though she is a little too fond of hunting, she is a nice girl, and I like her. And she is very pretty. You might do a great deal worse, Roland," said Rosalind, with maternal gravity, "than admire Ethel Plympton. She is quite a nice girl, not only when she is on horseback. But she would not have anything to say to you."

"That is just as well," said the young man, "for hers is not the sort of shrine I should ever worship at. The kind of girl I like doesn't hunt, though she goes like a bird when it strikes her fancy. She is the queen at home, she makes a room like this into heaven. She makes a man feel that there's nothing in life half so sweet as to be by her, whatever she is doing. She would make hard work and poverty and all that sort of thing delightful. She is—"

"A dreadful piece of perfection!" said Rosalind, with a slightly embarrassed laugh. "Don't you know nobody likes to have that sort of person held up to them? One always suspects girls that are too good. But I hope you sometimes think of other things than girls," she added, with an air of delightful gravity and disapproval. "I have wanted all this long time to know what you were going to do; and to find instead only that hyperbolical fiend, you know, that talks of nothing but ladies, is disappointing. What would you think of me," Rosalind continued, turning upon him with still more imposing dignity, "if I talked to you of nothing but gentlemen?"

"Rosalind!—that's blasphemy to think of; besides that I should feel like getting behind a hedge and shooting all of them," the young man cried.

"Yes, it is a sort of blasphemy; you would all think a girl a dreadful creature if she did so. But you think you are different, and that it doesn't matter; that is what everybody says; one law for men and one for women. But I, for one, will never give in to that. I want to know what you are going to do."

"And suppose," he cried, "that I were to return the question, since you say there must not be one law for men and one for women. Rosalind, what are you going to do?"

"I?" she said, and looked at him with surprise. "Alas! you know I have my work cut out for me, Roland. I have to bring up the children; they are very young, and it will be a great many years before they can do without me; there is no question about me. Perhaps it is a good thing to have your path quite clear before you, so that you can't make any mistake about it," she added, with a little sigh.

"But, Rosalind, that is completely out of the question, don't you know. Sacrifice yourself and all your life to those children—why, it would be barbarous; nobody would permit it."

"I don't know," said Rosalind, "who has any right to interfere. You think Uncle John, perhaps? Uncle John would never think of anything so foolish. It is much less his business than it is mine; and you forget that I am old enough to judge for myself."

"Rosalind, you can't really intend anything so dreadful! Oh, at present you are so young, you are all living in the same house, it does not make so much difference. But to sacrifice yourself, to give up your own life, to relinquish everything for a set of half—"

"You had better not make me angry," she said. He had sprung to his feet and was pacing about in great excitement, his figure relieved against the blaze of the fire, while she sat in the shadow at one side, protected from the glow. "What am I giving up? In the first place, I know nothing that I am giving up; and I confess that it amuses me, Roland, to see you so excited about my life. I should like to hear what you are going to do with your own."

"Can't you understand?" he cried, hastily and in confusion, "that the one might—that the one might—involve perhaps—" And here the young man stopped and looked helplessly at her, not daring to risk what he had for the uncertainty of something better. But it was very hard, when he had gone so far, to refrain.

"Might involve perhaps—No, I can't understand," Rosalind said, almost with unconcern. "What I do understand is that you can't hunt forever if you are going to be any good in life. And you don't even hunt as a man ought that means to make hunting his object. Do something, Roland, as if you meant it!—that is what I am always telling you."

"And don't I always tell you the same thing, that I am no hero. I can't hold on to an object, as you say. What do you mean by an object? I want a happy life. I should like very well to be kind to people, and do my duty and all that, but as for an object, Rosalind! If you expect me to become a reformer or a philanthropist or anything of that sort, or make a great man of myself—"

Rosalind shook her head softly in her shadowed corner. "I don't expect that," she said, with a tone of regret. "I might have done so, perhaps, at one time. At first one thinks every boy can do great things, but that is only for a little while, when one is without experience."

"You see you don't think very much of my powers, for all you say," he cried, hastily, with the tone of offence which the humblest can scarcely help assuming when taken at his own low estimate. Roland knew very well that he had no greatness in him, but to have the fact acknowledged with this regretful certainty was somewhat hard.

"That is quite a different matter," said Rosalind. "Only a few men (I see now) can be great. I know nobody of that kind," she added, with once more that tone of regret, shaking her head. "But you can always do something, not hang on amusing yourself, for that is all you ever do, so far as I can see."

"What does your Uncle John do?" he cried; "you have a great respect for him, and so have I; he is just the best man going. But what does he do? He loafs about; he goes out a great deal when he is in town; he goes to Scotland for the grouse, he goes to Homburg for his health, he comes down and sees you, and then back to London again. Oh, I think that's all right, but if I am to take him for my example—and I don't know where I could find a better—"

"There is no likeness between your case and his. Uncle John is old, he has nothing particular given him to do; he is—well, he is Uncle John. But you, Roland, you are just my age."

"I'm good five years older, if not more."

"What does that matter? You are my own age, or, according to all rules of comparison between boys and girls, a little younger than me. You have got to settle upon something. I am not like many people," said Rosalind, loftily; "I don't say do this or do that; I only say, for Heaven's sake do something, Roland; don't be idle all your life."

"I should not mind so much if you did say do this or do that. Tell me something to do, Rosalind, and I'll do it for your sake."

"Oh! that is all folly; that belongs to fairy tales—a shawl that will go through a ring, or a little dog that will go into a nutshell, or a golden apple. They are all allegories, I suppose; the right thing, however, is to do what is right for the sake of what is right, and not because any one in particular tells you."

"Shall I set up in chambers, and try to get briefs?" said Roland. "But then I have enough to live on, and half the poor beggars at the bar haven't; and don't you think it would be taking an unfair advantage, when I can afford to do without and they can't, and when everybody knows there isn't half enough business to keep all going? I ask you, Rosalind, do you think that would be fair?"

Here the monitress paused, and did not make her usual eager reply. "I don't know that it is right to consider that sort of thing, Roland. You see, it would be good for you to try for briefs, and then probably the other men who want them more might be—cleverer than you are."

"Oh, very well," cried Roland, who had taken a chair close to his adviser, springing up with natural indignation; "if it is only by way of mortification, as a moral discipline, that you want me to go in for bar work."

She put out her hand and laid it on his arm. "Oh, no! it would only be fair competition. Perhaps you would be cleverer than they—than some of them."

"That's a very doubtful perhaps," he cried, with a laugh. But he was mollified and sat down again—the touch was very conciliatory. "The truth is," he said, getting hold of the hand, which she withdrew very calmly after a moment, "I am in no haste; and," with timidity, "the truth is, Rosalind, that I shall never do work anyhow by myself. If I had some one with me to stir me up and keep me going, and if I knew it was for her interest as well as for my own—"

"You mean if you were to marry?" said Rosalind, in a matter-of-fact tone, rising from her chair. "I don't approve of a man who always has to be stirred up by his wife; but marry by all means, Roland, if you think that is the best way. Nobody would have the least objection; in short, I am sure all your best friends would like it, and I, for one, would give her the warmest welcome. But still I should prefer, you know, first to see you acting for yourself. Why, there is the quarter chiming, and I promised to let Saunders know when we went to dress. Aunt Sophy will be down-stairs directly. Ring the bell, and let us run; we shall be late again. But the firelight is so pleasant." She disappeared out of the room before she had done speaking, flying up-stairs to escape the inevitable response, and left poor Roland, tantalized and troubled, to meet the gloomy looks of Saunders, who reminded him that there was but twelve minutes and a half to dress in, and that Mrs. Lennox was very particular about the fish. Saunders took liberties with the younger visitors, and he too had known young Mr. Hamerton all his life.

CHAPTER XXIX

It was not on that day, but the next, that Uncle John arrived so suddenly, bringing with him the friend whom he had picked up in Switzerland. This was a man still young, but not so young as Roland Hamerton, with looks a little worn, as of a man who had been, as he himself said, "knocking about the world." Perhaps, indeed, they all thought afterwards, it was his dress which suggested this idea; for when he appeared dressed for the evening he turned out in reality a handsome man, with the very effective contrast of hair already gray, waving upwards from a countenance not old enough to justify that change, and lighted up with dark eyes full of light and humor and life. The hair which had changed its color so early had evidently been very dark in his youth, and Mrs. Lennox, who was always a little romantic, could not help suggesting, when Rosalind and she awaited the gentlemen in the drawing-room after dinner, that Mr. Rivers might be an example of one of the favorite devices of fiction, the turning gray in a single night, which is a possibility of which every one has heard. "I should not wonder if he has had a very remarkable life," Aunt Sophy said. "No doubt the servants and common people think him quite old, but when you look into it, it is a young face." She took her chair by the fireside, and arranged all her little paraphernalia, and unfolded her crewel-work, and had done quite half a leaf before she burst forth again, as if without any interval, "though full of lines, and what you might call wrinkles if you did not know better! In my young days such a man would have been thought like Lara or Conrad, or one of Byron's other heroes. I don't know who to compare him to nowadays, for men of that sort are quite out of fashion; but he is quite a hero, I have a conviction, and saved John's life."

"He says Uncle John was in no danger, and that he did nothing that a guide or a servant might not have done."

"My dear," said Aunt Sophy, "that is what they always say; the more they do the less they will give in to it."

"To call that old man like the Wandering Jew a hero!" said little Sophy. "Yes, I have seen him. I saw him arrive with Uncle John. He looked quite old and shabby; oh, not a bit like Lara, whose hair was jet-black, and who scowled when he looked at you."

"Why, how can you tell, you little—Rosalind, I am afraid Miss Robinson must be romantic, for Sophy knows—oh, a great deal more than a little girl ought to know."

"It was in your room that I found 'Lara,'" said Sophy, "and the 'Corsair' too; I have read them all. Oh, Miss Robinson never reads them; she reads little good books where everybody dies. I do not admire Mr. Rivers at all, and if Uncle John should intend to give him one of us because he has saved his life, I hope it will not be me."

"Sophy, I shall send you to bed if you talk so. Give him one of you! I suppose you think you are in a fairy tale. Mr. Rivers would laugh if you were offered to him. He would think it was a curious reward."

"He might like Rosalind better, perhaps, now, but Rosalind has gone off, Aunt Sophy. Ferriss says so. She is getting rather old. Don't you know she is in her twenty-first year?"

"Rosalind! why, I never saw her looking better in her life. Ferriss shall be sent away if she talks such impertinence. And she is just twenty! Going off! she is not the least going off: her complexion is just beautiful, and so fresh. I don't know what you mean, you or Ferriss either!" Mrs. Lennox cried. She had always a little inclination to believe what was suggested to her; and, notwithstanding the complete assurance of her words, she followed Rosalind, who was moving about at the other end of the room, with eyes that were full of sudden alarm.

"And I am in my thirteenth year," said Sophy; "it sounds much better than to say only twelve. I shall improve, but Rosalind will not improve. If he were sensible, he would like me best."

"Don't let your sister hear you talk such nonsense, Sophy: and remember that I forbid you to read the books in my room without asking me first. There are things that are very suitable for me, or even for Rosalind, but not for you. And what are you doing down-stairs at this hour, Sophy? I did not remember the hour, but it is past your bedtime. Miss Robinson should not let you have so much of your own way."

"It was because of Uncle John," said Rosalind. "What has she been saying about Lara and the Corsair? I could not hear, Saunders made so much noise with the tea. Here is your tea, Aunt Sophy, though you know Dr. Beaton says you ought not to take it after dinner, and that it keeps you from sleeping."

"Dr. Beaton goes upon the new-fashioned rules, my dear," said Mrs. Lennox. "It never keeps me from my sleep; nothing does that, thank God. It is the young people that are so delicate nowadays, that can't take this and that. I wonder if John has any news of Dr. Beaton. He had a great many fads like that about the tea, but he was very nice. What a comfort he was to poor Reginald, and took so much anxiety off Gra—"

"I declare," Aunt Sophy cried, coloring and coughing, "I have caught cold, though I have not been out of the house since the cold weather set in. My dear, I am so sorry," she added in an undertone; "I know I should not have said a word—"

"I have never been of that opinion," said Rosalind, shaking her head sadly. "I think you are all taking the wrong way."

"For Heaven's sake don't say a word, Rosalind; with John coming in, and that little thing with ears as sharp—"

"Is it me that have ears so sharp, Aunt Sophy? It is funny to hear you talk. You think I don't know anything, but I know everything. I know why Roland Hamerton is always coming here; and I know why Mr. Blake never comes, but only the old gentleman. And, Rosalind, you had better make up your mind and take some one, for you are getting quite passée, and you will soon be an old maid."

"Sophy! if you insult your sister—"

"Do you think that is insulting me?" Rosalind said. "I believe I shall be an old maid. That would suit me best, and it would be best for the children, who will want me for a long time."

"My dear," said Aunt Sophy, solemnly, "there are some things I will never consent to, and one of them is, a girl like you making such a sacrifice. That is what I will never give in to. Oh, go away, Sophy, you are a perfect nuisance! No, no, I will never give in to it. For such a sacrifice is always repented of. When the children grow up they will not be a bit grateful to you; they will never think it was for them you did it. They will talk of you as if it was something laughable, and as if you could not help it. An old maid! Yes, it is intended for an insult, and I won't have it, any more than I will have you do it, Rosalind."

"Oh, Uncle John," cried the enfant terrible, "there is Aunt Sophy with tears in her eyes because I said Rosalind was going to be an old maid. But it is not anything so very dreadful, is it? Why, Uncle John, you are an old maid."

"I don't think Rosalind's prospects need distress you, Sophy," said Uncle John. "We can take care of her in any case. She will not want your valuable protection."

"Oh, I was not thinking of myself; I don't mind at all," said Sophy; "but only she is getting rather old. Don't you see a great difference, Uncle John? She is in her twenty-first year."

"I shall not lose hope till she has completed her thirty-third," said Uncle John. "You may run away, Sophy; you are young enough, fortunately, to be sent to bed."

"I am in my thirteenth," said Sophy, resisting every step of her way to the door, dancing in front of her uncle, who was directing her towards it. When Sophy found that resistance was vain, she tried entreaty.

"Oh, Uncle John, don't send me away! Rosalind promised I should sit up to-night because you were coming home."

"Then Rosalind must take the consequences," said John Trevanion. All this time the stranger had been standing silent, with a slight smile on his face, watching the whole party, and forming those unconscious conclusions with which we settle everybody's character and qualities when we come into a new place. This little skirmish was all in his favor, as helping him to a comprehension of the situation; the saucy child, the indulgent old aunt, the disapproving guardian, of whom alone Sophy was a little afraid, made a simple group enough. But when he turned to the subject of the little disturbance, he found in Rosalind's smile a curious light thrown upon the altercation. Was she in real danger of becoming an old maid? He thought her looking older than the child had said, a more gracious and perfect woman than was likely to be the subject of such a controversy; and he saw, by the eager look and unnecessary indignation of Hamerton, sufficient evidence that the fate of the elder sister was by no means so certain as Sophy thought, and that, at all events, it was in her own hands. The young fellow had seemed to Mr. Rivers a pleasant young fellow enough in the after-dinner talk, but when he thus involuntarily coupled him with Rosalind, his opinion changed in a curious way. The young man was not good enough for her. A touch of indignation mingled, he could not tell why, in this conclusion; indignation against unconscious Roland, who aspired to one so much above him, and at the family who were so little aware that this girl was the only one of them the least remarkable. He smiled at himself afterwards for the earnestness with which he decided all this; settling the character of people whom he had never seen before in so unjustifiable a fashion. The little new world thus revealed to him had nothing very novel in it. The only interesting figure was the girl who was in her twenty-first year. She was good enough for the heroine of a romance of a higher order than any that could be involved in the mild passion of young Hamerton; and it pleased the stranger to think, from the unconcerned way in which Rosalind looked at her admirer, that she was evidently of this opinion too.

"Rosalind," said John Trevanion, after the episode of Sophy was over, and she was safely dismissed to bed, "will you show Rivers the miniatures? He is a tremendous authority on art."

"Bring the little lamp then, Uncle John; there is not light enough. We are very proud of them ourselves, but if Mr. Rivers is a great authority, perhaps they will not please him so much."

She took up the lamp herself as she spoke, and its light gave a soft illumination to her face, looking up at him with a smile. It was certain that there was nothing so interesting here as she was. The miniatures! well, yes, they were not bad miniatures. He suggested a name as the painter of the best among them which pleased John Trevanion, and fixed the date in a way which fell in entirely with family traditions. Perhaps he would not have been so gracious had the exhibitor been less interesting. He took the lamp, which she had insisted upon holding, out of her hand when the inspection was done, and set it down upon a table which was at some distance from the fireside group. It was a writing-table, with indications upon it of the special ownership of Rosalind. But this he could not be supposed to know. He thought it would be pleasant, however, to detain her here in conversation, apart from the others who were so much more ordinary, for he was a man who liked to appropriate to himself the best of everything. And fortune favored his endeavors. As he put down the lamp his eye was caught by a photograph framed in a sort of shrine, which stood upon the table. The doors of the little shrine were open, and he stooped to look at the face within, at the sight of which he uttered an exclamation. "I know that lady very well," he said.

In a moment the courteous attention which Rosalind had been giving him turned into eager interest. She made a hurried step forward, clasped her hands together, and raised to him eyes which all at once had filled with sudden tragic meaning, anxiety, and suspense. If there had seemed to him before much more in her than in any of the others, there was a hundredfold more now. He seemed in a moment to have got at the very springs of her life. "Oh, where, where have you seen her? When did you see her? Tell me all you know," Rosalind cried. She turned to him, betraying in her every gesture an excess of suddenly awakened feeling, and waited breathless, repeating her inquiry with her eyes.

"I was afraid, from the way in which her portrait was framed, that perhaps she was no longer—"

Rosalind gave a low cry, following the very movements of his lips with her eager eyes. Then she exclaimed, "No, no, she must be living, or we should have heard."

"What is it, Rosalind?" said John Trevanion, looking somewhat pale and anxious too, as he turned round to join them.

"Uncle John, Mr. Rivers knows her. He is going to tell me something."

"But really I have nothing to tell, Miss Trevanion. I fear I have excited your interest on false pretences. It is such an interesting face—so beautiful in its way."

"Oh, yes, yes."

"I met the lady last year in Spain. I cannot say that I know her, though I said so in the surprise of the moment. One could not see her without being struck with her appearance."

"Oh, yes, yes!" Rosalind cried again, eagerly, with her eyes demanding more.

"I met her several times. They were travelling out of the usual routes. I have exchanged a few chance words with her at the door of a hotel, or on the road, changing horses. I am sorry to say that was all, Miss Trevanion."

"Last year; that is later than we have heard. And was she well? Was she very sad? Did she say anything? But, oh, how could she say anything? for she could not tell," cried Rosalind, her eyes filling, "that you were coming here."

"Hush, Rosalind. You say they, Rivers. She was not alone, then?"

"Alone? oh, no, there was a man with her. I never could," said Rivers, lightly, "make out who he was—more like a son or brother than her husband. But, to be sure, you who know the lady—"

He paused, entirely unable to account for the effect he had produced. Rosalind had grown as pale as marble; her mouth quivered, her hands trembled. She gave him the most pathetic, reproachful look, as a woman might have done whom he had stabbed unawares, and, getting up quickly from his side, went away with an unsteady, wavering movement, as if it were all her strength could do to get out of the room. Hamerton rushed forward to open the door for her, but he was too late, and he too came to look at Rivers with inquiring, indignant looks, as if to say, What have you done to her? "What have I done—what is wrong, Trevanion? Have I said anything I ought not to have said?" Rivers cried.

The only answer John Trevanion made was to drop down upon the seat Rosalind had left, with a suppressed groan, and to cover his face with his hands.

CHAPTER XXX

Rosalind came down to breakfast next morning at the usual hour. She was the most important member of the household party, and everything depended upon her. Sometimes Aunt Sophy would have a little cold and did not appear. She considered it was her right to take her leisure in the mornings; but Rosalind was like the mother of the young ones, and indispensable. Rivers had come down early, which is an indiscreet thing for a stranger to do in a house with which he is unacquainted. He felt this when Rosalind came into the breakfast-room, and found Sophy, full of excitement and delight in thus taking the most important place, entertaining him. He thought Rosalind looked at him with a sort of question in her eyes, which she turned away the next moment; but afterwards put force upon herself and came up to him, bidding him good-morning. He was so much interested that he felt he could follow the processes in her mind; that she reproved herself for her distaste to him, and said within herself, it is no fault of his. He did not yet at all know what he had done, but conjectured that the woman whose photograph was on Rosalind's table must be some dear friend or relation who had either made an imprudent marriage, or, still worse, "gone wrong." It was the mention of the man who had been with her which had done all the mischief. He wished that he had bitten his tongue rather than made that unfortunate disclosure, which evidently had plunged them into trouble. But then, how was he to know? As for Rosalind, her pain was increased and complicated by finding this new visitor with the children; Sophy, her eyes dancing with excitement and pleasure, doing her utmost to entertain him. Sophy had that complete insensibility which is sometimes to be seen in a clever child whose satisfaction with her own cleverness overbalances all feeling. She was just as likely as not to have poured forth all the family history into this new-comer's ears; to have let him know that mamma had gone away when papa died, and that nobody knew where she had gone. This gave Rosalind an additional alarm, but overcame her repugnance to address the stranger who had brought news so painful, for it was better at once to check Sophy's revelations, whatever they might have been. That lively little person turned immediately upon her sister, knowing by instinct that her moment of importance was over. "What a ghost you do look, Rosie!" she cried; "you look as if you had been crying. Just as I do when Miss Robinson is nasty. But nobody can scold you except Aunt Sophy, and she never does; though—oh, I forgot, there is Uncle John."

"Miss Robinson will be here before you are ready for her, Sophy," said Rosalind. "I fear I am a little late. Has she been giving you the carte du pays, Mr. Rivers? She is more fond of criticism than little girls should be."

"I have had a few sketches of the neighborhood," he answered quickly, divining her fears. "She is an excellent mimic, I should suppose, but it is rather a dangerous quality. If you take me off, Miss Sophy, as you take off the old ladies, I shall not enjoy it."

Rosalind was relieved, he could see. She gave him a look that was almost grateful as she poured out his coffee, though he had done nothing to call forth her gratitude, any more than he had done anything last night to occasion her sorrow. A stranger in a new household, of which he has heard nothing before, being introduced into it, is like an explorer in an unknown country; he does not know when he may find himself on forbidden ground, or intruding into religious mysteries. He began to talk of himself, which seemed the safest subject; it was one which he was not eager to launch upon, but yet which had come in handy on many previous occasions. His life had been full of adventures. There were a hundred things in it to tell, and it had delivered him from many a temporary embarrassment to introduce a chapter out of his varied experiences. He had shot elephants in Africa and tigers in India. He had been a war-correspondent in the height of every military movement. "I have been one of the rolling stones that gather no moss," he said, "though it is a kind of moss to have so many stories to tell. If the worst comes to the worst, I can go from house to house and amuse the children." He did it so skilfully that Rosalind felt her agitation calmed. A man who could fall so easily into this narrative vein, and who was, apparently, so full of his own affairs, would not think twice, she reflected, of such a trifling incident as that of last night. If she had judged more truly, she would perhaps have seen that the observer who thus dismissed the incident totally, with such an absence of all consciousness on the subject, was precisely the one most likely to have perceived, even if he did not understand how, that it was an incident of great importance. But Rosalind was not sufficiently learned in moral philosophy to have found out that.

Her feelings were not so carefully respected by Roland Hamerton, who would have given everything he had in the world to please her, but yet was not capable of perceiving what, in this matter at least, was the right way to do so. He had, though he was not one of the group round the writing-table, heard enough to understand what had happened on the previous night, solely, it would seem, by that strange law which prevails in human affairs, by which the obstacles of distance and the rules of acoustics are set aside as soon as something is going on which it is undesirable for the spectators to hear. In this way Hamerton had made out what it was; that Madam had been seen by the stranger, travelling with a man. Rosalind's sudden departure from the room, her face of anguish, the speed with which she disappeared, and the confused looks of those whom she thus hastily left, roused young Hamerton to something like the agitation into which he had been plunged by the incidents of that evening, now so long past, when Madam Trevanion had appeared in the drawing-room at Highcourt with that guilty witness of her nocturnal expedition clinging to her dress. He had been then almost beside himself with the painful nature of the discovery which he had made. What should he do—keep the knowledge to himself, or communicate it to those who had a right to know? Roland was so unaccustomed to deal with difficulties of this kind that he had felt it profoundly, and at the end had held his peace, rather because it was the easiest thing to do than from any better reason. It returned to his mind now, with all the original trouble and perception of a duty which he could not define. Here was Rosalind, the most perfect, the sweetest, the girl whom he loved, wasting her best affections upon a woman who was unworthy of them; standing by her, defending her, insisting even upon respect and honor for her—and suffering absolute anguish, such as he had seen last night, when the veil was lifted for a moment from that mysterious darkness of intrigue and shame into which she had disappeared. If she only knew and could be convinced that Madam had been unworthy all the time, would not that deliver her? Roland thought that he was able to prove this; he had never wavered in his own judgment. All his admiration and regard for Mrs. Trevanion had been killed at a blow by the shock he had received, by what he had seen. He could not bear to think that such a woman should retain Rosalind's affection. And he thought he had it in his power to convince Rosalind, to make her see everything in its true light. This conviction was not come to without pain. The idea of opening such a subject at all, of speaking of what was impure and vile in Rosalind's hearing, of looking in her eyes, which knew no evil, and telling her such a tale, was terrible to the young man. But yet he thought it ought to be done. Certainly it ought to be done. Had she seen what he had seen, did she know what he knew, she would give up at once that championship which she had held so warmly. It had always been told him that though men might forgive a woman who had fallen, no woman ever did so; and how must an innocent girl, ignorant, incredulous of all evil, feel towards one who had thus sinned? What could she do but flee from her in terror, in horror, with a condemnation which would be all the more relentless, remorseless, from her own incapacity to understand either the sin or the temptation? But no doubt it would be a terrible shock to Rosalind. This was the only thing that held him back. It would be a blow which would shake the very foundations of her being: for she could not suspect, she could not even know of what Madam was suspected, or she would never stand by her so. Now, however, that her peace had been disturbed by this chance incident, there was a favorable opportunity for Roland. It was his duty now, he thought, to strike to the root of her fallacy. It was better for her that she should be entirely undeceived.

Thinking about this, turning it over and over in his mind, had cost him almost his night's rest: not altogether. If the world itself had gone to pieces, Roland would still have got a few hours' repose. He allowed to himself that he had got a few hours, but, as a matter of fact, he had been thinking of this the last thing when he went to sleep, and it was the first thing that occurred to him when he awoke. The frost had given way, but he said to himself that he would not hunt that day. He would go on to the Elms; he would manage somehow to see Rosalind by herself, and he would have it out. If in her pain her heart was softened, and she was disposed to turn to him for sympathy, then he could have it all out, and so get a little advantage out of his anxiety for her good. Indeed, she had snubbed him yesterday and made believe that she did not know who it was he wanted for his companion and guide; but that was nothing. Girls did so, he had often heard—staved off a proposal when they knew it was coming, even though they did not mean to reject it when it came. That was nothing. But when she was in trouble, when her heart was moved, who could say that she would not cling to him for sympathy? And there was nobody that could sympathize with her as he could. He pictured to himself how he would draw her close to him, and bid her cry as much as she liked on his faithful bosom. That faithful bosom heaved with a delicious throb. He would not mind her crying; she might cry us long as she pleased—there.

And, as it happened, by a chance which seemed to Roland providential, he found Rosalind alone when he entered the drawing-room at the Elms. Mrs. Lennox had taken Sophy with her in the carriage to the dentist at Clifton; Roland felt a certain satisfaction in knowing that Sophy, that little imp of mischief, was going to have a tooth drawn. The gentlemen were out, and Miss Rosalind was alone. Roland could have hugged Saunders for this information; he gave him a sovereign, which pleased the worthy man much better, and flew three steps at a time up-stairs. Rosalind was seated by her writing-table. It subdued him at once to see her attitude. She had been crying already. She had not waited for the faithful bosom. And he thought that when she was disturbed by the opening of the door, she had closed the little gates of that carved shrine in which Madam's picture dwelt; otherwise she did not move when she saw who her visitor was, but nodded to him, with relief, he thought. "Is it you, Roland? I thought you were sure to be out to-day," she said.

"No, I didn't go out. I hadn't the heart." He came and sat down by her where she had made Rivers sit the previous night; she looked up at him with a little surprise.

"Hadn't the heart! What is the matter, Roland? Have you had bad news—is there anything wrong at home?"

"No—nothing about my people. Rosalind, I haven't slept a wink all night"—which was exaggeration, the reader knows—"thinking about you."

"About me!" She smiled, then blushed a little, and then made an attempt to recover the composure with which yesterday she had so calmly ignored his attempts at love-making. "I don't see why you should lose your sleep about me; was it a little toothache—perhaps neuralgia? I know you are sometimes subject to that."

"Rosalind," he said, solemnly, "you must not laugh at me to-day. It is nothing to laugh at. I could not help hearing what that fellow said last night."

The color ebbed away out of Rosalind's face, but not the courage. "Yes!" she said, half affirmation, half interrogation; "that he had met mamma abroad."

"I can't bear to hear you call her mamma. And it almost killed you to hear what he said."

She did not make any attempt to defend herself, but grew whiter, as if she would faint, and her mouth quivered again. "Well," she said, "I do not deny that—that I was startled. Her dear name, that alone is enough to agitate me, and to hear of her like that without warning, in a moment."

The tears rose to her eyes, but she still looked him in the face, though she scarcely saw him through that mist.

"Well," she said again—she took some time to master herself before she was able to speak—"if I did feel it very much, that was not wonderful. I was taken by surprise. For the first moment, just in the confusion, knowing what wickedness people think, I—I—lost heart altogether. It was too dreadful and miserable, but I was not very well, I suppose. I am not going to shirk it at all, Roland. She was travelling with a gentleman—well! and what then?"

"Oh, Rosalind!" he cried, with a sort of horror, "after that, can you stand up for her still?"

"I don't know what there is to stand up for. My mother is not a girl like me. She is the best judge of what is right. When I had time to think, that became a matter of course, as plain as daylight."

"And you don't mind?" he said.

She turned upon him something of the same look which she had cast on Rivers, a look of anguish and pathos, reproachful, yet with a sort of tremulous smile.

"Oh, Rosalind," he cried, "I can't bear to look at you like that. I can't bear to see you so deceived. I'll tell you what I saw myself. Nobody was more fond of Madam than I. I'd have gone to the stake for her. But that night—that night, if you remember, when the thorn was hanging to her dress, I had gone away into the conservatory because I couldn't bear to hear your father going on. Rosalind, just hear out what I have got to say. And there I saw—oh, saw! with my own eyes—I saw her standing—with a man—I saw them part, he going away into the shadow of the shrubbery, she—Rosalind!"

She had risen up, and stood towering (as he felt) over him, as if she had grown to double her height in a moment. "Do you tell me this," she said, steadying herself with an effort, moistening her lips between her words to be able to speak—"do you tell me this to make me love you, or hate you?"

"Rosalind, to undeceive you, that you may know the truth."

"Go away!" she said. She pointed with her arm to the door. "Go away! It is not the truth. If it were the truth, I should never forgive you, I should never speak to you again. But it is not the truth. Go away!"

"Rosalind!"

"Must I put you out," she cried, in the passion which now and then overcame her, stamping her foot upon the floor, "with my own hands?"

Alas! he carried the faithful bosom which was of no use to her to cry upon, but which throbbed with pain and trouble all the same, out of doors. He was utterly cowed and subdued, not understanding her, nor himself, nor what had happened. It was the truth, she might deny it as she pleased; he had meant it for the best. But now he had done for himself, that was evident. And perhaps, after all, he was a cad to tell.

CHAPTER XXXI

Arthur Rivers had come to Clifton not to visit a new friend, but to see his own family, who lived there. They were not, perhaps, quite on the same level as the Trevanions and Mrs. Lennox, who did not know them. And so it came to pass that, after the few days which he passed at the Elms, and in which he did everything he could to obliterate the recollection of that first unfortunate reference on the night of his arrival, he was for some time in the neighborhood without seeing much of them. To the mistress of the house at least this was agreeable, and a relief. She had, indeed, taken so strong a step as to remonstrate with her brother on the subject.

"I am not quite sure that it was judicious to bring a man like that, so amusing and nice to talk to, into the company of a girl like Rosalind, without knowing who his people were," Mrs. Lennox said. "I don't like making a fuss, but it was not judicious—not quite judicious," she added, faltering a little as she felt the influence of John's eyes.

"What does it matter to us who his people are?" said John Trevanion (which was so like a man, Mrs. Lennox said to herself). "He is himself a capital fellow, and I am under obligations to him; and as for Rosalind—Rosalind is not likely to be fascinated by a man of that age; and, besides, if there had ever been any chance of that, he completely put his foot into it the first night."

"Do you think so?" said Aunt Sophy, doubtfully. "Now you know you all laugh at Mrs. Malaprop and her sayings. But I have always thought there was a great deal of good sense in one of them, and that is when she speaks of people beginning with a little aversion. Oh, you may smile, but it's true. It is far better than being indifferent. Rosalind will think a great deal more of the man because he made her very angry. And, as he showed after that, he could make himself exceedingly pleasant."

"He did not make her angry."

"Oh, I thought you said he did. Something about poor Grace—that he met her and thought badly of her—or something. I shall take an opportunity when he calls to question him myself. I dare say he will tell me more."

"Don't, unless you wish to distress me very much, Sophy; I would rather not hear anything about her, nor take him into our family secrets."

"Do you think not, John? Oh, of course I will do nothing to displease you. Perhaps, on the whole, indeed, it will be better not to have him come here any more on account of Rosalind, for of course his people—"

"Who are his people?—he is a man of education himself. I don't see why we should take it to heart whatever his people may be."

"Oh, well, there is a brother a doctor, I believe, and somebody who is a schoolmaster, and the mother and sister, who live in—quite a little out-of-the-way place."

"I thought you must mean a green-grocer," said John. "Let him alone, Sophy, that is the best way; everything of the kind is best left to nature. I shall be very happy to see him if he comes, and I will not break my heart if he doesn't come. It is always most easy, and generally best, to let things alone."

"Well, if you think so, John." There was a little hesitation in Mrs. Lennox's tone, but it was not in her to enforce a contrary view. And as it was a point he insisted upon that nothing should be said to Rosalind on the subject, that, too, was complied with. It was not, indeed, a subject on which Mrs. Lennox desired to tackle Rosalind. She had herself the greatest difficulty in refraining from all discussion of poor Grace, but she never cared to discuss her with Rosalind, who maintained Mrs. Trevanion's cause with an impetuosity which confused all her aunt's ideas. She could not hold her own opinion against professions of faith so strenuously made; and yet she did hold it in a wavering way, yielding to Rosalind's vehemence for the moment, only to resume her own convictions with much shaking of her head when she was by herself. It was difficult for her to maintain her first opinion on the subject of Mr. Rivers and his people. When he called he made himself so agreeable that Mrs. Lennox could not restrain the invitation that rushed to her lips. "John will be so sorry that he has missed you; won't you come and dine with us on Saturday?" she said, before she could remember that it was not desirable he should be encouraged to come to the house. And Rosalind had been so grateful to him for never returning to the subject of the photograph, or seeming to remember anything about it, that his natural attraction was rather increased than diminished to her by that incident. There were few men in the neighborhood who talked like Mr. Rivers. He knew everybody, he had been everywhere. Sometimes, when he talked of the beautiful places he had seen, Rosalind was moved by a thrill of expectation; she waited almost breathless for a mention of Spain, for something that would recall to him the interrupted conversation of the first evening. But he kept religiously apart from every mention of Spain. He passed by the writing-table upon which the shrine in which the portrait was enclosed stood, now always shut, without so much as a glance which betrayed any association with it, any recollection. Thank Heaven, he had forgotten all that, it had passed from his mind as a mere trivial accident without importance. She was satisfied, yet disappointed, too. But it never occurred to Rosalind that this scrupulous silence meant that Rivers had by no means forgotten; and he was instantly conscious that the portrait was covered; he lost nothing of these details. Though the story had faded out of the recollection of the Clifton people, to whom it had never been well known, he did not fail to discover something of the facts of the case; and, perhaps, it was the existence of a mystery which led him back to the Elms, and induced him to accept Mrs. Lennox's invitation to come on Saturday. This fact lessened the distance between the beautiful young Miss Trevanion, and the man whose "people" were not at all on the Highcourt level. He had thought at first that it would be his best policy to take himself away and see as little as might be of Rosalind. But when he heard that there was "some story about the mother," he ceased to feel the necessity for so much self-denial. When there is a story about a mother it does the daughter harm socially; and Rivers was not specially diffident about his own personal claims. The disadvantage on his side of having "people" who were not in society was neutralized on hers by having a mother who had been talked of. Neither of these facts harmed the individual. He, Arthur Rivers, was not less of a personage in his own right because his mother lived in a small street in Clifton and was nobody; and she, Rosalind Trevanion, was not less delightful because her mother had been breathed upon by scandal; but the drawback on her side brought them upon something like an equality, and did away with the drawback on his, which was not so great a drawback. This, at least, was how he reasoned. He did not even know that the lady about whom there was a story was not Rosalind's mother, and he could not make up his mind whether it was possible that the lady whom he had recognized could be that mother. But after he had turned the whole matter over in his mind, after a week had elapsed, and he had considered it from every point of view, he went over to the Elms and called. This was the result of his thoughts.

It must not be concluded from these reflections that he had fallen in love at first sight, according to a mode which has gone out of fashion. He had not, perhaps, gone so far as that. He was a man of his time, and took no such plunges into the unseen. But Rosalind Trevanion had somewhat suddenly detached herself from all other images when he came, after years of wandering, into the kind of easy acquaintance with her which is produced by living, even if it is only from Saturday to Monday, in the same house. He had met all kinds of women of the world, old and young—some of them quite young, younger than Rosalind—in the spheres which he had frequented most; but not any that were so fresh, so maidenly, so full of charm, and yet so little artificial; no child, but a woman, and yet without a touch of that knowledge which stains the thoughts. This was what had caught his attention amid the simple but conventional circumstances that surrounded her. Innocence is sometimes a little silly; or so, at least, this man of the world thought. But Rosalind understood as quickly, and had as much intelligence in her eyes, as any of his former acquaintances, and yet was as entirely without any evil knowledge as a child. It had startled him strangely to meet that look of hers, so pathetic, so reproachful, though he did not know why. Something deeper still was in that look; it was the look an angel might have given to one who drew his attention to a guilt or a misery from which he could give no deliverance. The shame of the discovery, the anguish of it, the regret and heart-breaking pity, all these shone in Rosalind's eyes. He had never been able to forget that look. And he could not get her out of his mind, do what he would. No, it was not falling in love; for he was quite cool and able to think over the question whether, as she was much younger, better off, and of more important connections than himself, he had not better go away and see her no more. He took this fully into consideration from every point of view, reflecting that the impression made upon him was slight as yet and might be wiped out, whereas if he remained at Clifton and visited the Elms it might become more serious, and lead him further than it would be prudent to go. But if there was a story about the mother—if it was possible that the mother might be wandering over Europe in the equivocal company of some adventurer—this was an argument which might prevent any young dukes from "coming forward," and might make a man who was not a duke, nor of any lofty lineage, more likely to be received on his own standing.

This course of thought took him some time, as we have said, during which his mother, a simple woman who was very proud of him, could not think why Arthur should be so slow to keep up with "his friends the Trevanions," who ranked among the county people, and were quite out of her humble range. She said to her daughter that it was silly of Arthur. "He thinks nothing of them because he is used to the very first society both in London and abroad," she said. "But he ought to remember that Clifton is different, and they are quite the best people here." "Why don't you go and see your fine friends?" she said to her son. "Oh, no, Arthur, I am not foolish; I don't expect Mrs. Lennox and Miss Trevanion to visit me and the girls; I think myself just as good in my way, but of course there is a difference; not for you though, Arthur, who have met the Prince of Wales and know everybody—I think it is your duty to keep them up." At this he laughed, saying nothing, but thought all the more; and at last, at the end of a week, he came round to his mother's opinion, and made up his mind that, if not his duty, it was at least a reasonable and not imprudent indulgence. And upon this argument he called, and was invited on the spot by Mrs. Lennox, who had just been saying how imprudent it was of John to have brought him to the house, to come and dine on Saturday. Thus things which have never appeared possible come about.

He went on Saturday and dined, and as a bitter frost had come on, and all the higher world of the neighborhood was coming on Monday to the pond near the Elms to skate, if the frost held, was invited for that too; and went, and was introduced to a great many people, and made himself quite a reputation before the day was over. There never had been a more successful début in society. And a Times' Correspondent! Nobody cared who was his father or what his family; he had enough in himself to gain admittance everywhere. And he had a distinguished look, with his gray hair and bright eyes, far more than the ordinary man of his age who is beginning to get rusty, or perhaps bald, which is not becoming. Mr. Rivers's hair was abundant and full of curl; there was no sign of age in his handsome face and vigorous figure, which made the whiteness of his locks piquant. Indeed, there was no one about, none of the great county gentlemen, who looked so imposing. Rosalind, half afraid of him, half drawn towards him, because, notwithstanding the dreadful disclosure he had made, he had admired and remembered the woman whom she loved, and more than half grateful to him for never having touched on the subject again, was half proud now of the notice he attracted, and because he more or less belonged to her party. She was pleased that he should keep by her side and manifestly devote himself to her. Thus it happened that she ceased to ask herself the question which has been referred to in previous pages, and began to think that the novels were right, after all, and that the commodity in which they dealt so largely did fall to every woman's lot.

CHAPTER XXXII

Roland Hamerton was not one of those on whom Mr. Rivers made this favorable impression. He would fain indeed have found something against him, something which would have justified him in stigmatizing as a "cad," or setting down as full of conceit, the new-comer about whom everybody was infatuated. Roland was not shabby enough to make capital out of the lowliness of Arthur's connections, though the temptation to do so crossed his mind more than once; but the young man was a gentleman, and could not, even in all the heat of rivalship, make use of such an argument. There was, indeed, nothing to be said against the man whom Roland felt, with a pang, to be so much more interesting than himself; a man who knew when to hold his tongue as well as when to speak; who would never have gone and done so ridiculous a thing as he (Hamerton) had done, trying to convince a girl against her will and to shake her partisan devotion. The young fellow perceived now what a mad idea this had been, but unfortunately it is not till after the event that a simple mind learns such a lesson. Rivers, who was older, had no doubt found it out by experience, or else he had a superior instinct and was a better diplomatist, or perhaps thought less of the consequences involved. It wounded Roland to think of the girl he loved as associated in any way with a woman who was under a stain. He could not bear to think that her robe of whiteness should ever touch the garments of one who was sullied. But afterwards, when he came to think, he saw how foolish he had been. Perhaps Rosalind felt, though she could not allow it, everything he had ventured to suggest; but, naturally, when it was said to her brutally by an outsider, she would flare up. Roland could remember, even in his own limited experience, corresponding instances. He saw the defects of the members of his own family clearly enough, but if any one else ventured to point them out! Yes, yes, he had been a fool, and he had met with the fate he deserved. Rosalind had said conditionally that if it were true she would never speak to him again, but that it was not true. She had thus left for herself a way of escape. He knew very well that it was all truth he had said, but he was glad enough to take advantage of her wilful scepticism when he perceived that it afforded a way of escape from the sentence of excommunication otherwise to be pronounced against him. He stayed away from the Elms for a time, which was also the time of the frost, when there was nothing to be done; but ventured on the third or fourth day to the pond to skate, and was invited by Mrs. Lennox, as was natural, to stay and dine, which he accepted eagerly when he perceived that Rosalind, though cold, was not inexorable. She said very little to him for that evening or many evenings after, but still she did not carry out her threat of never speaking to him again. But when he met the other, as he now did perpetually, it was not in human nature to preserve an unbroken amiability. He let Rivers see by many a silent indication that he hated him, and found him in his way. He became disagreeable, poor boy, by dint of rivalry and the galling sense he had of the advantages possessed by the new-comer. He would go so far as to sneer at travellers' tales, and hint a doubt that there might be another version of such and such an incident. When he had been guilty of suggestions of this kind he was overpowered with shame. But it is very hard to be generous to a man who has the better of you in every way; who is handsomer, cleverer, even taller; can talk far better, can amuse people whom you only bore; and when you attempt to argue can turn you, alas! inside out with a touch of his finger. The prudent thing for Roland to have done would have been to abstain from any comparison of himself with his accomplished adversary; but he was not wise enough to do this: few, very few, young men are so wise. He was always presenting his injured, offended, clouded face, by the side of the fine features and serene, secure look of the elder man, who was thus able to contemplate him, and, worse, to present him to others, in the aspect of a mad youngster, irritable and unreasoning. Roland was acutely, painfully aware that this was not his character at all, and yet that he had the appearance of it, and that Rosalind no doubt must consider him so. The union of pain, resentment, indignation at the thought of such injustice, with a sense that it scarcely was injustice, and that he was doing everything to justify it, made the poor young fellow as miserable as can be imagined. He did not deserve to be so looked upon, and yet he did deserve it; and Rivers was an intolerable prig and tyrant, using a giant's strength villainously as a giant, yet in a way which was too cunning to afford any opening for reproach. He could have wept in his sense of the intolerable, and yet he had not a word to say. Was there ever a position more difficult to bear? And poor Roland felt that he had lost ground in every way. Ever since that unlucky interference of his and disclosure of his private information (which he saw now was the silliest thing that could have been done) there was no lingering in the fire-light, no tête-à-tête ever accorded to him. When Mrs. Lennox went to dress for dinner, Rosalind went too. After a while she ceased to show her displeasure, and talked to him as usual when they met in the presence of the family, but he saw her by herself no more. He could not make out indeed whether that fellow was ever admitted to any such privilege, but it certainly was extended to himself no more.

The neighborhood began to take a great interest in the Elms when this rivalship first became apparent, which it need not have done had Hamerton shown any command of himself; for Mr. Rivers was perfectly well-bred, and there is nothing in which distinguished manners show more plainly than in the way by which, in the first stage of a love-making, a man can secure the object of his devotion from all remark. There can be no better test of a high-bred gentleman; and though he was only the son of an humble family with no pretension to be considered county people, he answered admirably to it. Rosalind was herself conscious of the special homage he paid her, but no one else would have been at all the wiser had it not been for the ridiculous jealousy of Roland, who could not contain himself in Rivers's presence.

The position of Rosalind between these two men was a little different from the ordinary ideal. The right thing to have done in her circumstances would have been, had she "felt a preference," as it was expressed in the eighteenth century, to have, with all the delicacy and firmness proper to maidenhood, so discouraged and put down the one who was not preferred as to have left him no excuse for persisting in his vain pretensions. If she had no preference she ought to have gently but decidedly made both aware that their homage was vain. As for taking any pleasure in it, if she did not intend in either case to recompense it—that would not be thought of for a moment. But Rosalind, though she had come in contact with so much that was serious in life, and had so many of its gravest duties to perform, was yet so young and so natural as not to be at all superior to the pleasure of being sought. She liked it, though her historian does not know how to make the admission. No doubt, had she been accused of such a sentiment, she would have denied it hotly and even with some indignation, not being at all in the habit of investigating the phenomena of her own mind; but yet she did not in her heart dislike to feel that she was of the first importance to more than one beholder, and that her presence or absence made a difference in the aspect of the world to two men. A sense of being approved, admired, thought much of, is always agreeable. Even when the sentiment does not go the length of love, there is a certain moral support in the consciousness in a girl's mind that she embodies to some one the best things in humankind. When the highest instincts of love touch the heart it becomes a sort of profanity, indeed, to think of any but the one who has awakened that divine inspiration; but, in the earlier stages, before any sentiment has become definite, or her thoughts begun to contemplate any final decision, there is a secret gratification in the mere consciousness. It may not be an elevated feeling, but it is a true one. She is pleased; there is a certain elation in her veins in spite of herself. Mr. Ruskin says that a good girl should have seven suitors at least, all ready to do impossibilities in her service, among whom she should choose, but not too soon, letting each have a chance. Perhaps in the present state of statistics this is somewhat impracticable, and it may perhaps be doubted whether the adoration of these seven gentlemen would be a very safe moral atmosphere for the young lady. It also goes rather against the other rule which insists on a girl falling in love as well as her lover; that is to say, making her selection by chance, by impulse, and not by proof of the worthiest. But at least it is a high authority in favor of a plurality of suitors, and might be adduced by the offenders in such cases as a proof that their otherwise not quite excusable satisfaction in the devotion of more than one was almost justifiable. The dogma had not been given forth in Rosalind's day, and she was not aware that she had any excuse at all, but blushed for herself if ever she was momentarily conscious of so improper a sentiment. She blushed, and then she withdrew from the outside world in which these two looked at her with looks so different from those they directed towards any other, and thought of neither of them. On such occasions she would return to her room with a vague cloud of incense breathing about her, a sort of faint atmosphere of flattered and happy sentiment in her mind, or sit down in the firelight in the drawing-room, which Aunt Sophy had left, and think. About whom? Oh, about no one! she would have said—about a pair of beautiful eyes which were like Johnny's, and which seemed to follow and gaze at her with a rapture of love and devotion still more wonderful to behold. This image was so abstract that it escaped all the drawbacks of fact. There was nothing to detract from it, no test of reality to judge it by. Sometimes she found it impossible not to laugh at Roland; sometimes she disagreed violently with something Mr. Rivers said; but she never quarrelled with the visionary lover, who had appeared out of the unknown merely to make an appeal to her, as it seemed, to frustrate her affections, to bid her wait until he should reveal himself. Would he come again? Should she ever see him again? All this was unreal in the last degree. But so is everything in a young mind at such a moment, when nature plays with the first approaches of fate.

"Mr. Rivers seems to be staying a long time in Clifton," Mrs. Lennox said one evening, disturbing Rosalind out of these dreams. Roland was in the room, though she could scarcely see him, and Rosalind had been guilty of what she herself felt to be the audacity of thinking of her unknown lover in the very presence of this visible and real one. She had been sitting very quiet, drawing back out of the light, while a gentle hum of talk went on on the other side of the fire. The windows, with the twilight stars looking in, and the bare boughs of the trees waving across, formed the background, and Mrs. Lennox, relieved against one of those windows, was the centre of the warm but uncertainly lighted room. Hamerton sat behind, responding vaguely, and intent upon the shadowed corner in which Rosalind was. "How can he be spared, I wonder, out of his newspaper work!" said the placid voice. "I have always heard it was a dreadful drudgery, and that you had to be up all night, and never got any rest."

"He is not one of the principal ones, perhaps," Roland replied.

"Oh, he must be a principal! John would not have brought a man here who is nothing particular to begin with, if he had not been a sort of a personage in his way."

"Well, then, perhaps he is too much of a principal," said Hamerton; "perhaps it is only the secondary people that are always on duty; and this, you know, is what they call the silly time of the year."

"I never knew much about newspaper people," said Aunt Sophy, in her comfortable voice, something like a cat purring by the warm glow of the fire. "We did not think much of them in my time. Indeed, there are a great many people who are quite important in society nowadays that were never thought of in my time. I never knew how important a newspaper editor was till I read that novel of Mr. Trollope's—do you remember which one it is, Rosalind?—where there is Tom something or other who is the editor of the Jupiter. That was said to mean the Times. But if Mr. Rivers is so important as that, how does he manage to stay so long at Clifton, where I am sure there is nothing going on?"

"Sometimes," said Hamerton, after a pause, "there are things going on which are more important than a man's business, though perhaps they don't show."

There was something in the tone with which he said this which called Rosalind out of her dreams. She had heard them talking before, but not with any interest; now she was roused, though she could scarcely tell why.

"That is all very well for you, Roland, who have no business. Oh! I know you're a barrister, but as you never did anything at the bar—A man, when he has money of his own and does not live by his profession, can please himself, I suppose; but when his profession is all he has, nothing, you know, ought to be more important than that. And if his family keep him from his work, it is not right. A mother ought to know better, and even a sister; they ought not to keep him, if it is they who are keeping him. Now, do you think, putting yourself in their place, that it is right?"

"I can't fancy myself in the place of Rivers's mother or sister," said Roland, with a laugh.

"Oh, but I can, quite! and I could not do such a thing; for my own pleasure injure him in his career! Oh, no, no! And if it was any one else," said Aunt Sophy, "I do think it would be nearly criminal. If it was a girl, for instance. Girls are the most thoughtless creatures on the face of the earth; they don't understand such things; they don't really know. I suppose, never having had anything to do themselves, they don't understand. But if a girl should have so little feeling, and play with a man, and keep him from his work, when perhaps it may be ruinous to him," said Mrs. Lennox—when she was not contradicted, she could express herself with some force, though if once diverted from her course she had little strength to stand against opposition—"I cannot say less than that it would be criminal," she said.

"Is any one keeping Mr. Rivers from his work?" said Rosalind, suddenly, out of her corner, which made Mrs. Lennox start.

"Dear me, are you there, Rosalind? I thought you had gone away" (which we fear was not quite true). "Keeping Mr. Rivers, did you say? I am sure, my dear, I don't know. I think something must be detaining him. I am sure he did not mean to stay so long when he first came here."

"But perhaps he knows best himself, Aunt Sophy, don't you think?" Rosalind said, rising up with youthful severity and coming forward into the ruddy light.

"Oh, yes, my dear, I have no doubt he does," Mrs. Lennox said, faltering; "I was only saying—"

"You were blaming some one; you were saying it was his mother's fault, or perhaps some girl's fault. I think he is likely to know much better than any girl; it must be his own fault if he is wasting his time. I shouldn't think he was wasting his time. He looks as if he knew very well what he was about—better than a girl, who, as you were saying, seldom has anything to do."

"Dear me, Rosalind, I did not know you were listening so closely. Yes, to be sure he must know best. You know, Roland, gossip is a thing that she cannot abide. And she knows you and I have been gossiping about our neighbors. It is not so; it is really because I take a great interest; and you too, Roland."

"Oh, no, I don't take any interest," cried Hamerton, hastily; "it was simple gossip on my part. If he were to lose ever so much time or money, or anything else, I shouldn't care!"

"It is of no consequence to any of us," Rosalind said. "I should think Mr. Rivers did what he pleased, without minding much what people say. And as for throwing the blame upon a girl! What could a girl have to do with it?" She stood still for a moment, holding out her hands in a sort of indignant appeal, and then turned to leave the room, taking no notice of the apologetic outburst from her aunt.

"I am sure I was not blaming any girl, Rosalind. I was only saying, if it was a girl; but to be sure, when one thinks of it, a girl couldn't have anything to do with it," came somewhat tremulously from Aunt Sophy's lips. Miss Trevanion took no notice of this, but went away through the partial darkness, holding her head high. She had been awakened for the moment out of her dreams. The two who were left behind felt guilty, and drew together for mutual support.

"She thinks I mean her," said Mrs. Lennox; "she thinks I was talking at her. Now I never talk at people, Roland, and really, when I began, I did think she had gone away. You don't suppose I ever meant it was Rosalind?" she cried.

"But it is Rosalind," said young Hamerton. "I can't be deceived about it. We are both in the same box. She might make up her mind and put us out of our misery. No, I don't want to be put out of my misery. I'd rather wait on and try, and think there was a little hope."

"There must be hope," cried Mrs. Lennox; "of course there is hope. Is it rational that she should care for a stranger with gray hair, and old enough to be her father, instead of you, whom she has known all her life? Oh, no, Roland, it is not possible. And even if it were, I should object, you may be sure. It may be fine to be a Times Correspondent, but what could he settle upon her? You may be sure he could settle nothing upon her. He has his mother and sister to think of. And then he is not like a man with money; he has only what he works for; there is not much in that that could be satisfactory to a girl's friends. No, no, I will never give my consent to it; I promise you that."

Roland shook his head notwithstanding. But he still took a little comfort from what Aunt Sophy said. Such words always afford a grain of consolation; though he knew that she was not capable of holding by them in face of any opposition, still there was a certain support even in hearing them said. But he shook his head. "If she liked him best I would not stand in their way," he said; "that is the only thing to be guided by. Thank you very much, Mrs. Lennox; you are my only comfort. But still, you know, if she likes him best—I don't think much of the gray hair and all that," he added somewhat tremulously. "I'm not the man he is, in spite of his gray hair. And girls are just as likely as not to like that best," said the honest young fellow. "I don't entertain any delusion on the subject. I would not stand in her way, not a moment, if she likes him best."

CHAPTER XXXIII

Rosalind herself was much aroused by this discussion. She thought it unjust and cruel. She had done nothing to call for such a reproach. She had not attempted to make Mr. Rivers love her, nor to keep him from his work, nor to interfere in any way with his movements. She had even avoided him at the first—almost disliked him, she said to herself—and that she should be exposed to remark on his account was not to be borne. She retired to her room, full of lively indignation against her aunt and Roland, and even against Rivers, who was entirely innocent, surely, if ever man was. This was another phase, one she had not thought of, in the chapter of life which had begun by that wonder in her mind why she had no lover. She had been surprised by the absence of that figure in her life, and then had seen him appear, and had felt the elation, the secret joy, of being worshipped. But now the matter had entered into another phase, and she herself was to be judged as an independent actor in it; she, who had been only passive, doing nothing, looking on with curiosity and interest, and perhaps pleasure, but no more. What had she to do with it? She had no part in the matter: it was their doing, theirs only, all through. She had done nothing to influence his fate. She had conducted herself towards him no otherwise than she did to old Sir John, or Mr. Penworthy, the clergyman, both of whom were Rosalind's good friends. If Mr. Rivers had taken up a different idea of her, that was his doing, not hers. She detain him, keep him from his business, interfere with his career! She thought Aunt Sophy must be mad, or dreaming. Rosalind was indignant to be made a party at all in the matter. It had thus entered a stage of which she had no anticipation. It had been pleasant inasmuch as it was entirely apart from herself, the attentions unsolicited, the admiration unsought. It was a new idea altogether that she should be considered accountable, or brought within the possibility of blame. What was she to do? Mr. Rivers was expected at the Elms that very evening, at one of Mrs. Lennox's everlasting dinner-parties. Rosalind had not hitherto looked upon them as everlasting dinner-parties. She had enjoyed the lively flow of society, which Aunt Sophy (who enjoyed it very much) considered herself obliged to keep up for Rosalind's sake, that she should have pleasant company and amusement. Now, however, Miss Trevanion was suddenly of opinion that she had hated them all along; that, above all, she had disliked the constant invitations to these men. It would be indispensable that she should put up with this evening's party, which it was now much too late to elude. But after to-night she resolved that she would make a protest. She would say to Aunt Sophy that henceforward she must be excused. Whatever happened, she must disentangle herself from this odious position as a girl who was responsible for the feeling, whatever it was, entertained for her by a gentleman. It was preposterous, it was insupportable. Whatever he chose to think, it was his doing, and not hers at all.

These sentiments gave great stateliness to Rosalind's aspect when she went down to dinner. They even influenced her dress, causing her to put aside the pretty toilet she had intended to make, and attire herself in an old and very serious garment which had been appropriated to evenings when the family was alone. Mrs. Lennox stared at her niece in consternation when she saw this visible sign of contrariety and displeasure. It disturbed her beyond measure to see how far Rosalind had gone in her annoyance: whereas the gentlemen, with their usual density, saw nothing at all the matter, but thought her more dazzling than usual in the little black dress, which somehow threw up all her advantages of complexion and the whiteness of her pretty arms and throat. She had put on manners, however, which were more repellent than her dress, and which froze Hamerton altogether, who had a guilty knowledge of what was the matter which Rivers did not share. Roland was frozen externally, but it cannot be denied that in his heart there was a certain guilty pleasure. He thought that the suggestion that she had encouraged Rivers was quite enough to make Rosalind henceforward so much the reverse of encouraging that his rival would see the folly of going on with his suit, and the field would be left free to himself, as before. Rosalind might not be the better inclined, in consequence, to himself: but it was worth something to get that fellow, whom nobody could help looking at, away. There were two or three indifferent people in the company this evening, to whose amusement Rosalind devoted herself, ignoring both the candidates for her favor; and, as is natural in such circumstances, she was more lively, more gay, than usual, and eager to please these indifferent persons. As for Rivers, he thought she was out of sorts, perhaps out of temper (for he was aware that in this point she was not perfect), her usual friendliness and sweetness clouded over. But a man of his age does not jump into despair as youth does, and he waited patiently, believing that the cloud would pass away. Rivers had been very wise in his way of approaching Rosalind. He had not tried openly to appropriate her society, to keep by her side, to make his adoration patent, as foolish Roland did. To-night, however, he, too, adopted a different course. Perhaps her changed aspect stirred him up, and he felt that the moment had come for a bolder stroke. However this might be, whether it was done by accident or on principle, the fact was that his tactics were changed. When Rosalind rose, by Mrs. Lennox's desire, and went to the writing-table to write an address, Rivers rose too, and followed her, drawing a chair near hers with the air of having something special to say. "I want to ask your advice, if you will permit me, Miss Trevanion," he said.

"My advice! oh, no!" said Rosalind; "I am not wise enough to be able to advise any one."

"You are young and generous. I do not want wisdom."

"Not so very young," said Rosalind. "And how do you know that I am generous at all? I do not think I am."

He smiled and went on, without noticing this protest. "My mother," he said, "wishes to come to London to be near me. I am sometimes sent off to the end of the world, and often in danger. She thinks she would hear of me more easily, be nearer, so to speak, though I might happen to be in India or Zululand."

Rosalind was taken much by surprise. Her thoughts of him, as of a man occupied above everything else by herself, seemed to come back upon her as if they had been flung in her face. His mother! was she the subject of his anxiety? She felt as though she had been indulging a preposterous vanity and the most unfounded expectations. The color flew to her face; for what had she to do with his mother, if his mother was what he was thinking of? She was irritated by the suggestion, she could scarcely tell why.

"I think it is very natural she should wish it, and you would be at home, I suppose, sometimes," she replied, with a certain stiffness.

"Do you think so? You know, Miss Trevanion, my family and I are in two different worlds; I should be a fool if I tried to hide it. Would the difference be less, do you think, between St. James's and Islington, or between London and Clifton? I think the first would tell most. They would not be happy with me, nor I, alas! with them. It is the penalty a man has to pay for getting on, as they call it. I have got on in my small way, and they—are just where they were. How am I to settle it? If you could imagine yourself, if that were possible, in my position, what would you do?"

There was a soft insinuation in his voice which would have gone to any girl's heart; and his eyes expressed a boundless faith in her opinion which could not be mistaken. The irritation which was entirely without cause died away, and, with the usual rebound of a generous nature, Rosalind, penitent, felt her heart moved to a return of the confidence he showed in her. She answered softly, "I would do what my mother wished." She was seated still in front of the writing-table where stood the portrait, the little carved door of the frame half closed on it. A sudden impulse seized her. She pointed to it quickly, without waiting to think: "That is the children's mother," she said.

He gave her a look of mingled sympathy and pain. "I had heard something."

"What did you hear, Mr. Rivers? Something that was not true? If you heard that she was not good, the best woman in the world, it was not true. I have always wanted to tell you. She went away not with her will; because she could not help it. The children have almost forgotten her, but I can never forget. She was all the mother I have ever known."

Rosalind did not know at all why at such a moment she should suddenly have opened her heart to him on this subject, through which he had given her such a wound. She took it up hastily, instinctively, in the quickening impulse of her disturbed thoughts. She added in a low voice, "What you said hurt me—oh, it hurt me, that night; but afterwards, when I came to think of it, the feeling went away."

"There was nothing to hurt you," said Rivers, hastily. "I saw it was so, but I could not explain. Besides, I was a stranger, and understood nothing. Don't you think I might be of use to you perhaps, if you were to trust me?" He looked at her with eyes so full of sympathy that Rosalind's heart was altogether melted. "I saw," he added quietly, "that there was a whole history in her face."

"Tell me all you saw—if you spoke to her—what she said. Oh! if she had only known you were coming here! But life seems like that—we meet people as it were in the dark, and we never know how much we may have to do with them. I could not let you go away without asking you. Tell me, before you go away."

"I will tell you. But I am not going away, Miss Trevanion."

"Oh!" cried Rosalind. She felt confused, as if she had gone through a world of conflicting experience since she first spoke. "I thought you must be going, and that this was why you asked me."

"About my mother? It was with a very different view I spoke. I wished you to know something more about me. I wished you to understand in what position I am, and to make you aware of her existence, and to find out what you thought about it; what would appear to you the better way." He was more excited and tremulous than became his years; and she was softened by the emotion more than by the highest eloquence.

"It must be always best to make her happy," Rosalind said.

"Shall I tell you what would make her happy? To see me sitting here by your side, to hear you counselling me so sweetly; to know that was your opinion, to hope perhaps—"

"Mr. Rivers, do not say any more about this. You make so much more than is necessary of a few simple words. What I want you to tell me is about her."

"I will tell you as much as I know," he said, with a pause and visible effort of self-restraint. "She was travelling by unusual routes, but without any mystery. She had a maid with her, a tall, thin, anxious woman."

"Oh, Jane!" cried Rosalind, clasping her hands together with a little cry of recognition and pleasure; this seemed to give such reality to the tale. She knew very well that the faithful maid had gone with Mrs. Trevanion; but to see her in this picture gave comfort to her heart.

"You knew her? She seemed to be very anxious about her mistress, very careful of her. Miss Trevanion, it may very well be that in my wanderings I may meet with them again. Shall I say anything? Shall I carry a message?"

Rosalind found her voice choked with tears. She made him a sign of assent, unable to do more.

"What shall I tell her? That you trust me—that I am a messenger from you? I would rather be your ambassador than the queen's. Shall I say that I have been so happy as to gain your confidence—or even perhaps—"

"Oh, a little thing will do," cried the girl; "she will understand you as soon as you say that Rosalind—"

He was leaning forward, his eyes fixed upon hers, his face full of emotion. He put out his hand and touched hers, which was leaning on the table. "Yes," he said, "I will say that Rosalind—so long as you give me an excuse for using that name."

Rosalind came to herself with a little shock. She withdrew her hand hastily. "Perhaps I am saying too much," she said. "It is only a dream, and you may never see her. But I could not bear that you should imagine we did not speak of her, or that I did not love her, and trust her," she added, drawing a long breath. "This is a great deal too much about me, and you had begun to tell me of your own arrangements," Rosalind said, drawing her chair aside a little in instinctive alarm. It was the sound she made in doing so which called the attention of John Trevanion—or, rather, which moved him to turn his steps that way, his attention having been already attracted by the fixed and jealous gaze of Roland, who had sat with his face towards the group by the writing-table ever since his rival had followed Rosalind there.

Rivers saw that his chance was over, with a sigh, yet not perhaps with all the vehement disappointment of a youth. He had made a beginning, and perhaps he was not yet ready to go any further, though his feelings might have hurried him on too hastily, injudiciously, had no interruption occurred. But he had half frightened without displeasing her, which, as he was an experienced man, was a condition of things he did not think undesirable. There is a kind of fright which, to be plunged into yet escape from, to understand without being forced to come to any conclusion, suits the high, fantastical character of a young maiden's awakening feelings. And then before he, who was of a race so different, could actually venture to ask a Miss Trevanion of Highcourt to marry him, a great many calculations and arrangements were necessary. He thought John Trevanion, who was a man of the world, looked at him with a certain surprise and disapproval, asking himself, perhaps, what such a man could have to offer, what settlements he could make, what establishment he could keep up.

"Are not you cold in this corner," John said, "so far from the fire, Rosalind?—and you are a chilly creature. Run away and get yourself warm." He took her chair as she rose, and sat down with an evident intention of continuing the conversation. As a matter of fact, John Trevanion was not asking himself what settlements a newspaper correspondent could make. He was thinking of other things. He gave a nod of his head towards the portrait, and said in a low tone, "She has been talking to you of her."

Rivers was half disappointed, half relieved. It proved to him, he thought, that he was too insignificant a pretender to arouse any alarm in Rosalind's relations, which was a galling thought. At the same time it was better that he should have made up his mind more completely what he was to say, before he exposed himself to any questioning on the subject. So he answered with a simple "Yes."

"We cannot make up our minds to think any harm of her," said Trevanion, leaning his head on his hand. "The circumstances are very strange, too strange for me to attempt to explain. And what you said seemed damaging enough. But I want you to know that I share somehow that instinctive confidence of Rosalind's. I believe there must be some explanation, even of the—companion—"

Rivers could not but smile a little, but he kept the smile carefully to himself. He was not so much interested in the woman he did not know as he was in the young creature who, he hoped, might yet make a revolution in his life.

CHAPTER XXXIV

It was not very long after this that one of "England's little wars" broke out—not a little war in so far as loss and cost went, but yet one of those convulsions that go on far from us, that only when they are identified by some dreadful and tragic incident really rouse the nation. It is more usual now than it used to be to have the note of horror struck in this way, and Rivers was one of the most important instructors of the English public in such matters. He went up to the Elms in the morning, an unusual hour, to tell his friends there that he was ordered off at once, and to bid them good-bye. He made as little as possible of his own special mission, but there was no disguising the light of excitement, anxiety, and expectation that was in his eyes.

"If I were a soldier," he said, "I should feel myself twice as interesting; and Sophy perhaps would give me her ribbon to wear in my cap; but a newspaper correspondent has his share of the kicks, and not much of the ha'pence, in the way of glory at least."

"Oh, I think quite the reverse," said Mrs. Lennox, always anxious to please and encourage; "because you know we should never know anything about it at home, but for you."

"And the real ha'pence do fall to your share, and not to the soldiers," said John.

"Well, perhaps it does pay better, which you will think an ignoble distinction," he said, turning to Rosalind with a laugh. "But picking up news is not without danger any more than inflicting death is, and the trouble we take to forestall our neighbors is as hard as greater generalship." He was very uneasy, looking anxiously from one to another. The impossibility of getting these people out of the way! What device would do it? he wondered. Mrs. Lennox sat in her chair by the fire with her crewel work as if she would never move; Sophy had a holiday and was pervading the room in all corners at once; and John

Trevanion was writing at Rosalind's table, with the composure of a man who had no intention of being disturbed. How often does this hopeless condition of affairs present itself when but one chance remains for the anxious lover! Had Rivers been a duke, the difficulty might easily have been got over, but he whose chief hope is not in the family, but in favor of the lady herself, has a more difficult task. Mrs. Lennox, he felt convinced, would have no desire to clear the way for him, and as for Mr. Trevanion, it was too probable that even had the suitor been a duke, on the eve of a long and dangerous expedition, he would have watched over Rosalind's tranquillity and would not have allowed her to be disturbed. It was a hopeless sort of glance which the lover threw round him, ending in an unspoken appeal. They were very kind to him; had he wanted money or help of influence, or any support to push him on in the world, John Trevanion, a true friend to all whom he esteemed, would have given it. But Rosalind—they would not give him five minutes with Rosalind to save his life.

Mrs. Lennox, however, whose amiability always overcame her prudence, caught the petition in his eyes and interpreted it after her own fashion.

"Dear me," she said, "how sorry we shall be to lose you! But you really must stay to lunch. The last time! You could not do less for us than that. And we shall drink your health and wish you a happy return."

"That will do him so much good; when he must have a hundred things to do."

"The kindness will do me good. Yes, I have a hundred things to do, but since Mrs. Lennox is so kind; it will do me more good than anything," Rivers said. His eyes were glistening as if there was moisture in them; and Rosalind, looking up and perceiving the restlessness of anxiety in his face, was affected by a sympathetic excitement. She began to realize what the position was—that he was going away, and might never see her again. She would be sorry too. It would be a loss of importance, a sort of coming down in the world, to have no longer this man—not a boy, like Roland; a man whose opinions people looked up to, who was one of the instructors and oracles of the world—depending upon her favor. There was perhaps more than this, a slightly responsive sentiment on her own part, not like his, but yet something—an interest, a liking. Her heart began to beat; there was a sort of anguish in his eyes which moved her more, she thought, than she had ever been moved before—a force of appeal to her which she could scarcely resist. But what could she do? She could not, any more than he could, clear the room of the principal persons in it, and give him the chance of speaking to her. Would she do it if she could?—she thought she would not. But yet she was agitated slightly, sympathetically, and gave him an answering look in which, in the excitement of the moment, he read a great deal more than there was to read. Was this to be all that was to pass between them before he went away? How commonplace the observations of the others seemed to them both! especially to Rivers, whose impatience was scarcely to be concealed, and who looked at the calm, every-day proceedings of the heads of the house with a sense that they were intolerable, yet a consciousness that the least sign of impatience would be fatal to him.

"Are you frightened, then, Mr. Rivers, that you look so strange?" said Sophy, planting herself in front of him, and looking curiously into his face.

"Sophy, how can you be so rude?" Mrs. Lennox said.

"I don't think I am frightened—not yet," he said, with a laugh. "It is time enough when the fighting begins."

"Are you very frightened then? It is not rudeness; I want to know. It must be very funny to go into battle. I should not have time to be frightened, I should want to know how people feel—and I never knew any one who was just going before. Did you ever want to run away?"

"You know," said Rivers, "I don't fight, except with another newspaper fellow, who shall get the news first."

"I am sure Mr. Rivers is frightened, for he has got tears in his eyes," said the enfant terrible. "Well, if they are not tears, it is something that makes your eyes very shiny. You have always rather shiny eyes. And you have never got a chair all this time, Mr. Rivers. Please sit down; for to move about like that worries Aunt Sophy. You are as bad as Rex when he comes home for the holidays. Aunt Sophy is always saying she will not put up with it."

"Child!" cried Mrs. Lennox, with dismay, "what I say to you is not meant for Mr. Rivers. Of course Mr. Rivers is a little excited. I am sure I shall look for the newspapers, and read all the descriptions with twice as much interest. Rosalind, I wish you would go and get some flowers. We have none for the table. You were so busy this morning, you did not pay any attention. Those we have here will do very well for to-day, but for the table we want something fresh. Get some of those fine cactuses. They are just the thing to put on the table for any one who is going to the wars."

"Yes, Aunt Sophy," said Rosalind, faintly. She saw what was coming, and it frightened, yet excited her. "There is plenty of time. It will do in—half an hour."

"My dear," said Mrs. Lennox, with an absurd insistence, as if she meant something, "you had better go at once."

"I am nervous, as Sophy has discovered, and can't keep still," said Rivers. "May I go too?"

Rosalind looked at him, on her side, with a kind of tremulous appeal, as he took her basket out of her hand. It seemed to say "Don't!" with a distinct sense that it was vain to say so. Aunt Sophy, with that foolish desire to please which went against all her convictions and baffled her own purpose, looked up at them as they stood, Rosalind hesitating and he so eager. "Yes, do; it will cheer you up a little," the foolish guardian said.

And John Trevanion wrote on calmly, thinking nothing. They abandoned her to her fate. It was such a chance as Rivers could not have hoped for. He could scarcely contain himself as he followed her out of the room. She went very slowly, hoping perhaps even now to be called back, though she scarcely wished to be called back, and would have been disappointed too, perhaps. She could not tell what her feelings were, nor what she was going to do. Yet there came before her eyes as she went out a sudden vision of the other, the stranger, he whom she did not know, who had wooed her in the silence, in her dreams, and penetrated her eyes with eyes not bright and keen, like those of Rivers, but pathetic, like little Johnny's. Was she going to forsake the visionary for the actual? Rosalind felt that she too was going into battle, not knowing what might come of it; into her first personal encounter with life and a crisis in which she must act for herself.

"I did not hope for anything like this," he said, hurriedly; "a good angel must have got it for me. I thought I should have to go without a word."

"Oh, no! there will be many more words; you have promised Aunt Sophy to stay to lunch."

"To see you in the midst of the family is almost worse than not seeing you at all. Miss Trevanion, you must know. Perhaps I am doing wrong to take advantage of their confidence, but how can I help it? Everything in the world is summed up to me in this moment. Say something to me! To talk of love in common words seems nothing. I know no words that mean half what I mean. Say you will think of me sometimes when I am away."

Rosalind trembled very much in spite of all she could do to steady herself. They had gone through the hall without speaking, and it was only when they had gained the shelter of the conservatory, in which they were safe from interruption, that he thus burst forth. The interval had been so breathless and exciting that every emotion was intensified. She did not venture to look up at him, feeling as if something might take flame at his eyes.

"Mr. Rivers, I could say that very easily, but perhaps it would not mean what you think."

"Yes," he said, "I see how it is; the words are too small for me, and you would mean just what they say. I want them to mean a great deal more, everything, as mine do. At my age," he said, with an agitated smile—"for I am too old for you, besides being not good enough in any way—at my age I ought to have the sense to speak calmly, to offer you as much as I can, which is no great things; but I have got out of my own control, Rosalind. Well, yes, let me say that—a man's love is worth that much, to call the girl whom he loves Rosalind—Rosalind. I could go on saying it, and die so, like Perdita's prince. All exaggerated nonsense and folly, I know, I know, and yet all true."

She raised her head for a moment and gave him a look in which there was a sort of tender gratitude yet half-reproach, as if entreating him to spare her that outburst of passion, to meet which she was so entirely prepared.

"I understand," he said; "I can see into your sweet mind as if it were open before me, I am so much older than you are. But the love ought to be most on the man's side. I will take whatever you will give me—a little, a mere alms!—if I cannot get any more. If you say only that, that you will think of me sometimes when I am away, and mean only that, and let me come back, if I come back, and see—what perhaps Providence may have done for me in the meantime—"

"Mr. Rivers, I will think of you often. Is it possible I could do otherwise after what you say? But when you come back, if you find that I do not—care for you more than now—"

"Do you care for me at all now, Rosalind?"

"In one way, but not as you want me. I must tell you the truth. I am always glad when you come, I shall be very glad when you come back, but I could not—I could not—"

"You could not—marry me, Rosalind?"

She drew back a little from his side. She said "No" in a quick, startled tone; then she added "Nor any one," half under her breath.

"Nor any one," he repeated; "that is enough. And you will think of me when I am away, and if I come back, I may come and ask? All this I will accept on my knees, and, at present, ask for no more."

"But you must not expect—you must not make sure of—when you come back—"

"I will wait upon Providence and my good angel, Rosalind!"

"What are you saying, Mr. Rivers, about angels and Rosalind? Do you call her by her name, and do you think she is an angel? That is how people talk in novels; I have read a great many. Why, you have got no flowers! What have you been doing all this time? I made Aunt Sophy send me to help you with the cactuses, and Uncle John said, 'Well, perhaps it will be better.' But, oh, what idle things you are! The cactuses are not here even. You look as if you had forgotten all about them, Rose."

"We knew you were sure to come, and waited for you," said Rivers; "that is to say, I did. I knew you were sure to follow. Here, Sophy, you and I will go for the cactuses, and Miss Trevanion will sit down and wait for us. Don't you think that is the best way?"

"You call her Miss Trevanion now, but you called her Rosalind when I was not here. Oh, and I know you don't care a bit for the flowers: you wanted only to talk to her when Uncle John and Aunt Sophy were out of the way."

"Don't you think that was natural, Sophy? You are a wise little girl. You are very fond of Uncle John and Aunt Sophy, but still now and then you like to get away for a time, and tell your secrets."

"Were you telling your secrets to Rosalind? I am not very fond of them. I like to see what is going on, and to find people out."

"Shall I give you something to find out for me while I am away?"

"Oh, yes, yes, do; that is what I should like," cried Sophy, with her little mischievous eyes dancing. "And I will write and tell you. But then you must give me your address; I shall be the only one in the house that knows your address; and I'll tell you what they are all doing, every one of them. There is nothing I should like so much," Sophy cried. She was so pleased with this idea that she forgot to ask what the special information required by her future correspondent was.

Meanwhile Rosalind sat among the flowers, hearing the distant sound of their voices, with her heart beating and all the color and brightness round flickering unsteadily in her eyes. She did not know what she had done, or if she had done anything; if she had pledged herself, or if she were still free.

CHAPTER XXXV

It happened after these events that sickness crept into Mrs. Lennox's cheerful house. One of the children had a lingering fever; and Aunt Sophy herself was troubled with headaches, and not up to the mark, the doctor said. This no doubt arose, according to the infallible decrees of sanitary science, from some deficiency in the drainage, notwithstanding that a great deal of trouble had already been taken, and that a local functionary and expert in such matters had been almost resident in the house for some months, to set right these sources of all evil. As soon, however, as it was understood that for the sixth or seventh time the house would have to be undermined, Mrs. Lennox came to a resolution which, as she said, she had "always intended;" and that was to "go abroad." To go abroad is a thing which recommends itself to most women as an infallible mode of procuring pleasure. They may not like it when they are there. Foreign "ways" may be a weariness to their souls, and foreign languages a series of unholy mysteries which they do not attempt to fathom; but going abroad is a panacea for all dulness and a good many maladies. The Englishwoman of simple mind is sure that she will be warmed and soothed, that the sun will always shine, the skies never rain, and everything go to her wish "abroad." She returns discontented; but she goes away always hopeful, scarcely able to conceive that gray skies and cold winds prevail anywhere except in her own island. Mrs. Lennox was of this simple-minded order. When she was driven to the depths of her recollection she could, indeed, remember a great many instances to the contrary, but in the abstract she felt that these were accidents, and, the likelihood was, would never occur again. And then it would be so good for the children! They would learn languages without knowing, without any trouble at all. With this happy persuasion English families every day convey their hapless babes into the depths of Normandy, for example, to learn French. Mrs. Lennox went to the Riviera, as was inevitable, and afterwards to other places, thinking it as well, as she said, while they were abroad, to see as much as possible. It was no small business to get the little caravansary under way, and when it was accomplished it may be doubted how much advantage it was to the children for whose good, according to Aunt Sophy, the journey was prolonged. Little Amy and Johnny wandered with big eyes after the nurse who had replaced Russell, through Rome and Florence, and gazed alarmed at the towers of Bologna, which the children thought were falling upon them, without deriving very much instruction from the sight.

It was a thoroughly English party, like many another, carrying its own little atmosphere about it and all its insular customs. The first thing they did on arriving at a new place was to establish a little England in the foreign hotel or chambres garnies which they occupied. The sitting-room at the inn took at once a kind of faux air of the dining-room at the Elms, Mrs. Lennox's work and her basket of crewels and her footstool being placed in the usual exact order, and a writing-table arranged for the family letters in the same light as that approved at home. And then there were elaborate arrangements for the nursery dinner at a proper nursery hour, and for roast mutton and rice pudding, such as were fit food for British subjects of the age of nine and seven. Then the whereabouts of the English church was inquired into, and the English chemist, and the bookshop where English books, and especially the editions of Baron Tauchnitz, and perhaps English newspapers, might be had. Having ascertained all this, and to the best of her power obliterated all difference between Cannes, or Genoa, or Florence, or even Rome, and the neighborhood of Clifton, Mrs. Lennox began to enjoy herself in a mild way. She took her daily drive, and looked at the Italians from her carriage with a certain disapproval, much curiosity, and sometimes amusement. She disapproved of them because they were not English, in a general way. She was too sweet-tempered to conclude, as some of the ladies did whom she met at the hotel, that they were universally liars, cheats, and extortioners; but they were not English; though, perhaps, poor things, that was not exactly their fault.

This was how she travelled, and in a sober way enjoyed it. She thought the Riviera very pretty, if there were not so many sick people about; and Florence very pretty too. "But I have been here before, you know, my dear," she said; therefore her admiration was calm, and never rose into any of the raptures with which Rosalind sometimes was roused by a new landscape. She lived just as she would have done if she had never stirred from home, and was moderately happy, as happy as a person of her age has any right to be. The children came to her at the same hours, they had their dinner and walk at the same hours, and they all went to church on Sunday just in the same way. The table d'hôte, at which she usually dined with Rosalind, was the only difference of importance between her life as a traveller and her life at home. She thought it was rather like a dinner-party without the trouble, and as she soon got to know a select little "set" of English of her own condition in her hotel, and sat with them, the public table grew more and more like a private one, except in so far as that all the guests had the delightful privilege of finding fault. The clergyman called upon her, and made little appeals to her for deserving cases, and pleaded that Rosalind should help in the music, and talked the talk of a small parish to her contented ears. All this made her very much at home, while still enjoying the gentle excitement of being abroad. And at the end of six months Mrs. Lennox began to feel that she was quite a cosmopolitan, able to adapt herself to all circumstances, and getting the full good of foreign travel, which, as she declared she was doing it entirely for the children, was a repayment of her goodness upon which she had not calculated. "I feel quite a woman of the world," was what Aunt Sophy said.

Perhaps, however, Rosalind, placed as she was between the children and their guardian, neither too old nor too young for such enjoyment, was, as lawyers say, the true beneficiary. She had the disadvantage of visiting a great many places of interest with companions who did not appreciate or understand them, it is true; with Aunt Sophy, who thought that the pictures as well as the views were pretty; and with the sharp little sister who thought picture-galleries and mountain landscapes equally a bore. But, notwithstanding, with that capacity for separating herself from her surroundings which belongs to the young, Rosalind was able to get a great deal of enjoyment as she moved along in Mrs. Lennox's train. Aunts in general are not expected to care for scenery; they care for being comfortable, for getting their meals, and especially the children's meals, at the proper time, and being as little disturbed in their ordinary routine as possible. When this is fully granted, a girl can usually manage to get a good deal of pleasure under their portly shadow. Rosalind saw everything as if nobody had ever seen it before; the most hackneyed scenes were newly created for her, and came upon her with a surprise almost more delightful than anything in life, certainly more delightful than anything that did not immediately concern the heart and affections. She thought, indeed, sometimes wistfully, that if it had been her mother, that never-to-be-forgotten and always trusted friend, who could have understood everything and felt with her, and added a charm wherever they went, the enjoyment would have been far greater. But then her heart would fall into painful questions as to where and with what companions that friend might now be, and rise into prayers, sometimes that they might meet to-morrow, sometimes that they might never meet—that nothing which could diminish her respect and devotion should ever be made known to her. Then, too, sometimes Rosalind would ask herself, in the leisure of her solitude, what this journey might have been had some one else been of the party? This some one else was not Roland Hamerton: that was certain. She could not say to herself, either, that it was Arthur Rivers. It was—well, some one with great eyes, dark and liquid, whose power of vision would be more refined, more educated than that of Rosalind, who would know all the associations and all the poetry, and make everything that was beautiful before more beautiful by the charm of his superior knowledge. Perhaps she felt, too, that it was more modest, more maidenly, to allow a longing for the companionship of one whom she did not know, who was a mere ideal, the symbol of love, or genius, or poetry, she did not know which, than to wish in straightforward terms for the lover whom she knew, who was a man, and not a symbol. Her imagination was too shy, too proud, to summon up an actual person, substantial and well known. It was more easy and simple, more possible, to fill that fancy with an image that had no actual embodiment, and to call to her side the being who was nothing more than a recollection, whose very name and everything about him was unknown to her. She accepted him as a symbol of all that a dreaming girl desires in a companion. He was a dream; there need be no bounds to the enthusiasm, the poetry, the fine imagination, with which she endowed him, any more than there need be to the devotion to herself, which was a mere dream also. He might woo her as men only woo in the imagination of girls, so delicately, so tenderly, with such ethereal worship. How different the most glorious road would be were he beside her! though in reality he was beside her all the way, saying things which were finer than anything but fancy, breathing the very soul of rapture into her being. The others knew nothing of all this; how should they? And Mrs. Lennox, for one, sometimes asked herself whether Rosalind was really enjoying her travels. "She says so little," that great authority said.

There was, however, little danger that she should forget one, at least, of her actual lovers. In the meantime a great deal had been going on in the world, and especially in that distant part of it to which Rivers had gone. The little war which he had gone to report had turned into a most exciting and alarming one; and there had been days in which the whole world, so to speak—all England at least, and her dependencies—had hung upon his utterance, and looked for his communications every morning almost before they looked at those which came from their nearest and dearest. And it was said that he had excelled himself in these communications. He had done things which were heroic, if not to hasten the conclusion of the war, to make it successful, yet at least to convey the earliest intelligence of any new action, and to make people at home feel as if they were present upon the very field, spectators of all the movements there.

This service involved him in as much danger as if he had been in the very front of the fighting; and, indeed, he was known to have done feats, for what is called the advantage of the public, to which the stand made by a mere soldier, even in the most urgent circumstances, was not to be compared. All this was extremely interesting, not to say exciting, to his friends. Mrs. Lennox had the paper sent after her wherever she travelled; and, indeed, it was great part of her day's occupation to read it, which she did with devotion. "The correspondent is a friend of ours," she said to the other English people in the hotels. "We know him, I may say, very well, and naturally I take a great interest." The importance of his position as the author of those letters which interested everybody, and even the familiar way in which he talked of generals and commanders-in-chief, impressed her profoundly. As for Rosalind, she said nothing, but she, too, read all about the war with an attention which was breathless, not quite sure in her mind that it was not under a general's helmet that those crisp locks of gray were curling, or that the vivid eyes which had looked into hers with such expression were not those of the hero of the campaign. It did not seem possible, somehow, that he could be less than a general. She took the paper to her room in the evening, when Aunt Sophy had done with it, and read and read. The charm was upon her that moved Desdemona, and it was difficult to remember that the teller of the tale was not the chief mover in it. How could she help but follow him in his wanderings wherever he went? It was the least thing she could do in return for what he had given to her—for that passion which had made her tremble—which she wondered at and admired as if it had been poetry. All this captivated the girl's fancy in spite of herself, and gave her an extraordinary interest in everything he said, and that was said of him. But, notwithstanding, it was not Mr. Rivers who accompanied her in the spirit on all the journeys she made, and to all the beautiful places which filled her with rapture. Not Mr. Rivers—a visionary person, one whose very name was to her unknown.

CHAPTER XXXVI

The events of the night on which Mrs. Trevanion left Highcourt had at this period of the family story fallen into that softened oblivion which covers the profoundest scars of the heart after a certain passage of time, except sometimes to the chief actor in such scenes, who naturally takes a longer period to forget.

She on whom the blow had fallen at a moment when she was unprepared for it, when a faint sense of security had begun to steal over her in spite of herself, had received it en plein cœur, as the French say. We have no word which expresses so well the unexpected, unmitigated shock. She had said to herself, like the captive king in the Bible, that the bitterness of death was past, and had gone, like that poor prince, "delicately," with undefended bosom, and heart hushed out of its first alarms, to meet her fate. The blow had gone through her very flesh, rending every delicate tissue before she had time to think. It does not even seem a metaphor to say that it broke her heart, or, rather, cut the tender structure sheer in two, leaving it bleeding, quivering, in her bosom. She was not a woman to faint or die at a stroke. She took the torture silently, without being vanquished by it. When nature is strong within us, and the force of life great, there is no pang spared. And while in one sense it was true that for the moment she expected nothing, the instantly following sensation in Madam's mind was that she had known all along what was going to happen to her, and that it had never been but certain that this must come. Even the details of the scene seemed familiar. She had always known that some time or other these men would look at her so, would say just those words to her, and that she would stand and bear it all, a victim appointed from the beginning. In the greater miseries of life it happens often that the catastrophe, however unexpected, bears, when it comes, a familiar air, as of a thing which has been mysteriously rehearsed in our consciousness all our lives. After the first shock, her mind sprang with a bound to those immediate attempts to find a way of existence on the other side of the impossible, which was the first impulse of the vigorous soul. She said little even to Jane until the dreary afternoon was over, the dinner, with its horrible formulas, and she had said what was really her farewell to everything at Highcourt. Then, when the time approached for the meeting in the park, she began to prepare for going out with a solemnity which startled her faithful attendant. She took from her desk a sum which she had kept in reserve (who can tell for what possibility?), and dressed herself carefully, not in her new mourning, with all its crape, but in simple black from head to foot. She always had worn a great deal of black lace; it had been her favorite costume always. She enveloped herself in a great veil which would have fallen almost to her feet had it been unfolded, doing everything for herself, seeking the things she wanted in her drawers with a silent diligence which Jane watched with consternation. At last the maid could restrain herself no longer.

"Am I to do nothing for you?" she cried, with anguish. "And, oh! where are you going? What are you doing? There's something more than I thought."

"You are to do everything for me, Jane," her mistress said, with a pathetic smile. "You are to be my sole companion all the rest of my life—unless, if it is not too late, that poor boy."

"Madam," Jane said, putting her hand to her heart with a natural tragic movement, "you are not going to desert—the children? Oh, no! you are not thinking of leaving the children?"

Her mistress put her hands upon Jane's shoulders, clutching her, and gave vent to a low laugh more terrible than any cry. "It is more wonderful than that—more wonderful—more, ah, more ridiculous. Don't cry. I can't bear it. They have sent me away. Their father—has sent me away!"

"Madam!" Jane's shriek would have rung through the house had it not been for Madam's imperative gesture and the hand she placed upon her mouth.

"Not a word! Not a word! I have not told you before, for I cannot bear a word. It is true, and nothing can be done. Dress yourself now, and put what we want for the night in your bag. I will take nothing. Oh, that is a small matter, a very small matter, to provide all that will be wanted for two poor women. Do you remember, Jane, how we came here?"

"Oh, well, well, Madam. You a beautiful bride, and nothing too much for you, nothing good enough for you."

"Yes, Jane; but leaving my duty behind me. And now it is repaid."

"Oh, Madam, Madam! He was too young to know the loss; and it was for his own sake. And besides, if that were all, it's long, long ago—long, long ago."

Mrs. Trevanion's hands dropped by her side. She turned away with another faint laugh of tragic mockery. "It is long, long ago; long enough to change everything. Ah, not so long ago but that he remembers it, Jane. And now the time is come when I am free, if I can, to make it up. I have always wondered if the time would ever come when I could try to make it up."

"Madam, you have never failed to him, except in not having him with you."

"Except in all that was my duty, Jane. He has known no home, no care, no love. Perhaps now, if it should not be too late—"

And then she resumed her preparations with that concentrated calm of despair which sometimes apes ordinary composure so well as to deceive the lookers-on. Jane could not understand what was her lady's meaning. She followed her about with anxious looks, doing nothing on her own part to aid, paralyzed by the extraordinary suggestion. Madam was fully equipped before Jane had stirred, except to follow wistfully every step Mrs. Trevanion took.

"Are you not coming?" she said at length. "Am I to go alone? For the first time in our lives do you mean to desert me, Jane?"

"Madam," cried the woman, "it cannot be—it cannot be! You must be dreaming; we cannot go without the children." She stood wringing her hands, beyond all capacity of comprehension, thinking her mistress mad or criminal, or under some great delusion—she could not tell which.

Mrs. Trevanion looked at her with strained eyes that were past tears. "Why," she said, "why—did you not say so seventeen years ago, Jane?"

"Oh, Madam," cried Jane, seizing her mistress by the hands, "don't do it another time! They are all so young, they want you. It can't do them any good, but only harm, if you go away. Oh, Madam, listen to me that loves you. Who have I but you in the world? But don't leave them. Oh, don't we both know the misery it brings? You may be doing it thinking it will make up. But God don't ask these kind of sacrifices," she cried, the tears running down her cheeks. "He don't ask it. He says, mind your duty now, whatever's been done in the past. Don't try to be making up for it, the Lord says, Madam; but just do your duty now; it's all that we can do."

Mrs. Trevanion listened to this address, which was made with streaming eyes and a face quivering with emotion, in silence. She kept her eyes fixed on Jane's face as if the sight of the tears was a refreshment to her parched soul. Her own eyes were dry, with that smile in them which answers at some moments in place of weeping.

"You cut me to the heart," she said, "every word. Oh, but I am not offering God any vain sacrifices, thinking to atone. He has taken it into his own hand. Life repeats itself, though we never think so. What I did once for my own will God makes me do over again not of my own will. He has his meaning clear through all, but I don't know what it is, I cannot fathom it." She said this quickly, with the settled quietness of despair. Then, the lines of her countenance melting, her eyes lit up with a forlorn entreaty, as she touched Jane on the shoulder, and asked, "Are you coming? You will not let me go alone—"

"Oh, Madam, wherever you go—wherever you go! I have never done anything but follow you. I can neither live nor die without you," Jane answered, hurriedly; and then, turning away, tied on her bonnet with trembling hands. Madam had done everything else; she had left nothing for Jane to provide. They went out together, no longer alarmed to be seen—two dark figures, hurrying down the great stairs. But the languor that follows excitement had got into the house: there were no watchers about; the whole place seemed deserted. She, who that morning had been the mistress of Highcourt, went out of the home of so many years without a soul to mark her going or bid her good-speed. But the anguish of the parting was far too great to leave room for any thought of the details. They stepped out into the night, into the dark, to the sobbing of the wind and the wildly blowing trees. The storm outside gave them a little relief from that which was within.

Madam went swiftly, softly along, with that power of putting aside the overwhelming consciousness of wretchedness which is possessed by those whose appointed measure of misery is the largest in this world. To die then would have been best, but not to be helpless and encounter the pity of those who could give no aid. She had the power not to think, to address herself to what was before her, and hold back "upon the threshold of the mind" the supreme anguish of which she could never be free, which there would be time enough, alas! and to spare, to indulge in. Perhaps, though she knew so much and was so experienced in pain, it did not occur to her at this terrible crisis of life to think it possible that any further pang might be awaiting her. The other, who waited for her within shade of the copse, drew back when he perceived that two people were coming towards him. He scarcely responded even when Mrs. Trevanion called him in a low voice by name. "Whom have you got with you?" he said, almost in a whisper, holding himself concealed among the trees.

"Only Jane."

"Only Jane," he said, in a tone of relief, but still with a roughness and sullenness out of keeping with his youthful voice. He added, after a moment, "What does Jane want? I hope there is not going to be any sentimental leave-taking. I want to stay and not to go."

"That is impossible now. Everything is altered. I am going with you, Edmund."

"Going with me—good Lord!" There was a moment's silence; then he resumed in a tone of satire, "What may that be for? Going with me! Do you think I can't take care of myself? Do you think I want a nurse at my heels?" Then another pause. "I know what you mean. You are going away for a change, and you mean me to turn up easily and be introduced to the family? Not a bad idea at all," he added, in a patronizing tone.

"Edmund," she said, "afterwards, when we have time, I will tell you everything. There is no time now; but that has come about which I thought impossible. I am—free to make up to you as much as I can, for the past—"

"Free," he repeated, with astonishment, "to make up to me?" The pause that followed seemed one of consternation. Then he went on roughly, "I don't know what you mean by making up to me. I have often heard that women couldn't reason. You don't mean that you are flinging over the others now, to make a romance—and balance matters? I don't know what you mean."

Madam Trevanion grasped Jane's arm and leaned upon it with what seemed a sudden collapse of strength, but this was invisible to the other, who probably was unaware of any effect produced by what he said. Her voice came afterwards through the dark with a thrill in it that seemed to move the air, something more penetrating than the wind.

"I have no time to explain," she said. "I must husband my strength, which has been much tried. I am going with you to London to-night. We have a long walk before we reach the train. On the way, or afterwards, as my strength serves me, I will tell you—all that has happened. What I am doing," she added, faintly, "is by no will of mine."

"To London to-night?" he repeated, with astonishment. "I am not going to London to-night."

"Yes, Edmund, with me. I want you."

"I have wanted," he said, "you—or, at least, I have wanted my proper place and the people I belonged to, all my life. If you think that now, when I am a man, I am to be burdened with two women always at my heels—Why can't you stay and make everything comfortable here? I want my rights, but I don't want you—more than is reasonable," he added after a moment, slightly struck by his own ungraciousness. "As for walking to the train, and going to London to-night—you, a fine lady, that have always driven about in your carriage!" He gave a hoarse little laugh at the ridiculous suggestion.

Mrs. Trevanion again clutched Jane's arm. It was the only outlet for her excitement. She said very low, "I should not have expected better—oh, no; how could he know better, after all! But I must go, there is no choice. Edmund, if anything I can do now can blot out the past—no, not that—but make up for it. You too, you have been very tyrannical to me these months past. Hush! let me speak, it is quite true. If you could have had patience, all might have been so different. Let us not upbraid each other—but if you will let me, all that I can do for you now—all that is possible—"

There was another pause. Jane, standing behind, supported her mistress in her outstretched arms, but this was not apparent, nor any other sign of weakness, except that her voice quivered upon the dark air which was still in the shadow of the copse.

"I have told you," he said, "again and again, what would please me. We can't be much devoted to each other, can we, after all! We can't be a model of what's affectionate. That was all very well when I was a child, when I thought a present was just as good, or better. But now I know what is what, and that something more is wanted. Why can't you stay still where you are and send for me? You can say I'm a relation. I don't want you to sacrifice yourself—what good will that do me? I want to get the advantage of my relations, to know them all, and have my chance. There's one thing I've set my heart upon, and you could help me in that if you liked. But to run away, good Lord! what good would that do? It's all for effect, I suppose, to make me think you are willing now to do a deal for me. You can do a deal for me if you like, but it will be by staying, not by running away."

"Jane," said Mrs. Trevanion, "he does not understand me; how should he? you did not understand me at first. It is not that he means anything. And how can I tell him?—not here, I am not able. After, when we are far away, when I am out of reach, when I have got a little—strength—"

"Madam!" said Jane, "if it is true, if you have to do it, if we must go to-night, don't stand and waste all the little strength you have got standing here."

He listened to this conversation with impatience, yet with a growing sense that something lay beneath which would confound his hopes. He was not sympathetic with her trouble. How could he have been so? Had not her ways been contrary to his all his life? But a vague dread crept over him. He had thought himself near the object of his hopes, and now disappointment seemed to overshadow him. He looked angrily, with vexation and gathering dismay, at the dark figures of the two women, one leaning against the other. What did she mean now? How was she going to baffle him this time—she who had been contrary to him all his life?

CHAPTER XXXVII

It was a long walk through the wind and blasts of rain, and the country roads were very dark and wet—not a night for a woman to be out in, much less a lady used to drive everywhere in her carriage, as he had said, and less still for one whose strength had been wasted by long confinement in a sick-room, and whose very life was sapped by secret pain. But these things, which made it less possible for Mrs. Trevanion to bear the fatigues to which she was exposed, reacted on the other side, and made her unconscious of the lesser outside evils which were as nothing in comparison with the real misery from which no expedient could set her free. She went along mechanically, conscious of a fatigue and aching which were almost welcome—which lulled a little the other misery which lay somewhere awaiting her, waiting for the first moment of leisure, the time when she should be clear-headed enough to understand and feel it all to the fullest. When they came into the light at the nearest railway station the two women were alone. They got into an empty carriage and placed themselves each in a corner, and, like St. Paul, wished for day; but yet the night was welcome too, giving their proceedings an air of something strange and out of all the habits of their life, which partially, momentarily, confused the every-day aspect of things around, and made this episode in existence all unnatural and unreal. It was morning, the dark, grim morning of winter, without light or color, when Mrs. Trevanion suddenly spoke for the first time. She said, as if thinking aloud, "It was not to be expected. Why should he, when he knows so little of me?" as if reasoning with herself.

"No, Madam," said Jane.

"If he had been like others, accustomed to these restraints—for no doubt it is a restraint—"

"Oh, yes, Madam."

"And perhaps with time and use," she said, sighing and faltering.

"Yes, Madam," said Jane.

"Why do you say no and yes," she cried, with sudden vehemence, "as if you had no opinion of your own?"

Then Jane faltered too. "Madam," she said, "everything is to be hoped from—time, as you say, and use—"

"You don't think so," her mistress replied, with a moan, and then all settled into silence again.

It is not supposed that anything save vulgar speed and practical convenience is to be got from the railway; and yet there is nothing that affords a better refuge and shelter from the painful thoughts that attend a great catastrophe in life, and those consultations which an individual in deep trouble holds with himself, than a long, silent journey at the desperate pace of an express train over the long, dark sweeps of the scarcely visible country, with the wind of rapid progress in one's face. That complete separation from all disturbance, the din that partially deadens in our ears the overwhelming commotion of brain and heart, the protection which is afforded by the roar and sweep of hot haste which holds us as in a sanctuary of darkness, peace, and solitude, is a paradox of every-day life which few think of, yet which is grateful to many. Mrs. Trevanion sank into it with a sensation which was almost ease. She lay back in her corner, as a creature wounded to death lies still after the anguish of medical care is ended, throbbing, indeed, with inevitable pain, yet with all horror of expectation over, and nothing further asked of the sufferer. If not the anguish, at least the consciousness of anguish was deadened by the sense that here no one could demand anything from her, any response, any look, any word. She lay for a long time dumb even in thought, counting the throbs that went through her, feeling the sting and smart of every wound, yet a little eased by the absolute separation between her and everything that could ask a question or suggest a thought. It is not necessary for us in such terrible moments to think over our pangs. The sufferer lies piteously contemplating the misery that holds him, almost glad to be left alone with it. For the most terrible complications of human suffering there is no better image still than that with which the ancients portrayed the anguish of Prometheus on his rock. There he lies, bound and helpless, bearing evermore the rending of the vulture's beak, sometimes writhing in his bonds, uttering hoarsely the moan of his appeal to earth and heaven, crying out sometimes the horrible cry of an endurance past enduring, anon lying silent, feeling the dew upon him, hearing soft voices of pity, comforters that tell him of peace to come, sometimes softening, sometimes only increasing his misery; but through all unending, never intermitting, the pain—"pain, ever, forever" of that torture from which there is no escape. In all its moments of impatience, in all its succumbings, the calm of anguish which looks like resignation, the struggle with the unbearable which looks like resistance, the image is always true. We lie bound and cannot escape. We listen to what is said about us, the soft consoling of nature, the voices of the comforters. Great heavenly creatures come and sit around us, and talk together of the recovery to come; but meanwhile without a pause the heart quivers and bleeds, the cruel grief tears us without intermission. "Ah me, alas, pain, ever, forever!"

If ever human soul had occasion for such a consciousness it was this woman, cut off in a moment from all she loved best—from her children, from her home, from life itself and honor, and all that makes life dear. Her good name, the last possession which, shipwrecked in every other, the soul in ruin and dismay may still derive some miserable satisfaction from, had to be yielded too. A faint smile came upon her face, the profoundest expression of suffering, when this thought, like another laceration, separated itself from the crowd. A little more or less, was that not a thing to be smiled at? What could it matter? All that could be done to her was done; her spiritual tormentors had no longer the power to give her another sensation; she had exhausted all their tortures. Her good name, and that even in the knowledge of her children! She smiled. Evil had done its worst. She was henceforward superior to any torture, as knowing all that pain could do.

There are some minds to which death is not a thought which is possible, or a way of escape which ever suggests itself. Hamlet, in his musings, in the sickness of his great soul, passes it indeed in review, but rejects it as an unworthy and ineffectual expedient. And it is seldom that a worthy human creature, when not at the outside verge of life, can afford to die. There is always something to do which keeps every such possibility in the background. To this thought after a time Mrs. Trevanion came round. She had a great deal to do; she had still a duty—a responsibility—was it perhaps a possibility, in life? There existed for her still one bond, a bond partially severed for long, apparently dropped out of her existence, yet never forgotten. The brief dialogue which she had held with Jane had betrayed the condition of her thoughts in respect to this one relationship which was left to her, as it betrayed also the judgment of Jane on the subject. Both of these women knew in their hearts that the young man who was now to be the only interest of their lives had little in him which corresponded with any ideal. He had not been kind, he had not been true; he thought of nothing but himself, and yet he was all that now remained to make, to the woman upon whom his folly had brought so many and terrible losses, the possibility of a new life. When she saw the cold glimmer of the dawn, and heard the beginnings of that sound of London, which stretches so far round the centre on every side, Mrs. Trevanion awoke again to the living problem which now was to occupy her wholly. She had been guilty towards him almost all his life, and she had been punished by his means; but perhaps it might be that there was still for her a place of repentance. She had much to do for him, and not a moment to lose. She had the power to make up to him now for all the neglect of the past. Realizing what he was, unlike her in thought, in impulse, in wishes, a being who belonged to her, yet who in heart and soul was none of hers, she rose up from the terrible vigil of this endless night, to make her life henceforward the servant of his, its guardian perhaps, its guide perhaps, but in any case subject to it, as a woman at all times is subject to those for whom she lives. She spoke again, when they were near their arrival, to her maid, as if they had continued the subject throughout the night: "He will be sure to follow us to-morrow night, Jane."

"I think so, Madam, for he will have nothing else to do."

"It was natural," said Mrs. Trevanion, "that he should hesitate to come off in a moment. Why should he, indeed? There was nothing to break the shock to him—as there was to us—"

"To break the shock?" Jane murmured, with a look of astonishment.

"You know what I mean," her mistress said, with a little impatience. "When things happen like the things that have happened, one does not think very much of a midnight journey. Ah, what a small matter that is! But one who has—nothing to speak of on his mind—"

"He ought to have a great deal on his mind," said Jane.

"Ought! Yes, I suppose I ought to be half dead, and, on the contrary, I am revived by the night journey. I am able for anything. There is no ought in such matters—it is according to your strength."

"You have not slept a wink," said Jane, in an injured voice.

"There are better things than sleep. And he is young, and has not learned yet the lesson that I have had such difficulty in learning."

"What lesson is that?" said Jane, quickly. "If it is to think of everything and every one's business, you have been indeed a long time learning, for you have been at it all your life."

"It takes a long time to learn," said Madam, with a smile; "the young do not take it in so easily. Come, Jane, we are arriving; we must think now of our new way of living."

"Madam," cried Jane, "if there had been an earthquake at Highcourt, and we had both perished in it trying to save the children—"

"Jane! do you think it is wise when you are in great trouble to fix your thoughts upon the greatest happiness in the world? To have perished at Highcourt, you and me, trying—" Her face shone for a moment with a great radiance. "You are a good woman," she said, shaking her head, with a smile, "but why should there be a miracle to save me? It is a miracle to give me the chance of making up—for what is past."

"Oh, Madam, I wish I knew what to say to you," cried Jane; "you will just try your strength and make yourself miserable, and get no return."

Mrs. Trevanion laughed with a strange solemnity. She looked before her into the vacant air, as if looking in the face of fate. What could make her miserable now? Nothing—the worst that could be done had been done. She said, but to herself, not to Jane, "There is an advantage in it, it cannot be done over again." Then she began to prepare for the arrival. "We shall have a great deal to do, and we must lose no time. Jane, you will go at once and provide some clothes for us. Whatever happens, we must have clothes, and we must have food, you know. The other things—life can go on without—"

"Madam, for God's sake, do not smile, it makes my blood run cold."

"Would you like me to cry, Jane? I might do that, too, but what the better should we be? If I were to cry all to-day and to-morrow, the moment would come when I should have to stop and smile again. And then," she said, turning hastily upon her faithful follower, "I can't cry—I can't cry!" with a spasm of anguish going over her face. "Besides, we are just arriving," she added, after a moment; "we must not call for remark. You and I, we are two poor women setting out upon the world—upon a forlorn hope. Yes, that is it—upon a forlorn hope. We don't look like heroes, but that is what we are going to do, without any banners flying, or music, but a good heart, Jane—a good heart!"

With these words, she stepped out upon the crowded pavement at the great London station. It was a very early hour in the morning, and there were few people except the travellers and the porters about. They had no luggage, which was a thing that confused Jane, and made her ashamed to the bottom of her heart. She answered the questions of the porter with a confused consciousness of something half disgraceful in their denuded condition, and gave her bag into his hands with a shrinking and trembling which made the poor soul, pallid with unaccustomed travelling, and out of her usual prim order, look like a furtive fugitive. She half thought the man looked at her as if she were a criminal escaping from justice. Jane was ashamed: she thought the people in the streets looked at the cab as it rattled out of the station with suspicion and surprise. She looked forward to the arrival at the hotel with a kind of horror. What would people think? Jane felt the real misery of the catastrophe more than any one except the chief sufferer: she looked forward to the new life about to begin with dismay; but nevertheless, at this miserable moment, to come to London without luggage gave her the deepest pang of all.

CHAPTER XXXVIII

Mrs. Trevanion remained for some time in London, where she was joined reluctantly, after a few days, by Edmund. This young man had not been educated on the level of Highcourt. He had been sent to a cheap school. He had never known any relations, nor had any culture of the affections to refine his nature. From his school, as soon as he was old enough, he had been transferred to an office in Liverpool, where all the temptations and attractions of the great town had burst upon him without defence. Many young men have to support this ordeal, and even for those who do not come through it without scathe, it is yet possible to do so without ruinous loss and depreciation. But in that case the aberration must be but temporary, and there must be a higher ideal behind to defend the mind against that extinction of all belief in what is good which is the most horrible result of vicious living. Whether Edmund fell into the absolute depths of vice at all it is not necessary to inquire. He fell into debt, and into unlawful ways of making up for his debts. When discovery was not to be staved off any longer he had fled, not even then touched with any compunction or shame, but with a strong certainty that the matter against him would never be allowed to come to a public issue, it being so necessary to the credit of the family that his relations with Highcourt should never be made known to the world. It was with this certainty that he had come to the village near Highcourt at the beginning of Mr. Trevanion's last illness. To prevent him from bursting into her husband's presence, and bringing on one of the attacks which sapped his strength, Mrs. Trevanion had yielded to his demands on her, and, as these increased daily, had exposed herself to remark and scandal, and, as it proved, to ruin and shame. Did she think of that as he sat opposite to her at the table, affording reluctantly the information she insisted upon, betraying by almost every word a mind so much out of tune with hers that the bond which connected them seemed impossible? If she did think of this it was with the bitterest self-reproach, rather than any complaint of him. "Poor boy," she said to herself, with her heart bleeding. She had informed him of the circumstances under which she had left home, but without a word of blame or intimation that the fault was his, and received what were really his reproaches on this matter silently, with only that heart-breaking smile in her eyes, which meant indulgence unbounded, forgiveness beforehand of anything he might do or say. When Russell, breathing hatred and hostility, came across her path, it was with the same sentiment that Madam had succored the woman who had played so miserable a part in the catastrophe. The whole history of the event was so terrible that she could bear no comment upon it. Even Jane did not venture to speak to her of the past. She was calm, almost cheerful, in what she was doing at the moment, and she had a great deal to do.

The first step she took was one which Edmund opposed with all his might, with a hundred arguments more or less valid, and a mixture of terror and temerity which it humiliated her to be a witness of. He was ready to abandon all possibility of after-safety or of recovery of character, to fly as a criminal to the ends of the earth, or to keep in hiding in holes and corners, liable to be seized upon at any moment; but to take any step to atone for what he had done, to restore the money, or attempt to recover the position of a man innocent, or at least forgiven, were suggestions that filled him with passion. He declared that such an attempt would be ineffectual, that it would end by landing him in prison, that it was madness to think she could do anything. She! so entirely ignorant of business as she was. He ended, indeed, by denouncing her as his certain ruin, when, in spite of all these arguments, she set out for Liverpool, and left him in a paroxysm of angry terror, forgetting both respect and civility in the passion of opposition. Madam Trevanion did not shrink from this any more than from the other fits of passion to which she had been exposed in her life. She went to Liverpool alone, without even the company and support of Jane. And there she found her mission not without difficulty. But the aspect of the woman to whom fate had done its worst, who was not conscious of the insignificant pain of a rebuff from a stranger, she who had borne every anguish that could be inflicted upon a woman, had an impressive influence which in the end triumphed over everything opposed to her. She told the young man's story with a composure from which it was impossible to divine what her own share in it was, but with a pathos which touched the heart of the master, who was not a hard man, and who knew the dangers of such a youth better than she did. In the end she was permitted to pay the money, and to release the culprit from all further danger. Her success in this gave her a certain hope. As she returned her mind went forward with something like a recollection of its old elasticity, to what was at least a possibility in the future. Thus made free, and with all the capacities of youth in him, might not some softening and melting of the young man's nature be hoped for—some development of natural affection, some enlargement of life? She said to herself that it might be so. He was not bad nor cruel—he was only unaccustomed to love and care, careless, untrained to any higher existence, unawakened to any better ideal. As she travelled back to London she said to herself that he must have repented his passion, that some compunction must have moved him, even, perhaps, some wish to atone. "He will come to meet me," she said to herself, with a forlorn movement of anticipation in her mind. She felt so sure as she thought of this expedient, by which he might show a wish to please her without bending his pride to confess himself in the wrong, that when she arrived and, amid the crowds at the railway, saw no one, her heart sank a little. But in a moment she recovered, saying to herself, "Poor boy! why should he come?" He had never been used to render such attentions. He was uneasy in the new companionship, to which he was unaccustomed. Perhaps, indeed, he was ashamed, wounded, mortified, by the poor part he played in it. To owe his deliverance even to her might be humiliating to his pride. Poor boy! Thus she explained and softened everything to herself.

But Mrs. Trevanion found herself now the subject of a succession of surprises very strange to her. She was brought into intimate contact with a nature she did not understand, and had to learn the very alphabet of a language unknown to her, and study impulses which left all her experience of human nature behind, and were absolutely new. When he understood that he was free, that everything against him was wiped off, that he was in a position superior to anything he had ever dreamed of, without need to work or deny himself, his superficial despair gave way to a burst of pleasure and self-congratulation. Even then he was on his guard not to receive with too much satisfaction the advantages of which he had in a moment become possessed, lest perhaps he should miss something more that might be coming. The unbounded delight which filled him when he found himself in London, with money in his pocket, and freedom, showed itself, indeed, in every look; but he still kept a wary eye upon the possibilities of the future, and would not allow that what he possessed was above his requirements or hopes. And when he perceived that the preparations for a further journey were by no means interrupted, and that Mrs. Trevanion's plan was still to go abroad, his disappointment and vexation were not to be controlled.

"What should you go abroad for?" he said. "We're far better in London. There is everything in London that can be desired. It is the right place for a young fellow like me. I have never had any pleasure in my life, nor the means of seeing anything. And here, the moment I have something in my power, you want to rush away."

"There is a great deal to see on the other side of the Channel, Edmund."

"I dare say—among foreigners whose language one doesn't know a word of. And what is it, after all? Scenery, or pictures, and that sort of thing. Whereas what I want to see is life."

She looked at him with a strange understanding of all that she would have desired to ignore, knowing what he meant by some incredible pang of inspiration, though she had neither any natural acquaintance with such a strain of thought nor any desire to divine it. "There is life everywhere," she said, "and I think it will be very good for you, Edmund. You are not very strong, and there are so many things to learn."

"I see. You think, as I am, that I am not much credit to you, Mrs. Trevanion, of Highcourt. But there might be different opinions about that." Offence brought a flush of color to his cheek. "Miss Trevanion, of Highcourt, was not so difficult to please," he added, with a laugh of vanity. "She showed no particular objections to me; but you have ruined me there, I suppose, once for all."

This attack left her speechless. She could not for the moment reply, but only looked at him with that appeal in her eyes, to which, in the assurance not only of his egotism, but of his total unacquaintance with what was going on in her mind, her motives and ways of thinking, he was utterly insensible. This, however, was only the first of many arguments on the subject which filled those painful days. When he saw that the preparations still went on, Edmund's disgust was great.

"I see Jane is still going on packing," he said. "You don't mind, then, that I can't bear it? What should you drag me away for? I am quite happy here."

"My dear," she said, "you were complaining yourself that you have not anything to do. You have no friends here."

"Nor anywhere," said Edmund; "and whose fault is that?"

"Perhaps it is my fault. But that does not alter the fact, Edmund. If I say that I am sorry, that is little, but still it does not mend it. In Italy everything will amuse you."

"Nothing will amuse me," said the young man. "I tell you I don't care for scenery. What I want to see is life."

"In travelling," said Mrs. Trevanion, "you often make friends, and you see how the people of other countries live, and you learn—"

"I don't want to learn," he cried abruptly. "You are always harping upon that. It is too late to go to school at my age. If I have no education you must put up with it, for it is your fault. And what I want is to stay here. London is the place to learn life and everything. And if you tell me that you couldn't get me plenty of friends, if you chose to exert yourself, I don't believe you. It's because you won't, not because you can't."

"Edmund!"

"Oh, don't contradict me, for I know better. There is one thing I want above all others, and I know you mean to go against me in that. If you stay here quiet, you know very well they will come to town like everybody else, for the season, and then you can introduce me. She knows me already. The last time she saw me she colored up. She knew very well what I was after. This has always been in my mind since the first time I saw her with you. She is fond of you. She will be glad enough to come, if it is even on the sly—"

He was very quick to see when he had gone wrong, and the little cry that came from her lips, the look that came over her face, warned him a moment too late. He "colored up," as he said, crimson to the eyes, and endeavored with an uneasy laugh to account for his slip. "The expression may be vulgar," he said, "but everybody uses it. And that's about what it would come to, I suppose."

"You mistake me altogether, Edmund," she said. "I will not see any one on the sly, as you say; and especially not—Don't wound me by suggesting what is impossible. If I had not known that I had no alternative, can you suppose I should have left them at all?"

"That's a different matter; you were obliged to do that; but nobody could prevent you meeting them in the streets, seeing them as they pass, saying 'How do you do?' introducing a relation—"

She rose up, and began to pace about the room in great agitation. "Don't say any more, don't torture me like this," she said. "Can you not understand how you are tearing me to pieces? If I were to do what you say, I should be dishonest, false both to the living and the dead. And it would be better to be at the end of the world than to be near them in a continual fever, watching, scheming, for a word. Oh, no! no!" she said, wringing her hands, "do not let me be tempted beyond my strength. Edmund, for my sake, if for no other, let us go away."

He looked at her with a sort of cynical observation, as she walked up and down the room with hurried steps at first, then calming gradually. He repeated slowly, with a half laugh, "For your sake? But I thought everything now was to be for my sake. And it is my turn; you can't deny that."

Mrs. Trevanion gave him a piteous look. It was true that it was his turn; and it was true that she had said all should be for him in her changed life. He had her at an advantage; a fact which to her finer nature seemed the strongest reason for generous treatment, but not to his.

"It is all very well to speak," he continued; "but if you really mean well by me, introduce me to Rosalind. That would be the making of me. She is a fine girl, and she has money; and she would be just as pleased—"

She stopped him, after various efforts, almost by force, seizing his arm. "There are some things," she said, "that I cannot bear. This is one of them. I will not have her name brought in—not even her name—"

"Why not? What's in her name more than another? A rose, don't you know, by any other name—" he said, with a forced laugh. But he was alarmed by Mrs. Trevanion's look, and the clutch which in her passion she had taken of his arm. After all, his new life was dependent upon her, and it might be expedient not to go too far.

This interlude left her trembling and full of agitation. She did not sleep all night, but moved about the room, in her dingy London lodging, scarcely able to keep still. A panic had seized hold upon her. She sent for him in the morning as soon as he had left his room, which was not early; and even he observed the havoc made in her already worn face by the night. She told him that she had resolved to start next day.

"I did not perceive," she said, "all the dangers of staying, till you pointed them out to me. If I am to be honest, if I am to keep any one's esteem, I must go away."

"I don't see it," he said, somewhat sullenly. "It's all your fancy. When a person's in hiding, he's safer in London than anywhere else."

"I am not in hiding," she said, hastily, with a sense of mingled irritation and despair. For what words could be used which he would understand, which would convey to him any conception of what she meant? They were like two people speaking different languages, incapable of communicating to each other anything that did not lie upon the surface of their lives. When he perceived at last how much in earnest she was, how utterly resolved not to remain, he yielded, but without either grace or good humor. He had not force enough in himself to resist when it came to a distinct issue. Thus they departed together into the world unknown—two beings absolutely bound to each other, each with no one else in the world to turn to, and yet with no understanding of each other, not knowing the very alphabet of each other's thoughts.

CHAPTER XXXIX

Thus Mrs. Trevanion went away out of reach and knowledge of everything that belonged to her old life. She had not been very happy in that life. The principal actor in it, her husband, had regarded her comfort less than that of his horses or hounds. He had filled her existence with agitations, but yet had not made life unbearable until the last fatal complications had arisen. She had been surrounded by people who understood her more or less, who esteemed and approved her, and she had possessed in Rosalind the sweetest of companions, one who was in sympathy with every thought, who understood almost before she was conscious of thinking at all; a creature who was herself yet not herself, capable of sharing everything and responding at every point. And, except her husband, there was no one who regarded Madam Trevanion with anything but respect and reverence. No one mistook the elevation of her character. She was regarded with honor wherever she went, her opinions prized, her judgment much considered. When a woman to whom this position has been given suddenly descends to find herself in the sole company of one who cares nothing for her judgment, to whom all her opinions are antiquated or absurd, and herself one of those conventional female types without logic or reason, which are all that some men know of women, the confusing effect which is produced upon earth and heaven is too wonderful for words. More than any change of events, this change of position confuses and overwhelms the mind. Sometimes it is the dismal result of an ill-considered marriage. Sometimes it appears in other relationships. She was pulled rudely down from the pedestal she had occupied so long, and rudely, suddenly, made to feel that she was no oracle, that her words had no weight because she said them, but rather carried with them a probability of foolishness because they were hers. The wonder of this bewildered at first; it confused her consciousness, and made her insecure of herself. And at last it produced the worse effect of making everything uncertain to her. Though she had been supposed so self-sustained and strong in character, she was too natural a woman not to be deeply dependent upon sympathy and the support of understanding. When these failed she tottered and found no firm footing anywhere. Perhaps she said to herself she was really foolish, as Edmund thought, unreasonable, slow to comprehend all character that was unlike her own. She was no longer young; perhaps the young were wiser, had stronger lights; perhaps her beliefs, her prejudices, were things of the past. All this she came to think with wondering pain when the support of general faith and sympathy was withdrawn. It made her doubtful of everything she had done or believed, timid to speak, watching the countenance of the young man whose attitude towards her had changed all the world to her. This was not part of the great calamity that had befallen her. It was something additional, another blow; to be parted from her children, to sustain the loss of all things dear to her, was her terrible fate, a kind of vengeance for what was past; but that her self-respect, her confidence, should thus be taken away from her was another distinct and severe calamity. Sometimes the result was a mental giddiness, a quiver about her of the atmosphere and all the solid surroundings, as though there was (but in a manner unthought of by Berkeley) nothing really existent but only in the thoughts of those who beheld it. Perhaps her previous experiences had led her towards this; for such had been the scope of all her husband's addresses to her for many a day. But she had not been utterly alone with him, she had felt the strong support of other people's faith and approval holding her up and giving her strength. Now all these accessories had failed her. Her world consisted of one soul, which had no faith in her; and thus, turned back upon herself, she faltered in all her moral certainties, and began to doubt whether she had ever been right, whether she had any power to judge, or perception, or even feeling, whether she were not perhaps in reality the conventional woman, foolish, inconsistent, pertinacious, which she appeared through Edmund's eyes.

The other strange, new sensations that Madam encountered in these years, while her little children throve and grew under the care of Mrs. Lennox, and Rosalind developed into the full bloom of early womanhood, were many and various. She had thought herself very well acquainted with the mysteries of human endurance, but it seemed to her now that at the beginning of that new life she had known nothing of them. New depths and heights developed every day; her own complete breaking down and the withdrawal from her of confidence in herself being the great central fact of all. On Edmund's side the development too was great. He had looked and wished for pleasure and ease and self-indulgence when he had very little power of securing them. When by a change of fortune so extraordinary and unexpected he actually obtained the means of gratifying his instincts, he addressed himself to the task with a unity of purpose which was worthy of a greater aim. He was drawn aside from his end by no glimmer of ambition, no impulse to make something better out of his life. His imperfect education and ignorance of what was best in existence had perhaps something to do with this. To him, as to many a laboring man, the power of doing no work, nor anything but what he pleased, seemed the most supreme of gratifications. He would not give himself the trouble to study anything, even the world, confident as only the ignorant are in the power of money, and in that great evidence that he had become one of the privileged classes, the fact that he did not now need to do anything for his living. He was not absolutely bad or cruel; he only preferred his own pleasure to anybody else's, and was a little contemptuous of a woman's advice and intolerant of her rule and impatient of her company. Perhaps her idea that she owed herself to him, that it was paying an old debt of long-postponed duty to devote herself to him now, to do her best for him, to give him everything in her power that could make him happy, was a mistaken one from the beginning. She got to believe that she was selfish in remaining with him, while still feeling that her presence was the only possible curb upon him. How was she to find a way of serving him best, of providing for all his wants and wishes, of keeping him within the bounds of possibility, yet letting him be free from the constraint of her presence? As time went on, this problem became more and more urgent, yet by the same progress of time her mind grew less and less clear on any point. The balance of the comparative became more difficult to carry. There was no absolute good within her reach, and she would not allow even to herself that there was any absolute bad in the young man's selfish life. It was all comparative, as life was. But to find the point of comparative advantage which should be best for him, where he should be free without being abandoned, and have the power of shaping his course as he pleased without the power of ruining himself and her—this became more and more the engrossing subject of her thoughts.

As for Edmund, though he indulged in many complaints and grumbles as to having always a woman at his heels, his impatience never went the length of emancipating himself. On the whole, his indolent nature found it most agreeable to have everything done for him, to have no occasion for thought. He had the power always of complaint, which gave him a kind of supremacy without responsibility. His fixed grievance was that he was kept out of London; his hope, varying as they went and came about the world, that somewhere they would meet the family from which Mrs. Trevanion had been torn, and that "on the sly," or otherwise (though he never repeated those unlucky words), he might find himself in a position to approach Rosalind. In the meantime he amused himself in such ways as were practicable, and spent a great deal of money, and got a certain amount of pleasure out of his life. His health was not robust, and when late hours and amusements told upon him he had the most devoted of nurses. On the whole, upon comparison with the life of a clerk on a small salary in a Liverpool office, his present existence was a sort of shabby Paradise.

About the time when Rosalind heard from Mr. Rivers of that chance encounter which revived all her longings for her mother, and at the same time all the horror of vague and miserable suspicion which surrounded Mrs. Trevanion's name, a kind of crisis had occurred in this strange, wandering life. Edmund had fallen ill, more seriously than before, and in the quiet of convalescence after severe suffering had felt certain compunctions cross his mind. He had acknowledged to his tender nurse that she was very kind to him. "If you would not nag a fellow so," he said, "and drive me about so that I don't know what I am doing, I think, now that I am used to your ways, we might get on."

Mrs. Trevanion did not defend herself against the charge of "nagging" or "driving" as she might perhaps have done at an earlier period, but accepted with almost grateful humility the condescension of this acknowledgment. "In the meantime," she said, "you must get well, and then, please God, everything will be better."

"If you like to make it so," he said, already half repentant of the admission he had made. And then he added, "If you'd only give up this fancy of yours for foreign parts. Why shouldn't we go home? You may like it, you speak the language, and so forth: but I detest it. If you want to please me and make me get well, let's go home."

"We have no home to go to, Edmund—"

"Oh, that's nonsense, you know. You don't suppose I mean the sort of fireside business. Nothing is so easy as to get a house in London; and you know that is what I like best."

"Edmund, how could I live in a house in London?" she said. "You must remember that a great deal has passed that is very painful. I could not but be brought in contact with people who used to know me—"

"Ah!" he cried, "here's the real reason at last. I thought all this time it was out of consideration for me, to keep me out of temptation, and that sort of thing; but now it crops up at last. It's for yourself, after all. It is always an advance to know the true reason. And what could they do to you, those people with whom you might be brought in contact?"

She would not perhaps have said anything about herself had he not beguiled her by the momentary softness of his tone. And now one of those rapid scintillations of cross light which were continually gleaming upon her life and motives flashed over her and changed everything. To be sure! it was selfishness, no doubt, though she had not seen it so. She answered, faltering a little: "They could do nothing to me. Perhaps you are right, Edmund. It may be that I have been thinking too much of myself. But I am sure London would not be good for you. To live there with comfort you must have something to do, or you must have—friends—"

"Well!" he said, with a kind of defiance.

"You have no friends, Edmund."

"Well," he repeated, "whose fault is that? It is true that I have no friends; but I could have friends and everything else if you would take a little trouble—more than friends; I might marry and settle. You could do everything for me in that way if you would take the trouble. That's what I want to do; but I suppose you would rather drag me forever about with you than see me happy in a place of my own."

Mrs. Trevanion had lost her beauty. She was pale and worn as if twenty additional years had passed over her head instead of two. But for a moment the sudden flush that warmed and lighted up her countenance restored to her something of her prime. "I think," she said, "Edmund, if you will let me for a moment believe what I am saying, that, to see you happy and prosperous, I would gladly die. I know you will say my dying would be little to the purpose; but the other I cannot do for you. To marry requires a great deal that you do not think of. I don't say love, in the first place—"

"You may if you please," he said. "I'm awfully fond of—Oh, I don't mind saying her name. You know who I mean. If you were good enough for her, I don't see why I shouldn't be good enough for her. You have only got to introduce me, which you can if you like, and all the rest I take in my own hands."

"I was saying," she repeated, "that love, even if love exists, is not all. Before any girl of a certain position would be allowed to marry, the man must satisfy her friends. His past, and his future, and the means he has, and how he intends to live—all these things have to be taken into account. It is not so easy as you think."

"That is all very well," said Edmund; though he paused with a stare of mounting dismay in his beautiful eyes, larger and more liquid than ever by reason of his illness—those eyes which haunted Rosalind's imagination. "That is all very well: but it is not as if you were a stranger: when they know who I am—when I have you to answer for me—"

A flicker of self-assertion came into her eyes. "Why do you think they should care for me or my recommendation? You do not," she said.

He laughed. "That's quite different. Perhaps they know more—and I am sure they know less—than I do. I should think you would like them to know about me for your own sake."

She turned away with once more a rapid flush restoring momentary youth to her countenance. She was so changed that it seemed to her, as she caught a glimpse of herself, languidly moving across the room, in the large, dim mirror opposite, that no one who belonged to her former existence would now recognize her. And there was truth in what he said. It would be better for her, for her own sake, that the family from whom she was separated should know everything there was to tell. After the first horror lest they should know, there had come a revulsion of feeling, and she had consented in her mind that to inform them of everything would be the best, though she still shrank from it. But even if she had strength to make that supreme effort it could do her no good. Nothing, they had said, no explanation, no clearing up, would ever remove the ban under which she lay. And it would be better to go down to her grave unjustified than to place Rosalind in danger. She looked back upon the convalescent as he resumed fretfully the book which was for the moment his only way of amusing himself. Illness had cleared away from Edmund's face all the traces of self-indulgence which she had seen there. It was a beautiful face, full of apparent meaning and sentiment, the eyes full of tenderness and passion—or at least what might seem so in other lights, and to spectators less dismally enlightened than herself. A young soul like Rosalind, full of faith and enthusiasm, might take that face for the face of a hero, a poet. Ah! this was a cruel thought that came to her against her will, that stabbed her like a knife as it came. She said to herself tremulously that in other circumstances, with other people, he might have been, might even be, all that his face told. Only with her from the beginning everything had gone wrong—which again, in some subtle way, according to those revenges which everything that is evil brings with it, was her fault and not his. But Rosalind must not be led to put her faith upon promises which were all unfulfilled. Rosalind must not run any such risk. Whatever should happen, she could not expose to so great a danger another woman, and that her own child.

But there were other means of setting the wheels of fate in motion, with which Madame Trevanion had nothing to do.

CHAPTER XL

Towards the end of the summer, during the height of which Mrs. Lennox's party had returned to the Italian lakes, one of the friends she made at Cadenabbia represented to that good woman that her rheumatism, from which she had suffered during the winter, though perhaps not quite so severely as she imagined, made it absolutely necessary to go through a "cure" at Aix-les-Bains, where, as everybody knows, rheumatism is miraculously operated upon by the waters. Aunt Sophy was very much excited by this piece of advice. In the company which she had been frequenting of late, at the tables d'hôte and in the public promenades, she had begun to perceive that it was scarcely respectable for a person of a certain age not to go through a yearly "cure" at some one or other of a number of watering-places. It indicated a state of undignified health and robustness which was not quite nice for a lady no longer young. There were many who went to Germany, to the different bads there, and a considerable number whose "cure" was in France, and some even who sought unknown springs in Switzerland and Italy; but, taken on the whole, very few indeed were the persons over fifty of either sex who did not reckon a "cure" occupying three weeks or so of the summer or autumn as a necessary part of the routine of life. To all Continental people it was indispensable, and there were many Americans who crossed the ocean for this purpose, going to Carlsbad or to Kissingen or somewhere else with as much regularity as if they had lived within a railway journey of the place. Only the English were careless on so important a subject, but even among them many become convinced of the necessity day by day.

Mrs. Lennox, when this idea fully penetrated her mind, and she had blushed to think how far she was behind in so essential a particular of life, had a strong desire to go to Homburg, where all the "best people" went, and where there was quite a little supplementary London season, after the conclusion of the genuine article. But, unfortunately, there was nothing the matter with her digestion. Her rheumatism was the only thing she could bring forward as entitling her to any position at all among the elderly ladies and gentlemen who in August were setting out for, or returning from, their "cures." "Oh, then, of course, it is Aix you must go to," her informants said; "it is a little late, perhaps, in September—most of the best people will have gone—still, you know, the waters are just as good, and the great heat is over. You could not do better than Aix." One of the ladies who thus instructed her was even kind enough to suggest the best hotel to go to, and to proffer her own services, as knowing all about it, to write and secure rooms for her friend. "It is a pity you did not go three weeks ago, when all the best people were there; but, of course, the waters are just the same," this benevolent person repeated. Mrs. Lennox became, after a time, very eager on this subject. She no longer blushed when her new acquaintances talked of their cure. She explained to new-comers, "It is a little late, but it did not suit my arrangements before; and, of course, the waters are the same, though the best people are gone." Besides, it was always, she said, on the way home, whatever might happen.

They set off accordingly, travelling in a leisurely way, in the beginning of September. Mrs. Lennox felt that it was expedient to go slowly, to have something of the air of an invalid before she began her "cure." Up to this moment she had borne a stray twinge of pain when it came, in her shoulder or her knee, and thought it best to say nothing about it; but now she made a little grimace when that occurred, and said, "Oh, my shoulder!" or complained of being stiff when she got out of the carriage. It was only right that she should feel her ailments a little more than usual when she began her cure.

The hotels were beginning to empty when the English party, so helpless, so used to comfort, so inviting to everybody that wanted to make money out of them, appeared. They were received, it is needless to say, with open arms, and had the best suites of rooms to choose from. Mrs. Lennox felt herself to grow in importance from the moment she entered the place. She felt more stiff than ever when she got out of the carriage and was led up-stairs, the anxious landlady suggesting that there was a chair in which she could be carried to her apartment if the stairs were too much for her. "Oh, I think I can manage to walk up if I am not hurried," Aunt Sophy said. It would have been quite unkind, almost improper, not to adopt the rôle which suited the place. She went up quite slowly, holding by the baluster, while the children, astonished, crowded up after her, wondering what had happened. "I think I will take your arm, Rosalind," murmured the simple woman. She did really feel much stiffer than usual; and then there was that pain in her shoulder. "I am so glad I have suffered myself to be persuaded to come. I wonder Dr. Tennant did not order me here long ago; for I really think in my present condition I never should have been able to get home." Even Rosalind was much affected by this suggestion, and blamed herself for never having discovered how lame Aunt Sophy was growing. "But it is almost your own fault, for you never showed it," she said. "My dear, I did not, of course, want to make you anxious," replied Mrs. Lennox.

The doctor came next morning, and everything was settled about the "cure." He told the new-comers that there were still a good many people in Aix, and that all the circumstances were most favorable. Mrs. Lennox was taken to her bath in a chair the day after, and went through all the operations which the medical man thought requisite. He spoke excellent English—which was such a comfort. He told his patient that the air of the place where the cure was to be effected often seemed to produce a temporary recrudescence of the disease. Aunt Sophy was much exhilarated by this word. She talked of this chance of a recrudescence in a soft and subdued tone, such as became her invalid condition, and felt a most noble increase of dignity and importance as she proceeded with her "cure."

Rosalind was one of the party who took least to this unexpected delay. She had begun to be very weary of the travelling, the monotony of the groups of new acquaintances all so like each other, the atmosphere of hotels, and all the vulgarities of a life in public. To the children it did not matter much; they took their walks all the same whether they were at the Elms or Aix-les-Bains, and had their nursery dinner at their usual hour, whatever happened. The absorption of Mrs. Lennox in her "cure" threw Rosalind now entirely upon the society of these little persons. She went with them, or rather they went with her, in her constant expeditions to the lake, which attracted her more than the tiresome amusements of the watering-place, and thus all their little adventures and encounters—incidents which in other circumstances might have been overlooked—became matters of importance to her.

It was perhaps because he was the only boy in the little feminine party, or because he was the youngest, that Johnny was invariably the principal personage in all these episodes of childish life. He it was whom the ladies admired, whom strangers stopped to talk to, who was the little hero of every small excitement. His beautiful eyes, the boyish boldness which contrasted so strongly with little Amy's painful shyness, and even with his own little pale face and unassured strength, captivated the passers-by. He was the favorite of the nursery, which was now presided over by a nurse much more enlightened than Russell, a woman recommended by the highest authorities, and who knew, or was supposed to know, nothing of the family history. Rosalind had heard vaguely, without paying much attention, of various admirers who had paid their tribute to the attractions of her little brother, but it was not until her curiosity was roused by the appearance of a present in the form of a handsome and expensive mechanical toy, the qualities of which Johnny expounded with much self-importance and in a loud voice, that she was moved to any remark. The children were on the floor near her, full of excitement. "Now it shall run round and round, and now it shall go straight home," Johnny said, while Amy watched and listened ecstatically, a little maiden of few words, whose chief qualities were a great power of admiration and a still greater of love.

Rosalind was seated musing by the window, a little tired, wondering when the "cure" would be over, and if Aunt Sophy would then recover the use of her limbs again, and consent to go home. Mrs. Lennox was always good and kind, and the children were very dear to their mother-sister; but now and then, not always, perhaps not often, there comes to a young woman like Rosalind a longing for companionship such as neither aunts or children can give. Neither the children nor her aunt shared her thoughts; they understood her very imperfectly on most occasions; they had love to give her, but not a great deal more. She sighed, as people do when there is something wanting to them, then turned upon herself with a kind of rage and asked, "What did she want?" as girls will do on whom it has been impressed that this wish for companionship is a thing that is wrong, perhaps unmaidenly. But, after all, there was no harm in it. Oh, that Uncle John were here! she said to herself. Even Roland Hamerton would have been something. He could have tried at least his very best to think as she did. Oh, that—! She did not put any name to this aspiration. She was not very sure who—which—it meant, and then she breathed a still deeper sigh, and tears came to her eyes. Oh! for her of whom nobody knew where she was wandering or in what circumstances she might be. She heard the children's voices vaguely through her thinking, and by and by a word caught her ear.

"The lady said I was to do it like this. She did it for me on the table out in the garden. It nearly felled down," said Johnny, "and then it would have broken itself, so she put it on the ground and went down on her knees."

"Oh, what did she go on her knees for, like saying her prayers, Johnny?"

"Nothin' of the sort. She just went down like this and caught hold of me. I expose," said Johnny, whose language was not always correct, "she is stiff, like Aunt Sophy; for I was far more stronger and kept her up."

"Who is this that he is talking of, Amy?" Rosalind said.

The little girl gave her a look which had some meaning in it, Rosalind could not tell what, and, giving Johnny a little push with her arm after the easy method of childhood, said, "Tell her," turning away to examine the toy.

"It was the lady," Johnny said, turning slightly round as on a pivot, and lifting to her those great eyes which Aunt Sophy had said were like—and which always went straight to Rosalind's heart.

"What lady, dear? and where did you get that beautiful toy?" Rosalind followed the description the child had been giving, and came and knelt on the carpet beside him. "How pretty it is! Did Aunt Sophy give you that?"

"It was the lady," Johnny repeated.

"What lady? Was it a stranger, Amy, that gave him such a beautiful toy?"

"I think, Miss Rosalind," said the nurse, coming to the rescue, "it is some lady that has lost her little boy, and that he must have been about Master Johnny's age. I said it was too much, and that you would not like him to take it; but she said the ladies would never mind if they knew it was for the sake of another—that she had lost."

"Poor lady!" Rosalind said; the tears came to her eyes in sudden sympathy; "that must be so sad, to lose a child."

"It is the greatest sorrow in this world, to be only sorrow," the woman said.

"Only sorrow! and what can be worse than that?" said innocent Rosalind. "Is the lady very sad, Johnny? I hope you were good and thanked her for it. Perhaps if I were with him some day she would speak to me."

"She doesn't want nobody but me," said Johnny. "Oh, look! doesn't it go. It couldn't go on the ground because of the stones. Amy, Amy, get out of the way, it will run you over. And now it's going home to take William a message. I whispered in it, so it knows what to say."

"But I want to hear about the lady, Johnny."

"Oh, look, look! it's falled on the carpet; it don't like the carpet any more than the stones. I expose it's on the floor it will go best, or on the grass. Nurse, come along, let's go out and try it on the grass."

"Johnny, stop! I want to know more about this lady, dear."

"Oh, there is nothing about her," cried the little boy, rushing after his toy. Sophy, who had been practising, got up from the piano and came forward to volunteer information.

"She's an old fright," said Sophy. "I've seen her back—dressed all in mourning, with a thick veil on. She never took any notice of us others that have more sense than Johnny. I could have talked to her, but he can't talk to anybody, he is so little and so silly. All he can say is only stories he makes up; you think that is clever, but I don't think it is clever. If I were his—aunt," said Sophy, with a momentary hesitation, "I would whip him. For all that is lies, don't you know? You would say it was lies if I said it, but you think it's poetry because of Johnny. Poetry is lies, Rosalind, yes, and novels too. They're not true, so what can they be but lies? that's why I don't care to read them. No, I never read them, I like what's true."

Rosalind caught her book instinctively, which was all she had left. "We did not ask you for your opinion about poetry, Sophy; but if this lady is so kind to Johnny I should like to go and thank her. Next time you see her say that Johnny's sister would like to thank her. If she has lost her little boy we ought to be very sorry for her," Rosalind said.

Sophy looked at her with an unmoved countenance. "I think people are a great deal better off that are not bothered with children," she said; "I should send the little ones home, and then we could do what we liked, and stay as long as we liked," quoth the little woman of the world.

CHAPTER XLI

Johnny's little social successes were so frequent that the memory of the poor lady who had lost her child at his age soon died away, and the toy got broken and went the way of all toys. Their life was spent in a very simple round of occupations. Rosalind, whose powers as an artist were not beyond the gentlest level of amateur art, took to sketching, as a means of giving some interest to her idle hours, and it became one of the habits of the family that Aunt Sophy, when well enough to go out for her usual afternoon drive, should deposit her niece and the children on the bank of the lake, the spot which Rosalind had chosen as the subject of a sketch. The hills opposite shone in the afternoon sun with a gray haze of heat softening all their outlines; the water glowed and sparkled in all its various tones of blue, here and there specked by a slowly progressing boat, carrying visitors across to the mock antiquity of Hautecombe.

After the jingle and roll of Mrs. Lennox's carriage had passed away, the silence of the summer heat so stilled the landscape that the distant clank of the oars on the water produced the highest effect. It was very warm, yet there was something in the haze that spoke of autumn, and a cool but capricious little breeze came now and then from the water. Rosalind, sitting in the shade, with her sketching-block upon her knee, felt that soft indolence steal over her, that perfect physical content and harmony with everything, which takes all impulse from the mind and makes the sweetness of doing nothing a property of the very atmosphere. Her sketch was very unsatisfactory, for one thing: the subject was much too great for her simple powers. She knew just enough to know that it was bad, but not how to do what she wished, to carry out her own ideal. To make out the open secret before her, and perceive how it was that Nature formed those shadows and poured down that light, was possible to her mind but not to her hand, which had not the cunning necessary for the task; but she was clever enough to see her incapacity, which is more than can be said of most amateurs. Her hands had dropped by her side, and her sketch upon her lap. After all, who could hope to put upon paper those dazzling lights, and the differing tones of air and distance, the shadows that flitted over the mountainsides, the subdued radiance of the sky? Perhaps a great artist, Turner or his chosen rival, but not an untrained girl, whose gifts were only for the drawing-room. Rosalind was not moved by any passion of regret on account of her failure. She was content to sit still and vaguely contemplate the beautiful scene, which was half within her and half without. The "inward eye which is the bliss of solitude" filled out the outline of the picture for her as she sat, not thinking, a part of the silent rapture of the scene. The children were playing near her, and their voices, softened in the warm air, made part of the beatitude of the moment—that, and the plash of the water on the shore, and the distant sound of the oars, and the breeze that blew in her face. It was one of those exquisite instants, without any actual cause of happiness in them, when we are happy without knowing why. Such periods come back to the mind as the great events which are called joyful never do—for with events, however joyful, there come agitations, excitements—whereas pure happiness is serene, and all the sweeter for being without any cause.

Thus Rosalind sat—notwithstanding many things in her life which were far from perfect—in perfect calm and pleasure. The nurse, seated lower down upon the beach, was busy with a piece of work, crochet or some other of those useless handiworks which are a refreshment to those who are compelled to be useful for the greater portion of their lives. The children were still nearer to the edge of the water, playing with a little pleasure-boat which was moored within the soft plash of the lake. It was not a substantial craft, like the boats native to the place, which are meant to convey passengers and do serious work, but was a little, gayly painted, pleasure skiff, belonging to an Englishman in the neighborhood, neither safe nor solid—one of the cockleshells that a wrong balance upsets in a moment. It was to all appearance safely attached to something on the land, and suggested no idea of danger either to the elder sister seated above or to the nurse on the beach.

Amy and Johnny had exhausted their imagination in a hundred dramatic plays; they had "pretended" to be kings and queens; to be a lady receiving visitors and a gentleman making a morning call; to be a clergyman preaching to a highly critical and unsatisfactory audience, which would neither stay quiet nor keep still; to be a procession chanting funeral hymns; even coming down sadly from that level of high art to keep a shop, selling pebbles and sand for tea and sugar. Such delights, however, are but transitory; the children, after a while, exhausted every device they could think of; and then they got into the boat, which it was very easy to do. The next thing, as was natural, was to "pretend" to push off and row. And, alas! the very first of these attempts was too successful. The boat had been attached, as it appeared, merely to a small iron rod thrust into the sand, and Johnny, being vigorous and pulling with all his little might—with so much might that he tumbled into the bottom of the boat head over heels in the revulsion of the effort—the hold gave way. Both nurse and sister sat tranquilly, fearing no evil, while this tremendous event took place, and it was not till the shifting of some bright lines in the foreground caught Rosalind's dreaming eye that the possibility of any accident occurred to her. She sprang to her feet then, with a loud cry which startled the nurse and a group of children playing farther on, on the beach, but no one who could be of any real assistance. The little bright vessel was afloat and already bearing away upon the shining water. In a minute it was out of reach of anything the women could do. There was not a boat or a man within sight; the only hope was in the breeze which directed the frail little skiff to a small projecting point farther on, to which, as soon as her senses came back to her, Rosalind rushed, with what intention she scarcely knew, to plunge into the water though she could not swim, to do something, if it should only be to drown along with them. The danger that the boat might float out into the lake was not all; for any frightened movement, even an attempt to help themselves on the part of the children, might upset the frail craft in a moment, and end their voyage forever.

She flew over the broken ground, stumbling in her hurry and agitation, doing her best to stifle the cries that burst from her, lest she should frighten the little voyagers. For the moment they were quite still, surprise and alarm and a temporary confusion as to what to do having quieted their usual restlessness. Amy's little face, with a smile on it, gradually growing fixed as fear crept over her which she would not betray, and Johnny's back as he settled himself on the rowing seat, with his arms just beginning to move towards the oars which Rosalind felt would be instant destruction did he get hold of them, stood out in her eyes as if against a background of flame. It was only the background of the water, all soft and glowing, with scarcely a ripple upon it, safe, so peaceful, and yet death. There could not have been a prettier picture. The boat was reflected in every tint, the children's dresses, its own lines of white and crimson, the foolish little flag of the same colors that fluttered at the bow—all prettiness, gayety, a picture that would have delighted a child, softly floating, double, boat and shadow. But never was any scene of prettiness looked at with such despair. "Keep still, keep still," Rosalind cried, half afraid even to say so much, as she flew along, her brain all one throb. If but the gentle breeze, the current so slight as to be scarcely visible, would drift them to the point! if only her feet would carry her there in time! Her sight seemed to fail her, and yet for years after it was like a picture ineffaceably printed upon her eyes.

She was rushing into the water in despair, with her hands stretched out, but, alas! seeing too clearly that the boat was still out of her reach, and restraining with pain the cry of anguish which would have startled the children, when she felt herself suddenly put aside and a coat, thrown off by some one in rapid motion, fell at her feet. Rosalind did not lose her senses, which were all strung to the last degree of vivid force and capability; but she knew nothing, did not think, was conscious neither of her own existence nor of how this came about, of nothing but the sight before her eyes. She stood among the reeds, her feet in the water, trying to smile to the children, to Amy, upon whom terror was growing, and to keep her own cries from utterance. The plunge of the new-comer in the water startled Johnny. He had got hold of the oar, and in the act of flinging it upon the water with the clap which used to delight him on the lake at home, turned sharply round to see what this new sound meant. Then the light vanished from Rosalind's eyes. She uttered one cry, which seemed to ring from one end of the lake to the other, and startled the rowers far away on the other side. Then gradually sight came back to her. Had it all turned into death and destruction, that shining water, with its soft reflections, the pretty outline, the floating colors? She heard a sound of voices, the tones of the children, and then the scene became visible again, as if a black shadow had been removed. There was the boat, still floating double, Amy's face full of smiles, Johnny's voice raised high—"Oh, I could have doned it!"—a man's head above the level of the water, a hand upon the side of the boat. Then some one called to her, "No harm done; I will take them back to the beach." The throbbing went out of Rosalind's brain and went lower down, till her limbs shook under her, and how to get through the reeds she could not tell. She lifted the coat instinctively and struggled along, taking, it seemed to her, half an hour to retrace the steps which she had made in two minutes in the access of terror which had left her so weak. The nurse, who had fallen helpless on the beach, covering her eyes with her hands not to see the catastrophe, had recovered and got the children in her arms before Rosalind reached them. They were quite at their ease, and skipped about on the shingle, when lifted from the boat, with an air of triumph. "I could have doned it if you had left me alone," said Johnny, careless of the mingled caresses and reproaches that fell upon him in a torrent—the "Oh, children, you've almost killed me!" of nurse, and the passionate clasp with which Rosalind seized upon them. "We were floating beautiful," said little Amy, oblivious of her terrors; and they began to descant both together upon the delights of their "sail." "Oh, it is far nicer than those big boats!" "And if he had let me get the oars out I'd have doned it myself," cried Johnny. The group of children which had been disturbed by the accident stood round, gaping open-mouthed in admiration, and the loud sound of hurrying oars from a boat rushing across the lake to the rescue added to the excitement of the little hero and heroine. Rosalind's dress was torn with her rush through the reeds, her shoes wet, her whole frame trembling; while nurse had got her tidy bonnet awry and her hair out of order. But the small adventurers had suffered no harm or strain of any kind. They were jaunty in their perfect success and triumph.

"I thought it safest to bring them round to this bit of beach, where they could be landed without any difficulty. Oh, pray don't say anything about it. It was little more than wading, the water is not deep. And I am amply—Miss Trevanion? I am shocked to see you carrying my coat!"

Rosalind turned to the dripping figure by her side with a cry of astonishment. She had been far too much agitated even to make any question in her mind who it was. Now she raised her eyes to meet—what? the eyes that were like Johnny's, the dark, wistful, appealing look which had come back to her mind so often. He stood there with the water running from him, in the glow of exertion, his face thinner and less boyish, but his look the same as when he had come to her help on the country road, and by the little lake at Highcourt. It flashed through Rosalind's mind that he had always come to her help. She uttered the "Oh!" which is English for every sudden wonder, not knowing what to say.

"I hope," he said, "that you may perhaps remember I once saw you at Highcourt in the old days, in a little difficulty with a boat. This was scarcely more than that."

"I recollect," she said, her breath coming fast; "you were very kind—and now—Oh, this is a great deal more; I owe you—their lives."

"Pray don't say so. It was nothing—any one would have done it, even if there had been a great deal more to do, but there was nothing; it was little more than wading." Then he took his coat from her hand, which she had been holding all the time. "It is far more—it is too much that you should have carried my coat, Miss Trevanion. It is more than a reward."

She had thought of the face so often, the eyes fixed upon her, and had forgotten what doubts had visited her mind when she saw him before. Now, when she met the gaze of those eyes again, all her doubts came back. There was a faint internal struggle, even while she remembered that he had saved the lives of the children. "I know," she said, recollecting herself, "that we have met before, and that I had other things to thank you for, though nothing like this. But you must forgive me, for I don't know your name."

"My name is Everard," he said, with a little hesitation and a quick flush of color. His face, which had always been refined in feature, had a delicacy that looked like ill-health, and as he pulled on his coat over his wet clothes he shivered slightly. Was it because he felt the chill, or only to call forth the sudden anxiety which appeared in Rosalind's face? "Oh," he said, "it was momentary. I shall take no harm."

"What can we do?" cried Rosalind, with alarm. "If it should make you ill! And you are here perhaps for the baths? and yet have plunged in without thought. What can we do? There is no carriage nor anything to be got. Oh, Mr. Everard! take pity upon me and hasten home."

"I will walk with you if you will let me."

"But we cannot go quick, the children are not able; and what if you catch cold! My aunt would never forgive me if I let you wait."

"There could be nothing improper," he said hastily, "with the nurse and the children."

Rosalind felt the pain of this mistaken speech prick her like a pin-point. To think in your innermost consciousness that a man is "not a gentleman" is worse than anything else that can be said of him in English speech. She hesitated and was angry with herself, but yet her color rose high. "What I mean," she said, with an indescribable, delicate pride, "is that you will take cold—you understand me, surely—you will take cold after being in the water. I beg you to go on without waiting, for the children cannot walk quickly."

"And you?" he said; still he did not seem to understand, but looked at her with a sort of delighted persuasion that she was avoiding the walk with him coyly, with that feminine withdrawal which leads a suitor on. "You are just as wet as I am. Could not we two push on and leave the children to follow?"

Rosalind gave him a look which was full of almost despairing wonder. The mind and the words conveyed so different an impression from that made by the refined features and harmonious face. "Oh, please go away," she said, "I am in misery to see you standing there so wet. My aunt will send to you to thank you. Oh, please go away! If you catch cold we will never forgive ourselves," Rosalind cried, with an earnestness that brought tears to her eyes.

"Miss Trevanion, that you should care—"

Rosalind, in her heat and eagerness, made an imperious gesture, stamping her foot on the sand in passionate impatience. "Go, go!" she cried. "We owe you the children's lives, and we shall not forget it—but go!"

He hesitated. He did not believe nor understand her! He looked in her eyes wistfully, yet with a sort of smile, to know how much of it was true. Could any one who was a gentleman have so failed to apprehend her meaning? Yet it did gleam on him at length, and he obeyed her, though reluctantly, turning back half a dozen times in the first hundred yards to see if she were coming. At last a turn in the road hid him from her troubled eyes.

CHAPTER XLII

When the party arrived at the hotel and Aunt Sophy was informed of what had happened, her excitement was great. The children were caressed and scolded in a breath. After a while, however, the enormity of their behavior was dwelt upon by all their guardians together.

"I was saying, ma'am, that I couldn't never take Miss Amy and Master Johnny near to that lake again. Oh, I couldn't! The hotel garden, I couldn't go farther, not with any peace of mind."

"You hear what nurse says, children," said Aunt Sophy; "she is quite right. It would be impossible for me to allow you to go out again unless you made me a promise, oh, a faithful promise."

Amy was tired with the long walk after all the excitement; and she was always an impressionable little thing. She began to cry and protest that she never meant any harm, that the boat was so pretty, and that she was sure it was fastened and could not get away. But Johnny held his ground. "I could have doned it myself," he said; "I know how to row. Nobody wasn't wanted—if that fellow had let us alone."

"Where is the gentleman, Rosalind?" cried Mrs. Lennox. "Oh, how could you be so ungrateful as to let him go without asking where he was to be found? To think he should have saved those precious children and not to know where to find him to thank him! Oh, children, only think, if you had been brought home all cold and stiff, and laid out there never to give any more trouble, never to go home again, never to speak to your poor, distracted auntie, or to poor Rosalind, or to—Oh, my darlings! What should I have done if you had been brought home to me like that? It would have killed me. I should never more have held up my head again."

At this terrible prospect, and at the sight of Aunt Sophy's tears, Amy flung her arms as far as they would go round that portly figure, and hid her sobs upon her aunt's bosom. Johnny began to yield; he grew pale, and his big eyes veiled themselves with a film of tears. To think of lying there cold and stiff, as Aunt Sophy said, daunted the little hero. "I could have doned it," he said, but faltered, and his mouth began to quiver.

"And Uncle John," cried Mrs. Lennox, "and Rex! what would you have said never, never to see them again?"

Johnny, in his own mind, piled up the agony still higher—and the rabbits, and the pigeons, and his own pet guinea-pig, and his pony! He flung himself into Aunt Sophy's lap, which was so large, and so soft, and so secure.

This scene moved Rosalind both to tears and laughter; for it was a little pathetic as well as funny, and the girl was overstrained. She would have liked to fling herself, too, into arms of love like Aunt Sophy's, which were full—arms as loving, but more strong. The children did not want their mother, but Rosalind did. Her mind was moved by sentiments more complex than Johnny's emotions, but she had no one to have recourse to. The afternoon brightness had faded, and the gray of twilight filled the large room, making everything indistinct. At this crisis the door opened and somebody was ushered into the room, some one who came forward with a hesitating, yet eager, step. "I hope I may be permitted, though I am without introduction, to ask if the children have taken any harm," he said.

"It is Mr. Everard, Aunt Sophy." Rosalind retired to the background, her heart beating loudly. She wanted to look on, to see what appearance he presented to a spectator, to know how he would speak, what he would say.

"Oh!" cried Mrs. Lennox, standing up with a child in each arm, "it is the gentleman who saved my darlings—it is your deliverer, children. Oh, sir, what can I say to you; how can I even thank you? You have saved my life too, for I should never have survived if anything had happened to them."

He stood against the light of one of the windows, unconscious of the eager criticism with which he was being watched. Perhaps the bow he made was a little elaborate, but his voice was soft and refined. "I am very glad if I have been of any service," he said.

"Oh, service! it is far, far beyond that. I hope Rosalind said something to you; I hope she told you how precious they were, and that we could never, never forget."

"There is nothing to thank me for, indeed. It was more a joke than anything else; the little things were in no danger so long as they sat still. I was scarcely out of my depth, not much more than wading all the time."

"Aunt Sophy, that is what I told you," said Johnny, withdrawing his head from under her arm. "I could have doned it myself."

"Oh, hush, Johnny! Whatever way it was done, what does that matter? Here they are, and they might have been at the bottom of the lake. And you risked your own life or your health, which comes to the same thing! Pray sit down, Mr. Everard. If you are here," Aunt Sophy went on, loosing her arms from the children and sitting down with the full purpose of enjoying a talk, "as I am, for the waters, to get drenched and to walk home in your wet clothes must have been madness—that is, if you are here for your health."

"I am here for the baths, but a trifle like that could harm no one."

"Oh, I trust not—oh, I anxiously trust not! It makes my heart stand still even to think of it. Are you getting any benefit? It is for rheumatism, I suppose? And what form does yours take? One sufferer is interested in another," Mrs. Lennox said.

He seemed to wince a little, and threw a glance behind into the dimness to look for Rosalind. To confess to rheumatism is not interesting. He said at last, with a faint laugh, "I had rheumatic fever some years ago. My heart is supposed to be affected, that is all; the water couldn't hurt that organ; indeed I think it did good."

Rosalind, in the background, knew that this was meant for her; but her criticism was disarmed by a touch of humorous sympathy for the poor young fellow, who had expected, no doubt, to appear in the character of a hero, and was thus received as a fellow-sufferer in rheumatism. But Mrs. Lennox naturally saw nothing ludicrous in the situation. "Mine," she said, "is in the joints. I get so stiff, and really to rise up after I have been sitting down for any time is quite an operation. I suppose you don't feel anything of that sort? To be sure, you are so much younger—but sufferers have a fellow-feeling. And when did you begin your baths? and how many do you mean to take? and do you think they are doing you any good? It is more than I can say just at present, but they tell me that it often happens so, and that it is afterwards that one feels the good result."

"I know scarcely any one here," said the young man, "so I have not been able to compare notes; but I am not ill, only taking the baths to please a—relation, who, perhaps," he said with a little laugh, "takes more interest in me than I deserve."

"Oh, I am sure not that!" said Aunt Sophy, with enthusiasm. "But, indeed, it is very nice of you to pay so much attention to your relation's wishes. You will never repent putting yourself to trouble for her peace of mind, and I am sure I sympathize with her very much in the anxiety she must be feeling. When the heart is affected it is always serious. I hope, Mr. —"

"Everard," he said with a bow, once more just a little, as the critic behind him felt, too elaborate for the occasion.

"I beg your pardon. Rosalind did tell me; but I was so much agitated, almost too much to pay any attention. I hope, Mr. Everard, that you are careful to keep yourself from all agitation. I can't think the shock of plunging into the lake could be good for you. Oh, I feel quite sure it couldn't be good. I hope you will feel no ill results afterwards. But excitement of any sort, or agitation, that is the worst thing for the heart. I hope, for your poor dear relation's sake, who must be so anxious, poor lady, that you will take every care."

He gave a glance behind Mrs. Lennox to the shadow which stood between him and the window. "That depends," he said, "rather on other people than on myself. You may be sure I should prefer to be happy and at ease if it were in my power."

"Ah, well!" said Aunt Sophy, "that is very true. Of course our happiness depends very much upon other people. And you have done a great deal for mine, Mr. Everard. It would not have done me much good to have people telling me to be cheerful if my poor little darlings had been at the bottom of the lake." Here Aunt Sophy stopped and cried a little, then went on. "You are not, I think, living at our hotel, but I hope you will stay and dine with us. Oh, yes, I cannot take any refusal. We may have made your acquaintance informally, but few people can have so good a reason for wishing to know you. This is my niece, Miss Trevanion, Mr. Everard; the little children you saved are my brother's children—the late Mr. Trevanion of Highcourt."

Rosalind listened with her heart beating high. Was it possible that he would receive the introduction as if he had known nothing of her before? He rose and turned towards her, made once more that slightly stiff, too elaborate bow, and was silent. No, worse than that, began to say something about being happy to make—acquaintance.

"Aunt Sophy," said Rosalind, stepping forward, "you are under a mistake. Mr. Everard knows us well enough. I met him before we left Highcourt." And then she, too, paused, feeling with sudden embarrassment that there was a certain difficulty in explaining their meetings, a difficulty of which she had not thought. It was he now who had the advantage which she had felt to lie with herself.

"It is curious how things repeat themselves," he said. "I had once the pleasure of recovering a boat that had floated away from Miss Trevanion on the pond at Highcourt, but I could not have ventured to claim acquaintance on so small an argument as that."

Rosalind was silenced—her mind began to grow confused. It was not true that this was all, and yet it was not false. She said nothing; if it were wrong, she made herself an accomplice in the wrong; and Aunt Sophy's exclamations soon put an end to the incident.

"So you had met before!" she cried. "So you know Highcourt! Oh, what a very small world this is!—everybody says so, but it is only now and then that one is sensible. But you must tell us all about it at dinner. We dine at the table d'hôte, if you don't mind. It is more amusing, and I don't like to shut up Rosalind with only an old lady like me for her company. You like it too? Oh, well, that is quite nice. Will you excuse us now, Mr. Everard, while we prepare for dinner? for that is the dressing-bell just ringing, and they allow one so little time. Give me your hand, dear, to help me up. You see I am quite crippled," Mrs. Lennox said, complacently, forgetting how nimbly she had sprung from her chair with a child under each arm to greet their deliverer. She limped a little as she went out of the room on Rosalind's arm. She was quite sure that her rheumatism made her limp; but sometimes she forgot that she had rheumatism, which is a thing that will happen in such cases now and then.

The room was still dark. It was not Mrs. Lennox's custom to have it lighted before dinner, and when the door closed upon the ladies the young man was left alone. His thoughts were full of triumph and satisfaction, not unmingled with praise. He had attained by the chance of a moment what he had set his heart upon, he said to himself; for years he had haunted Highcourt for this end; he had been kept cruelly and unnaturally (he thought) from realizing it. Those who might have helped him, without any harm to themselves, had refused and resisted his desire, and compelled him to relinquish it. And now in a moment he had attained what he had so desired. Introduced under the most flattering circumstances, with every prepossession in his favor, having had it in his power to lay under the deepest obligation the family, the guardians as well as the girl who, he said to himself, was the only girl he had ever loved. Did he love Rosalind? He thought so, as Mrs. Lennox thought she had rheumatism. Both were serious enough—and perhaps this young stranger was not clearly aware how much it was he saw in Rosalind besides herself. He saw in her a great deal that did not meet the outward eye, though he also saw the share of beauty she possessed, magnified by his small acquaintance with women of her kind. He saw her sweet and fair and desirable in every way, as the truest lover might have done. And there were other advantages which such a lover as Roland Hamerton would have scorned to take into consideration, which Rivers—not able at his more serious age to put them entirely out of his mind—yet turned from instinctively as if it were doing her a wrong to remember them, but which this young man realized vividly and reminded himself of with rising exhilaration. With such a wife what might he not do? Blot out everything that was against him, attain everything he had ever dreamed of, secure happiness, advancement, wealth. He moved from window to window of the dim room, waiting for the ladies, in a state of exaltation indescribable. He had been raised at once from earth to heaven. There was not a circumstance that was not in his favor. He was received by them as an intimate, he was to be their escort, to be introduced by them, to form one of their party; and Rosalind! Rosalind! she was the only girl whom he had ever loved.

CHAPTER XLIII

He was placed between the ladies at the table d'hôte. Mrs. Lennox, on her side, told the story of what had happened to the lady on her other side, and Rosalind was appealed to by her left-hand neighbor to know what was the truth of the rumor which had begun to float about the little community. It was reported all down the table, so far, at least, as the English group extended, "That is the gentleman next to Mrs. Lennox—the children were drowning, and he plunged in and saved both." "What carelessness to let them go so near the water! It is easy to see, poor things, that they have no mother." "And did he save them both? Of course, they must both be safe or Mrs. Lennox and Miss Trevanion would not have appeared at the table d'hôte." Such remarks as these, interspersed with questions, "Who is the young fellow?—where has he sprung from? I never saw him before," buzzed all about as dinner went on. Mr. Everard was presented by Mrs. Lennox, in her gratitude, to the lady next to her, who was rather a great lady, and put up her glass to look at him. He was introduced to the gentleman on Rosalind's other hand by that gentleman's request. Thus he made his appearance in society at Aix with greatest éclat. When they rose from the table he followed Rosalind out of doors into the soft autumnal night. The little veranda and the garden walks under the trees were full of people, under cover of whose noisy conversation there was abundant opportunity for a more interesting tête-à-tête. "You are too kind," he said, "in telling this little story. Indeed, there was nothing to make any commotion about. You could almost have done it, without any help from me."

"No," she said. "I could not have done it; I should have tried and perhaps been drowned, too. But it is not I who have talked, it is Aunt Sophy. She is very grateful to you."

"She has no occasion," he said. "Whatever I could do for you, Miss Trevanion—" and then he stopped, somewhat breathlessly. "It was curious, was it not? that the boat on the pond should have been so much the same thing, though everything else was so different. And that is years ago."

"Nearly two years."

"Then you remember?" he said, in a tone of delighted surprise.

"I have much occasion to remember. It was at a very sad moment. I remember everything that happened."

"To be sure," said the young man. "No, I did not forget. It was only that in the pleasure of seeing you everything else went out of my mind. But I have never forgotten, Miss Trevanion, all your anxiety. I saw you, you may remember, the day you were leaving home."

Rosalind raised her eyes to him with a look of pain. "It is not a happy recollection," she said.

"Oh, Miss Rosalind. I hope you will forgive me for recalling to you what is so painful."

"The sight of you recalls it," she said; "it is not your fault, Mr. Everard, you had relations near Highcourt."

"Only one, but nobody now—nobody. It was a sort of chance that took me there at all. I was in a little trouble, and then I left suddenly, as it happened, the same day as you did, Miss Trevanion. How well I remember it all! You were carrying the same little boy who was in the boat to-day—was it the same?—and you would not let me help you. I almost think if you had seen it was me you would not have allowed me to help you to-day."

"If I had seen it was—" Rosalind paused with troubled surprise. Sometimes his fine voice and soft tones lulled her doubts altogether, but, again, a sudden touch brought them all back. He was very quick, however, to observe the changes in her, and changed with them with a curious mixture of sympathy and servility.

"Circumstances have carried me far away since then," he said; "but I have always longed to know, to hear, something. If I could tell you the questions I have asked myself as to what might be going on; and how many times I have tried to get to England to find out!"

"We have never returned to Highcourt," she said, confused by his efforts to bring back those former meetings, and not knowing how to reply. "I think we shall not till my brother comes of age. Yes, my little brother was the same. He is very much excited about what happened to-day; neither of them understood it at first, but now they begin to perceive that it is a wonderful adventure. I hope the wetting will do you no harm."

"Please," he said in a petulant tone, "if you do not want to vex me, say no more of that. I am not such a weak creature; indeed, there is nothing the matter with me, except in imagination."

"I think," said Rosalind, with a little involuntary laugh, "that the baths of Aix are good for the imagination. It grows by what it feeds on; though rheumatism does not seem to be an imaginative sort of malady."

"You forget," he cried, almost with resentment; "the danger of it is that it affects the heart, which is not a thing to laugh at."

"Oh, forgive me!" Rosalind cried. "I should not have spoken so lightly. It was because you were so determined that nothing ailed you. And I hope you are right. The lake was so beautiful to-day. It did not look as if it could do harm."

"You go there often? I saw you had been painting."

"Making a very little, very bad, sketch, that was all. Mr. Everard, I think I must go in. My aunt will want me."

"May I come, too? How kind she is! I feared that being without introduction, knowing nobody—But Mrs. Lennox has been most generous, receiving me without a question—and you, Miss Trevanion."

"Did you expect me to stop you from saving the children till I had asked who you were?" cried Rosalind, endeavoring to elude the seriousness with which he always returned to the original subject. "It is a pretty manner of introduction to do us the greatest service, the greatest kindness."

"But it was nothing. I can assure you it was nothing," he said. He liked to be able to make this protestation. It was a sort of renewing of his claim upon them. To have a right, the very strongest right, to their gratitude, and yet to declare it was nothing—that was very pleasant to the young man. And in a way it was true. He would have done anything that it did not hurt him very much to do for Rosalind, even for her aunt and her little brothers and sisters, but to feel that he was entitled to their thanks and yet waived them was delightful to him. It was a statement over and over again of his right to be with them. He accompanied Rosalind to the room in which Aunt Sophy had established herself, with mingled confidence and timidity, ingratiating himself by every means that was possible, though he did not talk very much. Indeed, he was not great in conversation at any time, and now he was so anxious to please that he was nervous and doubtful what to say.

Mrs. Lennox received the young people with real pleasure. She liked, as has been said in a previous part of this history, to have a young man about, in general attendance, ready to go upon her errands and make himself agreeable. It added to the ease and the gayety of life to have a lover upon hand, one who was not too far gone, who still had eyes for the other members of the party, and a serious intention of making himself generally pleasant. She had never concealed her opinion that an attendant of this description was an advantage. And Mrs. Lennox was imprudent to the bottom of her heart. She had plenty of wise maxims in store as to the necessity of keeping ineligible persons at a distance, but it did not occur to her to imagine that a well-looking young stranger attaching himself to her own party might be ineligible. Of Arthur Rivers she had known that his family lived in an obscure street in Clifton, which furnished her with objections at once. But of Mr. Everard, who had saved the children's lives, she had no doubts. She did, indeed, mean to ask him if he belonged to the Everards of Essex, but in the meantime was quite willing to take that for granted.

"It is so curious," she said, making room for him to bring a chair beside her, "that you and Rosalind should have met before, and how fortunate for us! Oh, yes, Highcourt is a fine place. Of course we think so, Rosalind and I, having both been born there. We think there is no place in the world like it; but I have a right to feel myself impartial, for I have been a good deal about; and there is no doubt it is a fine place. Did you see over the house, Mr. Everard? Oh, no, of course it was when my poor brother was ill. There were so many trying circumstances," she added, lowering her voice, "that we thought it best just to leave it, you know, and the Elms does very well for the children as long as they are children. Of course, when Reginald comes of age—Do you know the neighborhood of Clifton, Mr. Everard? Oh, you must come and see me there. It is a capital hunting country, you know, and that is always an inducement to a gentleman."

"I should have no need of any inducement, if you are so kind."

"It is you that have been kind," Mrs, Lennox said. "I am sure if we can do anything to make our house agreeable to you—Now tell me how you get on here. How often do you take the baths? Oh, I hope you are regular—so much depends upon regularity, they tell me. Lady Blashfield, whom I was talking to at dinner, tells me that if you miss one it is as bad as giving up altogether. It is the continuity, she says. Young men are very difficult to guide in respect to their health. My dear husband, that is, Mr. Pulteney, my first dear husband, whom I lost when we were both quite young, might have been here now, poor dear fellow, if he had only consented to be an invalid, and to use the remedies. You must let one who has suffered so much say a word of warning to you, Mr. Everard. Use the remedies, and youth will do almost everything for you. He might have been here now—" Mrs. Lennox paused and applied her handkerchief to her eyes.

Young Everard listened with the most devout attention, while Rosalind, on her side, could not refrain from an involuntary reflection as to the extreme inconvenience of Mr. Pulteney's presence now. If that had been all along possible, was not Aunt Sophy guilty of a kind of constructive bigamy? To hear her dwelling upon this subject, and the stranger listening with so much attention, gave Rosalind an insane desire to laugh. Even Roland Hamerton, she thought, would have seen the humor of the suggestion; but Everard was quite serious, lending an attentive ear. He was very anxious to please. There was an absence of ease about him in his anxiety. Not the ghost of a smile stole to his lips. He sat there until Mrs. Lennox got tired, and remembered that the early hour at which she began to bathe every morning made it expedient now to go to bed. He was on the alert in a moment, offering his arm, and truly sympathetic about the difficulty she expressed in rising from her chair. "I can get on when once I am fairly started," she said; "thank you so much, Mr. Everard. Rosalind is very kind, but naturally in a gentleman's arm there is more support."

"I am so glad that I can be of use," he said fervently. And Rosalind followed up-stairs, carrying Aunt Sophy's work, half pleased, half amused, a little disconcerted by the sudden friendship which had arisen between them. She was, herself, in a very uncertain, somewhat excited state of mind. The re-appearance of the stranger who had achieved for himself, she could not tell how, a place in her dreams, disturbed the calm in which she had been living, which in itself was a calm unnatural at her age. Her heart beat with curious content, expectation, doubt, and anxiety. He was not like the other men whom she had known. There was something uncertain about him, a curiosity as to what he would do or say, a suppressed alarm in her mind as to whether his doings and sayings would be satisfactory. He might make some terrible mistake. He might say something that would set in a moment a great gulf between him and her. It was uncomfortable, and yet perhaps it had a certain fascination in it. She never knew what was the next thing he might say or do. But Aunt Sophy was loud in his praises when they reached their own apartment. "What a thoroughly nice person!" she said. "What a modest, charming young man! not like so many, laughing in their sleeve, in a hurry to get away, taking no trouble about elder people. Mr. Everard has been thoroughly well brought up, Rosalind; he must have had a nice mother. That is always what I think when I see a young man with such good manners. His mother must have been a nice woman. I am sure if he had been my own nephew he could not have been more attentive to me."

Rosalind said little in reply to this praise. She was pleased, and yet an intrusive doubt would come in. To be a little original, not like all the others, is not that an advantage? and yet—She went to her own room, thoughtful, yet with a sensation of novelty not without pleasure in her mind, and paused, in passing, at the children's door to pay them her usual visit, and give them the kiss when they were asleep which their mother was not near to give. This visit had a twofold meaning to Rosalind. It was a visit of love to the little ones, that they might not be deprived of any tenderness that she could give; and it was a sort of pilgrimage of faithful devotion to the shrine which the mother had left empty. A pang of longing for that mother, and of the wondering pain which her name always called forth, was in her heart when she stooped over the little beds. Ordinarily, everything was dim—the faint night-light affording guidance to where they lay, and no more—and still, with nothing but the soft breathing of the two children, one in the outer and the other in the inner room. But to-night there was a candle burning within and the sound of nurse's voice soothing Johnny, who, sitting up in his bed, was looking round him with eyes full of light, and that large childish wakefulness which seems a sort of protest against ever sleeping again.

"Oh, Miss Rosalind, I don't know what to do with Master Johnny; he says a lady came and looked at him. You've not been here, have you, miss? I tell him there is no lady. He must just have dreamed it."

"I didn't dreamed it," said Johnny. "It was a beautiful lady. She came in there, and stood here. I want her to come again," the child said, gazing about him with his great eyes.

"But it is impossible, Miss Rosalind," said the nurse; "the door is locked, and there is no lady. He just must have been dreaming. He is a little upset with the accident."

"We wasn't a bit upsetted," said Johnny. "I could have doned it myself. I wanted to tell the lady, Rosy, but she only said, 'Go to sleep.'"

"That was the very wisest thing she could say. Go to sleep, and I will sit by you," said Rosalind.

It was some time, however, before Johnny accomplished the feat of going to sleep. He was very talkative and anxious to fight his battles over again, and explain exactly how he would have "doned" it. When the little eyes closed at last, and all was still, Rosalind found the nurse waiting in the outer room in some anxiety.

"Yes, Miss Rosalind, I am sure he was off his head a little—not to call wandering, but just a little off his head. For how could any lady have got into this room? It is just his imagination. I had once a little boy before who was just the same, always seeing ladies and people whenever he was the least excited. I will give him a dose in the morning, and if he sees her again I would just send for the doctor. It is all physical, miss, them sort of visions," said the nurse, who was up to the science of her time.

CHAPTER XLIV

Mrs. Lennox's cure went on through the greater part of the month of September, and the friendship that had been begun so successfully grew into intimacy perhaps in a shorter time than would have been credible had the conditions of life been less easy. In the space of two or three days Mr. Everard had become almost a member of Mrs. Lennox's party. He dined with them two evenings out of three. He walked by the elder lady's chair when she went to her bath, he was always ready to give her his arm when she wished it, to help her to her favorite seat in the garden, to choose a place for her from which she could most comfortably hear the music. All these services to herself Aunt Sophy was quite aware were the price the young man paid for permission to approach Rosalind, to admire and address her, to form part of her surroundings, and by degrees to become her almost constant companion. Mrs. Lennox agreed with Mr. Ruskin that this sort of apprenticeship in love was right and natural. If in spite of all these privileges he failed to please, she would have been sorry for him indeed, but would not have felt that he had any right to complain. It was giving him his chance like another; and she was of opinion that a lover or two on hand was a cheerful thing for a house. In the days of Messrs. Hamerton and Rivers the effect had been very good, and she had liked these unwearied attendants, these unpaid officers of the household, who were always ready to get anything or do anything that might happen to be wanted. It was lonely to be without one of those hangers-on, and she accepted with a kind of mild enthusiasm the young man who had begun his probation by so striking an exhibition of his fitness for the post. It may be objected that her ready reception of a stranger without any introduction or guarantee of his position was imprudent in the extreme, for who could undertake that Rosalind might not accept this suitor with more ready sympathy than she had shown for the others? And there can be no doubt that this was the case; but as a matter of fact Mrs. Lennox was not prudent, and it was scarcely to be expected that she should exercise a virtue unfamiliar to her in respect to the young man who had, as she loved to repeat, saved the lives of the children. He was one of the Essex Everards, she made no doubt. She had always forgotten to ask him, and as, she said, they had never got upon the subject of his family, he had said nothing to her about them. But there was nothing wonderful in that. It is always pleasant when a young man does talk about his people, and lets you know how many brothers and sisters he has, and all the family history, but a great many young men don't do so, and there was nothing at all wonderful about it in this case. A young man who is at Aix for the baths, who has been at most places where the travelling English go, who can talk like other people about Rome and Florence, not to speak of a great many out-of-the-way regions—it would be ridiculous to suppose that he was not "of our own class." Even Aunt Sophy's not very fastidious taste detected a few wants about him. He was not quite perfect in all points in his manners; he hesitated when a man in society would not have hesitated. He had not been at any university, nor even at a public school. All these things, however, Mrs. Lennox accounted for easily—when she took the trouble to think of them at all—by the supposition that he had been brought up at home, most likely in the country. "Depend upon it, he is an only child," she said to Rosalind, "and he has been delicate—one can see that he is delicate still—and they have brought him up at home. Well, perhaps it is wrong—at least, all the gentlemen say so; but if I had an only child I think I should very likely do the same, and I am sure I feel very much for his poor mother. Why? Oh, because I don't think he is strong, Rosalind. He colors like a girl when he makes any little mistake. He is not one of your bold young men that have a way of carrying off everything. He does make little mistakes, but then that is one of the things that is sure to happen when you bring boys up at home."

Rosalind, who became more and more inclined as the days went on to take the best view of young Everard's deficiencies, accepted very kindly this explanation. It silenced finally, she believed, that chill and horrible doubt, that question which she had put to herself broadly when she saw him first, which she did not even insinuate consciously now, but which haunted her, do what she would. Was he, perhaps, not exactly a gentleman? No, she did not ask that now. No doubt Aunt Sophy (who sometimes hit upon the right explanation, though she could not be called clever) was right, and the secret of the whole matter was that he had been brought up at home. There could be no doubt that the deficiencies which had at first suggested this most awful of all questions became rather interesting than otherwise when you came to know him better. They were what might be called ignorances, self-distrusts, an unassured condition of mind, rather than deficiencies; and his blush over his "little mistakes," as Mrs. Lennox called them, and the half-uttered apology and the deprecatory look, took away from a benevolent observer all inclination towards unkindly criticism. Mrs. Lennox, who soon became "quite fond of" the young stranger, told him frankly when he did anything contrary to the code of society, and he took such rebukes in the very best spirit, but was unfortunately apt to forget and fall into the same blunder again. There were some of these mistakes which kept the ladies in amusement, and some which made Rosalind, as she became more and more "interested," blush with hot shame—a far more serious feeling than that which made the young offender blush. For instance, when he found her sketch-book one morning, young Everard fell into ecstasies over the sketch Rosalind had been making of the lake on that eventful afternoon which had begun their intercourse. It was a very bad sketch, and Rosalind knew it. That golden sheet of water, full of light, full of reflections, with the sun blazing upon it, and the hills rising up on every side, and the sky looking down into its depths, had become a piece of yellow mud with daubs of blue and brown here and there, and the reeds in the foreground looked as if they had been cut out of paper and pasted on. "Don't look at it. I can't do very much, but yet I can do better than that," she had said, finding him in rapt contemplation of her unsatisfactory performance, and putting out her hand to close the book. He looked up at her, for he was seated by the table, hanging over the sketch with rapture, with the most eager deprecation.

"I think it is lovely," he said; "don't try to take away my enjoyment. I wonder how any one can turn a mere piece of paper into a picture!"

"You are laughing at me," said Rosalind, with a little offence.

"I—laughing! I would as soon laugh in church. I think it is beautiful. I can't imagine how you do it. Why, there are the reflections in the water just as you see them. I never thought before that it was so pretty."

"Oh!" Rosalind cried, drawing a long breath. It hurt her that he should say so, and it hurt still more to think that he was endeavoring to please her by saying so. "I am sure it is your kindness that makes you praise it; but, Mr. Everard, you must know that I am not quite ignorant. When you say such things of this daub it sounds like contempt—as if you thought I did not know better."

"But suppose I don't know any better?" he said, looking up at her with lustrous eyes full of humility, without even his usual self-disgust at having said something wrong. "Indeed, you must believe me, I don't. It is quite true. Is it a fault, Miss Trevanion, when one does not know?"

What could Rosalind say? She stood with her hand put out towards the book, looking down upon the most expressive countenance, a face which of itself was a model for a painter. There was very little difference between them in age, perhaps a year or so to his advantage, not more; and something of the freemasonry of youth was between them, besides the more delicate link of sentiment. Yes, she said to herself, it was a fault. A man, a gentleman, should not be so ignorant. Something must be wrong before such ignorance could be. But how say this or anything like it to her companion, who threw himself so entirely upon her mercy? She closed the book that had been open before him and drew it hastily away.

"I am afraid," she said, "your eye is not good; of course it is no fault except to think that I could be so silly, that I could accept praise which I don't deserve."

"Ah!" he said, "I see what you mean. You despise me for my ignorance, and it is true I am quite ignorant; but then how could I help it? I have never been taught."

"Oh!" cried Rosalind again, thinking the apology worse than the fault, bad as that was. "But you have seen pictures—you have been in the galleries?"

"Without any instruction," he said. "I do admire that, but I don't care for the galleries. Oh, but I never say so except to you."

She was silent in the dreadful situation in which she found herself. She did not know how to behave, such unutterable want of perception had never come in her way before.

"Then I suppose," she said, with awful calm, "the chromo-lithographs, those are what you like? Mine is something like them, that is why you approve of it, I suppose?"

"I like it," he said simply, "because you were doing it that day, and because that is where I saw you sitting when everything happened. And because the lake and the mountains and the sky all seem yours to me now."

This speech was of a character very difficult to ignore and pass over as if it meant nothing. But Rosalind had now some experience, and was not unused to such situations. She said hurriedly, "I see—it is the association that interests you. I remember a very great person, a great author, saying something like that. He said it was the story of the pictures he liked, and when that pleased him he did not think so much about the execution. If he had not been a great person he would not have dared to say it. An artist, a true artist, would shiver to hear such a thing. But that explains why you like my daub. It is better than if you really thought it itself worthy of praise."

"But I—" here young Everard paused; he saw by her eyes that he must not go any further, there was a little kindling of indignation in them. Where had he been all his life that he did not know any better than that? Had he gone on, Rosalind might not have been able to contain herself, and there were premonitory symptoms in the air.

"I wish," he said, "that you would tell me what is nice and what isn't."

"Nice! Oh, Mr, Everard!" Rosalind breathed out with a shudder. "Perhaps you would call Michael Angelo nice," she added, with a laugh.

"It is very likely that I might; you must forgive me. I have a relation who laughs at me in the same way, but how can one know if one has never been taught?"

"One is never taught such things," it was on Rosalind's lips to say, but with an impatient sigh she forbore. Afterwards, when she began to question herself on the subject, Rosalind took some comfort from the thought that Roland Hamerton knew almost as little about art as it is possible for a well-bred young Englishman to know. Ah! but that made all the difference. He knew enough to have thought her sketch a dreadful production; he knew enough to abhor the style of the chromo-lithograph. Even a man who has been brought up at home must have seen the pictures on his own walls. This thought cast her down again, but she began after this to break up into small morsels adapted to her companion's comprehension the simplest principles of art, and to give him little hints about the fundamental matters which are part of a gentleman's education in this respect, and even to indicate to him what terms are commonly used. He was very quick; he did not laugh out at her efforts as Roland would have done; he picked up the hints and adopted every suggestion—all which compliances pleased Rosalind in a certain sense, yet in another wrapped her soul in trouble, reviving again and again that most dreadful of all possible doubts, just when she thought that it had been safely laid to rest.

And yet all the while this daily companion made his way into something which, if not the heart, was dangerously near it, a sort of vestibule of the heart, where those who enter may hope to go further with good luck. He was ignorant in many ways. He did not know much more of books than of pictures—sometimes he expressed an opinion which took away her breath—and he was always on the watch for indications how far he might go; a sort of vigilance which was highly uncomfortable, and suggested some purpose on his part, some pursuit which was of more consequence to him than his natural opinions or traditions, all of which he seemed ready to sacrifice at a word. Rosalind was used to the ease of society, an ease, perhaps, more apparent than real, and this eagerness disconcerted her greatly. It was true that it might bear a flattering interpretation, if it was to recommend himself to her that he was ready to make all these sacrifices, to change even his opinions, to give up everything that could displease her. If all expedients are fair in love, is it not justifiable to watch that no word may offend, to express no liking unless it is sure to be in harmony with the tastes of the object loved, to be always on the alert and never to forget the purpose aimed at? This question might, perhaps, by impartial persons, be considered open to a doubt, but when one is one's self the object of such profound homage it is natural that the judgment should be slightly biassed. And there was a certain personal charm about him notwithstanding all his deficiencies. It was difficult for a girl not to be touched by the devotion which shone upon her from such a pair of wonderful eyes.

CHAPTER XLV

While this intercourse was going on, and Mr. Everard became more and more the associate of the ladies, the little shock that had been given them by the result of Johnny's excitement on the night of the accident grew into something definite and rather alarming. Johnny was not ill—so far as appeared, he was not even frightened; but he continued to see "the lady" from time to time, and more than once a cry from the room in which he slept had summoned Rosalind, and even Mrs. Lennox, forgetful of her rheumatism. On these occasions Johnny would be found sitting up in his bed, his great eyes like two lamps, shining even in the dim glow of the night-light. It was at an hour when he should have been asleep, when nurse had gone to her supper, and to that needful relaxation which nurses as well as other mortals require. The child was not frightened, but there was a certain excitement about this periodical awakening. "The lady! the lady!" he said. "Oh, my darling," cried Aunt Sophy, trembling; "what lady? There could be no lady. You have been dreaming. Go to sleep, Johnny, and think of it no more."

"I sawed her," cried the child. He pushed away Mrs. Lennox and clung to Rosalind, who had her arms round him holding him fast. "I never was asleep at all, Rosy; I just closed my eyes, and then I opened them and I sawed the lady."

"Oh, Rosalind, he has just been dreaming. Oh, Johnny dear, that is all nonsense; there was no lady!" Aunt Sophy cried.

"Tell me about her," said Rosalind. "Was it a strange lady? Did you know who she was?"

"It is just the lady," cried Johnny, impatiently. "I told you before. She is much more taller than Aunt Sophy, with a black thing over her head. She wouldn't stay, because you came running, and she didn't want you. But I want the lady to speak to me—I want her to speak to me. Go away, Rosy!" the little fellow cried.

"Dear, the lady will not come back again to-night. Tell me about her. Johnny, did you know who she was?"

"I told you: she's just the lady," cried Johnny, with the air of one whose explanation leaves nothing to be desired.

"Oh, Rosalind, you are just encouraging him in his nonsense. He was dreaming. My darling, you were dreaming. Nurse, here is this little boy been dreaming again about the lady, as he calls her. You must give him a dose. He must have got his little digestion all wrong. It can be nothing but that, you know," Aunt Sophy said. She drew the nurse, who had hastened up from her hour's relaxation in alarm, with her into the outer room. Mrs. Lennox herself was trembling. She clutched the woman's arm with a nervous grasp. "What does he mean about this lady? Is there any story about a lady? I am quite sure it is all nonsense, or that it is just a dream," said Mrs. Lennox, with a nervous flutter in the bow of her cap. "Is there any story (though it is all nonsense) of a haunted room or anything of that sort? If there is, I sha'n't stay here, not another day."

The nurse, however, had heard no such story: she stood whispering with her mistress, talking over this strange occurrence, while Rosalind soothed and quieted the excited child. Amy's little bed was in the outer room, but all was still there, the child never stirring, so absolutely noiseless that her very presence was forgotten by the two anxious women comparing notes. "He always keeps to the same story," said nurse. "I can't tell what to make of it, ma'am, but Master Johnny always was a little strange."

"What do you mean by a little strange? He is a dear child, he never gives any trouble, he is just a darling," Aunt Sophy said. "It is his digestion that has got a little wrong. A shock like that of the other day—it sometimes will not tell for some time, and as often as not it puts their little stomachs wrong. A little medicine will set everything right."

Nurse demurred to this, having notions of her own, and the discussion went on till Rosalind, who had persuaded Johnny to compose himself, and sat by him till he fell asleep, came out and joined them. "It will be better for you not to leave him without calling me or some one," she said.

"Miss Rosalind!" cried nurse, with natural desperation, "children is dreadfully tiring to have them all day long, and every day. And nurses is only flesh and blood like other people. If I'm never to have a moment's rest, day nor night, I think I shall go off my head."

All this went on in the room where little Amy lay asleep. She was so still that she was not considered at all. She was, indeed, at all times so little disposed to produce herself or make any call upon the attention of those about her, that the family, as is general, took poor little Amy at her own showing and left her to herself. It did not even seem anything remarkable that she was so still—and nobody perceived the pair of wide-open eyes with which she watched all that was going on under the corner of the coverlet. Even Rosalind scarcely looked towards her little sister's bed, and all the pent-up misery and terror which a child can conceal (and how much that implies) lay unconsoled and unlightened in poor little Amy's breast. Meanwhile Johnny had fallen fast asleep, untroubled by any further thought of the apparition which only he was supposed to have seen.

This brought a great deal of trouble into the minds of Johnny's guardians. Mrs. Lennox was so nearly breaking down under a sense of the responsibility that her rheumatism, instead of improving with her baths, grew worse than ever, and she became so stiff that Rosalind and Everard together were needed, each at one arm, to raise her from her chair. The doctor was sent for, who examined Johnny, and, after hearing all the story, concluded that it was suppressed gout in the child's system, and that baths to bring it out would be the best cure. He questioned Mrs. Lennox so closely as to her family and all their antecedents that it very soon appeared a certain fact that all the Trevanions had suffered from suppressed gout, which explained everything, and especially all peculiarities in the mind or conduct. "The little boy," said the doctor, who spoke English so well, "is the victim of the physiological sins of his forefathers. Pardon, madam; I do not speak in a moral point of view. They drank Oporto wine and he sees what you call ghosts; the succession is very apparent. This child," turning to Amy, who stood by, "she also has suppressed gout."

"Oh, Amy is quite well," cried Aunt Sophy; "there is nothing at all the matter with Amy. But it cannot be denied that there is gout in the family. Indeed, when gentlemen come to a certain age they always suffer in that way, though I am sure I don't know why. My poor father and grandfather, too, as I have always heard. Your papa, Rosalind, with him it was the heart."

"They are all connected. Rheumatism, it is the brother of gout, and rheumatism is the tyrant which affects the heart. No, my dear young lady, it is not the emotions, nor love, nor disappointment, nor any of the pretty things you think; it is rheumatism that is most fatal for the heart. I will settle for the little boy a course of baths, and he will see no more ladies; that is," said the doctor, with a wave of his hand, "except the very charming ladies whom he has a right to see. But this child, she has it more pronounced; she is more ill than the little boy."

"Oh, no, doctor, it is only that Amy is always pale; there is nothing the matter with her. Do you feel anything the matter with you, Amy, my dear?"

"No, Aunt Sophy," said the little girl in a very low voice, turning her head away.

"I told you so; there is nothing the matter with her. She is a pale little thing. She never has any color. But Johnny! Doctor, oh, I hope you will do your best for Johnny! He quite destroys all our peace and comfort. I am afraid to open my eyes after I go to bed, lest I should see the lady too; for that sort of thing is very catching. You get it into your mind. If there is any noise I can't account for, I feel disposed to scream. I am sure I shall be seeing it before long if Johnny gets no better. But I have always supposed in such cases that it was the digestion that was out of order," Mrs. Lennox said, returning, but doubtfully, to her original view.

"It is all the same thing," said the doctor, cheerfully waving his hand; and then he patted Johnny on the head, who was half overawed, half pleased, to have an illness which procured unlimited petting without any pain. The little fellow began his baths immediately, but next night he saw the lady again. This time he woke and found her bending over him, and gave forth the cry which was now so well known by all the party. Mrs. Lennox, who rushed into the room the first, being in her own chamber, which was near Johnny's, had to be led back to the sitting-room in a state of nervous prostration, trembling and sobbing. When she was placed in her chair and a glass of wine administered to her, she declared that she had seen it too. "Oh, how can you ask me what it was? I saw something move. Do you think," with a gasp, "Rosalind, that one can keep one's wits about one, with all that going on? I am sure I saw something—something black go out of the door—or at least something moved. The curtain? oh, how can you say it was the curtain? I never thought of that. Are you sure you didn't see anything, Rosalind?"

"I saw the wind in the curtain, Aunt Sophy: the window was open, and it blew out and almost frightened me too."

"Oh, I could not say I was frightened," said Mrs. Lennox, grasping Rosalind's hand tight. "A curtain does bulge out with the wind, doesn't it? I never thought of that. I saw something—move—I—wasn't frightened, only a little nervous. Perhaps it was—the wind in the curtain. You are sure you were frightened too."

"It blew right out upon me, like some one coming to meet me."

Aunt Sophy grasped Rosalind's hand tight. "It must have some explanation," she said. "It couldn't be anything super—You don't believe in—that sort of thing, Rosalind?"

"Dear Aunt Sophy, I am sure it was the curtain. I saw it too. I would not say so if I did not feel—sure—"

"Oh, my dear, what a comfort it is to have a cool head like yours. You're not carried away by your feelings like me. I'm so sympathetic, I feel as other people feel; to hear Johnny cry just made me I can't tell how. It was dreadfully like some one moving, Rosalind."

"Yes, Aunt Sophy. When the wind got into the folds, it was exactly like some one moving."

"You are sure it was the curtain, Rosalind."

Poor Rosalind was as little sure as any imaginative girl could be; she, too, was very much shaken by Johnny's vision; at her age it is so much more easy to believe in the supernatural than in spectral illusions or derangement of the digestion. She did not believe that the stomach was the source of fancy, or that imagination only meant a form of suppressed gout. Her nerves were greatly disturbed, and she was as ready to see anything, if seeing depended upon an excited condition, as any young and impressionable person ever was. She was glad to soothe Mrs. Lennox with an easy explanation. But Rosalind did not believe that it was the curtain which had deceived Johnny. Neither did she believe in the baths, or in the suppressed gout. She was convinced in her mind that the child spoke the truth, and that it was some visitor from the unseen who came to him. But who was it? Dark fears crossed her mind, and many a wistful wonder. There were no family warnings among the Trevanions, or it is to be feared that reason would have yielded in Rosalind's mind to nature and faith. As it was, her heart grew feverish and expectant. The arrival of the letters from England every morning filled her with terror. She dreaded to see a black-bordered envelope, a messenger of death.

CHAPTER XLVI

Johnny throve, notwithstanding his visions. He woke up in the morning altogether unaffected, so far as appeared, by what he saw at night. He had always been more or less the centre of interest, both by dint of being the only male member of the party and because he was the youngest, and he was more than ever the master of the situation now. He did not mind his baths, and he relished the importance of his position. So much time as Mrs. Lennox had free from her "cure" was entirely occupied with Johnny. She thought he wanted "nourishment" of various dainty kinds, to which the little fellow had not the least objection. Secretly in her heart Aunt Sophy was opposed to the idea of suppressed gout, and clung to that of impaired digestion. Delicate fricassees of chicken, game, the earliest products of la chasse, she ordered for him instead of the roast mutton of old. He had fine custards and tempting jellies, while Sophy and Amy ate their rice pudding; and in the intervals between his meals Aunt Sophy administered glasses of wine, cups of jelly, hunches of spongecake, to the boy. He took it all with the best grace in the world—and an appetite which it was a pleasure to see—and throve and grew, but nevertheless still saw the lady at intervals with a pertinacity which was most discouraging. It may be supposed that an incident so remarkable had not passed without notice in the curious little community of the hotel. And the first breath of it, whispered by nurse in the ear of some confidante, brought up the landlady from the bureau in a painful condition of excitement, first to inquire and then to implore that complete secrecy might be kept on the matter. Madame protested that there was no ghost in her well-regulated house. If the little boy saw anything it must be a ghost whom the English family had brought with them: such things, it was well known, did exist in English houses. But there were no ghosts in Aix, much less in the Hotel Venat. To request ladies in the middle of their cure to find other quarters was impossible, not to say that Madame Lennox and her charming family were quite the most distinguished party at the hotel, and one which she would not part with on any consideration; but if the little monsieur continued to have his digestion impaired (and she could recommend a most excellent tisane that worked marvels), might she beg ces dames to keep silence on the subject? The reputation of a hotel was like that of a woman, and if once breathed upon—Mrs. Lennox remained in puzzling and puzzled silence for some time after this visit was over. About a quarter of an hour after her thought burst forth.

"Rosalind! I don't feel at all reassured by what that woman said. Why should she make all that talk about the house if there wasn't some truth in it? It is a very creepy, disagreeable thing to think of, and us living on the very brink of it, so to speak. But, after all, what if Johnny's lady should be something—some—appearance, some mystery about the house?"

"You thought it was Johnny's digestion, Aunt Sophy."

"So I did: but then, you know, one says that sort of thing when one can't think of anything else. I believe it is his digestion, but, at the same time, how can one tell what sort of things may have happened in great big foreign houses, and so many queer people coming and going? There might have been a murder or something, for anything we know."

This suggestion awoke a tremor in Rosalind's heart, for she was not very strong-minded, nor fortified by any consistent opinion in respect to ghosts. She said somewhat faintly, with a laugh, "I never heard of a ghost in a hotel."

"In a hotel? I should think a hotel was just the sort of place, with all kinds of strange people. Mind, however," said Aunt Sophy after a pause, "I don't believe in ghosts at all, not at all; there are no such things. Only foolish persons, servants and the uneducated, put any faith in them (it was the entrance of Amy and Sophy in the midst of this discussion that called forth such a distinct profession of faith); and now your Uncle John is coming," she added cheerfully, "and it will all be cleared up and everything will come right."

"Will Uncle John clear up about the lady?" said Sophy, with a toss of her little impertinent head. "He will just laugh, I know. He will say he wished he had ladies come to see him like that. Uncle John," said this small critic, "is never serious at all about us children. Oh, perhaps about you grown-up people; but he will just laugh, I know. And so shall I laugh. All the fuss that is made is because Johnny is the boy. Me and Amy, we might see elephants and you would not mind, Aunt Sophy. It is because Johnny is the boy."

"You are a little impertinent! I think just as much about Amy—and the child is looking pale, don't you think so, Rosalind? But you are never disturbed in your sleep, my pet, nor take things in your little head. You are the quietest little woman. Indeed, I wish she would be naughty sometimes, Rosalind. What is the matter with you, dear? Don't you want me to talk to you? Well, if my arm is disagreeable, Amy—"

"Oh, no, no, Aunt Sophy!" cried the child, with an impetuous kiss, but she extricated herself notwithstanding, and went away to the farther window, where she sat down on a footstool, half hidden among the curtains. The two ladies, looking at her, began to remember at the same moment that this had become Amy's habitual place. She was always so quiet that to become a little quieter was not remarked in her as it would have been in the other children: she had always been pale, but not so pale as now. The folds of the long white curtain, falling half over her, added to the delicacy of her aspect. She seemed to shrink and hide herself from their gaze, though she was not conscious of it.

"Dear me!" said Aunt Sophy, "perhaps there is something after all in the doctor's idea of suppressed gout being in the family. You don't show any signs of it, Rosalind, Heaven be praised! or Sophy either; but just look at that child, how pale she is!"

Rosalind did not make any reply. She called her little sister to her presently, but Amy declared that she was "reading a book," which was, under Mrs. Lennox's sway, a reason above all others for leaving the little student undisturbed. Mrs. Lennox had not been used to people who were given to books, and she admired the habit greatly. "Don't call her if she is reading, Rosalind. I wonder how it is the rest of you don't read. But Amy always has her book. Perhaps it is because of reading so much that she is so pale. Well, Uncle John is coming to-morrow, and he will want the children to take long walks, and I dare say all this little confusion will blow away. I wish John had come a little sooner; he might have tried the 'cure' as well as me, for I am sure he has rheumatism, if not gout. Gentlemen always have one or the other when they come to your uncle's age, and it might have saved him an illness later," said Aunt Sophy. She had to go away in her chair, in a few minutes, for her bath, and it was this that made her think what an excellent thing it would be for John.

When she had gone, Rosalind sat very silent with her two little sisters in the room. Sophy went on talking, while Rosalind mused and kept silent. She was so well accustomed to Sophy talking that she took little notice of it. When the little girl said anything of sufficient importance to penetrate the mist of self-abstraction in which her sister sat, Rosalind would answer her. But generally she took little notice. She woke up, however, in the midst of one of Sophy's sentences which caught her ear, she could not tell why.

"Think it's a real lady?" Sophy said. It was at the end of a long monologue, during which her somewhat sharp voice had run on monotonous without variety. "Think it's a real lady? There could be no ghost here, or if there was, why should it go to Johnny, who don't understand, who has no sense. I think it's a real lady that comes in to look at the children. Perhaps she is fond of children; perhaps she's not in her right mind," said Sophy; "perhaps she has lost a little boy like Johnny; perhaps—" here she clapped her hands together, which startled Rosalind greatly, and made little Amy, looking up with big eyes from within the curtain, jump from her seat; "I know who it is—it is the lady that gave him the toy."

"The toy—what toy?"

"Oh, you know very well, Rosalind. That is what it is—the lady that had lost a child like Johnny, that brought him that thing that you wind up, that runs, that nurse says must have cost a mint of money. She says mint of money, and why shouldn't I? I shall watch to-night, and try if I can't see her," cried Sophy; "that is the lady! and Johnny is such a little silly he has never found it out. But it is a real lady, that I am quite certain, whatever the children say."

"But Amy has never seen anything, Sophy, or heard anything," Rosalind said.

"Oh, Rosalind, how soft you are! How could she help hearing about it, with Aunt Sophy and you rampaging in the room every night! You don't know how deep she is; she would just go on and go on, and never tell."

"Amy, come here," said Rosalind.

"Oh, please, Rosy! I am in such an interesting part."

"Amy, come here—you can go back to your book after. Sophy says you have heard about the lady Johnny thinks he sees."

"Yes, Rosalind."

"You have known about her perhaps all the time, though we thought you slept so sound and heard nothing! You don't mean that you have seen her too?"

Amy stood by her sister's knee, her hand reluctantly allowing itself to be held in Rosalind's hand. She submitted to this questioning with the greatest reluctance, her little frame all instinct with eagerness to get away. But here she gave a hasty look upward as if drawn by the attraction of Rosalind's eyes. How strange that no one had remarked how white and small she had grown! She gave her sister a solemn, momentary look, with eyes that seemed to expand as they looked, but said nothing.

"Amy, can't you answer me?" Rosalind cried.

Amy's eyelids grew big with unwilling tears, and she made a great effort to draw away her hand.

"Tell me, Amy, is there anything you can't tell Rosalind? You shall not be worried or scolded, but tell me."

There was a little pause, and then the child flung her arms round her sister's neck and hid her face. "Oh, Rosalind!"

"Yes, my darling, what is it? Tell me!"

Amy clung as if she would grow there, and pressed her little head, as if the contact strengthened her, against the fair pillar of Rosalind's throat. But apparently it was easier to cling there and give vent to a sob or two than to speak. She pressed closer and closer, but she made no reply.

"She has seen her every time," said Sophy, "only she's such a story she won't tell. She is always seeing her. When you think she's asleep she is lying all shivering and shaking with the sheet over her head. That is how I found out. She is so frightened she can't go to sleep. I said I should tell Rosalind; Rosalind is the eldest, and she ought to know. But then, Amy thinks—"

"What, Sophy?"

"Well, that you are only our half-sister. You are only our half-sister, you know. We all think that, and perhaps you wouldn't understand."

To Rosalind's heart this sting of mistrust went sharp and keen, notwithstanding the close strain of the little girl's embrace which seemed to protest against the statement. "Is it really, really so?" she cried, in a voice of anguish. "Do you think I am not your real sister, you little ones? Have I done anything to make you think—"

"Oh, no, no! Oh, Rosalind, no! Oh, no, no!" cried the little girl, clasping closer and closer. The ghost, if it was a ghost, the "lady" who, Sophy was sure, was a "real lady," disappeared in the more immediate pressure of this poignant question. Even Rosalind, who had now herself to be consoled, forgot, in the pang of personal suffering, to inquire further.

And they were still clinging together in excitement and tears when the door was opened briskly, and Uncle John, all brown and dusty and smiling, a day too soon, and much pleased with himself for being so, suddenly marched into the room. A more extraordinary change of sentiment could not be conceived. The feminine tears dried up in a moment, the whole aspect of affairs changed. He was so strong, so brown, so cordial, so pleased to see them, so full of cheerful questions, and the account of what he had done. "Left London only yesterday," he said, "and here I am. What's the matter with Amy? Crying! You must let her off, Rosalind, whatever the sin may be, for my sake."

CHAPTER XLVII

The arrival of John Trevanion made a great difference to the family group, which had become absorbed, as women are so apt to be, in the circle of little interests about them, and to think Johnny's visions the most important things in the world. Uncle John would hear nothing at all of Johnny's visions. "Pooh!" he said. Mrs. Lennox was half disposed to think him brutal and half to think him right. He scoffed at the fricassee of chicken and the cups of jelly. "He looks as well as possible," said Uncle John. "Amy is a little shadow, but the boy is fat and flourishing," and he laughed with an almost violent effusion of mirth at the idea of the suppressed gout. "Get them all off to some place among the hills, or, if it is too late for that, come home," he said.

"But, John, my cure!" cried Mrs. Lennox; "you don't know how rheumatic I have become. If it was not a little too late I should advise you to try it too; for, of course, we have gout in the family, whatever you may say, and it might save you an illness another time. Rosalind, was not Mr. Everard coming to lunch? I quite forgot him in the pleasure of seeing your uncle. Perhaps we ought to have waited, but, then, John, coming off his journey, wanted his luncheon; and I dare say Mr. Everard will not mind. He is always so obliging. He would not mind going without his luncheon altogether to serve a friend."

"Who is Mr. Everard?" said John Trevanion. He was pleased to meet them all, and indisposed to find fault with anything. Why should he go without his lunch?

"Oh, he is very nice," said Aunt Sophy somewhat evasively; "he is here for his 'cure,' like all the rest. Surely I wrote to you, or some one wrote to you, about the accident with the boat, and how the children's lives were saved? Well, this is the gentleman. He has been a great deal with us ever since. He is quite young, but I think he looks younger than he is, and he has very nice manners," Mrs. Lennox continued, with a dim sense, which began to grow upon her, that explanations were wanted, and a conciliatory fulness of detail. "It is very kind of him making himself so useful as he does. I ask him quite freely to do anything for me; and, of course, being a young person, it is more cheerful for Rosalind."

Here she made a little pause, in which for the first time there was a consciousness of guilt, or, if not of guilt, of imprudence. John might think that a young person who made things more cheerful for Rosalind required credentials. John might look as gentlemen have a way of looking at individuals of their own sex introduced in their absence. Talk of women being jealous of each other, Aunt Sophy said to herself, but men are a hundred times more! and she began to wish that Mr. Everard might forget his engagement, and not walk in quite so soon into the family conclave. Rosalind's mind, too, was disturbed by the same thought; she felt that it would be better if Mr. Everard did not come, if he would have the good taste to stay away when he heard of the new arrival. But Rosalind, though she had begun to like him, and though her imagination was touched by his devotion, had not much confidence in Everard's good taste. He would hesitate, she thought, he would ponder, but he would not be so wise as to keep away. As a matter of fact this last reflection had scarcely died from her mind when Everard came in, a little flushed and anxious, having heard of the arrival, but regarding it from an opposite point of view. He thought that it would be well to get the meeting over while John Trevanion was still in the excitement of the reunion and tired with his journey. There were various changes in his own appearance since he had been at Highcourt, and he was three years older, but on the other side he remembered so well his own meeting with Rosalind's uncle that he could not suppose himself to be more easily forgotten. In fact, John Trevanion had a slight movement of surprise at sight of the young intruder, and a vague sense of recognition as he met the eyes which looked at him with a mixture of anxiety and deprecation. But he got up and held out his hand, and said a few words of thanks for the great service which Mr. Everard had rendered to the family, with the best grace in the world, and though the presence of a stranger could scarcely be felt otherwise than as an intrusion at such a moment, Everard himself was perhaps the person least conscious of it. Rosalind, on the other hand, was very conscious of it, and uncomfortably conscious that Everard was not, yet ought to have been, aware of the inappropriateness of his appearance. There was thus a certain cloud over the luncheon hour, which would have been very merry and very pleasant but for the one individual who did not belong to the party, and who, though wistfully anxious to recommend himself, to do everything or anything possible to make himself agreeable, yet could not see that the one thing to be done was to take himself away. When he did so at last, John Trevanion broke off what he was saying hurriedly—he was talking of Reginald, at school, a subject very interesting to them all—and, turning to Rosalind, said, "I know that young fellow's face; where have I seen him before?"

"I know, Uncle John," cried Sophy; "he is the gentleman who was staying at the Red Lion in the village, don't you remember, before we left Highcourt. Rosalind knew him directly, and so did I."

"Yes," said Rosalind, faltering a little. "You remember I met you once when he had done me a little service; that," she said, with a sense that she was making herself his advocate, and a deprecating, conciliatory smile, "seems to be his specialty, to do people services."

"The gentleman who was at the Red Lion!" cried John Trevanion with a start. "The fellow who—" and then he stopped short and cast upon his guileless sister a look which made Mrs. Lennox tremble.

"Oh, dear, dear, what have I done?" Aunt Sophy cried.

"Nothing; it is of no consequence," said he; but he got up, thrusting his hands deep into his pockets, and walked about from one window to another, and stared gloomily forth, without adding any more.

"But he is very nice now," said Sophy; "he is much more nicely dressed, and I think he is handsome—rather. He is like Johnny a little. It was nice of him, don't you think, Uncle John, to save the children? They weren't anything to him, you know, and yet he went plunging into the water with his clothes on—for, of course, he could not stop to take off his clothes, and he couldn't have done it either before Rosalind—and had to walk all the way home in his wet trousers, all for the sake of these little things. Everybody would not have done it," said Sophy, with importance, speaking as one who knew human nature. "It was very nice, don't you think, of Mr. Everard."

"Everard! Was that the name?" said Uncle John, incoherently; and he did not sit down again, but kept walking up and down the long room in a way some men have, to the great annoyance of Mrs. Lennox, who did not like to see people, as she said, roving about like wild beasts. A certain uneasiness had got into the atmosphere somehow, no one could tell why, and when the children were called out for their walk Rosalind too disappeared, with a consciousness, that wounded her and yet seemed somehow a fault in herself, that the elders would be more at ease without her presence.

When they were all gone John turned upon his sister. "Sophy," he said, "I remember how you took me to task for bringing Rivers, a man of character and talent, to the house, because his parentage was somewhat obscure. Have you ever asked yourself what your own meaning was in allowing a young adventurer, whose very character, I fear, will not bear looking into, to make himself agreeable to Rosalind?"

"John!" cried Mrs. Lennox, with a sudden scream, sitting up very upright in her chair, and in her fright taking off her spectacles to see him the better.

"Yes," cried John Trevanion, "I mean what I say. He has managed to make himself agreeable to Rosalind. She takes his part already. She is troubled when he puts himself in a false position."

"But, John, what makes you think he is an adventurer? I am quite sure he is one of the Essex Everards, who are as good a family and as well thought of—"

"Did he tell you he was one of the Essex Everards?"

Mrs. Lennox put on a very serious air of trying to remember. She bit her lips, she contracted her forehead, she put up her hand to her head. "I am sure," she said, "I cannot recollect whether he ever said it, but I have always understood. Why, what other Everards could he belong to?" she added, in the most candid tone.

"That is just the question," said John Trevanion; "the same sort of Everards perhaps as my friend's Riverses, or most likely not half so good. Indeed, I'm not at all sure that your friend has any right even to the name he claims. I both saw and heard of him before we left Highcourt. By Jove!" He was not a man to swear, even in this easy way, but he jumped up from the seat upon which he had thrown himself and grew so red that Aunt Sophy immediately thought of the suppressed gout in the family, and felt that it must suddenly have gone to his head.

"Oh, John, my dear! what is it?" she cried.

He paced about the room back and forward in high excitement, repeating to himself that exclamation. "Oh, nothing, nothing! I can't quite tell what it is," he said.

"A twinge in your foot," cried Mrs. Lennox. "Oh, John, though it is late, very late, in the season, and you could not perhaps follow out the cure altogether, you might at least take some of the baths as they are ordered for Johnny. It might prevent an illness hereafter. It might, if you took it in time—"

"What is a 'cure'?" said John. Mrs. Lennox pronounced the word, as indeed it is intended that the reader should pronounce it in this history, in the French way; but this in her honest mouth, used to good, downright English pronunciation, sounded like koor, and the brother did not know what it was. He laughed so long and so loudly at the idea of preventing an illness by the cure, as he called it with English brutality, and at the notion of Johnny's baths, that Mrs. Lennox was quite disconcerted and could not find a word to say.

Rosalind had withdrawn with her mind full of disquietude. She was vexed and annoyed by Everard's ignorance of the usages of society and the absence of perception in him. He should not have come up when he heard that Uncle John had arrived; he should not have stayed. But Rosalind reflected with a certain resentment and impatience that it was impossible to make him aware of this deficiency, or to convey to him in any occult way the perceptions that were wanting. This is not how a girl thinks of her lover, and yet she was more disturbed by his failure to perceive than any proceeding on the part of a person in whom she was not interested could have made her. She had other cares in her mind, however, which soon asserted a superior claim. Little Amy's pale face, her eyes so wistful and pathetic, which seemed to say a thousand things and to appeal to Rosalind's knowledge with a trust and faith which were a bitter reproach to Rosalind, had given her a sensation which she could not overcome. Was she too wanting in perception, unable to divine what her little sister meant? It was well for her to blame young Everard and to blush for his want of perception, she, who could not understand little Amy! Her conversation with the children had thrown another light altogether on Johnny's vision. What if it were no trick of the digestion, no excitement of the spirit, but something real, whether in the body or out of the body, something with meaning in it? She resolved that she would not allow this any longer to go on without investigation, and, with a little thrill of excitement in her, arranged her plans for the evening. It was not without a tremor that Rosalind took this resolution. She had already many times taken nurse's place without any particular feeling on the subject, with the peaceful result that Johnny slept soundly and nobody was disturbed; but this easy watch did not satisfy her now. Notwithstanding the charm of Uncle John's presence, Rosalind hastened up-stairs after dinner when the party streamed forth to take coffee in the garden, denying herself the pleasant stroll with him which she had looked forward to, and which he in his heart was wounded to see her withdraw from without a word. She flew along the half-lighted passages with her heart beating high.

The children's rooms were in their usual twilight, the faint little night-lamp in its corner, the little sleepers breathing softly in the gloom. Rosalind placed herself unconsciously out of sight from the door, sitting down behind Johnny's bed, though without any intention by so doing of hiding herself. If it were possible that any visitor from the unseen came to the child's bed, what could it matter that the watcher was out of sight? She sat down there with a beating heart in the semi-darkness which made any occupation impossible, and after a while fell into the thoughts which had come prematurely to the mother-sister, a girl, and yet with so much upon her young shoulders. The arrival of her uncle brought back the past to her mind. She thought of all that had happened, with the tears gathering thick in her eyes. Where was she now that should have had these children in her care? Oh, where was she? would she never even try to see them, never break her bonds and claim the rights of nature? How could she give them up—how could she do it? Or could it be, Rosalind asked herself—or rather did not ask herself, but in the depths of her heart was aware of the question which came independent of any will of hers—that there was some reason, some new conditions, which made the breach in her life endurable, which made the mother forget her children? The girl's heart grew sick as she sat thus thinking, with the tears silently dropping from her eyes, wondering upon the verge of that dark side of human life in which such mysteries are, wondering whether it were possible, whether such things could be?

A faint sound roused her from this preoccupation. She turned her head. Oh, what was it she saw? The lady of Johnny's dream had come in while Rosalind had forgotten her watch, and stood looking at him in his little bed. Rosalind's lips opened to cry out, but the cry seemed stifled in her throat. The spectre, if it were a spectre, half raised the veil that hung about her head and gazed at the child, stooping forward, her hands holding the lace in such an attitude that she seemed to bless him as he lay—a tall figure, all black save for the whiteness of the half-seen face. Rosalind had risen noiselessly from her chair; she gazed too as if her eyes would come out of their sockets, but she was behind the curtain and unseen. Whether it was that her presence diffused some sense of protection round, or that the child was in a more profound sleep than usual, it was impossible to tell, but Johnny never moved, and his visitor stood bending towards him without a breath or sound. Rosalind, paralyzed in body, overwhelmed in her mind with terror, wonder, confusion, stood and looked on with sensations beyond description, as if her whole soul was suspended on the event. Had any one been there to see, the dark room, with the two ghostly, silent figures in it, noiseless, absorbed, one watching the other, would have been the strangest sight. But Rosalind was conscious of nothing save of life suspended, hanging upon the next movement or sound, and never knew how long it was that she stood, all power gone from her, watching, scarcely breathing, unable to speak or think. Then the dark figure turned, and there seemed to breathe into the air something like a sigh. It was the only sound; not even the softest footfall on the carpet or rustle of garments seemed to accompany her movements, slow and reluctant, towards the doorway. Then she seemed to pause again on the threshold between the two rooms, within sight of the bed in which Amy lay. Rosalind followed, feeling herself drawn along by a power not her own, herself as noiseless as a ghost. The strain upon her was so intense that she was incapable of feeling, and stood mechanically, her eyes fixed, her heart now fluttering wildly, now standing still altogether. The moment came, however, when this tension was too much. Beyond the dark figure in the doorway she saw, or thought she saw, Amy's eyes, wild and wide open, appealing to her from the bed. Her little sister's anguish of terror and appeal for help broke the spell and made Rosalind's suspense intolerable. She made a wild rush forward, her frozen voice broke forth in a hoarse cry. She put out her hands and grasped or tried to grasp the draperies of the mysterious figure; then, as they escaped her, fell helpless, blind, unable to sustain herself, but not unconscious, by Amy's bed, upon the floor.

CHAPTER XLVIII

Down below, in the garden of the hotel, all was cheerful enough, and most unlike the existence of any mystery here or elsewhere. The night was very soft and mild, though dark, the scent of the mignonette in the air, and most of the inhabitants of the hotel sitting out among the dark, rustling shrubs and under the twinkling lights, which made effects, too strong to be called picturesque, of light and shade among the many groups who were too artificial for pictorial effect, yet made up a picture like the art of the theatre, effective, striking, full of brilliant points. The murmur of talk was continuous, softened by the atmosphere, yet full of laughter and exclamations which were not soft. High above, the stars were shining in an atmosphere of their own, almost chill with the purity and remoteness of another world. At some of the tables the parties were not gay; here and there a silent English couple sat and looked on, half disapproving, half wistful, with a look in their eyes that said, how pleasant it must be when people can thus enjoy themselves, though in all likelihood how wrong! Among these English observers were Mrs. Lennox and John Trevanion.

Mrs. Lennox had no hat on, but a light white shawl of lacey texture over her cap, and her face full in the light. She was in no trouble about Rosalind's absence, which she took with perfect calm. The girl had gone, no doubt, to sit with the children, or she had something to do up-stairs—Mrs. Lennox was aware of all the little things a girl has to do. But she was dull, and did not find John amusing. Mrs. Lennox would have thought it most unnatural to subject a brother to such criticism in words, or to acknowledge that it was necessary for him to be amusing to make his society agreeable. Such an idea would have been a blasphemy against nature, which, of course, makes the society of one's brother always delightful, whether he has or has not anything to say. But granting this, and that she was, of course, a great deal happier by John's side, and that it was delightful to have him again, still she was a little dull. The conversation flagged, even though she had a great power of keeping it up by herself when need was; but when you only get two words in answer to a question which it has taken you five minutes to ask, the result is discouraging; and she looked round her with a great desire for some amusement and a considerable envy of the people at the next table, who were making such a noise! How they laughed, how the conversation flew on, full of fun evidently, full of wit, no doubt, if one could only understand. No doubt it is rather an inferior thing to be French or Russian or whatever they were, and not English; and to enjoy yourself so much out of doors in public is vulgar perhaps. But still Mrs. Lennox envied a little while she disapproved, and so did the other English couple on the other side. Aunt Sophy even had begun to yawn and to think it would perhaps be better for her rheumatism to go in and get to bed, when she perceived the familiar figure of young Everard amid the shadows, looking still more wistfully towards her. She made him a sign with great alacrity and pleasure, as she was in the habit of doing, for indeed he joined them every night, or almost every night. When she had done this, and had drawn a chair towards her for him, then and not till then Mrs. Lennox suddenly remembered that John might not like it. That was very true—John might not like it! What a pity she had not thought of it sooner? But why shouldn't John like such a very nice, friendly, serviceable young man. Men were so strange! they took such fancies about each other. All this flashed through her mind after she had made that friendly sign to Everard, and indicated the chair.

"Is any one coming?" asked John, roused by these movements.

"Only Mr. Everard, John; he usually comes in the evening—please be civil to him," she cried in dismay.

"Oh, civil!" said John Trevanion; he pushed away his chair almost violently, with the too rapid reflection, so easily called forth, that Sophy was a fool and had no thought, and the intention of getting up and going away. But then he bethought himself that it would be well to see what sort of fellow this young man was. It would be necessary, he said to himself sternly, that there should be an explanation before the intimacy went any further, but, in the meantime, as fortunately Rosalind was absent (he said this to himself with a forlorn sort of smile at his former disappointment), it would be a good opportunity to see what was in him. Accordingly he did not get up as he intended, but only pushed his chair away, as the young man approached with a hesitating and somewhat anxious air. John gave him a gruff nod, but said nothing, and sat by, a grim spectator, taking no part in the conversation, as Mrs. Lennox broke into eager, but, in consequence of his presence, somewhat embarrassed and uneasy talk.

"I thought we were not to see you to-night," she said. "I thought there might be something going on, perhaps. We never know what is going on except when you bring us word, Mr. Everard. I do think, though the Venat is supposed to be the best hotel, that madame is not at all enterprising about getting up a little amusement. To be sure, the season is almost over. I suppose that is the cause."

"I don't think there is anything going on except the usual music and the weekly dance at the Hotel d'Europe, and—"

"I think French people are always dancing," said Mrs. Lennox, with a little sigh, "or rattling on in that way, laughing and jesting as if life were all a play. I am sure I don't know how they keep it up, always going on like that. But Rosalind does not care for those sort of dances. Had there been one in our own hotel among people we know—But I must say madame is rather remiss: she does not exert herself to provide amusement. If I came here another year, as I suppose I must, now that I have begun to have a koor—"

"Oh, yes, they will keep you to it. This is the second year I have been made to come. I hope you will be here, Mrs. Lennox, for then I shall be sure to see you, and—" Here he paused a little and added "the children," in a lower voice.

"It is so nice of you, a young man, to think of the children," said Aunt Sophy, gratefully; "but they say it does make you like people when you have done them a great service. As to meeting us, I hope we shall meet sooner than that. When you come to England you must—" Here Mrs. Lennox paused, feeling John's malign influence by her side, and conscious of a certain kick of his foot and the suppressed snort with which he puffed out the smoke of his cigar. She paused; but then she reflected that, after all, the Elms was her own, and she was not in the habit of consulting John as to whom she should ask there. And then she went on, with a voice that trembled slightly, "Come down to Clifton and see me; I shall be so happy to see you, and I think I know some of your Essex relations," Mrs. Lennox said.

John Trevanion, who had been leaning back with the legs of his chair tilted in the air, came down upon them with a dint in the gravel, and thus approached himself nearer to the table in his mingled indignation at his sister's foolishness, and eagerness to hear what the young fellow would find to say. This, no doubt, disturbed the even flow of the response, making young Everard start.

"I don't think I have any relations in Essex," he said. "You are very kind. But I have not been in England for some years, and I don't think I am very likely to go."

"Dear me!" said Mrs. Lennox, "I am very sorry. I hope you have not got any prejudice against home. Perhaps there is more amusement to be found abroad, Mr. Everard, and no doubt that tells with young men like you; but I am sure you will find after a while what the song says, that there is no place like home."

"Oh, no, I have no prejudice," he said hurriedly. "There are reasons—family reasons." Then he added, with what seemed to John, watching him eagerly, a little bravado, "The only relative I have is rather what you would call eccentric. She has her own ways of thinking. She has been ill-used in England, or at least she thinks so, and nothing will persuade her—Ladies, you know, sometimes take strange views of things."

"Oh," said Mrs. Lennox, "I cannot allow you to say anything against ladies. For my part I think it is men that take strange views. But, my dear Mr. Everard, because your relative has a prejudice (which is so very unnatural in a woman), that is not to say that a young man like you is to be kept from home. Oh, no, you may be sure she doesn't mean that."

"It does seem absurd, doesn't it?" the young man said.

"And I would not," said Aunt Sophy, strong in the sense of superiority over a woman who could show herself so capricious, "I would not, though it is very nice of you, and everybody must like you the better for trying to please her, I would not yield altogether in a matter like this. For, you know, if you are thinking of public life, or of any way of distinguishing yourself, you can only do that at home. Besides, I think it is everybody's duty to think of their own country first. A tour like this we are all making is all very well, for six months or even more. We shall have been nine months away in a day or two, but then I am having my drains thoroughly looked to, and it was necessary. Six months is quite enough, and I would not stay abroad for a permanency, oh! not for anything. Being abroad is very nice, but home—you know what the song says, there is—Rosalind! Good heavens, what is the matter? It can't be Johnny again?"

Rosalind seemed to rush upon them in a moment, as if she had lighted down from the skies. Even in the flickering artificial light they could see that she was as white as her dress and her face drawn and haggard. She came and stood by the table with her back to all the fluttering crowd beyond and the light streaming full upon her. "Uncle John," she said, "mamma is dead, I have seen her; Amy and I have seen her. You drove her away, but she has come back to the children. I knew—I knew—that sometime she would come back."

"Rosalind!" Mrs. Lennox rose, forgetting her rheumatism, and John Trevanion rushed to the girl and took her into his arms. "My darling, what is it? You are ill—you have been frightened."

She leaned against his arm, supporting herself so, and lifted her pale face to his. "Mamma is dead, for I have seen her," Rosalind said.

CHAPTER XLIX

When Rosalind came to herself she had found little Amy in her white nightgown standing by her, clinging round her, her pretty hair, all tumbled and in disorder, hanging about the cheeks which were pressed against her sister's, wet with tears. For a moment they said nothing to each other. Rosalind raised herself from her entire prostration and sat on the carpet holding Amy in her arms. They clung to each other, two hearts beating, two young souls full of anguish, yet exaltation; they were raised above all that was round them, above the common strain of speech and thought. The first words that Rosalind said were very low.

"Amy, did you see her?"

"Oh, yes, yes, Rosalind!"

"Did you know her?"

"Yes, Rosalind."

"Have you seen her before?"

"Oh, every night!"

"Amy, and you never said it was mamma!"

They trembled both as if a blast of wind had passed over them, and clasped each other closer. Was it Rosalind that had become a child again and Amy that was the woman? She whispered, with her lips on her sister's cheek,

"How was I to tell? She came to me—to me and Johnny. We belong to her, Rosalind."

"And not I!" the girl exclaimed, with a great cry. Then she recovered herself, that thought being too keen to pass without effect.

"Amy! you are hers without her choice, but she took me of her own will to be her child; I belong to her almost more than you. Oh, not more, not more, Amy! but you were so little you did not know her like me."

Little Amy recognized at last that in force of feeling she was not her sister's equal, and for a time they were both silent. Then the child asked, looking round her with a wild and frightened glance, "Rosalind, must mamma be dead?"

This question roused them both to a terror and panic such as in the first emotion and wonder they had not been conscious of. Instead of love came fear; they had been raised above that tremor of the flesh, but now it came upon them in a horror not to be put aside. Even Rosalind, who was old enough to take herself to task, felt with a painful thrill that she had stood by something that was not flesh and blood, and in the intensity of the shuddering terror forgot her nobler yearning sympathy and love. They crept together to the night-lamp and lit the candles from it, and closed all the doors, shrinking from the dark curtains and shadows in the corners as if spectres might be lurking there. They had lit up the room thus when nurse returned from her evening's relaxation down-stairs, cheerful but tired, and ready to go to bed. She stood holding up her head and gazing at them with eyes of amazement. "Lord, Miss Rosalind, what's the matter? You'll wake the children up," she cried.

"Oh, it is nothing, nurse. Amy was awake," said Rosalind, trembling. "We thought the light would be more cheering." Her voice shook so that she could with difficulty articulate the words.

"And did you think, Miss Rosalind, that the child could ever go to sleep with all that light; and telling her stories, and putting things in her head? I don't hold with exciting them when it is their bedtime. It may not matter so much for a lady that comes in just now and then, but for the nurse as is always with them—And children are tiresome at the best of times. No one knows how tiresome they are but those that have to do for them day and night."

"We did not mean to vex you. We were very sad, Amy and I; we were unhappy, thinking of our mother," said Rosalind, trying to say the words firmly, "whom we have lost."

"Oh, Rosalind, do you think so too?" cried Amy, flinging herself into her sister's arms.

Rosalind took her up trembling and carried her to bed. The tears had begun to come, and the terrible iron hand that had seemed to press upon her heart relaxed a little. She kissed the child with quivering lips. "I think it must be so," she said. "We will say our prayers, and ask God, if there is anything she wants us to do, to show us what it is." Rosalind's lips quivered so that she had to stop to subdue herself, to make her voice audible. "Now she is dead, she can come back to us. We ought to be glad. Why should we be frightened for poor mamma? She could not come back to us living, but now, when she is dead—"

"Miss Rosalind," said the nurse, "I don't know what you are saying, but you will put the child off her sleep and she won't close an eye all the night."

"Amy, that would grieve mamma," said the girl. "We must not do anything to vex her now that she has come back."

And so strong is nature and so weak is childhood, that Amy, wearied and soothed and comforted, with Rosalind's voice in her ears and the cheerful light within sight, did drop to sleep, sobbing, before half an hour was out. Then Rosalind bathed the tears from her eyes, and, hurrying through the long passages with that impulse to tell her tale to some one which to the simple soul is a condition of life, appeared suddenly in her exaltation and sorrow amid all the noisy groups in the hotel garden. Her head was light with tears and suffering, she scarcely felt the ground she trod upon, or realized what was about her. Her only distinct feeling was that which she uttered with such conviction, leaning her entire weight on Uncle John's kind arm and lifting her colorless face to his—"Mamma is dead; and she has come back to the children." How natural it seemed! the only thing to be expected; but Mrs. Lennox gave a loud cry and fell back in her chair, in what she supposed to be a faint, good woman, having happily little experience. It was now that young Everard justified her good opinion of him. He soothed her back out of this half-faint, and, supporting her on his arm, led her up-stairs. "I will see to her; you will be better alone," he said, as he passed the other group. Even John Trevanion, when he had time to think of it, felt that it was kind, and Aunt Sophy never forgot the touching attention he showed to her, calling her maid, and bringing her eau-de-cologne after he had placed her on the sofa. "He might have been my son," Mrs. Lennox said; "no nephew was ever so kind." But when he came out of the room, and stood outside in the lighted corridor, there was nothing tender in the young man's face. It was pale with passion and a cruel force. He paused for a moment to collect himself, and then, turning along a long passage and up another staircase, made his way, with the determined air of a man who has a desperate undertaking in hand, to an apartment with which he was evidently well acquainted, on the other side of the house.

CHAPTER L

The Hotel Venat that night closed its doors upon many anxious and troubled souls. A certain agitation seemed to have crept through the house itself. The landlady was disturbed in her bureau, moving about restlessly, giving short answers to the many inquirers who came to know what was the matter. "What is there, do you ask?" she said, stretching out her plump hands, "there is nothing! there is that mademoiselle, the young Anglaise, has an attaque des nerfs. Nothing could be more simple. The reason I know not. Is it necessary to inquire? An affair of the heart! Les Anglaises have two or three in a year. Mademoiselle has had a disappointment. The uncle has come to interfere, and she has a seizure. I do not blame her; it is the weapon of a young girl. What has she else, pauvre petite, to avenge herself?"

"But, madame, they say that something has been seen—a ghost, a—"

"There are no ghosts in my house," the indignant landlady said; and her tone was so imperious and her brow so lowering that the timid questioners scattered in all directions. The English visitors were not quite sure what an attaque des nerfs was. It was not a "nervous attack;" it was something not to be defined by English terms. English ladies do not have hysterics nowadays; they have neuralgia, which answers something of the same purpose, but then neuralgia has no sort of connection with ghosts.

In Mrs. Lennox's sitting-room up-stairs, which was so well lighted, so fully occupied, with large windows opening upon the garden, and white curtains fluttering at the open windows, a very agitated group was assembled. Mrs. Lennox was seated at a distance from the table, with her white handkerchief in her hand, with which now and then she wiped off a few tears. Sometimes she would throw a word into the conversation that was going on, but for the most part confined herself to passive remonstrances and appeals, lifting up now her hands, now her eyes, to heaven. It was half because she was so overcome by her feelings that Mrs. Lennox took so little share in what was going on, and half because her brother had taken the management of this crisis off her hands. She did not think that he showed much mastery of the situation, but she yielded it to him with a great and consolatory consciousness that, whatever should now happen, she could not be held as the person to blame.

Rosalind's story was that which the reader already knows, with the addition of another extracted from little Amy, who had one of those wonderful tales of childish endurance and silence which seem scarcely credible, yet occur so often, to tell. For many nights past, Amy, clinging to her sister, with her face hidden on Rosalind's shoulder, declared that she had seen the same figure steal in. She had never clearly seen the face, but the child had been certain from the first that it was mamma. Mamma had gone to Johnny first, and then had come to her own little bed, where she stood for a moment before she disappeared. Johnny's outcry had been always, Amy said, after the figure disappeared, but she had seen it emerge from out of the dimness, and glide away, and by degrees this mystery had become the chief incident in her life. All this Rosalind repeated with tremulous eloquence; and excitement, as she stood before the two elder people, on her defence.

"But I saw her, Uncle John; what argument can be so strong as that? You have been moving about, you have not got your letters; and perhaps—perhaps—" cried Rosalind with tears—"perhaps it has happened only now, only to-night. A woman who was far from her children might come and see them—and see them," she struggled to say through her sobs, "on her way to heaven."

"Oh, Rosalind! it is a fortnight since it begun," Mrs. Lennox said.

"Do people die in a moment?" cried Rosalind. "She may have been dying all this time; and perhaps when they thought her wandering in her mind it might be that she was here. Oh, my mother; who would watch over her, who would be taking care of her? and me so far away!"

John Trevanion sprang from his chair. It was intolerable to sit there and listen and feel the contagion of this excitement, which was so irrational, so foolish, gain his own being. Women take a pleasure in their own anguish, which a man cannot bear. "Rosalind," he cried, "this is too terrible, you know. I cannot stand it if you can; I tell you, if anything had happened, I must have heard. All this is simply impossible. You have all got out of order, the children first, and their fancies have acted upon you."

"It is their digestion, I always said so—or gout in the system," said Aunt Sophy, lifting her handkerchief to her eyes.

"It is derangement of the brain, I think," said John. "I see I must get you out of here; one of you has infected the other. Come, Rosalind, you have so much sense—let us see you make use of it."

"Uncle John, what has sense to do with it? I have seen her," Rosalind said.

"This is madness, Rosalind."

"What is madness? Are my eyes mad that saw mamma? I was not thinking of seeing her. In a moment I lifted up my eyes, and she was there. Is it madness that she should die? Oh no, more wonderful how she can live; or madness to think that her heart would fly to us—oh, like an arrow, the moment it was free?"

"Rosalind," said Mrs. Lennox, "poor Grace was a very religious woman; at that moment she would be thinking about her Maker."

"Do you think she would be afraid of him?" cried Rosalind, "afraid that our Lord would be jealous, that he would not like her to love her children? Oh, that's not what my mother thought! My religion is what I got from her. She was not afraid of him—she loved him. She would know that he would let her come, perhaps bring her and stand by her; perhaps," the girl cried, clasping her hands, "if I had been better, more religious, more like my mother, I should have seen him in the room too."

John Trevanion seized her hands almost fiercely. Short of giving up his own self-control, and yielding to this stormy tide of emotion, it was the only thing he could do. "I must have an end of this," he said. "Rosalind, you must be calm—we shall all go distracted if you continue so. She was a good woman, as Sophy says. She never could, I don't believe it, have gratified herself at your expense like this. I shall telegraph the first thing in the morning to the lawyers, to know if they have any news. Will that satisfy you? Suspend your judgment till I hear; if then it turns out that there is any cause—" Here his voice broke and yielded to the strain of emotion; upon which Rosalind, whose face had been turned away, rose up suddenly and flung herself upon him as Amy had done upon her, crying, "Oh, my mother! oh, my mother! you loved her too, Uncle John."

Thus the passion of excited feeling extended itself. For a moment John Trevanion sobbed too, and the girl felt, with a sensation of awe which calmed her, the swelling of the man's breast. He put her down in her chair next moment with a tremulous smile. "No more, Rosalind—we must not all lose our senses. I promise you if there is any truth in your imagination you shall not want my sympathy. But I am sure you are exciting yourself unnecessarily; I know I should have heard had there been anything wrong. My dear, no more now."

Next morning John Trevanion was early astir. He had slept little, and his mind was full of cares. In the light of the morning he felt a little ashamed of the agitation of last night, and of the credulity to which he himself had been drawn by Rosalind's excitement. He said to himself that no doubt it was in the imagination of little Amy that the whole myth had arisen. The child had been sleepless, as children often are, and no doubt she had formed to herself that spectre out of the darkness which sympathy and excitement and solitude had embodied to Rosalind also. Nothing is more contagious than imagination. He had himself been all but overpowered by Rosalind's impassioned certainty. He had felt his own firmness waver; how much more was an emotional girl likely to waver, who did not take into account the tangle of mental workings even in a child? As he came out into the cool morning air it all seemed clear enough and easy; but the consequences were not easy, nor how he was to break the spell, and recall the visionary child and the too sympathetic girl to practical realities, and dissipate these fancies out of their heads. He was not very confident in his own powers; he thought they were quite as likely to overcome him as he to restore them to composure. But still something must be done, and the scene changed at least. As he came along the corridor from his room, with a sense of being the only person waking in this part of the house, though the servants had long been stirring below, his ear was caught by a faint, quick sound, and a whispering call from the apartment occupied by his sister. He looked round quickly, fearful, as one is in a time of agitation, of every new sound, and saw another actor in the little drama, one whose name had not yet been so much as mentioned as taking any part in it—the sharp, inquisitive, matter-of-fact little Sophy, who was the one of the children he liked least. Sophy made energetic gestures to stop him, and with elaborate precaution came out of her room attired in a little dressing-gown of blue flannel, with bare feet in slippers, and her hair hanging over her shoulders. He stood still in the passage with great impatience while she elaborately closed the door behind her, and came towards him on her toes, with an evident enjoyment of the mystery. "Oh, Uncle John! hush, don't make any noise," Sophy said.

"Is that all you want to tell me?" he asked severely.

"No, Uncle John; but we must not wake these poor things, they are all asleep. I want to tell you—do you think we are safe here and nobody can hear us? Please go back to your room. If any one were to come and see me, in bare feet and my dressing-gown—"

He laughed somewhat grimly, indeed with a feeling that he would like to whip this important little person; but Sophy detected no under-current of meaning. She cried "Hush!" again, with the most imperative energy, under her breath, and swinging by his arm drew him back to his room, which threw a ray of morning sunshine down the passage from its open door. The man was a little abashed by the entrance of this feminine creature, though she was but thirteen, especially as she gave a quick glance round of curiosity and sharp inspection. "What an awfully big sponge, and what a lot of boots you have!" she said quickly. "Uncle John! they say one ought never to watch or listen or anything of that sort; but when everybody was in such a state last night, how do you think I could just stay still in bed? I saw that lady come out of the children's room, Uncle John."

The child, though her eyes were dancing with excitement and the delight of meddling, and the importance of what she had to say, began at this point to change color, to grow red and then pale.

"You! I did not think you were the sort of person, Sophy—"

"Oh, wait a little, Uncle John! To see ghosts you were going to say. But that is just the mistake. I knew all the time it was a real lady. I don't know how I knew. I just found out, out of my own head."

"A real lady! I don't know, Sophy, what you mean."

"Oh, but you do, it is quite simple. It is no ghost, it is a real lady, as real as any one. I stood at the door and saw her come out. She went quite close past me, and I felt her things, and they were as real as mine. She makes no noise because she is so light and thin. Besides, there are no ghosts," said Sophy. "If she had been a ghost she would have known I was there, and she never did, never found me out though I felt her things. She had a great deal of black lace on," the girl added, not without meaning, though it was a meaning altogether lost upon John Trevanion. Though she was so cool and practical, her nerves were all in commotion. She could not keep still; her eyes, her feet, her fingers, all were quivering. She made a dart aside to his dressing-table. "What big, big brushes—and no handles to them! Why is everything a gentleman has so big? though you have so little hair. Her shoes were of that soft kind without any heels to them, and she made no noise. Uncle John!"

"This is a very strange addition to the story, Sophy. I am obliged to you for telling me. It was no imagination, then, but somebody, who for some strange motive—I am very glad you had so much sense, not to be deceived."

"Uncle John!" Sophy said. She did not take any notice of this applause, as in other circumstances she would have done; everything about her twitched and trembled, her eyes seemed to grow large like Amy's. She could not stand still. "Uncle John!"

"What is it, Sophy? You have something more to say."

The child's eyes filled with tears. So sharp they were, and keen, that this liquid medium seemed inappropriate to their eager curiosity and brightness. She grew quite pale, her lips quivered a little. "Uncle John!" she said again, with an hysterical heave of her bosom, "I think it is mamma."

"Sophy!" He cried out with such a wildness of exclamation that she started with fright, and those hot tears dropped out of her eyes. Something in her throat choked her. She repeated, in a stifled, broken voice, "I am sure it is mamma."

"Sophy! you must have some reason for saying this. What is it? Don't tell me half, but everything. What makes you think—?"

"Oh, I don't think at all," cried the child. "Why should I think? I saw her. I would not tell the others or say anything, because it would harm us all, wouldn't it, Uncle John? but I know it is mamma."

He seized her by the shoulder in hot anger and excitement. "You little—! Could you think of that when you saw your mother—if it is your mother? but that's impossible. And you can't be such a little—such a demon as you make yourself out."

"You never said that to any one else," cried Sophy, bursting into tears; "it was Rex that told me. He said we should lose all our money if mamma came back. We can't live without our money, can we, Uncle John? Other people may take care of us, and—all that. But if we had no money what would become of us? Rex told me. He said that was why mamma went away."

John Trevanion gazed at the little girl in her precocious wisdom with a wonder for which he could find no words. Rex, too, that fresh and manly boy, so admirable an example of English youth; to think of these two young creatures talking it over, coming to their decision! He forgot even the strange light, if it were a light, which she had thrown upon the events of the previous evening, in admiration and wonder at this, which was more wonderful. At length he said, with perhaps a tone of satire too fine for Sophy, "As you are the only person who possesses this information, Sophy, what do you propose to do?"

"Do?" she said, looking at him with startled eyes; "I am not going to do anything, Uncle John. I thought I would tell you—"

"And put the responsibility on my shoulders? Yes, I understand that. But you cannot forget what you have seen. If your mother, as you think, is in the house, what shall you do?"

"Oh, Uncle John," said Sophy, pale with alarm. "I have not really, really seen her, if that is what you mean. She only just passed where I was standing. No one could punish me just for having seen her pass."

"I think you are a great philosopher, my dear," he said.

At this, Sophy looked very keenly at him, and deriving no satisfaction from the expression of his face, again began to cry. "You are making fun of me, Uncle John," she said. "You would not laugh like that if it had been Rosalind. You always laugh at us children whatever we may say."

"I have no wish to laugh, Sophy, I assure you. If your aunt or some one wakes and finds you gone from your bed, how shall you explain it?"

"Oh, I shall tell her that I was—I know what I shall tell her," Sophy said, recovering herself; "I am not such a silly as that."

"You are not silly at all, my dear. I wish you were not half so clever," said John. He turned away with a sick heart. Sophy and those unconscious, terrible revelations of hers were more than the man could bear. The air was fresh outside, the day was young; he seemed to have come out of an oppressive atmosphere of age and sophistication, calculating prudence and artificial life, when he left the child behind him. He was so much overwhelmed by Sophy that for the moment, he did not fully realize the importance of what she had told him, and it was not till he had walked some distance, and reconciled himself to nature in the still brightness of the morning, that he awoke with a sudden sensation which thrilled through and through him to the meaning of what the little girl had said. Her mother—was it possible? no ghost, but a living woman. This was indeed a solution of the problem which he had never thought of. At first, after Madam's sudden departure from Highcourt, John Trevanion went nowhere without a sort of vague expectation of meeting her suddenly, in some quite inappropriate place—on a railway, in a hotel. But now, after years had passed, he had no longer that expectation. The world is so small, as it is the common vulgarity of the moment to say, but nevertheless the world is large enough to permit people who have lost each other in life to drift apart, never to meet, to wander about almost within sight of each other, yet never cross each other's paths. He had not thought of that—he could scarcely give any faith to it now. It seemed too natural, too probable to have happened. And yet it was not either natural or probable that Mrs. Trevanion, such as he had known her, a woman so self-restrained, so long experienced in the act of subduing her own impulses, should risk the health of her children and shatter their nerves by secret visits that looked like those of a supernatural being. It was impossible to him to think this of her. She who had not hesitated to sacrifice herself entirely to their interests once, would she be so forgetful now? And yet, a mother hungering for the sight of her children's faces, severed from them, without hope, was she to be judged by ordinary rules? Was there any expedient which she might not be pardoned for taking—any effort which she might not make to see them once more?

The immediate question, however, was what to do. He could not insist upon carrying the party away, which was his first idea; for various visitors were already on their way to join them, and it would be cruel to interrupt the "koor" which Mrs. Lennox regarded with so much hope. The anxious guardian did as so many anxious guardians have done before—he took refuge in a compromise. Before he returned to the hotel he had hired one of the many villas in the neighborhood, the white board with the inscription à louer coming to him like a sudden inspiration. Whether the appearance which had disturbed them was of this world or of another, the change must be beneficial.

The house stood upon a wooded height, which descended with its fringe of trees to the very edge of the water, and commanded the whole beautiful landscape, the expanse of the lake answering to every change of the sky, the homely towers of Hautecombe opposite, the mountains on either side, reflected in the profound blue mirror underneath. Within this enclosure no one could make a mysterious entry; no one, at least, clothed in ordinary flesh and blood. To his bewildered mind it was the most grateful relief to escape thus from the dilemma before him; and in any case he must gain time for examination and thought.

CHAPTER LI

Mrs. Lennox was struck dumb with amazement when she heard what her brother's morning's occupation had been. "Taken a house!" she cried, with a scream which summoned the whole party round her. But presently she consoled herself, and found it the best step which possibly could have been taken. It was a pretty place; and she could there complete her "koor" without let or hinderance. The other members of the party adapted themselves to it with the ease of youth; but there were many protests on the part of the people in the hotel; and to young Everard the news at first seemed fatal. He could not understand how it was that he met none of the party during the afternoon. In ordinary circumstances he crossed their path two or three times at least, and by a little strategy could make sure of being in Rosalind's company for a considerable part of every day, having, indeed, come to consider himself, and being generally considered, as one of Mrs. Lennox's habitual train. He thought at first that they had gone away altogether, and his despair was boundless. But very soon the shock was softened, and better things began to appear possible. Next day he met Mrs. Lennox going to her bath, and not only did she stop to explain everything to him, and tell him all about the new house, which was so much nicer than the hotel, but, led away by her own flood of utterance, and without thinking what John would say, she invited him at once to dinner.

"Dinner is rather a weak point," she said, "but there is something to eat always, if you don't mind taking your chance."

"I would not mind, however little there might be," he said, beaming. "I thought you had gone away, and I was in despair."

"Oh, no," Mrs. Lennox said. But then she began to think what John would say.

John did not say very much when, in the early dusk, Everard, in all the glories of evening dress, made his appearance in the drawing-room at Bonport, which was furnished with very little except the view. But then the view was enough to cover many deficiencies. The room was rounded, almost the half of the wall being window, which was filled at all times, when there was light enough to see it, with one of those prospects of land and water which never lose their interest, and which take as many variations, as the sun rises and sets upon them, and the clouds and shadows flit over them, and the light pours out of the skies, as does an expressive human face. The formation of the room aided the effect by making this wonderful scene the necessary background of everything that occurred within; in that soft twilight the figures were as shadows against the brightness which still lingered upon the lake. John Trevanion stood against it, black in his height and massive outline, taking the privilege of his manhood and darkening for the others the remnant of daylight that remained. Mrs. Lennox's chair had been placed in a corner, as she liked it to be, out of what she called the draught, and all that appeared of her was one side of a soft heap, a small mountain, of drapery; while on the other hand, Rosalind, slim and straight, a soft whiteness, appeared against the trellis of the veranda. The picture was all in shadows, uncertain, visionary, save for the outline of John Trevanion, which was very solid and uncompromising, and produced a great effect amid the gentle vagueness of all around. The young man faltered on the threshold at sight of him, feeling none of the happy, sympathetic security which he had felt in the company of the ladies and the children. Young Everard was in reality too ignorant of society and its ways to have thought of the inevitable interviews with guardians and investigations into antecedents which would necessarily attend any possible engagement with a girl in Rosalind's position. But there came a cold shiver over him when he saw the man's figure opposite to him as he entered, and a prevision of an examination very different from anything he had calculated upon came into his mind. For a moment the impulse of flight seized him; but that was impossible, and however terrible the ordeal might be it was evident that he must face it. It was well for him, however, that it was so dark that the changes of his color and hesitation of his manner were not so visible as they would otherwise have been. Mrs. Lennox was of opinion that he was shy—perhaps even more shy than usual from the fact that John was not so friendly as, in view of what Mr. Everard had done for the children, he ought to have been. And she did her best accordingly to encourage the visitor. The little interval before dinner, in the twilight, when they could not see each other, was naturally awkward, and, except by herself, little was said; but she had a generally well-justified faith in the effect of dinner as a softening and mollifying influence. When, however, the party were seated in the dining-room round the shaded lamp, which threw a brilliant light on the table, and left the faces round it in a sort of pink shadow, matters were little better than before. The undesired guest, who had not self-confidence enough to appear at his ease, attempted, after a while, to entertain Mrs. Lennox with scraps of gossip from the hotel, though always in a deprecating tone and with an apologetic humility; but this conversation went on strangely in the midst of an atmosphere hushed by many agitations, where the others were kept silent by thoughts and anxieties too great for words. John Trevanion, who could scarcely contain himself or restrain his inclination to take this young intruder by the throat and compel him to explain who he was, and what he did here, and Rosalind, who had looked with incredulous apathy at the telegram her uncle had received from Mrs. Trevanion's lawyers, informing him that nothing had happened to her, so far as they were aware, sat mute, both of them, listening to the mild chatter without taking any part in it. Mrs. Lennox wagged, if not her head, at least the laces of her cap, as she discussed the company at the table d'hôte. "And these people were Russians, after all?" she said. "Why, I thought them English, and you remember Rosalind and you, Mr. Everard, declared they must be German; and all the time they were Russians. How very odd! And it was the little man who was the lady's husband! Well, I never should have guessed that. Yes, I knew our going away would make a great gap—so many of us, you know. But we have got some friends coming. Do you mean to take rooms at the Venat for Mr. Rivers, John? And then there is Roland Hamerton—"

"Is Roland Hamerton coming here?"

"With Rex, I think. Oh, yes, he is sure to come—he is great friends with Rex. I am so glad the boy should have such a steady, nice friend. But we cannot take him in at Bonport, and of course he never would expect such a thing. Perhaps you will mention at the bureau, Mr. Everard, that some friends of mine will be wanting rooms."

"I had no idea," said John, with a tone of annoyance, "that so large a party was expected."

"Rex?" said Mrs. Lennox, with simple audacity. "Well, I hope you don't think I could refuse our own boy when he wanted to come."

"He ought to have been at school," the guardian grumbled under his breath.

"John! when you agreed yourself he was doing no good at school; and the masters said so, and everybody. And he is too young to go to Oxford; and whatever you may think, John, I am very glad to know that a nice, good, steady young man like Roland Hamerton has taken such a fancy to Rex. Oh, yes, he has taken a great fancy to him—he is staying with him now. It shows that though the poor boy may be a little wilful, he is thoroughly nice in his heart. Though even without that," said Mrs. Lennox, ready to weep, "I should always be glad to see Roland Hamerton, shouldn't you, Rosalind? He is always good and kind, and we have known him, and Rosalind has known him, all his life."

Rosalind made no reply to this appeal. She was in no mood to say anything, to take any part in common conversation. Her time of peace and repose was over. If there had been nothing else, the sudden information only now conveyed to her of the coming of Rivers and of Hamerton, with what motive she knew too well, would have been enough to stop her mouth. She heard this with a thrill of excitement, of exasperation, and at the same time of alarm, which is far from the state of mind supposed by the visionary philosopher to whom it seems meet that a good girl should have seven suitors. Above all, the name of Rivers filled her with alarm. He was a man who was a stranger, who would insist upon an answer, and probably think himself ill-used if that answer was not favorable. With so many subjects of thought already weighing upon her, to have this added made her brain swim. And when she looked up and caught, from the other side of the table, a wistful gaze from those eyes which had so long haunted her imagination, Rosalind's dismay was complete. She shrank into herself with a troubled consciousness that all the problems of life were crowding upon her, and at a moment when she had little heart to consider any personal question at all, much less such a one as this.

The party round the dinner-table was thus a very agitated one, and by degrees less and less was said. The movements of the servants—Mrs. Lennox's agile courier and John Trevanion's solemn English attendant, whose face was like wood—became very audible, the chief action of the scene. To Everard the silence, broken only by these sounds and by Mrs. Lennox's voice coming in at intervals, was as the silence of fate. He made exertions which were really stupendous to find something to say, to seize the occasion and somehow divert the catastrophe which, though he did not know what it would be, he felt to be hanging over his head; but his throat was dry and his lips parched, notwithstanding the wine which he swallowed in his agitation, and not a word would come. When the ladies rose to leave the table, he felt that the catastrophe was very near. He was paralyzed by their sudden movement, which he had not calculated upon, and had not even presence of mind to open the door for them as he ought to have done, but stood gazing with his mouth open and his napkin in his hand, to find himself alone and face to face with John Trevanion. He had not thought of this terrible ordeal. In the hotel life to which he had of late been accustomed, the awful interval after dinner is necessarily omitted, and Everard had not been brought up in a society which sits over its wine. When he saw John Trevanion bearing down upon him with his glass of wine in his hand, to take Mrs. Lennox's place, he felt that he did not know to what trial this might be preliminary, and turned towards his host with a sense of danger and terror which nothing in the circumstances seemed to justify, restraining with an effort the gasp in his throat. John began, innocently enough, by some remark about the wine. It was very tolerable wine, better than might have been expected in a country overrun by visitors. "But I suppose the strangers will be going very soon, as I hear the season is nearly over. Have you been long here?"

"A month—six weeks I mean—since early in August."

"And did you come for the 'cure'? You must have taken a double allowance."

"It was not exactly for the cure; at least I have stayed on—for other reasons."

"Pardon me if I seem inquisitive," said John Trevanion. "It was you, was it not, whom I met in the village at Highcourt two years ago?"

"Yes, it was I."

"That was a very unlikely place to meet; more unlikely than Aix. I must ask your pardon again, Mr. Everard; you will allow that when I find you here, almost a member of my sister's family, I have a right to inquire. Do you know that there were very unpleasant visitors at Highcourt in search of you after you were gone?"

The young man looked at him with eyes expanding and dilating—where had he seen such eyes?—a deep crimson flush, and a look of such terror and anguish that John Trevanion's good heart was touched. He had anticipated a possible bravado of denial, which would have given him no difficulty, but this was much less easy to deal with.

"Mr. Trevanion," Everard said, with lips so parched that he to moisten them before he could speak, "that was a mistake, it was indeed! That was all arranged; you would not put me to shame for a thing so long past, and that was entirely a mistake! It was put right in every way, every farthing was paid. A great change happened to me at that time of my life. I had been kept out of what I had a right to, and badly treated. But after that a change occurred. I can assure you, and the people themselves would tell you. I can give their address."

"I should not have spoken to you on the subject if I had not been disposed to accept any explanation you could make," said John Trevanion; which was but partially true so far as his intention went, although it was impossible to doubt an explanation which was so evidently sincere. After this there ensued a silence, during which Everard, the excitement in his mind growing higher and higher, turned over every subject on which he thought it possible that he could be questioned further. He thought, as he sat there drawn together on his defence, eagerly yet stealthily examining the countenance of this inquisitor, that he had thought of everything and could not be taken by surprise. Nevertheless his heart gave a great bound of astonishment when John Trevanion spoke again. The question he put was perhaps the only one for which the victim was unprepared. "Would you mind telling me," he said, with great gravity and deliberation, "what connection there was between you and my brother, the late Mr. Trevanion of Highcourt?"

CHAPTER LII

The moon was shining in full glory upon the lake, so brilliant and broad that the great glittering expanse of water retained something like a tinge of its natural blue in the wonderful splendor of the light. It was not a night on which to keep in-doors. Mrs. Lennox, in the drawing-room, after she had left her protégé to the tender mercies of John, had been a little hysterical, or, at least, as she allowed, very much "upset." "I don't know what has come over John," she said; "I think his heart is turned to stone. Oh, Rosalind, how could you keep so still? You that have such a feeling for the children, and saw the way that poor young fellow was being bullied. It is a thing I will not put up with in my house—if it can be said that this is my house. Yes, bullied. John has never said a word to him! And I am sure he is going to make himself disagreeable now, and when there is nobody to protect him—and he is so good and quiet and takes it all so well," said Mrs. Lennox, with a great confusion of persons, "for our sakes."

Rosalind did her best to soothe and calm her aunt's excitement, and at last succeeded in persuading her that she was very tired, and had much better go to bed. "Oh, yes, I am very tired. What with my bath, and the trouble of removing down here, and having to think of the dinners, and all this trouble about Johnny and Amy, and your uncle that shows so little feeling—of course, I am very tired. Most people would have been in bed an hour ago. If you think you can remember my message to poor Mr. Everard: to tell him never to mind John; that it is just his way and nobody takes any notice of it; and say good-night to him for me. But you know you have a very bad memory, Rosalind, and you will never tell him the half of that."

"If I see him, Aunt Sophy; but he may not come in here at all."

"Oh, you may trust him to come in," Aunt Sophy said; and with a renewed charge not to forget, she finally rang for her maid, and went away, with all her little properties, to bed. Rosalind did not await the interview which Mrs. Lennox was so certain of. She stole out of the window, which stood wide open like a door, into the moonlight. Everything was so still that the movements of the leaves, as they rustled faintly, took importance in the great quiet; and the dip of an oar into the water, which took place at slow intervals, somewhere about the middle of the lake, where some romantic visitors were out in the moonlight, was almost a violent interruption. Rosalind stepped out into the soft night with a sense of escape, not thinking much perhaps of the messages with which she had been charged. The air was full of that faint but all-pervading fragrance made up of odors, imperceptible in themselves, which belong to the night, and the moon made everything sacred, spreading a white beatitude even over the distant peaks of the hills. The girl, in her great trouble and anxiety, felt soothed and stilled, without any reason, by those ineffable ministrations of nature which are above all rule. She avoided the gravel, which rang and jarred under her feet, and wandered across the dry grass, which was burned brown with the heat, not like the verdant English turf, towards the edge of the slope. She had enough to think of, but, for the moment, in the hush of the night, did not think at all, but gave herself over to the tranquillizing calm. Her cares went from her for the time; the light and the night together went to her heart. Sometimes this quiet will come unsought to those who are deeply weighted with pain and anxiety; and Rosalind was very young; and when all nature says it so unanimously, how is a young creature to contradict, and say that all will not be well? Even the old and weary will be deceived, and take that on the word of the kind skies and hushed, believing earth. She strayed about among the great laurels and daphnes, under the shadow of the trees, with her spirit calmed and relieved from the pressure of troublous events and thoughts. She had forgotten, in that momentary exaltation, that any interruption was possible, and stood, clearly visible in the moonlight, looking out upon the lake, when she heard the sound behind her of an uncertain step coming out upon the veranda, then, crossing the gravel path, coming towards her. She had not any thought of concealing herself, nor had she time to do so, when Everard came up to her, breathless with haste, and what seemed to be excitement. He said quickly, "You were not in the drawing-room, and the window was open. I thought you would not mind if I came after you." Rosalind looked up at him somewhat coldly, for she had forgotten he was there.

"I thought you had gone," she said, turning half towards him, as if—which was true—she did not mean to be disturbed. His presence had a jarring effect, and broke the enchantment of the scene. He was always instantly sensitive to any rebuff.

"I thought," he repeated apologetically, "that you would not mind. You have always made me feel so much—so much at home."

These ill-chosen words roused Rosalind's pride. "My aunt," she said, "has always been very glad to see you, Mr. Everard, and grateful to you for what you have done for us."

"Is that all?" he said hastily; "am I always to have those children thrown in my teeth? I thought now, by this time, that you might have cared for me a little for myself; I thought we had taken to each other," he added, with a mixture of irritation and pathos, with the straightforward sentiment of a child; "for you know very well," he cried, after a pause, "that it is not for nothing I am always coming; that it is not for the children, nor for your aunt, nor for anything but you. You know that I think of nothing but you."

The young man's voice was hurried and tremulous with real feeling, and the scene was one, above all others, in harmony with a love tale; and Rosalind's heart had been touched by many a soft illusion in respect to the speaker, and had made him, before she knew him, the subject of many a dream; but at this supreme moment a strange effect took place in her. With a pang, acute as if it had been cut off by a blow, the mist of illusion was suddenly severed, and floated away from her, leaving her eyes cold and clear. A sensation of shame that she should ever have been deceived, that she could have deceived him, ran hot through all her being. "I think," she said quickly, "Mr. Everard, that you are speaking very wildly. I know nothing at all of why you come, of what you are thinking." Her tone was indignant, almost haughty, in spite of herself.

"Ah!" he cried, "I know what you think; you think that I am not as good as you are, that I'm not a gentleman. Rosalind, if you knew who I was you would not think that. I could tell you about somebody that you are very, very fond of; ay! and make it easy for you to see her and be with her as much as ever you pleased, if you would listen to me. If you only knew, there are many, many things I could do for you. I could clear up a great deal if I chose. I could tell you much you want to know if I chose. I have been fighting off John Trevanion, but I would not fight off you. If you will only promise me a reward for it; if you will let your heart speak; if you will give me what I am longing for, Rosalind!"

He poured forth all this with such impassioned haste, stammering with excitement and eagerness, that she could but partially understand the sense, and not at all the extraordinary meaning and intention with which he spoke. She stood with her face turned to him, angry, bewildered, feeling that the attempt to catch the thread of something concealed and all-important in what he said was more than her faculties were equal to; and on the surface of her mind was the indignation and almost shame which such an appeal, unjustified by any act of hers, awakens in a sensitive girl. The sound of her own name from his lips seemed to strike her as if he had thrown a stone at her. "Mr. Everard," she cried, scarcely knowing what words she used, "you have no right to call me Rosalind. What is it you mean?"

"Ah!" he cried, with a laugh, "you ask me that! you want to have what I can give, but give me nothing in return."

"I think," said Rosalind, quickly, "that you forget yourself, Mr. Everard. A gentleman, if he has anything to tell, does not make bargains. What is it, about some one, whom you say I love—" She began to tremble very much, and put her hands together in an involuntary prayer! "Oh, if it should be—Mr. Everard! I will thank you all my life if you will tell me—"

"Promise me you will listen to me, Rosalind; promise me! I don't want your thanks; I want your—love. I have been after you for a long, long time; oh, before anything happened. Promise me—"

He put out his hands to clasp hers, but this was more than she could bear. She recoiled from him, with an unconscious revelation of her distaste, almost horror, of these advances, which stung his self-esteem. "You won't!" he cried, hoarsely; "I am to give everything and get nothing? Then I won't neither, and that is enough for to-night—"

He had got on the gravel again, in his sudden, angry step backward, and turned on his heel, crushing the pebbles with a sound that seemed to jar through all the atmosphere. After he had gone a few steps he paused, as if expecting to be called back. But Rosalind's heart was all aflame. She said to herself, indignantly, that to believe such a man had anything to tell her was folly, was a shame to think of, was impossible. To chaffer and bargain with him, to promise him anything—her love, oh Heaven! how dared he ask it?—was intolerable. She turned away with hot, feminine impulse, and a step in which there was no pause or wavering; increasing the distance between them at a very different rate from that achieved by his lingering steps. It seemed that he expected to be recalled after she had disappeared altogether and hidden herself, panting, among the shadows; for she could still hear his step pause with that jar and harsh noise upon the gravel for what seemed to her, in her excitement, an hour of suspense. And Rosalind's heart jarred, as did all the echoes. Harsh vibrations of pain went through and through it. The rending away of her own self-illusion in respect to him, which was not unmingled with a sense of guilt—for that illusion had been half voluntary, a fiction of her own creating, a refuge of the imagination from other thoughts—and at the same time a painful sense of his failure, and proof of the floating doubt and fear which had always been in her mind on his account, wounded and hurt her with almost a physical reality of pain. And what was this suggestion, cast into the midst of this whirlpool of agitated and troubled thought?—"I could tell you; I could make it easy for you to see; I could clear up—" What? oh what, in the name of Heaven! could he mean?

She did not know how long she remained pondering these questions, making a circuitous round through the grounds, under the shadows, until she got back again, gliding noiselessly to the veranda, from which she could dart into the house at any return of her unwelcome suitor. But she still stood there after all had relapsed into the perfect silence of night in such a place. The tourists in the boat had rowed to the beach and disembarked, and disappeared on their way home. The evening breeze dropped altogether and ceased to move the trees, while she still stood against the trellis-work scarcely visible in the gloom, wondering, trying to think, trying to satisfy the questions that arose in her mind, with a vague sense that if she but knew what young Everard meant, there might be in it some guide, some clue to the mystery which weighed upon her soul. But this was not all that Rosalind was to encounter. While she stood thus gazing out from her with eyes that noted nothing, yet could not but see, she was startled by something, a little wandering shadow, not much more substantial than her dreams, which flitted across the scene before her. Her heart leaped up with a pang of terror. What was it? When the idea of the supernatural has once gained admission into the mind the mental perceptions are often disabled in after-emergencies. Her strength abandoned her. She covered her eyes with her hands, with a rush of the blood to her head, a failing of all her powers. Something white as the moonlight flitting across the moonlight, a movement, a break in the stillness of nature. When she looked up again there was nothing to be seen? With a sick flutter of her heart, searching the shadows round with keen eyes, she had just made sure that there was nothing on the terrace, when a whiteness among the shrubs drew her eyes farther down. Her nerves, which had played her false for a moment, grew steady again, though her heart beat wildly. There came a faint sound like a footstep, which reassured her a little. In such circumstances sound is salvation. She herself was a sight to have startled any beholder, as timidly, breathlessly, under the impulse of a visionary terror, she came out, herself all white, into the whiteness of the night. She called "Is there any one there?" in a very tremulous voice. No answer came to her question; but she could now see clearly the other moving speck of whiteness, gliding on under the dark trees, emerging from the shadows, on to a little point of vision from which the foliage had been cleared a little farther down. It stood there for a moment, whiteness on whiteness, the very embodiment of a dream. A sudden idea flashed into Rosalind's mind, relieving her brain, and, without pausing a moment, she hurried down the path, relieved from one fear only to be seized by another. She reached the little ghost as it turned from that platform to continue the descent. The whiteness of the light had stolen the color out of the child's hair. She was like a little statue in alabaster, her bare feet, her long, half-curled locks, the folds of her nightdress, all softened and rounded in the light. "Amy!" cried Rosalind—but Amy did not notice her sister. Her face had the solemn look of sleep, but her eyes were open. She went on unconscious, going forward to some visionary end of her own from which no outward influence could divert her. Rosalind's terror was scarcely less great than when she thought it an apparition. She followed, with her heart and her head both throbbing, the unconscious little wanderer. Amy went down through the trees and shrubs to the very edge of the lake, so close that Rosalind behind hovered over her, ready at the next step to seize upon her, her senses coming back, but her mind still confused, in her perplexity not knowing what to do. Then there was for a moment a breathless pause. Amy turned her head from side to side, as if looking for some one; Rosalind seated herself on a stone to wait what should ensue. It was a wonderful scene. The dark trees waved overhead, but the moon, coming down in a flood of silver, lit up all the beach below. It might have been an allegory of a mortal astray, with a guardian angel standing close, watching, yet with no power to save. The water moving softly with its ceaseless ripple, the soft yet chill air of night rustling in the leaves, were the only things that broke the stillness. The two human figures in the midst seemed almost without breath.

Rosalind did not know what to do. In the calm of peaceful life such incidents are rare. She did not know whether she might not injure the child by awaking her. But while she waited, anxious and trembling, Nature solved the question for her. The little wavelets lapping the stones came up with a little rush and sparkle in the light an inch or two farther than before, and bathed Amy's bare feet. The cold touch broke the spell in a moment. The child started and sprang up with a sudden cry. What might have happened to her had she woke to find herself alone on the beach in the moonlight, Rosalind trembled to think. Her cry rang along all the silent shore, a cry of distracted and bewildering terror: "Oh, mamma! mamma! where are you?" then Amy, turning suddenly round, flew, wild with fear, fortunately into her sister's arms.

"Rosalind! is it Rosalind? And where is mamma? oh, take me to mamma. She said she would be here." It was all Rosalind could do to subdue and control the child, who nearly suffocated her, clinging to her throat, urging her on: "I want mamma—take me to mamma!" she cried, resisting her sister's attempts to lead her up the slope towards the house. Rosalind's strength was not equal to the struggle. After a while her own longing burst forth. "Oh, if I knew where I could find her!" she said, clasping the struggling child in her arms. Amy was subdued by Rosalind's tears. The little passion wore itself out. She looked round her, shuddering in the whiteness of the moonlight. "Rosalind! are we all dead, like mamma?" Amy said.

The penetrating sound of the child's cry reached the house and far beyond it, disturbing uneasy sleepers all along the edge of the lake. It reached John Trevanion, who was seated by himself, chewing the cud of fancy, bitter rather than sweet, and believing himself the only person astir in the house. There is something in a child's cry which touches the hardest heart; and his heart was not hard. It did not occur to him that it could proceed from any of the children of the house, but it was too full of misery and pain to be neglected. He went out, hastily opening the great window, and was, in his terror, almost paralyzed by the sight of the two white figures among the trees, one leaning upon the other. It was only after a momentary hesitation that he hurried towards them, arriving just in time, when Rosalind's strength was about giving way, and carried Amy into the house. The entire household, disturbed, came from all corners with lights and outcries. But Amy, when she had been warmed and comforted, and laid in Rosalind's bed, and recovered from her sobbing, had no explanations to give. She had dreamed she was going to mamma, that mamma was waiting for her down on the side of the lake. "Oh, I want mamma, I want mamma!" the child cried, and would not be comforted.

CHAPTER LIII

Arthur Rivers had come home on the top of the wave of prosperity; his little war was over, and if it were not he who had gained the day, he yet had a large share of its honors. It was he who had made it known to all the eager critics in England, and given them the opportunity to let loose their opinion. He had kept the supply of news piping hot, one supply ready to be served as soon as the other was despatched, to the great satisfaction of the public and of his "proprietors." His well-known energy, daring, and alertness, the qualities for which he had been sent out, had never been so largely manifested before. He had thrown himself into the brief but hot campaign with the ardor of a soldier. But there was more in it than this. It was with the ardor of a lover that he had labored—a lover with a great deal to make up to bring him to the level of her he loved. And his zeal had been rewarded. He was coming home, to an important post, with an established place and position in the world, leaving his life of adventure and wandering behind him. They had their charms, and in their time he had enjoyed them; but what he wanted now was something that it would be possible to ask Rosalind to share. Had he been the commander, as he had only been the historian of the expedition; had he brought back a baronetcy and a name famous in the annals of the time, his task would have been easier. As it was, his reputation—though to its owner very agreeable—was of a kind which many persons scoff at. The soldiers, for whom he had done more than anybody else could do, recommending them to their country as even their blood and wounds would never have recommended them without his help, did not make any return for his good offices, and held him cheap; but, on the other hand, it had procured him his appointment, and made it possible for him to put his question to Rosalind into a practical shape and repeat it to her uncle. He came home with his mind full of this and of excitement and eagerness. He had no time to lose. He was too old for Rosalind as well as not good enough for her, not rich enough, not great enough. Sir Arthur Rivers, K.C.B., the conquering hero—that would have been the right thing. But since he was not that, the only thing he could do was to make the most of what he was. He could give her a pretty house in London, where she would see the best of company; not the gentle dulness of the country, but all the wits, all that was brilliant in society, and have the cream of those amusements and diversions which make life worth living in town. That is always something to offer, if you have neither palaces nor castles, nor a great name, nor a big fortune. Some women would think it better than all these; and he knew that it would be full of pleasures and pleasantness, not dull—a life of variety and brightness and ease. Was it not very possible that these things would tempt her, as they have tempted women more lofty in position than Rosalind? And he did not think her relations would oppose it if she so chose. His family was very obscure; but that has ceased to be of the importance it once was. He did not believe that John Trevanion would hesitate on account of his family. If only Rosalind should be pleased! It was, perhaps, because he was no longer quite young that he thought of what he had to offer; going over it a thousand times, and wondering if this and that might not have a charm to her as good, perhaps better, than the different things that other people had to offer. He was a man who was supposed to know human nature and to have studied it much, and had he been writing a book he would no doubt have scoffed at the idea of a young girl considering the attractions of different ways of living and comparing what he had to give with what other people possessed. But there was a certain humility in the way in which his mind approached the subject in his own case, not thinking of his own personal merits. He could give her a bright and full and entertaining life. She would never be dull with him. That was better even than rank, he said to himself.

Rivers arrived a few days after the Trevanion party had gone to Bonport. He was profoundly pleased and gratified to find John Trevanion waiting at the station, and to receive his cordial greeting. "My sister will expect to see you very soon," he said. "They think it is you who are the hero of the war; and, indeed, so you have been, almost as much as Sir Ruby, and with fewer jealousies; and the new post, I hear, is a capital one. I should say you were a lucky fellow, if you had not worked so well for it all."

"Yes, I hear it is a pleasant post; and to be able to stay at home, and not be sent off to the end of the earth at a moment's notice—"

"How will you bear it? that is the question," said John Trevanion. "I should not wonder if in a year you were bored to death."

Rivers shook his head, with a laugh. "And I hope all are well," he said; "Mrs. Lennox and Miss Trevanion."

He did not venture as yet to put the question more plainly.

"We are all well enough," said John, "though there are always vexations. Oh! nothing of importance, I hope; only some bother about the children and Rosalind. That's why I removed them; but Rex is coming, and another young fellow, Hamerton—perhaps you recollect him at Clifton. I hope they will cheer us up a little. There is their train coming in. Let us see you soon. Good-night!"

Another young fellow, Hamerton! Then it was not to meet him, Rivers, that Trevanion was waiting. There was no special expectation of him. It was Rex, the schoolboy, and young Hamerton who was to cheer them up—Rex, a sulky young cub, and Hamerton, a thick-headed rustic. John went off quite unconscious of the arrow he had planted in his friend's heart, and Rivers turned away, with a blank countenance, to his hotel, feeling that he had fallen down—down from the skies into a bottomless abyss. All this while, during so many days of travel, he had been coming towards her; now he seemed to be thrown back from her—back into uncertainty and the unknown. He lingered a little as the train from Paris came in, and heard John Trevanion's cheerful "Oh, here you are!" and the sound of the other voices. It made his heart burn to think of young Hamerton—the young clodhopper!—going to her presence, while he went gloomily to the hotel. His appearance late for dinner presented a new and welcome enigma to the company who dined at the table d'hôte. Who was he? Some one fresh from India, no doubt, with that bronzed countenance and hair which had no right to be gray. There was something distinguished about his appearance which everybody remarked, and a little flutter of curiosity to know who he was awoke, especially among the English people, who, but that he seemed so entirely alone, would have taken him for Sir Ruby himself. Rivers took a little comfort from the sense of his own importance and of the sensation made by his appearance. But to arrive here with his mind full of Rosalind, and to find himself sitting alone at a foreign table d'hôte, with half the places empty and not a creature he knew, chilled him ridiculously—he who met people he knew in every out-of-the-way corner in the earth. And all the time Hamerton at her side—Hamerton, a young nobody! There was no doubt that it was very hard to bear. As soon as dinner was over he went out to smoke his cigar and go over again, more ruefully than ever, his prospects of success. It was a brilliant moonlight night, the trees in the hotel garden standing, with their shadows at their feet, in a blackness as of midnight, while between, every vacant space was full of the intense white radiance. He wandered out and in among them, gloomily thinking how different the night would have been had he been looking down upon the silver lake by the side of Rosalind. No doubt that was what she was doing. Would there be any recollection of him among her thoughts, or of the question he had asked her in the conservatory at the Elms? Would she think he was coming for his answer, and what in all this long interval had she been making up her mind to reply?

He was so absorbed in these thoughts that he took no note of the few people about. These were very few, for though the night was as warm as it was bright, it was yet late in the season, and the rheumatic people thought there was a chill in the air. By degrees even the few figures that had been visible at first dwindled away, and Rivers at last awoke to the consciousness that there was but one left, a lady in black, very slight, very light of foot, for whose coming he was scarcely ever prepared when she appeared, and who shrank into the shadow as he came up, as if to avoid his eye. Something attracted him in this mysterious figure, he could not tell what, a subtle sense of some link of connection between her and himself; some internal and unspoken suggestion which quickened his eyes and interest, but which was too indefinite to be put into words. Who could she be? Where had he seen her? he asked, catching a very brief, momentary glimpse of her face; but he was a man who knew everybody, and it was little wonder if the names of some of his acquaintances should slip out of his recollection. It afforded him a sort of occupation to watch for her, to calculate when in the round of the garden which she seemed to be making she would come to that bare bit of road, disclosed by the opening in the trees, where the moonlight revealed in a white blaze everything that passed. He was for the moment absorbed in this pursuit—for it was in reality a pursuit, a sort of hunt through his own mind for some thread of association connected with a wandering figure like this—when some one else, a new-comer, came hastily into the garden, and established himself at a table close by. There was no mistaking this stranger—a robust young Englishman still in his travelling dress, whom Rivers recognized with mingled satisfaction and hostility. He was not then spending the evening with Rosalind, this young fellow who was not worthy to be admitted to her presence. That was a satisfaction in its way. He had been received to dinner because he came with the boy, but that was all. Young Hamerton sat down in the full moonlight where no one could make any mistake about him. He recognized Rivers with a stiff little bow. They said to each other, "It is a beautiful night," and then relapsed respectively into silence. But in the heat of personal feeling thus suddenly evoked, Rivers forgot the mysterious lady for a moment, and saw her no more. After some time the new-comer said to him, with a sort of reluctant abruptness, "They are rather in trouble over there," making a gesture with his hand to indicate some locality on the other side of the darkly waving trees.

"In trouble—"

"Oh, not of much importance, perhaps. The children—have all been—upset; I don't understand it quite. There was something that disturbed them—in the hotel here. Perhaps you know—"

"I only arrived this evening," Rivers said.

The other drew a long breath. Was it of relief? Perhaps he had spoken only to discover whether his rival had been long enough in the neighborhood to have secured any advantage. "We brought over the old nurse with us—the woman, you know, who—Oh, I forgot, you don't know," Hamerton added, hastily. This was said innocently enough, but it offended the elder suitor, jealous and angry after the unreasonable manner of a lover, that any one, much less this young fellow, whose pretensions were so ridiculous, should have known her and her circumstances before and better than himself.

"I prefer not to know anything that the Trevanions do not wish to be known," he said sharply. It was not true, for his whole being quivered with eagerness to know everything about them, all that could be told; but at the same time there was in his harsh tones a certain justness of reproach that brought the color to young Hamerton's face.

"You are quite right," he said; "it is not my business to say word."

And then there was silence again. It was growing late. The verandas of the great hotel, a little while ago full of chattering groups, were all vacant; the lights had flitted up-stairs; a few weary waiters lounged about the doors, anxiously waiting till the two Englishmen—so culpably incautious about the night air and the draughts, so brutally indifferent to the fact that Jules and Adolphe and the rest had to get up very early in the morning and longed to be in bed—should come in, and all things be shut up; but neither Hamerton nor Rivers thought of Adolphe and Jules.

Finally, after a long silence, the younger man spoke again. His mind was full of one subject, and he wanted some one to speak to, were it only his rival. "This cannot be a healthy place," he said; "they are not looking well—they are all—upset. I suppose it is bad for—the nerves—"

"Perhaps there may be other reasons," said Rivers. His heart stirred within him at the thought that agitation, perhaps of a nature kindred to his own, might be affecting the one person who was uppermost in the thoughts of both—for he did not doubt that Hamerton, who had said them, meant Rosalind. That she might be pale with anticipation, nervous and tremulous in this last moment of suspense! the idea brought a rush of blood to his face, and a warm flood of tender thoughts and delight to his heart.

"I don't know what other reasons," said Hamerton. "She thinks—I mean there is nothing thought of but those children. Something has happened to them. The old nurse, the woman—I told you—came over with us to take them in hand. Poor little things? it is not much to be wondered at—" he said, and then stopped short, with the air of a man who might have a great deal to say.

A slight rustling in the branches behind caught Rivers' attention. All his senses were very keen, and he had the power, of great advantage in his profession, of seeing and hearing without appearing to do so. He turned his eyes, but not his head, in the direction of that faint sound, and saw with great wonder the lady whom he had been watching, an almost imperceptible figure against the opaque background of the high shrubs, standing behind Hamerton. Her head was a little thrust forward in the attitude of listening, and the moon just caught her face. He was too well disciplined to suffer the cry of recognition which came to his lips to escape from them, but in spite of himself expressed his excitement in a slight movement—a start which made the rustic chair on which he was seated quiver, and displaced the gravel under his feet. Hamerton did not so much as notice that he had moved at all, but the lady's head was drawn back, and the thick foliage behind once more moved as by a breath, and all was still. Rivers was very much absorbed in one pursuit and one idea, which made him selfish; but yet his heart was kind. He conquered his antipathy to the young fellow who was his rival, whom (on that ground) he despised, yet feared, and forced himself to ask a question, to draw him on. "What has happened to the children," he said; "are they ill?" There was a faint breeze in the tree-tops, but none down here in the solid foliage of the great bushes; yet there was a stir in the laurel as of a bird in its nest.

"They are not ill, but yet something has happened. I believe the little things have been seeing ghosts. They sent for this woman, Russell, you know—confound her—"

"Why confound her?"

"Oh, it's a long story—confound her all the same! There are some women that it is very hard for a man not to wish to knock down. But I suppose they think she's good for the children. That is all they think of, it appears to me," Roland said, dejectedly. "The children—always the children—one cannot get in a word. And as for anything else—anything that is natural—"

This moved Rivers on his own account. Sweet hope was high in his heart. It might very well be that this young fellow could not get in a word. Who could tell that the excuse of the children might not be made use of to silence an undesired suitor, to leave the way free for—His soul melted with a delicious softness and sense of secret exultation. "Let us hope their anxiety may not last," he said, restraining himself, keeping as well as he could the triumph out of his voice. Hamerton looked at him quickly, keenly; he felt that there was exultation—something exasperating—a tone of triumph in it.

"I don't see why it shouldn't last," he said. "Little Amy is like a little ghost herself; but how can it be otherwise in such an unnatural state of affairs—the mother gone, and all the responsibility put upon one—upon one who—For what is Mrs. Lennox?" he cried, half angrily; "oh yes, a good, kind soul—but she has to be taken care of too—and all upon one—upon one who—"

"You mean Miss Trevanion?"

"I don't mean—to bring in any names. Look here," cried the young man, "you and I, Rivers—we are not worthy to name her name."

His voice was a little husky; his heart was in his mouth. He felt a sort of brotherly feeling even for this rival who might perhaps, being clever (he thought), be more successful than he, but who, in the meantime, had more in common with him than any other man, because he too loved Rosalind. Rivers did not make any response. Perhaps he was not young enough to have this feeling for any woman. A man may be very much in love—may be ready even to make any exertion, almost any sacrifice, to win the woman he loves, and yet be unable to echo such a sentiment. He could not allow that he was unworthy to name her name. Hamerton scarcely noticed his silence, and yet was a little relieved not to have any response.

"I am a little upset myself," he said, "because you know I've been mixed up with it all from the beginning, which makes one feel very differently from those that don't know the story. I couldn't help just letting out a little. I beg your pardon for taking up your time with what perhaps doesn't interest you."

This stung the other man to the quick. "It interests me more, perhaps, than you could understand," he cried. "But," he added, after a pause, "it remains to be seen whether the family wish me to know—not certainly at second-hand."

Hamerton sprang to his feet in hot revulsion of feeling. "If you mean me by the second-hand," he said; then paused, ashamed both of the good impulse and the less good which had made him thus betray himself. "I beg your pardon," he added; "I've been travelling all day, and I suppose I'm tired and apt to talk nonsense. Good-night."

Jules and Adolphe were glad. They showed the young Englishman to his room with joy, making no doubt that the other would follow. But the other did not follow. He sat for a time silently, with his head on his hand. Then he rose, and walking to the other side of the great bouquet of laurels, paused in the profound shadow, where there stood, as he divined rather than saw, a human creature in mysterious anguish, anxiety, and pain. He made out with difficulty a tall shadow against the gloomy background of the close branches. "I do not know who you are," he said; "I do not ask to know; but you are deeply interested in what that—that young fellow was saying?"

The voice that replied to him was very low. "Oh, more than interested; it is like life and death to me. For God's sake, tell me if you know anything more."

"I know nothing to-night—but to-morrow—You are the lady whom I met in Spain two years ago, whose portrait stands on Rosalind Trevanion's writing-table."

There was a low cry; "Oh! God bless you for telling me! God bless you for telling me!" and the sound of a suppressed sob.

"I shall see her to-morrow," he said. "I have come thousands of miles to see her. It is possible that I might be of use to you. May I tell her that you are here?"

The stir among the branches seemed to take a different character as he spoke, and the lady came out towards the partial light. She said firmly, "No; I thank you for your kind intentions;" then paused. "You will think it strange that I came behind you and listened. You will think it was not honorable. But I heard their name, and Roland Hamerton knows me. When a woman is in great trouble she is driven to strange expedients. Sir," she cried, after another agitated pause, "I neither know your name nor who you are, but if you will bring me news to-morrow after you have seen them—if you will tell me—it will be a good deed—it will be a Christian deed."

"Say something more to me than that," he cried, with a passion that surprised himself; "say that you will wish me well."

She moved along softly, noiselessly, with her head turned to him, moving towards the moonlight, which was like the blaze of day, within a few steps from where they had been standing. The impression which had been upon his mind of a fugitive—a woman abandoned and forlorn—died out so completely that he felt ashamed ever to have ventured upon such a thought. And he felt, with a sudden sense of imperfection quite unfamiliar to him, that he was being examined and judged. He felt, too, with an acute self-consciousness, that the silver in his hair shone in the white light, and that the counterbalancing qualities of fine outline and manly color must be wanting in that wan and colorless illumination. He could not see her face, except as an abstract paleness, turned towards him, over-shadowed by the veil which she had put back, but which still threw a deep shade; but she gazed into his, which he could not but turn towards her in the full light of the moon. The end of the examination was not very consolatory to his pride. She sighed and turned away. "The man whom she chooses will want no other blessing," she said.

A few minutes after Jules and Adolphe were happy, shutting up the doors, putting out the lights, betaking themselves to the holes and corners under the stairs, under the roofs, in which these sufferers for the good of humanity slept.

CHAPTER LIV

The incident of that evening had a very disturbing effect upon the family at Bonport. Little Amy, waking next morning much astonished to find herself in Rosalind's room, and very faintly remembering what had happened, was subjected at once to questionings more earnest than judicious—questionings which brought everything to her mind, with a renewal of all the agitation of the night. But the child had nothing to say beyond what she had said before—that she had dreamed of mamma, that mamma had called her to come down to the lake, and be taken home; that she wanted to go home, to go to mamma—oh, to go to mamma! but Rosalind said she was dead, and Sophy said they were never, never to see her again. Then Amy flung herself upon her sister's breast, and implored to be taken to her mother. "You don't know how wicked I was, Rosalind. Russell used to say things till I stopped loving mamma—oh, I did, and did not mind when she went away! But now! where is she, where is she? Oh, Rosalind! oh, Rosalind! will she never come back? Oh, do you think she is angry, or that she does not care for me any more? Oh, Rosalind, is she dead, and will she never come back?" This cry seemed to come from Amy's very soul. She could not be stilled. She lay in Rosalind's bed, as white as the hangings about her, not much more than a pair of dark eyes looking out with eagerness unspeakable. And Rosalind, who had gone through so many vicissitudes of feeling—who had stood by the mother who was not her mother with so much loyalty, yet had yielded to the progress of events, and had not known, in the ignorance of her youth, what to do or say, or how to stand against it—Rosalind was seized all at once by a vehement determination and an intolerable sense that the present position of affairs was impossible, and could not last.

"Oh, my darling!" she cried; "get well and strong, and you and I will go and look for her, and never, never be taken from her again!"

"But, Rosalind, if mamma is dead?" cried little Amy.

The elder people who witnessed this scene stole out of the room, unable to bear it any longer.

"It must be put a stop to," John Trevanion said, in a voice that was sharp with pain.

"Oh, who can put a stop to it?" cried Mrs. Lennox, weeping, and recovering herself and weeping again. "I should not have wondered, not at all, if it had happened at first; but, after these years! And I that thought children were heartless little things, and that they had forgot!"

"Can Russell do nothing, now you have got her here?" he cried with impatience, walking up and down the room. He was at his wits' end, and in his perplexity felt himself incapable even of thought.

"Oh, John, did you not hear what that little thing said? She put the children against their mother. Amy will not let Russell come near her. If I have made a mistake, I meant it for the best. Russell is as miserable as any of us. Johnny has forgotten her, and Amy cannot endure the sight of her. And now it appears that coming to Bonport, which was your idea, is a failure too, though I am sure we both did it for the best."

"That is all that could be said for us if we were a couple of well-intentioned fools," he cried. "And, indeed, we seem to have acted like fools in all that concerns the children," he added, with a sort of bitterness. For what right had fate to lay such a burden upon him—him who had scrupulously preserved himself, or been preserved by Providence, from any such business of his own?

"John," said Mrs. Lennox, drying her eyes, "I don't think there is so much to blame yourself about. You felt sure it would be better for them being here; and when you put it to me, so did I. You never thought of the lake. Why should you think of the lake? We never let them go near it without somebody to take care of them in the day, and how could any one suppose that at night—"

Upon this her brother seized his hat and hurried from the house. The small aggravation seemed to fill up his cup so that he could bear no more, with this addition, that Mrs. Lennox's soft purr of a voice roused mere exasperation in him, while his every thought of the children, even when the cares they brought threatened to overwhelm him, was tender with natural affection. But, in fact, wherever he turned at this moment he saw not a gleam of light, and there was a bitterness as of the deferred and unforeseen in this sudden gathering together of clouds and dangers which filled him almost with awe. The catastrophe itself had passed over much more quietly than could have been thought. But, lo, here, when no fear was, the misery came. His heart melted within him when he thought of Amy's little pale face and that forlorn expedition in the stillness of the night to the side of the lake which betrayed, as nothing else could have done, the feverish working of her brain and the disturbance of her entire being. What madness of rage and jealousy must that have been that induced a man to leave this legacy of misery behind him to work in the minds of his little children years after he was dead! and what appalling cruelty and tyranny it was which made it possible for a dead man, upon whom neither argument nor proof could be brought to bear, thus to blight by a word so many lives! All had passed with a strange simplicity at first, and with such swift and silent carrying-out of the terrible conditions of the will that there had been no time to think if any expedient were possible. Looking back upon it, it seemed to him incredible that anything so extraordinary should have taken place with so little disturbance. She had accepted her fate without a word, and every one else had accepted it. The bitterness of death seemed to have passed, except for the romance of devotion on Rosalind's part, which he believed had faded in the other kind of romance more natural at her age. No one but himself had appeared to remember at all this catastrophe which rent life asunder. But now, when no one expected it, out of the clear sky came the explosions of the storm. He had decided too quickly that all was over. The peace had been but a pretence, and now the whole matter would have to be re-opened again.

The cause of the sudden return of all minds to the great family disaster and misery seemed to him more than ever confused by this last event. The condition which had led to Amy's last adventure seemed to make it more possible, notwithstanding Sophy's supposed discovery, that the story of the apparition was an illusion throughout. The child, always a visionary child, must have had, in the unnatural and strained condition of her nerves and long repression of her feelings, a dream so vivid as, like that of last night, to take the aspect of reality; and Rosalind, full of sympathy, and with all her own keen recollections ready to be called forth at a touch, must have received the contagion from her little sister, and seen what Amy had so long imagined she saw. Perhaps, even, it was the same contagion, acting on a matter-of-fact temperament, which had induced Sophy to believe that she, too, had seen her mother, but in real flesh and blood. Of all the hypotheses that could be thought of this seemed to him the most impossible. He had examined all the hotel registers, and made anxious inquiries everywhere, without finding a trace of Mrs. Trevanion. She had not, so far as he was aware, renounced her own name. And, even had she done so, it was impossible that she could have been in the hotel without some one seeing her, without leaving some trace behind. Notwithstanding this certainty, John Trevanion, even while he repeated his conviction to himself, was making his way once more to the hotel to see whether, by any possibility, some light might still be thrown upon a subject which had become so urgent. Yet even that, though it was the first thing that presented itself to him, had become, in fact, a secondary matter. The real question in this, as in all difficulties, was what to do next. What could be done to unravel the fatal tangle? Now that he contemplated the matter from afar, it became to him all at once a thing intolerable—a thing that must no longer be allowed to exist. What was publicity, what was scandal, in comparison with this wreck of life? There must be means, he declared to himself, of setting an unrighteous will aside, whatever lawyers might say. His own passiveness seemed incredible to him, as well as the extraordinary composure with which everybody else had acquiesced, accepting the victim's sacrifice. But that was over. Even though the present agitation should pass away, he vowed to himself that it should not pass from him until he had done all that man could do to set the wrong right.

While these thoughts were passing through his mind, he was walking into Aix with the speed of a man who has urgent work before him, though that work was nothing more definite or practical than the examination over again of the hotel books to see if there he could find any clew. He turned them over and over in his abstraction, going back without knowing it to distant dates, and roaming over an endless succession of names which conveyed no idea to his mind. He came at last, on the last page, to the name of Arthur Rivers, with a dull sort of surprise. "To be sure, Rivers is here!" he said to himself aloud.

"Yes, to be sure I am here. I have been waiting to see if you would find me out," Rivers said behind him. John did not give him so cordial a welcome as he had done on the previous night.

"I beg your pardon," he said. "I have so much on my mind I forget everything. Were you coming out to see my sister? We can walk together. The sun is warm, but not too hot for walking. That's an advantage of this time of the year."

"It is perhaps too early for Mrs. Lennox," Rivers said.

"Oh, no, not too early. The truth is we are in a little confusion. One of the children has been giving us a great deal of anxiety."

"Then, perhaps," said Rivers, with desperate politeness, "it will be better for me not to go." He felt within himself, though he was so civil, a sort of brutal indifference to their insignificant distresses, which were nothing in comparison with his own. To come so far in order to eat his breakfast under the dusty trees, and dine at the table d'hôte in a half-empty hotel at Aix, seemed to him so great an injustice and scorn in the midst of his fame and importance that even the discovery he had made, though it could not but tell in the situation, passed from his mind in the heat of offended consequence and pride.

John Trevanion, for his part, noticed the feeling of the other as little as Rivers did his. "One of the children has been walking in her sleep," he said. "I don't want to get a fool of a doctor who thinks of nothing but rheumatism. One of them filled my good sister's mind with folly about suppressed gout. Poor little Amy! She has a most susceptible brain, and I am afraid something has upset it. Do you believe in ghosts, Rivers?"

"As much as everybody does," said Rivers, recovering himself a little.

"That is about all that any one can say. This child thinks she has seen one. She is a silent little thing. She has gone on suffering and never said a word, and the consequence is, her little head has got all wrong."

By this time Rivers, having cooled down, began to see the importance of the disclosure he had to make. He said, "Would you mind telling me what the apparition was? You will understand, Trevanion, that I don't want to pry into your family concerns, and that I would not ask without a reason."

John Trevanion looked at him intently with a startled curiosity and earnestness. "I can't suppose," he said, "when it comes to that, much as we have paid for concealment, that you have not heard something—"

"Miss Trevanion told me," said Rivers—he paused a moment, feeling that it was a cruel wrong to him that he should be compelled to say Miss Trevanion—he who ought to have been called to her side at once, who should have been in a position to claim her before the world as his Rosalind—"Miss Trevanion gave me to understand that the lady whom I had met in Spain, whose portrait was on her table, was—"

"My sister-in-law—the mother of the children—yes, yes—and what then?" John Trevanion cried.

"Only this, Trevanion—that lady is here."

John caught him by the arm so fiercely, so suddenly, that the leisurely waiters standing about, and the few hotel guests who were moving out and in in the quiet of the morning stopped and stared with ideas of rushing to the rescue. "What do you mean?" he said. "Here? How do you know? It is impossible."

"Come out into the garden, where we can talk. It may be impossible, but it is true. I also saw her last night."

"You must be mad or dreaming, Rivers. You too—a man in your senses—and—God in heaven!" he said, with a sudden bitter sense of his own unappreciated friendship—unappreciated even, it would seem, beyond the grave—"that she should have come, whatever she had to say, to you—to any one—and not to me!"

"Trevanion, you are mistaken. This is no apparition. There was no choice, of me or any one. That poor lady, whether sinned against or sinning I have no knowledge, is here. Do you understand me? She is here."

They were standing by this time in the shadow of the great laurel bushes where she had sheltered on the previous night. John Trevanion said nothing for a moment. He cast himself down on one of the seats to recover his breath. It was just where Hamerton had been sitting. Rivers almost expected to see the faint stir in the bushes, the evidence of some one listening, to whom the words spoken might, as she said, be death or life.

"This is extraordinary news," said Trevanion at last. "You will pardon me if I was quite overwhelmed by it. Rivers, you can't think how important it is. Where can I find her? You need not fear to betray her—oh, Heaven, to betray her to me, her brother! But you need not fear. She knows that there is no one who has more—more regard, more respect, or more—Let me know where to find her, my good fellow, for Heaven's sake!"

"Trevanion, it is not any doubt of you. But, in the first place, I don't know where to find her, and then—she did not disclose herself to me. I found her out by accident. Have I any right to dispose of her secret? I will tell you everything I know," he added hastily, in answer to the look and gesture, almost of despair, which John could not restrain. "Last night your friend, young Hamerton, was talking—injudiciously, I think"—there was a little sweetness to him in saying this, even in the midst of real sympathy and interest—"he was talking of what was going on in your house. I had already seen some one walking about the garden whose appearance I seemed to recollect. When Hamerton mentioned your name" (he was anxious that this should be made fully evident), "she heard it; and by and by I perceived that some one was listening, behind you, just there, in the laurels."

John started up and turned round, gazing at the motionless, glistening screen of leaves, as if she might still be there. After a moment—"And what then?"

"Not much more. I spoke to her afterwards. She asked me, for the love of God, to bring her news, and I promised—what I could—for to-night."

John Trevanion held out his hand, and gave that of Rivers a strong pressure. "Come out with me to Bonport. You must hear everything, and perhaps you can advise me. I am determined to put an end to the situation somehow, whatever it may cost," he said.

CHAPTER LV

The two men went out to Bonport together, and on the way John Trevanion, half revolted that he should have to tell it, half relieved to talk of it to another man, and see how the matter appeared to a person unconcerned, with eyes clear from prepossession of any kind, either hostile or tender, gave his companion all the particulars of his painful story. It was a relief; and Rivers, who had been trained for the bar, gave it at once as his opinion that the competent authorities would not hesitate to set such a will aside, or at least, on proof that no moral danger would arise to the children, would modify its restrictions greatly. "Wills are sacred theoretically; but there has always been a power of revision," he said. And he suggested practical means of bringing this point to a trial—or at least to the preliminary trial of counsel's advice, which gave his companion great solace. "I can see that we all acted like fools," John Trevanion confessed, with a momentary over-confidence that his troubles might be approaching an end. "We were terrified for the scandal, the public discussion, that would have been sure to rise—and no one so much as she. Old Blake was all for the sanctity of the will, as you say, and I—I was so torn in two with doubts and—miseries—"

"But I presume," Rivers said, "these have all been put to rest. There has been a satisfactory explanation—"

"Explanation!" cried John. "Do you think I could ask, or she condescend to give, what you call explanations? She knew her own honor and purity; and she knew," he added with a long-drawn breath, "that I knew them as well as she—"

"Still," said Rivers, "explanations are necessary when it is brought before the public."

"It shall never be brought before the public!"

"My dear Trevanion! How then are you to do anything, how set the will aside?"

This question silenced John; and it took further speech out of the mouth of his companion, who felt, on his side, that if he were about to be connected with the Trevanion family, it would not be at all desirable, on any consideration, that this story should become public. He had been full of interest in the woman whose appearance had struck him before he knew anything about her, and who had figured so largely in his first acquaintance with Rosalind. But when it became a question of a great scandal occupying every mind and tongue, and in which it was possible his own wife might be concerned—that was a very different matter. In a great family such things are treated with greater case. If it is true that an infringement on their honor, a blot on the scutcheon, is supposed to be of more importance where there is a noble scutcheon to tarnish, it is yet true that a great family history would lose much of its interest if it were not crossed now and then by a shadow of darkness, a tale to make the hearers shudder; and that those who are accustomed to feel themselves always objects of interest to the world bear the shame of an occasional disclosure far better than those sprung from a lowlier level whose life is sacred to themselves, and who guard their secrets far more jealously than either the great or the very small. Rivers, in the depth of his nature, which was not that of a born patrician, trembled at the thought of public interference in the affairs of a family with which he should be connected. All the more that it would be an honor and elevation to him to be connected with it, he trembled to have its secrets published. It was not till after he had given his advice on the subject that this drawback occurred to him. He was not a bad man, to doom another to suffer that his own surroundings might go free; but when he thought of it he resolved that, if he could bring it about, Rosalind's enthusiasm should be calmed down, and she should learn to feel for her stepmother only that calm affection which stepmothers at the best are worthy of, and which means separation rather than unity of interests. He pondered this during the latter part of the way with great abstraction of thought. He was very willing to take advantage of his knowledge of Mrs. Trevanion, and of the importance it gave him to be their only means of communication with her; but further than this he did not mean to go. Were Rosalind once his, there should certainly be no room in his house for a stepmother of blemished fame.

And there were many things in his visit to Bonport which were highly unsatisfactory to Rivers. John Trevanion was so entirely wrapped in his own cares as to be very inconsiderate of his friend, whose real object in presenting himself at Aix at all he must no doubt have divined had he been in possession of his full intelligence. He took the impatient lover into the grounds of the house where Rosalind was, and expected him to take an interest in the winding walks by which little Amy had strayed down to the lake, and all the scenery of that foolish little episode. "If her sister had not followed her, what might have happened? The child might have been drowned, or, worse still, might have gone mad in the shock of finding herself out there all alone. It makes one shudder to think of it." Rivers did not shudder; he was not very much interested about Amy. But his nerves were all jarred by the contrariety of the circumstances as he looked up through the shade of the trees to the house at the top of the little eminence, where Rosalind was, but as much out of his reach as if she had been at the end of the world. He did not see her until much later, when he returned at John Trevanion's invitation to dinner. Rosalind was very pale, but blushed when she met him with a consciousness which he scarcely knew how to interpret. Was there hope in the blush, or was it embarrassment—almost pain? She said scarcely anything during dinner, sitting in the shadow of the pink abat-jour, and of her aunt Sophy, who, glad of a new listener, poured forth her soul upon the subject of sleep-walking, and told a hundred stories, experiences of her own and of other people, all tending to prove that it was the most usual thing in the world, and that, indeed, most children walked in their sleep. "The thing to do is to be very careful not to wake them," Mrs. Lennox said. "That was Rosalind's mistake. Oh, my dear, there is no need to tell me that you didn't mean anything that wasn't for the best. Nobody who has ever seen how devoted you are to these children—just like a mother—could suppose that; but I understand," said Aunt Sophy with an air of great wisdom, "that you should never wake them. Follow, to see that they come to no harm, and sometimes you may be able to guide them back to their own room—which is always the best thing to do—but never wake them; that is the one thing you must always avoid."

"I should think Rivers has had about enough of Amy's somnambulism by this time," John said. "Tell us something about yourself. Are you going to stay long? Are you on your way northwards? All kinds of honor and glory await you at home, we know."

"My movements are quite vague. I have settled nothing," Rivers replied. And how could he help but look at Rosalind, who, though she never lifted her eyes, and could not have seen his look, yet changed color in some incomprehensible way? And how could he see that she changed color in the pink gloom of the shade, which obscured everything, especially such a change as that? But he did see it, and Rosalind was aware he did so. Notwithstanding his real interest in the matter, it was hard for him to respond to John Trevanion's questions about the meeting planned for this evening. It had been arranged between them that John should accompany Rivers back to the hotel, that he should be at hand should the mysterious lady consent to see him; and the thought of this possible interview was to him as absorbing as was the question of Rosalind's looks to his companion. But they had not much to say to each other, each being full of his own thoughts as they sat together for those few minutes after dinner which were inevitable. Then they followed each other gloomily into the drawing-room, which was vacant, though a sound of voices from outside the open window betrayed where the ladies had gone. Mrs. Lennox came indoors as they approached. "It is a little cold," she said, with a shiver. But Rivers found it balm as he stepped out and saw Rosalind leaning upon the veranda among the late roses, with the moonlight making a sort of silvery gauze of her light dress. He came out and placed himself by her; but the window stood open behind, with John Trevanion within hearing, and Mrs. Lennox's voice running on quite audibly close at hand. Was it always to be so? He drew very near to her, and said in a low voice, "May I not speak to you?" Rosalind looked at him with eyes which were full of a beseeching earnestness. She did not pretend to be ignorant of what he meant. The moonlight gave an additional depth of pathetic meaning to her face, out of which it stole all the color.

"Oh, Mr. Rivers, not now!" she said, with an appeal which he could not resist. Poor Rivers turned and left her in the excitement of the moment. He went along the terrace to the farther side with a poor pretence of looking at the landscape, in reality to think out the situation. What could he say to recommend himself, to put himself in the foreground of her thoughts? A sudden suggestion flashed upon him, and he snatched at it without further consideration. When he returned to where he had left her, Rosalind was still there, apparently waiting. She advanced towards him shyly, with a sense of having given him pain. "I am going in now to Amy," she said; "I waited to bid you good-night."

"One word," he said. "Oh, nothing about myself, Miss Trevanion. I will wait, if I must not speak. But I have a message for you."

"A message—for me!" She came a little nearer to him, with that strange divination which accompanies great mental excitement, feeling instinctively that what he was about to say must bear upon the subject of her thoughts.

"You remember," he said, "the lady whom I told you I had met? I have met her again, Miss Trevanion."

"Where?" She turned upon him with a cry, imperative and passionate.

"Miss Trevanion, I have never forgotten the look you gave me when I said that the lady was accompanied by a man. I want to explain; I have found out who it was."

"Mr. Rivers!"

"Should I be likely to tell you anything unfit for your ears to hear? I know better now. The poor lady is not happy, in that any more than in any other particular of her lot. The man was her son."

"Her son!" Rosalind's cry was such that it made Mrs. Lennox stop in her talk; and John Trevanion, from the depths of the dark room behind, came forward to know what it was.

"I felt that I must tell you; you reproached me with your eyes when I said—But, if I wronged her, I must make reparation. It was in all innocence and honor; it was her son."

"Mr. Rivers!" cried Rosalind, turning upon him, her breast heaving, her lips quivering, "this shows it is a mistake. I might have known all the time it was a mistake. She had no son except—It was not the same. Thank you for wishing to set me right; but it could not be the same. It is no one we know. It is a mistake."

"But when I tell you, Miss Trevanion, that she said—"

"No, no, you must not say any more. We know nothing; it is a mistake." Disappointment, with, at the same time, a strange, poignant smart, as of some chance arrow striking her in the dark, which wounded her without reason, without aim, filled her mind. She turned quickly, eluding the hand which Rivers had stretched out, not pausing even for her uncle, and hastened away without a word. John Trevanion turned upon Rivers, who came in slowly from the veranda with a changed and wondering look. "What have you been saying to Rosalind? You seem to have frightened her," he said.

"Oh, it seems all a mistake," he replied vaguely. He was, in fact, greatly cast down by the sudden check he had received. In the height of his consciousness that his own position as holding a clew to the whereabouts of this mysterious woman was immeasurably advantaged, there came upon him this chill of doubt lest perhaps after all—But then she had herself declared that to hear of the Trevanions was to her as life and death. Rivers did not know how to reconcile Rosalind's instant change of tone, her evident certainty that his information did not concern her, with the impassioned interest of the woman whom he half felt that he had betrayed. How he had acquired the information which he had thought it would be a good thing for him thus to convey he could scarcely have told. It had been partly divination, partly some echo of recollection; but he felt certain that he was right; and he had also felt certain that to hear it would please Rosalind. He was altogether cast down by her reception of his news. He did not recover himself during all the long walk back to Aix in the moonlight, which he made in company with John Trevanion. But John was absorbed in the excitement of the expected meeting, and did not disturb him by much talking. They walked along between the straight lines of the trees, through black depths of shadow and the white glory of the light, exchanging few words, each wrapped in his own atmosphere. When the lights of the town were close to them John spoke. "Whether she will speak to me or not, you must place me where I can see her, Rivers. I must make sure."

"I will do the best I can," said Rivers; "but what if it should all turn out to be a mistake?"

"How can it be a mistake? Who else would listen as you say she did? Who else could take so much interest? But I must make sure. Place me, at least, where I may see her, even if I must not speak."

The garden was nearly deserted, only one or two solitary figures in shawls and overcoats still lingering in the beauty of the moonlight. Rivers placed John standing in the shadow of a piece of shrubbery, close to the open space which she had crossed as she made her round of the little promenade, and he himself took the seat under the laurels which he had occupied on the previous night. He thought there was no doubt that she would come to him, that after the hotel people had disappeared she would be on the watch, and hasten to hear what he had to tell her. When time passed on and no one appeared, he got up again and began himself to walk round and round, pausing now and then to whisper to John Trevanion that he did not understand it—that he could not imagine what could be the cause of the delay. They waited thus till midnight, till the unfortunate waiters on the veranda were nearly distracted, and every intimation of the late hour which these unhappy men could venture to give had been given. When twelve struck, tingling through the blue air, John Trevanion came, finally, out of his hiding-place, and Rivers from his chair. They spoke in whispers, as conspirators instinctively do, though there was nobody to hear. "I cannot understand it," said Rivers, with the disconcerted air of a man whose exhibition has failed. "I don't think it is of any use waiting longer," said John. "Oh, of no use. I am very sorry, Trevanion. I confidently expected—" "Something," said John, "must have happened to detain her. I am disappointed, but still I do not cease to hope; and if, in the meantime, you see her, or any trace of her—" "You may be sure I will do my best," Rivers said, ashamed, though it was no fault of his, and, notwithstanding Rosalind's refusal to believe, with all his faith in his own conclusions restored.

They shook hands silently, and John Trevanion went away downcast and disappointed. When he had gone down the narrow street and emerged into the Place, which lay full in the moonlight, he saw two tall, dark shadows in the very centre of the white vacancy and brightness in the deserted square. They caught his attention for the moment, and he remembered after that a vague question crossed his mind what two women could be doing out so late. Were they sisters of charity, returning from some labor of love? Thus he passed them quickly, yet with a passing wonder, touched, he could not tell how, by something forlorn in the two solitary women, returning he knew not from what errand. Had he but known who these wayfarers were!

CHAPTER LVI

Two days after this, while as yet there had appeared no further solution of the mystery, Roland Hamerton came hastily one morning up the sloping paths of Bonport into the garden, where he knew he should find Rosalind. He was in the position of a sort of outdoor member of the household, going and coming at his pleasure, made no account of, enjoying the privileges of a son and brother rather than of a lover. But the advantages of this position were great. He saw Rosalind at all hours, in all circumstances, and he was himself so much concerned about little Amy, and so full of earnest interest in everything that affected the family, that he was admitted even to the most intimate consultations. To Rosalind his presence had given a support and help which she could not have imagined possible; especially in contrast with Rivers, who approached her with that almost threatening demand for a final explanation, and shaped every word and action so as to show that the reason for his presence here was her and her only. Roland's self-control and unfeigned desire to promote her comfort first of all, before he thought of himself, was in perfect contrast to this, and consolatory beyond measure. She had got to be afraid of Rivers; she was not at all afraid of the humble lover who was at the same time her old friend, who was young like herself, who knew everything that had happened. This was the state to which she had come in that famous competition between the three, who ought, as Mr. Ruskin says, to have been seven. One she had withdrawn altogether from, putting him out of the lists with mingled repulsion and pity. Another she had been seized with a terror of, as of a man lying in wait to devour her. The third—he was no one; he was only Roland; her lover in the nursery, her faithful attendant all her life. She was not afraid of him, nor of any exaction on his part. Her heart turned to him with a simple reliance. He was not clever, he was not distinguished; he had executed for her none of the labors either of Hercules or any other hero. He had on his side no attractions of natural beauty, or any of those vague appeals to the imagination which had given Everard a certain power over her; and he had not carried her image with him, as Rivers had done, through danger and conflict, or brought back any laurels to lay at her feet. If it had been a matter of competition, as in the days of chivalry, or in the scheme of our gentle yet vehement philosopher, Roland would have had little chance. But after the year was over in which Rosalind had known of the competition for her favor, he it was who remained nearest. She glanced up with an alarmed look to see who was coming, and her face cleared when she saw it was Roland. He would force no considerations upon her, ask no tremendous questions. She gave him a smile as he approached. She was seated under the trees, with the lake gleaming behind for a background through an opening in the foliage. Mrs. Lennox's chair still stood on the same spot, but she was not there. There were some books on the table, but Rosalind was not reading. She had some needlework in her hands, but that was little more than a pretence; she was thinking, and all her thoughts were directed to one subject. She smiled when he came up, yet grudged to lose the freedom of those endless thoughts. "I thought," she said, "you were on the water with Rex."

"No, I told you I wanted something to do. I think I have got what I wanted, but I should like to tell you about it, Rosalind."

"Yes?" she said, looking up again with a smiling interrogation. She thought it was about some piece of exercise or amusement, some long walk he was going to take, some expedition which he wanted to organize.

"I have heard something very strange," he said. "It appears that I said something the other night to Rivers, whom I found when I went back to the hotel, and that somebody, some lady, was seen to come near and listen. I was not saying any harm, you may suppose, but only that the children were upset. And this lady came around to hear what I was saying."

His meaning did not easily reach Rosalind, who was preoccupied, and did not connect Roland at all with the mystery around her. She said, "That was strange; who could it be; some one who knew us in the hotel?"

"Rosalind, I have never liked to say anything to you about—Madam."

"Don't!" she said, holding up her hand; "oh, don't, Roland. The only time you spoke to me about her you hurt me—oh, to the very heart; not that I believed it; but it was so grievous that you could think, that you could say—that you could see even, anything—"

"I have thought it over a hundred times since then, and what you say is true, Rosalind. One has no right even to see things that—there are some people who are above even—I know now what you mean, and that it is true. You knew her better than any one else, and your faith is mine. That is why I came to tell you. Rosalind—who could that woman be but one? She came behind the bushes to hear what I was saying. She was all trembling—who else could that be?"

"Roland!" Rosalind had risen up, every tinge of color ebbing from her face; "you too!—you too—!"

"No," he said, rising also, taking her hand; "not that, not that, Rosalind. If she were dead, as you think, would she not know everything? She would not need to listen to me. This is what I am sure of, that she is here and trying every way—"

She grasped his hands as if her own were iron, and then let them go, and threw herself into her seat, and sobbed, unable to speak, "Oh, Roland! oh, Roland!" with a cry that went to his heart.

"Rosalind," he said, leaning over her, touching her shoulder, and her hair, with a sympathy which filled his eyes with tears, and would not be contented with words, "listen; I am going to look for her now. I sha'n't tire of it, whoever tires. I shall find her, Rosalind. And then, if she will let me take care of her, stand by her, bring her news of you all—! I have wronged her more than anybody, for I thought that I believed; see if I don't make up for it now. I could not go without telling you—I shall find her, Rosalind," the young man cried.

She rose up again, trembling, and uncovered her face. Her cheeks were wet with tears, her eyes almost wild with hope and excitement. "I'll come with you," she said. "I had made up my mind before. I will bear it no longer. Let them take everything; what does it matter? I am not only my father's daughter, I am myself first of all. If she is living, Roland—"

"She is living, I am sure."

"Then as soon as we find her—oh no, she would go away from me; when you find her Roland—I put all my trust in you."

"And then," he cried breathlessly, "and then? No, I'll make no bargains; only say you trust me, dear. You did say you trusted me, Rosalind."

"With all my heart," she said.

And as Rosalind looked at him, smiling with her eyes full of tears, the young man turned and hurried away. When he was nearly out of sight he looked back and waved his hand: she was standing up gazing after him as if—as if it were the man whom she loved was leaving her. That was the thought that leaped up into his heart with an emotion indescribable—the feeling of one who has found what he had thought lost and beyond his reach. As if it were the man she loved! Could one say more than that? "But I'll make no bargains, I'll make no bargains," he said to himself. "It's best to be all for love and nothing for reward."

While this scene was being enacted in the garden, another, of a very different description, yet bearing on the same subject, was taking place in the room which John Trevanion, with the instinct of an Englishman, called his study. The expedient of sending for Russell had not been very successful so far as the nursery was concerned. The woman had arrived in high elation and triumph, feeling that her "family" had found it impossible to go on any longer without her, and full of the best intentions, this preliminary being fully acknowledged. She had meant to make short work with Johnny's visions and the dreams of Amy, and to show triumphantly that she, and she only, understood the children. But when she arrived at Bonport her reception was not what she had hoped. The face of affairs was changed. Johnny, who saw no more apparitions, no longer wanted any special care, and Russell found the other woman in possession, and indisposed to accept her dictation, or yield the place to her, while Amy, now transferred to Rosalind's room and care, shrank from her almost with horror. All this had been bitter to her, a disappointment all the greater that her hopes had been so high. She found herself a supernumerary, not wanted by any one in the house, where she had expected to be regarded as a deliverer. The only consolation she received was from Sophy, who had greatly dropped out of observation during recent events, and was as much astonished and as indignant to find Amy the first object in the household, and herself left out, as Russell was in her humiliation. The two injured ones found great solace in each other in these circumstances. Sophy threw herself with enthusiasm into the work of consoling, yet embittering, her old attendant's life. Sophy told her all that had been said in the house before her arrival, and described the distaste of everybody for her with much graphic force. She gave Russell also an account of all that had passed, of the discovery which she believed she herself had made, and further, though this of itself sent the blood coursing through Russell's veins, of the other incidents of the family life, and of Rosalind's lovers; Mr. Rivers, who had just come from the war, and Mr. Everard, who was the gentleman who had been at the Red Lion. "Do you think he was in love with Rosalind then, Russell?" Sophy said, her keen eyes dancing with curiosity and eagerness. Russell said many things that were very injudicious, every word of which Sophy laid up in her heart, and felt with fierce satisfaction that her coming was not to be for nothing, and that the hand of Providence had brought her to clear up this imbroglio. She saw young Everard next day, and convinced herself of his identity, and indignation and horror blazed up within her. Russell scarcely slept all night, and as she lay awake gathered together all the subjects of wrath she had, and piled them high. Next morning she knocked at John Trevanion's door, with a determination to make both her grievances and her discovery known at once.

"Mr. Trevanion," said Russell, "may I speak a word with you, sir, if you please?"

John Trevanion turned around upon his chair, and looked at her with surprise, and an uncomfortable sense of something painful to come. What had he to do with the women-servants? That, at least, was out of his department. "What do you want?" he asked in a helpless tone.

"Mr. John," said Russell, drawing nearer, "there is something that I must say. I can't say it to Mrs. Lennox, for she's turned against me like the rest. But a gentleman is more unpartial like. Do you know, sir, who it is that is coming here every day, and after Miss Rosalind, as they tell me? After Miss Rosalind! It's not a thing I like to say of a young lady, and one that I've brought up, which makes it a deal worse; but she has no proper pride. Mr. John, do you know who that Mr. Everard, as they call him, is?"

"Yes, I know who he is. You had better attend to the affairs of the nursery, Russell."

This touched into a higher blaze the fire of Russell's wrath. "The nursery! I'm not allowed in it. There is another woman there that thinks she has the right to my place. I'm put in a room to do needlework, Mr. John. Me! and Miss Amy in Miss Rosalind's room, that doesn't know no more than you do how to manage her. But I mustn't give way," the woman cried, with an effort. "Do you know as the police are after him, Mr. John? Do you know it was all along of him as Madam went away?"

John Trevanion sprang from his chair. "Be silent, woman!" he cried; "how dare you speak so to me?"

"I've said it before, and I will again!" cried Russell—"a man not half her age. Oh, it was a shame!—and out of a house like Highcourt—and a lady that should know better, not a poor servant like them that are sent out of the way at a moment's notice when they go wrong. Don't lift your hand to me, Mr. John. Would you strike a woman, sir, and call yourself a gentleman? And you that brought me here against my will when I was happy at home. I won't go out of the room till I have said my say."

"No," said John, with a laugh which was half rage, though the idea that he was likely to strike Russell was a ludicrous exasperation. "No, as you are a woman I can't, unfortunately, knock you down, whatever impertinence you may say."

"I am glad of that, sir," said Russell, "for you looked very like it; and I've served the Trevanions for years, though I don't get much credit for it, and I shouldn't like to have to say as the lady of the house forgot herself for a boy, and a gentleman of the house struck a woman. I've too much regard for them to do that."

Here she paused to take breath, and then resumed, standing in an attitude of defence against the door, whither John's threatening aspect had driven her: "You mark my words, sir," cried Russell, "where that young man is, Madam's not far off. Miss Sophy, that has her wits about her, she has seen her—and the others that is full of fancies they've seen what they think is a ghost; and little Miss Amy, she is wrong in the head with it. This is how I find things when I'm telegraphed for, and brought out to a strange place, and then told as I'm not wanted. But it's Providence as wants me here. Mrs. Lennox—she always was soft—I don't wonder at her being deceived; and, besides, she wasn't on the spot, and she don't know. But, Mr. Trevanion, you were there all the time. You know what goings-on there were. It wasn't the doctor or the parson Madam went out to meet, and who was there besides? Nobody but this young man. When a woman's bent on going wrong, she'll find out the way. You're going to strike me again! but it's true. It was him she met every night, every night, out in the cold. And then he saw Miss Rosalind, and he thought to himself—here's a young one, and a rich one, and far nicer than that old—Mr. John! I know more than any of you know, and I'll put up with no violence, Mr. John!"

John Trevanion's words will scarcely bear repeating. He put her out of the room with more energy than perhaps he ought to have employed with a woman; and he bade her go to the devil with her infernal lies. Profane speech is not to be excused, but there are times when it becomes mere historical truth and not profanity at all. They were infernal lies, the language and suggestion of hell even if—even if—oh, that a bleeding heart should have to remember this!—even if they were true. John shut the door of his room upon the struggling woman and came back to face himself, who was more terrible still. Even if they were true! They brought back in a moment a suggestion which had died away in his mind, but which never had been definitely cast forth. His impulse when he had seen this young Everard had been to take him by the collar and pitch him forth, and refuse him permission even to breathe the same air: "Dangerous fellow, hence; breathe not where princes are!" but then a sense of confusion and uncertainty had come in and baffled him. There was no proof, either, that Everard was the man, or that there was any man. It was not Madam's handwriting, but her husband's, that had connected the youth with Highcourt; and though he might have a thousand faults, he did not look the cold-blooded villain who would make his connection with one woman a standing ground upon which to establish schemes against another. John Trevanion's brow grew quite crimson as the thought went through his mind. He was alone, and he was middle-aged and experienced in the world; and two years ago many a troublous doubt, and something even like a horrible certainty, had passed through his mind. But there are people with whom it is impossible to associate shame. Even if shame should be all but proved against them, it will not hold. When he thought an evil thought of Madam—nay, when that thought had but a thoroughfare through his mind against his will, the man felt his cheek redden and his soul faint. And here, too, were the storm-clouds of that catastrophe which was past, rolling up again, full of flame and wrath. They had all been silent then, awestricken, anxious to hush up and pass over, and let the mystery remain. But now this was no longer possible. A bewildering sense of confusion, of a darkness through which he could not make his way, of strange coincidences, strange contradictions, was in John Trevanion's mind. He was afraid to enter upon this maze, not knowing to what conclusion it might lead him. And yet now it must be done.

Only a very short time after another knock came to his door, and Rosalind entered, with an atmosphere about her of urgency and excitement. She said, without any preface:

"Uncle John, I have come to tell you what I have made up my mind to do. Do you remember that in two days I shall be of age, and my own mistress? In two days!"

"My dear," he said, "I hope you have not been under so hard a taskmaster as to make you impatient to be free."

"Yes," said Rosalind. "Oh, not a hard taskmaster; but life has been hard, Uncle John! As soon as I am my own mistress I am going, Amy and I, to—you know. I cannot rest here any longer. Amy will be safe; she can have my money. But this cannot go on any longer. If we should starve, we must find my mother. I know you will say she is not my mother. And who else, then? She is all the mother I have ever known. And I have left her these two years under a stain which she ought not to bear, and in misery which she ought not to bear. Was it ever heard of before that a mother should be banished from her children? I was too young to understand it all at first; and I had no habit of acting for myself; and perhaps you would have been right to stop me; but now—"

"Certainly I should have stopped you. But, Rosalind, I have come myself to a similar resolution," he said. "It must all be cleared up. But not by you, my dear, not by you. If there is anything to discover that is to her shame—"

"There is nothing, Uncle John."

"My dear, you don't know how mysterious human nature is. There are fine and noble creatures such as she is—as she is! don't think I deny it, Rosalind—who may have yet a spot, a stain, which a man like me may see and grieve for and forgive, but you—"

"Oh, Uncle John, say that a woman like me may wash away with tears, if you like, but that should never, never be betrayed to the eyes of a man!"

He took her into his arms, weeping as she was, and he not far from it. "Rosalind, perhaps yours is the truest way; but yet, as common people think, and according to the way of the world—"

"Which is neither your way nor mine," cried the girl.

"And you can say nothing to change my mind; I was too young at the time. But now—if she has died," Rosalind said, with difficulty swallowing down the "climbing sorrow" in her throat, "she will know at least what we meant. And if she is living there is no rest but with our mother for Amy and me. And the child shall not suffer, Uncle John, for she shall have what is mine."

"Rosalind, you are still in the absolute stage—you see nothing that can modify your purposes. My dear, you should have had your mother to speak to on this subject. There are two men here, Rosalind, to whom—have you not some duty, some obligation? They both seem to me to be waiting—for what, Rosalind?"

Rosalind detached herself from her uncle's arm. A crimson flush covered her face. "Is it—dishonorable?" she said.

In the midst of his emotion John Trevanion could not suppress a smile. "That is, perhaps, a strong word."

"It would be dishonorable in a man," she cried, lifting her eyes with a hot color under them which seemed to scorch her.

"It would be impossible in a man, Rosalind," he said gravely; "the circumstances are altogether different. And yet you too owe something to Roland, who has loved you all his life, poor fellow, and to Rivers, who has come here neglecting everything for your sake. I do not know," he added, in a harsher tone, "whether there may not be still another claim."

"I think you are unjust, Uncle John," she said, with tremulous dignity. "And if it is as you say, these gentlemen have followed their own inclinations, not mine. Am I bound because they have seen fit—But that would be slavery for a woman." Then her countenance cleared a little, and she added, "When you know all that is in my mind you will not disapprove."

"I hope you will make a wise decision, Rosalind," he said. "But at least do nothing—make up your mind to do nothing—till the time comes." He spoke vaguely, and so did she, but in the excitement of their minds neither remarked this in the other. For he had not hinted to her, nor her to him, the possibility of some great new event which might happen at any moment and change all plans and thoughts.

Rosalind left her uncle with the thrill of her resolution in all her veins. She met, as she crossed the ante-room, Rivers, who had just come in and was standing waiting for a reply to the petition to be admitted to see her which he had just sent by a servant. She came upon him suddenly while he stood there, himself wound up to high tension, full of passion and urgency, feeling himself ill-used, and determined that now, at last, this question should be settled. He had failed indeed in pushing his suit by means of the mysterious stranger whom he had not seen again; but this made him only return with additional vehemence to his own claim, the claim of a man who had waited a year for his answer. But when he saw Rosalind there came over him that instant softening which is so apt to follow an unusual warmth of angry feeling, when we are "wroth with those we love." He thought at first that she had come to him in answer to his message, granting all he asked by that gracious personal response. "Rosalind!" he cried, putting out his hands. But next moment his countenance reflected the blush in hers, as she turned to him startled, not comprehending and shrinking from this enthusiastic address. "I beg your pardon," he said, crushing his hat in his hands. "I was taken by surprise. Miss Trevanion, I had just sent to ask—"

Rosalind was seized by a sort of helpless terror. She was afraid of him and his passion. She said, "Uncle John is in his room. Oh, forgive me, please! If it is me, will you wait—oh, will you be so kind as to wait till Thursday? Everything will be settled then. I shall know then what I have to do. Mr. Rivers, I am very sorry to give you so much trouble—"

"Trouble!" he cried; his voice was almost inarticulate in the excess of emotion. "How can you use such words to me? As if trouble had anything to do with it; if you would send me to the end of the earth, so long as it was to serve you, or give me one of the labors of Hercules—Yes, I know I am extravagant. One becomes extravagant in the state of mind in which—And to hear you speak of trouble—"

"Mr. Rivers," said Rosalind, humble in her sense of guilt, "I have a great many things to think of. You don't know how serious it is; but on Thursday I shall be of age, and then I can decide. Come then, if you will, and I will tell you. Oh, let me tell you on Thursday—not now!"

"That does not sound very hopeful for me," he said. "Miss Trevanion, remember that I have waited a year for my answer—few men do that without—without—"

And then he paused, and looked at her with an air which was at once fierce and piteous, defiant and imploring. And Rosalind shrank with a sense of guilt, feeling that she had no right to hold him in suspense, yet frightened by his vehemence, and too much agitated to know what to say.

"On Thursday," she said, mechanically; "on Thursday—You shall not complain of me any more." She held out her hand to him with a smile, apologetic and deprecatory, which was very sweet, which threw him into a bewilderment unspeakable. She was cruel without knowing it, without intending it. She had, she thought, something to make up to this man, and how could she do it but by kindness—by showing him that she was grateful—that she liked and honored him? He went away asking himself a thousand questions, going over and over her simple words, extracting meanings from them of which they were entirely innocent, framing them at last to the signification which he wished. He started from Bonport full of doubt and uneasiness, but before he reached his hotel a foolish elation had got the better of these sadder sentiments. He said to himself that these words could have but one meaning. "You shall not complain of me any more." But if she cast him off after this long probation he would have very good reason to complain. It was impossible that she should prepare a refusal by such words; and, indeed, if she had meant to refuse him, could she have postponed her answer again? Is it not honor in a woman to say "No" without delay, unless she means to say "Yes?" It is the only claim of honor upon her, who makes so many claims upon the honor of men, to say "No," if she means "No." No one could mistake that primary rule. When she said "Thursday," was it not the last assurance she could give before a final acceptance, and "You shall not complain of me any more?" This is a consequence of the competitive system in love which Mr. Ruskin evidently did not foresee, for Rosalind, on the other hand, was right enough when she tried to assure herself that she had not wished for his love, had not sought it in any way, that she should be made responsible for its discomfiture. Rivers employed his time of suspense in making arrangements for his departure. He was a proud man, and he would not have it said that he had left Aix hastily in consequence of his disappointment. In the evening he wrote some letters, vaguely announcing a speedy return. "Perhaps almost as soon as you receive this," he said, always guarding against the possibility of a sudden departure; and then he said to himself that such a thing was impossible. This was how he spent the intervening days. He had almost forgotten by this time, in the intensity of personal feeling, the disappointment and shock to his pride involved in the fact that the lady of the garden had appeared no more.

In the meantime, while all this was going on, Reginald was out on the shining water in a boat, which was the first thing the English boy turned to in that urgent necessity for "something to do" which is the first thought of his mind. He had taken Sophy with him condescendingly for want of a better, reflecting contemptuously all the time on the desertion of that beggar Hamerton, with whom he was no longer the first object. But Sophy was by no means without advantages as a companion. He sculled her out half a mile from shore with the intention of teaching her how to row on the way back; but Sophy had made herself more amusing in another way by that time, and he was willing to do the work while she maintained the conversation. Sophy was nearly as good as Scheherazade. She kept up her narrative, or series of narratives, with scarcely a pause to take breath, for she was very young and very long-winded, with her lungs in perfect condition, and her stories had this advantage, to the primitive intelligence that is, that they were all true; which is to say that they were all about real persons, and spiced by that natural inclination to take the worst view of everything, which, unfortunately, is so often justified by the results, and makes a story-teller piquant, popular, and detested. Sophy had a great future before her in this way, and in the meantime she made Reginald acquainted with everything, as they both concluded, that he ought to know. She told him about Everard, and the saving of Amy and Johnny, which he concluded to be a "plant," and "just like the fellow;" and about the encouragement Rosalind gave him, at which Rex swore, to the horror, yet delight, of his little sister, great, real oaths. And then the story quickened and the interest rose as she told him about the apparitions, about what the children saw, and, finally, under a vow of secrecy (which she had also administered to Russell), what she herself saw, and the conclusion she had formed. When she came to this point of her story, Reginald was too much excited even to swear. He kept silence with a dark countenance, and listened, leaning forward on his oars with a rapt attention that flattered Sophy. "I told Uncle John," cried the child, "and he asked me what I was going to do? How could I do anything, Rex? I watched because I don't believe in ghosts, and I knew it could not be a ghost. But what could I do at my age? And, besides, I did not actually see her so as to speak to her. I only touched her as she passed."

"And you are sure it was—" The boy was older than Sophy, and understood better. He could not speak so glibly of everything as she did.

"Mamma? Yes, of course I am sure. I don't take fits like the rest; I always know what I see. Don't you think Uncle John was the one to do something about it, Rex? And he has not done anything. It could never be thought that it was a thing for me."

"I'll tell you what, Sophy," said Rex, almost losing his oars in his vehemence; "soon it'll have to be a thing for me. I can't let things go on like this with all Aunt Sophy's muddlings and Uncle John's. The children will be driven out of their senses; and Rosalind is just a romantic—I am the head of the family, and I shall have to interfere."

"But you are only seventeen," said Sophy, her eyes starting from their sockets with excitement and delight.

"But I am the head of the house. John Trevanion may give himself as many airs as he likes, but he is only a younger son. After all, it is I that have got to decide what's right for my family. I have been thinking a great deal about it," he cried. "If—if—Mrs. Trevanion is to come like this frightening people out of their wits—"

"Oh, Reginald," cried Sophy, with a mixture of admiration and horror, "how can you call mamma Mrs. Trevanion?"

"That's her name," said the boy. His lips quivered a little, to do him justice, and his face was darkly red with passion, which was scarcely his fault, so unnatural were all the circumstances. "I am going to insist that she should live somewhere, so that a fellow may say where she lives. It's awful when people ask you where's your mother, not to be able to say. I suppose she has enough to live on. I shall propose to let her choose where she pleases, but to make her stay in one place, so that she can be found when she is wanted. Amy could be sent to her for a bit, and then the fuss would be over—"

"But, Rex, you said we should lose all our money—"

"Oh, bother!" cried the boy. "Who's to say anything? Should I make a trial and expose everything to take her money from Amy? (It isn't so very much you have, any of you, that I should mind.) I suppose even, if I insisted, they might take a villa for her here or somewhere. And then one could say she lived abroad for her health. That is what people do every day. I know lots of fellows whose father, or their mother, or some one, lives abroad for their health. It would be more respectable. It would be a thing you could talk about when it was necessary," Rex said.

Sophy's mind was scarcely yet open to this view of the question. "I wish you had told me," she said peevishly, "that one could get out of it like that; for I should have liked to speak to mamma—"

"I don't know that we can get out of it like that. The law is very funny; it may be impossible, perhaps. But, at all events," said Reginald, recovering his oars, and giving one great impulse forward with all his strength, which made the boat shoot along the lake like a living thing, "I know that I won't let it be muddled any longer if I can help it, and that I am going to interfere."

CHAPTER LVIII

Roland Hamerton did not find any trace of her. He had pledged himself easily, in utter ignorance of all ways and means, to find her, knowing nothing, neither how to set about such a search, or where he was likely to meet with success in it. It is easy for a young man, in his fervor, to declare that he is able to do anything for the girl he loves, and to feel that in that inspiration he is sure to carry all before him. But love will not trace the lost even when it is the agony of love for the lost, and that passion of awful longing, anxiety, and fear which is, perhaps, the most profound of all human emotions. The fact that he loved Rosalind did not convert him into that sublimated and heroic version of a detective officer which is to be found more often in fiction than reality. He, too, went to all the hotels, as John Trevanion had done; he walked about incessantly, looking at everybody he met, and trying hard, in his bad French, to push cunning inquiries everywhere—inquiries which he thought cunning, but which were in reality only very innocently anxious, betraying his object in the plainest way. "A tall lady, English, with remains of great beauty." "Oui, monsieur, nous la connaissons;" a dozen such lively responses were made to him, and he was sent in consequence to wander about as many villas, to prowl in the gardens of various hotels, rewarded by the sight of some fine Englishwomen and some scarecrows, but never with the most distant glimpse of the woman he sought. He did, however, meet and recognize almost at every turn the young fellow whose appearances at Bonport had been few since Rosalind's repulse, but whom he had seen several times in attendance upon Mrs. Lennox, and of whom he knew that he was understood to have been seen in the village at Highcourt, presumably on account of Rosalind, and was therefore a suitor too, and a rival. Something indefinable in his air, though Roland did not know him sufficiently to be a just judge, had increased at first the natural sensation of angry scorn with which a young lover looks upon another man who has presumed to lift his eyes to the same objet adoré; but presently there arose in his mind something of that same sensation of fellowship which had drawn him, on the first night of his arrival, towards Rivers. They were in "the same box." No doubt she was too good for any of them, and Everard had not the sign and seal of the English gentleman about him—the one thing indispensable; but yet there was a certain brotherhood even in the rivalry. Roland addressed him at last when he met him coming round one of the corners, where he himself was posted, gazing blankly at an English lady pointed out to him by an officious boatman from the lake. His gaze over a wall, his furtive aspect when discovered, all required, he felt, explanation. "I think we almost know each other," he said, in a not unfriendly tone. Everard took off his hat with the instinct of a man who has acquired such breeding as he has in foreign countries, an action for which, as was natural, the Englishman mildly despised him. "I have seen you, at least, often," he replied. And then Roland plunged into his subject.

"Look here! You know the Trevanions, don't you? Oh yes, I heard all about it—the children and all that. I am a very old friend;" Roland dwelt upon these words by way of showing that a stranger was altogether out of competition with him in this respect at least. "There is a lady in whom they are all—very much interested, to say the least, living somewhere about here; but I don't know where, and nobody seems to know. You seem to be very well up to all the ways of the place; perhaps you could help me. Ros—I mean," said Roland, with a cough to obliterate the syllable—"they would all be very grateful to any one who would find—"

"What," said Everard, slowly, looking in Roland's face, "is the lady's name?"

It was the most natural question; and yet the one man put it with a depth of significance which to a keener observer than Roland would have proved his previous knowledge; while the other stood entirely disconcerted, and not knowing how to reply. It was perfectly natural; but somehow he had not thought of it as a probable question. And he was not prepared with an answer.

"Oh—ah—her name. Well, she is a kind of a relation, you know—and her name would be—Trevanion."

"Oh, her name would be Trevanion? Is there supposed to be any chance that she would change her name?"

"Why do you ask such a question?"

"I thought, by the way you spoke, as if there might be a doubt."

"No," said Roland, after a moment, "I never thought—I don't think it's likely. Why should she change her name?"

Everard answered with great softness, "I don't know anything about it. Something in your tone suggested the idea, but no doubt I am wrong. No, I cannot say, all in a moment, that I am acquainted—" Here his want of experience told like Roland's. He was very willing, nay anxious, to deceive, but did not know how. He colored, and made a momentary pause. "But I will inquire," he said, "if it is a thing that the—Trevanions want to find out."

Roland looked at him with instinctive suspicion, but he did not know what he suspected. He had no desire, however, to put this quest out of his own hands into those of a man who might make capital of it as he himself intended to do. He said hastily, "Oh, I don't want to put you to trouble. I think I am on the scent. If you hear anything, however, and would come in and see me at the hotel—to-night."

The other looked at him with something in his face which Roland did not understand. Was it a kind of sardonic smile? Was it offence? He ended by repeating, "I will inquire," and took off his hat again in that Frenchified way.

And Roland went on, unaided, somewhat discouraged, indeed, with his inquiries. Sometimes he saw in the distance a figure in the crowd which he thought he recognized, and hurried after it, but never with any success. For either it was gone when he reached the spot, or turned out to be one of the ordinary people about; for of course there were many tall ladies wearing black to be seen about the streets of Aix, and most of them English. He trudged about all that day and the next with a heavy heart, his high hopes abandoning him, and the search seeming hopeless. He became aware when night fell that he was not alone in his quest. There drifted past him at intervals, hurried, flushed, and breathless, with her cloak hanging from her shoulders, her bonnet blown back from her head, her eyes always far in front of her, investigating every corner, a woman so instinct with keen suspicion and what looked like a thirst for blood that she attracted the looks even of the careless passers-by, and was followed, till she outstripped him, by more than one languid gendarme. Her purpose was so much more individual than she was that, for a time, in the features of this human sleuth-hound he failed to recognize Russell. But it was Russell, as he soon saw, with a mixture of alarm and horror. It seemed to him that some tragic force of harm was in this woman's hand, and that while he wandered vaguely round and round discovering nothing, she, grim with hatred and revenge, was on the track.

CHAPTER LIX

When John Trevanion questioned Everard, as already recorded, the young man, though greatly disconcerted, had made him a very unexpected reply. He had the boldness to say what was so near the truth that there was all the assurance of conviction in his tone; and John, on his side, was confounded. Everard had declared to him that there was a family connection, a relationship, between himself and Mr. Trevanion, though, on being more closely questioned, he declined to explain how it was; that is, he postponed the explanation, saying that he could only make the matter clear by reference to another relation, who could give him the exact information. It was a bold thought, conceived at the moment, and carried through with the daring of desperation. He felt, before it was half said, that John Trevanion was impressed by the reality in his tone, and that if he dared further, and told all his tale, the position of affairs might be changed. But Rosalind's reply to the sudden declaration which in his boldness he had made, and to his vague, ill-advised promises to reward her if she would listen to him, had driven for some days everything out of his mind; and when he met Roland Hamerton he was but beginning to recall his courage, and to say to himself that there was still something which might be done, and that things were not perhaps so hopeless as they seemed. From that brief interview he went away full of a sudden resolution. If, after all, this card was the one to play, did not he hold it in his hand? If it were by means of the lost mother that Rosalind was to be won, it was by the same means alone that he could prove to John Trevanion, all he had promised to prove, and thus set himself right with Rosalind's guardian. Thoughts crowded fast upon him as he turned away, instinctively making a round to escape Hamerton's scrutiny. This led him back at length to the precincts of the hotel, where he plunged among the shrubbery, passing round behind the house, and entered by a small door which was almost hid by a clump of laurels. A short stair led from this to a small, entirely secluded apartment separated from the other part of the hotel. The room which young Everard entered with a sort of authoritative familiarity was well lighted with three large windows opening upon the garden, but seemed to be a sort of receptacle for all the old furniture despised elsewhere. It had but one occupant, who put down the book when Everard came in, and looked up with a faint, inquiring smile. The reader does not need to be told who was the banished woman who sat here, shut out and separated from the external world. She had thought it wise, amid the risks of travel, to call herself by the name he bore, and had been living here, as everywhere, in complete retirement, before the arrival of the Trevanions. The apartment which she occupied was cheap and quiet, one of which recommendations was of weight with her in consequence of Edmund's expenses; the other for reasons of her own. She had changed greatly in the course of these two years, not only by becoming very thin and worn, but also from a kind of moral exhaustion which had taken the place of that personal power and dignity which were once the prevailing expression of her face. She had borne much in the former part of her life without having the life itself crushed out of her; but her complete transference to a strange world, her absorption in one sole subject of interest which presented nothing noble, nothing elevated, and, finally, the existence of a perpetual petty conflict in which she was always the loser, a struggle to make a small nature into a great one, or, rather, to deal with the small nature as if it were a great one, to attribute to it finer motives than it could even understand, and to appeal with incessant failure to generosities which did not exist—this had taken the strength out of Mrs. Trevanion. Her face had an air of exhausted and hopeless effort. She saw the young man approaching with a smile, which, though faint, was yet one of welcome. To be ready to receive him whenever he should appear, to be always ready and on the watch for any gleam of higher meaning, to be dull to no better impulse, but always waiting for the good—that was the part she had to play. But she was no longer impatient, no longer eager to thrust him into her own world, to convey to him her own thoughts. That she knew was an endeavor without hope. And, as a matter of fact, she had little hope in anything. She had done all that she knew how to do. If anything further were possible she was unaware what it was; and her face, like her heart, was worn out. Yet she looked up with what was not unlike a cheerful expectation. "Well, Edmund?" she said.

He threw down his hat on the table, giving emphasis to what he said.

"I have brought you some news. I don't know if you will like it or not, or if it will be a surprise. The Trevanions are after you."

The smile faded away from her face, but seemed to linger pathetically in her eyes as she looked at him and repeated, "After me!" with a start.

"Yes. Of course all those visits and apparitions couldn't be without effect. You must have known that; and you can't say I did not warn you. They are moving heaven and earth—"

"How can they do that?" she asked; and then, "You reproach me justly, Edmund; not so much as I reproach myself. I was made to do it, and frighten—my poor children."

"More than that," he said, as if he took a pleasure in adding color to the picture; "the little girl has gone all wrong in her head. She walks in her sleep and says she is looking for her mother."

The tears sprang to Mrs. Trevanion's eyes. "Oh, Edmund!" she said, "you wring my heart; and yet it is sweet! My little girl! she does not forget me!"

"Children don't forget," he said gloomily. "I didn't. I cried for you often enough, but you never came to me."

She gave him once more a piteous look, to which the tears in her eyes added pathos. "Not—till it was too late," she said.

"Not—till you were obliged; till you had no one else to go to," said he. "And you have not done very much for me since—nothing that you could help. Look here! You can make up for that now, if you like; there's every opportunity now."

"What is it, Edmund?" She relapsed into the chair, which supplied a sort of framework on which mind and body seemed alike to rest.

Edmund drew a chair opposite to her, close to her, and threw himself down in it. His hand raised to enhance his rhetoric was almost like the threat of a blow.

"Look here," he repeated; "I have told you before all I feel about Rosalind!"

"And I have told you," she said, with a faint, rising color, "that you have no right to call her by that name. There is no sort of link between Miss Trevanion and you."

"She does not think so," he answered, growing red. "She has always felt there was a link, although she didn't know what. There are two other fellows after her now. I know that one of them, and I rather think both of them, are hunting for you, by way of getting a hold on Rosalind. One of them asked me just now if I wouldn't help him. Me! And that woman that was nurse at Highcourt, that began all the mischief, is here. So you will be hunted out whatever you do. And John Trevanion is at me, asking me what had I to do with his brother? I don't know how he knows, but he does know. I've told him there was a family connection, but that I couldn't say what till I had consulted—"

"You said that, Edmund? A—family connection!"

"Yes, I did. What else could I say? And isn't it true? Now, here are two things you can do: one would be kind, generous, all that I don't expect from you; the other would, at least, leave us to fight fair. Look here! I believe they would be quite glad. It would be a way of smoothing up everything and stopping all sorts of scandal. Come up there with me straight and tell them who I am; and tell Rosalind that you want her to cast off the others and marry me. She will do whatever you tell her."

"Never, never, Edmund." She had begun to shake her head, looking at him, for some time before he would permit her voice to be heard. "Oh, ask me anything but that!"

"Anything but the only thing," he said; "that is like you; that is always the way. Can't you see it would be a way of smoothing over everything? It would free Rosalind—it would free them all; if she were my—"

She put out her hand to stop him. "No, Edmund, you must not say it. I cannot permit it. That cannot be. You do not understand her, nor she you. I can never permit it, even if—even if—"

"Even if—? You mean to say if she were—fond of me—"

Mrs. Trevanion uttered a low cry. "Edmund, I will rather go and tell her, what I have told you—that you could never understand each other—that you are different, wholly different—that nothing of the kind could be—"

He glared at her with a fierce rage, by which she was no longer frightened, which she had seen before, but which produced in her overwrought mind a flutter of the old, sickening misery which had fallen into so hopeless a calm. "That is what you will do for me—when affairs come to an issue!—that is all after everything you have promised, everything you have said—that is all; but I might have known—"

She made no reply. She was so subdued in her nature by all the hopeless struggles of the past that she did not say a word in self-defence.

"Then," he said, rising up from his chair, throwing out his hands as though putting her out of her place, "go! That's the only other thing you can do for me. Get out of this. Why stay till they come and drag you out to the light and expose you—and me? If you won't do the one thing for me, do the other, and make no more mischief, for the love of heaven—if you care for heaven or for love either," he added, making a stride towards the table and seizing his hat again. He did not, however, rush away then, as seemed his first intention, but stood for a moment irresolute, not looking at her, holding his hat in his hand.

"Edmund," she said, "you are always sorry afterwards when you say such things to me."

"No," he said, "I'm not sorry—don't flatter yourself—I mean every word I say. You've been my worst enemy all my life. And since you've been with me it's been worst of all. You've made me your slave; you've pretended to make a gentleman of me, and you've made me a slave. I have never had my own way or my fling, but had to drag about with you. And now, when you really could do me good—when you could help me to marry the girl I like, and reform, and everything, you won't. You tell me point-blank you won't. You say you'll rather ruin me than help me. Do you call that the sort of a thing a man has a right to expect—after all I have suffered in the past?"

"Edmund, I have always told you that Miss Trevanion—"

"Rosalind!" he said. "Whatever you choose to call her, I shall call her by her name. I have been everything with them till now, when this friend of yours, this Uncle John, has come. And you can put it all right with him, if you please, in a moment, and make my way clear. And now you say you won't! Oh, yes, I know you well enough. Let all those little things go crazy and everybody be put out, rather than lend a real helping hand to me—"

"Edmund!" she called to him, holding out her hands as he rushed to the door; but he felt he had got a little advantage and would not risk the loss of it again. He turned round for a moment and addressed her with a sort of solemnity.

"To-morrow!" he said. "I'll give you till to-morrow to think it over, and then—I'll do for myself whatever I find it best to do."

For a minute or two after the closing of the door, which was noisy and sharp, there was no further movement in the dim room. Mrs. Trevanion sat motionless, even from thought. The framework of the chair supported her, held her up, but for the moment, as it seemed to her, nothing else in earth and heaven. She sat entirely silent, passive, as she had done so often during these years, all her former habits of mind arrested. Once she had been a woman of energy, to whom a defeat or discouragement was but a new beginning, whose resources were manifold; but all these had been exhausted. She sat in the torpor of that hopelessness which had become habitual to her, life failing and everything in life. As she sat thus an inner door opened, and another figure, which had grown strangely like her own in the close and continual intercourse between them, came in softly. Jane was noiseless as her mistress, almost as worn as her mistress, moving like a shadow across the room. Her presence made a change in the motionless atmosphere. Madam was no longer alone; and with the softening touch of that devotion which had accompanied all her wanderings for so great a portion of her life, there arose in her a certain re-awakening, a faint flowing of the old vitality. There were, indeed, many reasons why the ice should be broken and the stream resume its flowing. She raised herself a little in her chair, and then she spoke. "Jane," she said; "Jane, I have news of the children—"

"God bless them," said Jane. She put the books down out of her hands, which she had been pretending to arrange, and turned her face towards her mistress, who said "Amen!" with a sudden gleam and lighting-up of her pale face like the sky after a storm.

"I have done very wrong," said Mrs. Trevanion; "there is never self-indulgence in the world but some one suffers for it. Jane, my little Amy is ill. She dreams about her poor mother. She has taken to walking in her sleep."

"Well, Madam, that's no great harm. I have heard of many children who did—"

"But not through—oh, such selfish folly as mine! I have grown so weak, such a fool! And they have sent for Russell, and Russell is here. You may meet her any day—"

"Russell!" Jane said, with an air of dismay, clasping her hands; "then, Madam, you must make up your mind what you will do, for Russell is not one to be balked. She will find us out."

"Why should I fear to be found out?" said Mrs. Trevanion, with a faint smile. "No one now can harm me. Jane, everything has been done that can be done to us. I do not fear Russell or any one. And sometimes it seems to me that I have been wrong all along. I think now I have made up my mind—"

"To what? oh, to what, Madam?" Jane cried.

"I am not well," said Mrs. Trevanion; "I am only a shadow of myself. I am not at all sure but perhaps I may be going to die. No, no—I have no presentiments, Jane. It is only people who want to live who have presentiments, and life has few charms for me. But look at me; you can see through my hands almost. I am dreadfully tired coming up those stairs. I should not be surprised if I were to die."

She said this apologetically, as if she were putting forth a plea to which perhaps objections might be made.

"You have come through a deal, Madam," said Jane, with the matter-of-fact tone of her class. "It is no wonder if you are thin; you have had a great deal of anxiety. But trouble doesn't kill."

"Sometimes," said her mistress, with a smile, "in the long run. But I don't say I am sure. Only, if that were so—there would be no need to deny myself."

"You will send for the children and Miss Rosalind." Jane clasped her hands with a cry of anticipation in which her whole heart went forth.

"That would be worth dying for," said Madam, "to have them all peaceably for perhaps a day or two. Ah! but I would need to be very bad before we could do that; and I am not ill, not that I know. I have thought of something else, Jane. It appears that they have found out, or think they have found out, that I am here. I cannot just steal away again as I did before. I will go to them and see them all. Ah, don't look so pleased; that probably means that we shall have to leave afterwards at once. Unless things were to happen so well, you know," she said, with a smile, "as that I should just really—die there; which would be ideal—but therefore not to be hoped for."

"Oh, Madam," said Jane, with a sob, "you don't think, when you say that—"

"Of you, my old friend? But I do. You would be glad to think, after a while, that I had got over it all. And what could happen better to me than that I should die among my own? I am of little use to Edmund—far less than I hoped. Perhaps I had no right to hope. One cannot give up one's duties for years, and then take them back again. God forgive me for leaving him, and him for all the faults that better training might have saved him from. All the tragedy began in that, and ends in that. I did wrong, and the issue is—this."

"So long ago, Madam—so long ago. And it all seemed so simple."

"To give up my child for his good, and then to be forced to give up my other children, not for their good or mine? I sometimes wonder how it was that I never told John Trevanion, who was always my friend. Why did I leave Highcourt so, without a word to any one? It all seems confused now, as if I might have done better. I might have cleared myself, at least; I might have told them. I should like to give myself one great indulgence, Jane, before I die."

"Madam!" Jane cried, with a panic which her words belied, "I am sure that it is only fancy; you are not going to die."

"Perhaps," said her mistress; "I am not sure at all. I told you so; but only I should not be surprised. Whether it is death or whether it is life, something new is coming. We must be ghosts no longer; we must come back to our real selves, you and I, Jane. We will not let ourselves be hunted down, but come out in the eye of day. It would be strange if Russell had the power to frighten me. And did I tell you that Reginald is here, too, and young Roland Hamerton, who was at Highcourt that night? They are all gathered together again for the end of the tragedy, Jane."

"Oh, Madam," cried Jane, "perhaps for setting it all right."

Her mistress smiled somewhat dreamily. "I do not see how that can be. And, even if it were so, it will not change the state of affairs. But we are not going to allow ourselves to be found out by Russell," she added, with a curious sense of the ludicrous. The occasion was not gay, and yet there was something natural, almost a sound of amusement, in the laugh with which she spoke. Jane looked at her wistfully, shaking her head.

"When I think of all that you have gone through, and that you can laugh still!—but perhaps it is better than crying," Jane said.

Mrs. Trevanion nodded her head in assent, and there was silence in the dim room where these two women spent their lives. It gave her a certain pleasure to see Jane moving about. There was a sort of lull of painful sensation, a calm, and disinclination for any exertion on her own part; a mood in which it was grateful to see another entirely occupied with her wants; anxious only to invent more wants for her, and means of doing her service. In the languor of this quiet it was not wonderful that Mrs. Trevanion should feel her life ebbing away. She began to look forward to the end of the tragedy with a pleased acquiescence. She had yielded to her fate at first, understanding it to be hopeless to strive against it; with, perhaps, a recoil from actual contact with the scandal and the shame which was as much pride as submission; but at that time her strength was not abated, nor any habit of living lost. Now that period of anguish seemed far off, and she judged herself and her actions not without a great pity and understanding, but yet not without some disapproval. She thought over it all as she sat lying back in the great chair, with Jane moving softly about. She would not repeat the decisive and hasty step she had once taken. She could not now, alas, believe in the atonement which she then thought might still be practicable in respect to the son whom she had given up in his childhood; nor did she think that it was well, as she had done then, to abandon everything without a word—to leave her reputation at the mercy of every evil-speaker. To say nothing for herself, to leave her dead husband's memory unassailed by any defence she could put forth, and to cut short the anguish of parting, for her children as well as for herself, had then seemed to her the best. And she had fondly thought, with what she now called vanity and the delusion of self-regard, that, by devoting herself to him who was the cause of all her troubles, she might make up for the evils which her desertion of him had inflicted. These were mistakes, she recognized now, and must not be repeated. "I was a fool," she said to herself softly, with a realization of the misery of the past which was acute, yet dim, as if the sufferer had been another person. Jane paused at the sound of her voice, and came towards her—"Madam, did you speak?"

"No, except to myself. My faithful Jane, you have suffered everything with me. We are not going to hide ourselves any longer," she replied.

CHAPTER LX

A resolution thus taken is not, however, strong enough to overcome the habits which have grown with years. Mrs. Trevanion had been so long in the background that she shrank from the idea of presenting herself again to what seemed to her the view of the world. She postponed all further steps with a conscious cowardice, at which, with faint humor, she was still able to smile.

"We are two owls," she said. "Jane, we will make a little reconnaissance first in the evening. There is still a moon, though it is a little late, and the lake in the moonlight is a fine sight."

"But, Madam, you were not thinking of the lake," said Jane.

"No," her mistress said; "the sight of a roof and four walls within which are—that is more to you and me than the most beautiful scenery in the world. And to think for how many years I had nothing to do but to walk from my room to the nursery to see them all!"

Jane shook her head with silent sympathy. "And it will be so again," she said, soothingly, "when Mr. Rex is of age. I have always said to myself it would come right then."

It was now Madam's turn to shake her head. The smile died away from her face. "I would rather not," she said, hurriedly, "put him to that proof. It would be a terrible test to put a young creature to. Oh, no, no, Jane! If he failed, how could I bear it?—or did for duty what should be done for love? No, no; the boy must not be put to such a test."

In the evening she carried out her idea of making a reconnaissance. She set out when the moon was rising in a vaporous autumnal sky, clearing slowly as the light increased. Madam threw back the heavy veil which she usually wore, and breathed in the keen, sweet air with almost a pang of pleasure. She grasped Jane's arm as they drove slowly round the tufted mound upon which the house of Bonport stood; then, as the coachman paused for further instructions in the shade of a little eminence on the farther side, she whispered breathlessly that she would walk a little way, and see it nearer. They got out, accordingly, both mistress and maid, tremulous with excitement. All was so still; not a creature about; the lighted windows shining among the trees; there seemed no harm in venturing within the gate, which was open, in ascending the slope a little way. Mrs. Trevanion had begun to say faintly, half to herself, half to her companion, "This is vanity; it is no use," when, suddenly, her grasp upon Jane's arm tightened so that the faithful maid had to make an effort not to cry out. "What is that?" she said, in a shrill whisper, at Jane's ear. It was nothing more than a little speck, but it moved along under the edge of the overhanging trees, with evident life in it; a speck which, as it emerged into the moonlight, became of a dazzling whiteness, like a pale flame gliding across the solid darkness. They both stood still for a moment in awe and wonder, clinging to each other. Then Madam forsook her maid's arm, and went forward with a swift and noiseless step very different from her former lingering. Jane followed, breathless, afraid, not capable of the same speed. No doubt had been in Mrs. Trevanion's mind from the first. The night air lifted now and then a lock of the child's hair, and blew cold through her long, white night-dress, but she went on steadily towards the side of the lake. Once more Amy was absorbed in her dream that her mother was waiting for her there; and, and unconscious, wrapped in her sleep, had set out to find the one great thing wanting in her life. The mother followed her, conscious of nothing save a great throbbing of head and heart. Thus they went on till the white breadth of the lake, flooded with moonlight, lay before them. Then, for the first time, Amy wavered. She came to a pause; something disturbed the absorption of her state, but without awaking her. "Mamma," she said, "where are you, mamma?"

"I am here, my darling." Mrs. Trevanion's voice was choked, and scarcely audible, in the strange mystery of this encounter. She dared not clasp her child in her arms, but stood trembling, watching every indication, terrified to disturb the illusion, yet hungering for the touch of the little creature who was her own. Amy's little face showed no surprise, its lines softened with a smile of pleasure; she put out her cold hand and placed it in that which trembled to receive it. It was no wonder to Amy, in her dream, to put her hand into her mother's. She gave herself up to this beloved guidance without any surprise or doubt, and obeyed the impulse given her without the least resistance, with a smile of heavenly satisfaction on her face. All Amy's troubles were over when her hand was in her mother's hand. Nor was her little soul, in its soft confusion and unconsciousness, aware of any previous separation, or any transport of reunion. She went where her mother led, calm as if that mother had never been parted from her. As for Mrs. Trevanion, the tumult of trouble and joy in her soul is impossible to describe. She made an imperative gesture to Jane, who had come panting after her, and now stood half stupefied in the way, only prevented by that stupor of astonishment from bursting out into sobs and cries. Her mistress could not speak; her face was not visible in the shadow as she turned her back upon the lake which revealed this wonderful group fully against its shining background. There was no sound audible but the faint stir of the leaves, the plash of the water, the cadence of her quick breathing. Jane followed in an excitement almost as overpowering. There was not a word said. Mrs. Trevanion turned back and made her way through the trees, along the winding path, with not a pause or mistake. It was dark among the bushes, but she divined the way, and though both strength and breath would have failed her in other circumstances, there was no sign of faltering now. The little terrace in front of the house, to which they reached at last, was brilliant with moonlight. And here she paused, the child standing still in perfect calm, having resigned her very soul into her mother's hands.

Then, for the first time, a great fainting and trembling seized upon her. She held out her disengaged hand to Jane. "What am I to do?" she said, with an appeal to which Jane, trembling, could give no reply. The closed doors, the curtained windows, were all dark. A momentary struggle rose in Mrs. Trevanion's mind, a wild impulse to carry the child away, to take her into her bosom, to claim her natural rights, if never again, yet for this night—mingled with a terror that seemed to take her senses from her, lest the door should suddenly open, and she be discovered. Her strength forsook her when she most wanted it. Amy stood still by her side, without a movement, calm, satisfied, wrapped in unconsciousness, knowing nothing save that she had attained her desire, feeling neither cold nor fear in the depth of her dream.

"Madam," said Jane, in an anxious whisper, "the child will catch her death. I'd have carried her. She has nothing on but her nightdress. She will catch her death."

This roused the mother in a moment, with the simplest but most profound of arguments. She bade Jane knock at the door, and, stooping over Amy, kissed her and blessed her. Then she transferred the little hand in hers to that of her faithful maid. A shiver passed through the child's frame, but she permitted herself to be led to the door. Jane was not so self-restrained as her mistress. She lifted the little girl in her arms and began to chafe and rub her feet. The touch, though was warm and kind, woke the little somnambulist, as the touch of the cold water had done before. She gave a scream and struggled out of Jane's arms.

And then there was a great sound of movement and alarm from the house. The door was flung open and Rosalind rushed out and seized Amy in her arms. She was followed by half the household, the servants hurrying out one after another; and there arose a hurried tumult of questions in the midst of which Jane stole away unnoticed and escaped among the bushes, like her mistress. Mrs. Trevanion stood quite still supporting herself against a tree while all this confused commotion went on. She distinguished Russell, who came out and looked so sharply about among the dark shrubs that for a moment she felt herself discovered, and John Trevanion, who appeared with a candle in his hand, lifting it high above his head, and inquiring who it was that had brought the child back. John's face was anxious and full of trouble; and behind him came a tall boy, slight and fair, who said there was nobody, and that Amy must have come back by herself. Then Mrs. Lennox came out with a shawl over her head, the flickering lights showing her full, comfortable person—"Who is it, John? Is there anybody? Oh, come in then, come in; it is a cold night, and the child must be put to bed." All of them stood about in their individuality, as she had left them, while she looked on in the darkness under the rustling boughs, invisible, her eyes sometimes blurred with moisture, a smile growing about her mouth. They had not changed, except the boy—her boy! She kept her eyes on his face, through the thick shade of the leaves and the flickering of the candles. He was almost a man, God bless him—a slight mustache on his upper lip, his hair darker—and so tall, like the best of the Trevanions—God bless him! But no, no, he must not be put to that test—never to that test. She would not permit it, she said to herself, with a horrible sensation in her heart, which she did not put into words, that he could not bear it. She did not seem able to move from the support of her tree even after the door was closed and all was silent again. Jane, in alarm, groped about the bushes till she had found her mistress, but did not succeed in leading her away. "A little longer," she said, faintly. After a while a large window on the other side of the door opened and John Trevanion came out again into the moonlight, walking up and down on the terrace with a very troubled face. By and by another figure appeared, and Rosalind joined him. "I came to tell you she is quite composed now—going to sleep again," said Rosalind. "Oh, Uncle John, something is going to happen; it is coming nearer and nearer. I am sure that, either living or dead, Amy has seen mamma."

"My dear, all these agitations are too much for you," said John Trevanion. "I think I must take you away."

"Uncle John, it is not agitation. I was not agitated to-night; I was quite at ease, thinking about—oh, thinking about very different things; I am ashamed of myself when I remember how little I was thinking. Russell is right, and I was to blame."

"My dear, I believe there is a safeguard against bodily ailments in that condition. We must look after her better again."

"But she has seen mamma, Uncle John!"

"Rosalind, you are so full of sense—"

"What has sense to do with it?" she cried. "Do you think the child came back by herself? And yet there was no one with her—no one. Who else could have led her back? Mamma took away her hand and she awoke. Uncle John, none of you can find her; but if she is not dead—and you say she is not dead—my mother must be here."

Jane had dropped upon her knees, and was keeping down by force, with her face pressed against her mistress's dress, her sobs and tears. But Mrs. Trevanion clung to her tree and listened and made no sound. There was a smile upon her face of pleasure that was heartrending, more pitiful than pain.

"My dear Rosalind," said John, in great distress, "my dearest girl! I have told you she is not dead. And if she is here we shall find her. We are certain to find her. Rosalind, if she were here, what would she say to you? Not to agitate and excite yourself, to try to be calm, to wait. My dear," he said, with a tremble in his voice, "your mother would never wish to disturb your life; she would like you to be—happy; she would like you—you know—your mother—"

It appeared that he became incoherent, and could say no more.

The house was closed again and all quiet before Jane, who had been in despair, could lead Mrs. Trevanion away. She yielded at length from weakness; but she did not hear what her faithful servant said to her. Her mind had fallen, or rather risen, into a state of semi-conscious exaltation, like the ecstasy of an ascetic, as her delicate and fragile form grew numb and powerless in the damp and cold.

"Did you think any one could stand and hear all that and never make a sign?" she said. "Did you see her face, Jane? It was like an angel's. I think that must be her window with the light in it. And he said her mother—John was always my friend. He said her mother—Where do you want me to go? I should like to stay in the porch and die there comfortably, Jane. It would be sweet; and then there could be no more quarrelling or questions, or putting any one to the test. No test! no test! But dying there would be so easy. And Sophy Lennox would never forbid it. She would take me in, and lay me on her bed, and bury me—like a good woman. I am not unworthy of it. I am not a bad woman, Jane."

"Oh, Madam," Jane cried, distracted, "do you know the carriage is waiting all this time? And the people of the hotel will be frightened. Come back, for goodness sake, come back!"

"The carriage," she said, with a wondering air. "Is it the Highcourt carriage, and are we going home?"

CHAPTER LXI

The day had come which Rosalind had looked forward to as the decisive moment. The day on which her life of submission was to be over, her independent action to begin. But to Rivers it was a day of almost greater import, the day on which he was to know, so far as she was concerned, what people call his fate. It was about noon when he set out from Aix, at a white heat of excitement, to know what was in store for him. He walked, scarcely conscious what he trod on, along the commonplace road; everything appeared to him as through a mist. His whole being was so absorbed in what was about to happen that at last his mind began to revolt against it. To put this power into the hands of a girl—a creature without experience or knowledge, though with all the charms which his heart recognized; to think that she, not much more than a child in comparison with himself, should thus have his fate in her hands, and keep his whole soul in suspense, and be able to determine even the tenor of his life. It was monstrous, it was ridiculous, yet true. If he left Bonport accepted, his whole career would be altered; if not—There was a nervous tremor in him, a quiver of disquietude, which he was not able conquer. To talk of women as wanting votes or freedom, when they had in their hands such unreasonable, such ridiculous, and monstrous power as this! His mind revolted though his heart obeyed. She would not, it was possible, be herself aware of the full importance of the decision she was about to make; and yet upon that decision his whole existence would turn. A great deal has been said about the subduing power of love, yet it was maddening to think that thus, in spite of reason and every dictate of good sense, the life of a man of high intelligence and mature mind should be at the disposal of a girl. Even while he submitted to that fate he felt in his soul the revolt against it. To young Roland it was natural and beautiful that it should be so, but to Rivers it was not beautiful at all; it was an inconceivable weakness in human nature—a thing scarcely credible when you came to think of it. And yet, unreasonable as it was, he could not free himself or assert his own independence. He was almost glad of this indignant sentiment as he hurried along to know his fate. When he reached the terrace which surrounded the house, looking back before he entered, he saw young Everard coming in at the gate below with an enormous bouquet in his hand. What were the flowers for? Did the fool mean to propitiate her with flowers? or had he—good heavens! was it possible to conceive that he had acquired a right to bring presents to Rosalind? This idea seemed to fill his veins with fire. The next moment he had entered into the calm of the house, which, so far as external appearances went, was so orderly, so quiet, thrilled by no excitement. He could have borne noise and confusion better. The stillness seemed to take away his breath.

And in another minute Rosalind was standing before him. She came so quickly that she must have been looking for him. There was an alarmed look in her eyes, and she, too, seemed breathless, as if her heart were beating more quickly than usual. Her lips were apart, as if already in her mind she had begun to speak, not waiting for any question from him. All this meant, must mean, a participation in his excitement. What was she going to say to him? It was in the drawing-room, the common sitting-room, with its windows open to the terrace, whence any one wandering about looking at the view, as every fool did, might step in at any moment and interrupt the conference. All this he was conscious of instantaneously, finding material in it both for the wild hope and the fierce despite which had been raging in him all the morning—to think not only that his fate was in this girl's hands, but that any vulgar interruption, any impertinent caller, might interfere! And yet what did that matter if all was to go well?

"Mr. Rivers," Rosalind said at once, with an eagerness which was full of agitation, "I have asked you to come—to tell you I am afraid you will be angry. I almost think you have reason to be angry. I want to tell you; it has not been my fault."

He felt himself drop down from vague, sunlit heights of expectation, down, down, to the end of all things, to cold and outer darkness, and looked at her blankly in the sternness and paleness of a disappointment all the greater that he had said to himself he was prepared for the worst. He had hoped to cheat fate by arming himself with that conviction; but it did not stand him in much stead. It was all he could do to speak steadily, to keep down the impulse of rising rage. "This beginning," he said, "Miss Trevanion, does not seem very favorable."

"Oh, Mr. Rivers! If I give you pain I hope you will forgive me. Perhaps I have been thoughtless—I have so much to think of, so much that has made me unhappy—and now it has all come to a crisis."

Rivers felt that the smile with which he tried to receive this, and reply to her deprecating, anxious looks, was more like a scowl than a smile. "If this is so," he said, "I could not hope that my small affair should dwell in your mind."

"Oh, do not say so. If I have been thoughtless it is not—it is not," cried Rosalind, contradicting herself in her haste, "for want of thought. And when I tell you I have made up my mind, that is scarcely what I mean. It is rather that one thing has taken possession of me, that I cannot help myself. If you will let me tell you—"

"Tell me that you have resolved to make another man happy and not me? That is very gracious, condescending," he cried, scarcely able to keep control of himself; "but perhaps, Miss Trevanion—"

"It is not that," she cried, "it is not that. It is something which it will take a long time to tell." She came nearer to him as she spoke, and putting out her hand touched his arm timidly. The agitation in his face filled her with grief and self-reproach. "Oh," she said, "forgive me if I have given you pain! When you spoke to me at the Elms, you would not let me answer you; and when you came here my mind was full—oh, full—so that I could not think of anything else."

He broke into a harsh laugh. "You do me too much honor, Miss Trevanion; perhaps I am not worthy of it. A story of love when it is not one's own is—Bah! what a savage I am! and you so kindly condescending, so sorry to give me pain! Perhaps," he cried, more and more losing the control of himself, "you may think it pleasant to drag a man like me at your chariot-wheels for a year; but I scarcely see the jest. You think, perhaps, that for a man to stake his life on the chance of a girl's favor is nothing—that to put all one's own plans aside, to postpone everything, to suspend one's being—for the payment of—a smile—" He paused for breath. He was almost beside himself with the sense of wrong—the burning and bitterness that was in his mind. He had a right to speak; a man could not thus be trifled with and the woman escape scot-free.

Rosalind stood, looking at him, turning from red to pale, alarmed, bewildered, overcome. How was she, a girl hemmed in by all the precautions of gentle life, to know what was in the heart of a man in the bitterness of his disappointment and humiliation? Sorry to have given him pain! that was all she had thought of. But it had never occurred to her that the pain might turn to rage and bitterness, and that instead of the pathos of a rejected lover, she might find herself face to face with the fury of a man who felt himself outraged, and to whom it had been a matter of resentment even that she, a slight girl, should have the disposal of his fate. She turned away to leave him without a word. But feeling something in her that must be spoken, paused a moment, holding her head high.

"I think you have forgotten yourself," she said, "but that is for you to judge. You have mistaken me, however, altogether, all through. What I meant to explain to you was something different—oh, very different. But there is no longer any room for that. And I think we have said enough to each other, Mr. Rivers." He followed her as she turned towards the door. He could not let her go, neither for love nor for hate. And by this time he began to see that he had gone too far; he followed her, entreating her to pause a moment, in a changed and trembling voice. But just then there occurred an incident which brought all his fury back. Young Everard, whom he had seen on the way, and whose proceedings were so often awkward, without perception, instead of entering in the ordinary way, had somehow strayed on to the terrace with his bouquet, perhaps because no one had answered his summons at the door, perhaps from a foolish hope that he might be allowed to enter by the window, as Mrs. Lennox, in her favor for him, had sometimes permitted him to do. He now came in sight, hesitating, in front of the open window. Rosalind was too much excited to think of ordinary rules. She was so annoyed and startled by his appearance that she made a sudden imperative movement of her hand, waving him away. It was made in utter intolerance of his intrusion, but it seemed to Rivers like the private signal of a mutual understanding too close for words, as the young fellow's indiscretion appeared to him the evidence of privileges only to be accorded to a successful lover. He stopped short with the prayer for pardon on his lips, and bursting once more into a fierce laugh of fury, cried, "Ah, here we have the explanation at last!"

Rosalind made no reply. She gave him a look of supreme indignation and scorn, and left him without a word—left him in possession of the field—with the other, the accepted one, the favored lover—good heavens!—standing, hesitating, in his awkward way, a shadow against the light. Rivers had come to a point at which the power of speech fails. It was all he could do to keep himself from seizing the bouquet and flinging it into the lake, and the bearer after it. But what was the use? If she, indeed, loved this fellow, there could be nothing further said. He turned round with furious impatience, and flung open the door into the ante-room—to find himself, breathing fire and flame as he was, and bearing every sign of his agitation in his face, in the midst of the family party streaming in from different quarters, for luncheon, all in their ordinary guise. For luncheon! at such a moment, when the mere outside appearances of composure seemed impossible to him, and his blood was boiling in his veins.

"Why, here is Rivers," said John Trevanion, "at a good moment; we are just going to lunch, as you see."

"And I am going away from Aix," said Rivers, with a sharpness which he felt to be like a gun of distress.

"Going away! that is sudden; but so much the more reason to sit down with us once more. Come, we can't let you go."

"Oh no, impossible to let you go, Mr. Rivers, without saying good-bye," said the mellow voice of Mrs. Lennox. "What a good thing we all arrived in time. The children and Rosalind would have been so disappointed to miss you. And though we are away from home, and cannot keep it as we ought, this is a little kind of feast, you know, for it is Rosalind's birthday; so you must stay and drink her health. Oh, and here is Mr. Everard too. Tell him to put two more places directly, Sophy. And how did you know it was Rosalind's birthday, Mr. Everard? What a magnificent bouquet! Come in, come in; we cannot let you go. You must drink Rosalind's health on such an important day."

Rivers obeyed, as in a dream; he was exhausted with his outbreak, remorseful, beginning to wonder whether, after all, that was the explanation? Rosalind came in alone after the rest. She was very pale, as if she had suffered too, and very grave; not a smile on her face in response to all the smiles around. For, notwithstanding the excitement and distress in the house, the family party, on the surface, was cheerful enough, smiling youthfulness and that regard for appearances which is second nature carrying it through. The dishes were handed round as usual, a cheerful din of talk arose; Rex had an appetite beyond all satisfaction, and even John Trevanion—ill-timed as it all seemed—bore a smiling face. As for Mrs. Lennox, her voice ran on with scarcely a pause, skimming over those depths with which she was totally unacquainted. "And are you really going away, Mr. Rivers?" she said. "Dear me, I am very sorry. How we shall miss you. Don't you think we shall miss Mr. Rivers dreadfully, Rosalind? But to be sure you must want to see your own people, and you must have a great deal of business to attend to after being so long away. We are going home ourselves very soon. Eh! What is that? Who is it? What are you saying, John? Oh, some message for Rosalind, I suppose."

There was a commotion at the farther end of the room, the servants attempting to restrain some one who forced her way in, in spite of them, calling loudly upon John Trevanion. It was Russell, flushed and wild—in her out-door clothes, her bonnet half falling off her head, held by the strings only, her cloak dropping from her shoulders. She pushed her way forward to John Trevanion at the foot of the table.

"Mr. John," she cried, panting, "I've got on the track of her! I told you it was no ghost. I've got on the tracks of her; and there's some here could tell you more than me."

"What is she talking about? Oh, I think the woman must have gone mad, John? She thinks since we brought her here that she may say anything. Send her away, send her away."

"I'll not be sent away," cried Russell. "I've come to do my duty to the children, and I'll do it. Mr. John, I tell you I am on her tracks, and there's two gentlemen here that can tell you all about her. Two, the young one and another. Didn't I tell you?" The woman was intoxicated with her triumph. "That one with the gray hair, that's a little more natural, like her own age—and this one," cried the excited woman, sharply, striking Everard on the shoulder, "that ran off with her. And everything I ever said is proved true."

Rivers rose to his feet instinctively as he was pointed out, and stood, asking with wonder, "What is it? What does she mean? What have I done?" Everard, who had turned round sharply when he was touched, kept his seat, throwing a quick, suspicious glance round him. John Trevanion had risen too, and so did Rex, who seized his former nurse by the arm and tried to drag her away. The boy was furious. "Be off with you, you—or I'll drag you out," he cried, crimson with passion.

At this moment, when the whole party was in commotion, the wheels of a carriage sounded in the midst of the tumult outside, and a loud knocking was heard at the door.

CHAPTER LXII

IT was difficult to explain the impulse which drew them one after another into the ante-room. On ordinary occasions it would have been the height of bad manners; and there was no reason, so far as most of the company knew, why common laws should be postponed to the exigencies of the occasion. John Trevanion hurried out first of all, and Rosalind after him, making no apology. Then Mrs. Lennox, with a troubled face, put forth her excuses—"I am sure I beg your pardon, but as they seem to be expecting somebody, perhaps I had better go and see—" Sophy, who had devoured Russell's communications with eyes dancing with excitement, had slipped from her seat at once and vanished. Rex, with a moody face and his hands in his pockets, strolled to the door, and stood there, leaning against the opening, divided between curiosity and disgust. The three men who were rivals alone remained, looking uneasily at each other. They were all standing up, an embarrassed group, enemies, yet driven together by stress of weather. Everard was the first to move; he tried to find an outlet, looking stealthily from one door to another.

"Don't you think," he said at last, in a tremulous voice, "that if there is—any family bother—we had better—go away?"

"I suppose," said Roland Hamerton, with white lips, "it must be something about Mrs. Trevanion." And he too pushed forward into the ante-room, too anxious to think of politeness, anxious beyond measure to know what Rosalind was about to do.

A little circular hall, with a marble floor, was between this ante-room and the door. The sound of the carriage driving up, the knocking, the little pause while a servant hurried through to open, gave time for all these secondary proceedings. Then there was again an interval of breathless expectation. Mrs. Lennox's travelling servant was a stranger, who knew nothing of the family history. He preceded the new-comer with silent composure, directing his steps to the drawing-room; but when he found that all the party had silently thronged into the ante-room, he made a formal pause half-way. No consciousness was in his unfaltering tones. He drew his feet into the right attitude, and then he announced the name that fell among them like a thunderbolt—"Mrs. Trevanion"—at the top of a formal voice.

She stood upon the threshold without advancing, her black veil thrown back, her black dress hanging in heavy folds about her worn figure, her face very pale, tremulous with a pathetic smile. She was holding fast by Jane with one hand to support herself. She seemed to stand there for an indefinite time, detached and separated from everything but the shadow of her maid behind her, looking at them all, on the threshold of the future, on the verge of the past; but in reality it was only for a moment. Before, in fact, they had time to breathe, a great cry rang through the house, and Rosalind flung herself, precipitated herself, upon the woman whom she adored. "Mother!" It rang through every room, thrilling the whole house from its foundations, and going through and through the anxious spectators, to whom were now added a circle of astonished servants, eager, not knowing what was happening. Mrs. Trevanion received the shock of this young life suddenly flung upon her with a momentary tottering, and, but for Jane behind her, might have fallen, even as she put forth her arms and returned the vehement embrace. Their faces met, their heads lay together for a moment, their arms closed upon each other, there was that murmur without words, of infinite love, pain, joy, undistinguishable. Then, while Rosalind still clasped and clung to her, without relaxing a muscle, holding fast as death what she had thus recovered, Mrs. Trevanion raised her head and looked round her. Her eyes were wistful, full of a yearning beyond words. Rosalind was here, but where were the others, her own, the children of her bosom? Rex stood in the doorway, red and lowering, his brows drawn down over his eyes, his shoulders up to his ears, a confused and uneasy embarrassment in every line of his figure. He said not a word, he looked straight before him, not at her. Sophy had got behind a curtain, and was peering out, her restless eyes twinkling and moving, her small figure concealed behind the drapery. The mother looked wistfully out over the head of Rosalind lying on her bosom, supporting the girl with her arms, holding her close, yet gazing, gazing, making a passionate, pathetic appeal to her very own. Was there to be no reply? Even on the instant there was a reply; a door was flung open, something white flashed across the ante-room, and added itself like a little line of light to the group formed by the two women. Oh, happiness that overflows the heart! Oh misery that cuts it through like a knife! Of all that she had brought into the world, little Amy alone!

"My mistress is not able to bear it. I told her she was not able to bear it. Let her sit down. Bring something for her; that chair, that chair! Have pity upon her!" cried Jane, with urgent, vehement tones, which roused them from the half-stupefaction with which the whole bewildered assembly was gazing. John Trevanion was the first to move, and with him Roland Hamerton. The others all stood by looking on; Rivers with the interest of a spectator at a tragedy, the others with feelings so much more personal and such a chaos of recollections and alarms. The two who had started forward to succor her put Mrs. Trevanion reverently into the great chair; John with true affection and anguish, Roland with a wondering reverence which the first glance of her face, so altered and pale, had impressed upon him. Then Mrs. Lennox bustled forward, wringing her hands; how she had been restrained hitherto nobody ever knew.

"Oh, Grace, Grace! oh, my poor Grace! oh, how ill she is looking! Oh, my dear, my dear, haven't you got a word for me? Oh, Grace, where have you been all this time, and why didn't you come to me? And how could you distrust me, or think I ever believed, or imagine I wasn't your friend! Grace, my poor dear! Oh,

Jane, is it a faint! What is it? Who has got a fan? or some wine. Bring some wine! Oh, Jane, tell us, can't you tell us, what we ought to do?"

"Nothing," said Mrs. Trevanion, rousing herself; "nothing, Sophy. I knew you were kind always. It is only—a little too much—and I have not been well. John—oh, yes, that is quite easy—comfortable. Let me rest for a moment, and then I will tell you what I have come to say."

They were all silent for that brief interval; even Mrs. Lennox did nothing but wring her hands; and those who were most concerned became like the rest, spectators of the tragedy. Little Amy, kneeling, half thrown across her mother's lap, made a spot of light upon the black dress with her light streaming hair. Rosalind stood upright, very upright, by the side of the mother whom she had found again, confronting all the world in a high, indignant championship, which was so strangely contrasted with the quiet wistfulness and almost satisfaction in the face of the woman by whom she stood. Jane, very anxious, watching every movement, her attention concentrated upon her mistress, stood behind the chair.

When Mrs. Trevanion opened her eyes she smiled. John Trevanion stood by her on one side, Rosalind on the other. She had no lack of love, of sympathy, or friendship. She looked from between them over Amy's bright head with a quivering of her lips. "Oh, no test, no test!" she said to herself. She had known how it would be. She withdrew her eyes from the boy standing gloomy in the doorway. She began to speak, and everybody but he made some unconscious movement of quickened attention. Rex did not give any sign, nor one other, standing behind, half hidden by the door.

"Sophy," she said quietly, "I have always had the fullest trust in your kindness; and if I come to your house on Rosalind's birthday that can hurt no one. This dreadful business has been going on too long—too long. Flesh and blood cannot bear it. I have grown very weak—in mind, I mean in mind. When I heard the children were near me I yielded to the temptation and went to look at them. And all this has followed. Perhaps it was wrong. My mind has got confused; I don't know."

"Oh, Grace, my dear, how could it be wrong to look at your little children, your own children, whom you were so cruelly, cruelly parted from?"

Mrs. Lennox began to cry. She adopted her sister-in-law's cause in a moment, without hesitation or pause. Her different opinion before mattered nothing now. Mrs. Trevanion understood all and smiled, and looked up at John Trevanion, who stood by her with his hand upon the chair, very grave, his face full of pain, saying nothing. He was a friend whom she had never doubted, and yet was it not his duty to enforce the separation, as it had been his to announce it to her?

"I know," she cried, "and I know what is your duty, John. Only I have a hope that something may come which will make it your duty no longer. But in the meantime I have changed my mind about many things. I thought it best before to go away without any explanations; I want now to tell you everything."

Rosalind clasped her hand more closely. "Dear mother, what you please; but not because we want explanations," she said, her eyes including the whole party in one high, defiant gaze.

"Oh no, dear, no. We want nothing but just to enjoy your society a little," cried Mrs. Lennox. "Give dear Grace your arm, and bring her into the drawing-room, John. Explanations! No, no! If there is anything that is disagreeable let it just be forgotten. We are all friends now; indeed we have always been friends," the good woman cried.

"I want to tell you how I left home," Mrs. Trevanion said. She turned to her brother-in-law, who was stooping over the back of her chair, his face partially concealed. "John, you were right, yet you were all wrong. In those terrible evenings at Highcourt"—she gave a slight shudder—"I did indeed go night after night to meet—a man in the wood. When I went away I went with him, to make up to him—the man, poor boy! he was scarcely more than a boy—was—" She paused, her eye caught by a strange combination. It brought the keenest pang of misery to her heart, yet made her smile. Everard had been drawn by the intense interest of the scene into the room. He stood in the doorway close to young Rex, who leaned against it, looking out under the same lowering brows, in the same attitude of sullen resistance. She gazed at them for a moment with sad certainty, and yet a wonder never to be extinguished. "There," she said, with a keen sharpness of anguish in her voice, "they stand together; look and you will see. My sons—both mine—and neither with anything in his heart that speaks for me!"

These words, and the unconscious group in the doorway, who were the only persons in the room unaffected by what was said, threw a sudden illumination upon the scene and the story and everything that had been. A strange thrill ran through the company as every individual turned round and gazed, and perceived, and understood. Mrs. Lennox gave a sudden cry, clasping her hands together, and Rosalind, who was holding Mrs. Trevanion's hand, gave it such a sudden pressure, emphatic, almost violent, that the sufferer moved involuntarily with the pain. John Trevanion raised his head from where he had been leaning on her chair. He took in everything with a glance. Was it an older Rex, less assured, less arrogant, but not less determined to resist all softening influences? But the effect on John was not that of an explanation, but of an alarming, horrifying discovery. He withdrew from Mrs. Trevanion's chair. A tempest of wonder and fear arose in his mind. The two in the doorway moved uneasily under the observation to which they were suddenly subjected. They gave each other a naturally defiant glance. Neither of them realized the revelation that had been made, not even Everard, though he knew it—not Rex, listening with jealous repugnance, resisting all the impulses of nature. Neither of them understood the wonderful effect that was produced upon the others by the sight of them standing side by side.

John Trevanion had suddenly taken up a new position; no one knew why he spoke in harsh, distinct tones, altogether unlike his usual friendly and gentle voice. "Let us know, now, exactly what this means; and, for God's sake, no further concealment, no evasion. Speak out for that poor boy's sake."

There was surprise in Mrs. Trevanion's eyes as she raised them to his face. "I have come to tell you everything," she said.

"Sir," said Jane, "my poor lady is far from strong. Before she says more and brings on one of her faints, let her rest—oh, let her rest."

For once in his life John Trevanion had no pity. "Her faints," he said; "does she faint? Bring wine, bring something; but I must understand this, whatever happens. It is a matter of life or death."

"Uncle John," said Rosalind, "I will not have her disturbed. Whatever there is amiss can be told afterwards. I am here to take care of her. She shall not do more than she is able for; no, not even for you."

"Rosalind, are you mad? Don't you see what hangs upon it? Reginald's position—everything, perhaps. I must understand what she means. I must understand what that means." John Trevanion's face was utterly without color; he could not stand still—he was like a man on the rack. "I must know everything, and instantly; for how can she stay here, unless—She must not stay."

This discussion, and his sharp, unhappy tone seemed to call Madam to herself.

"I did not faint," she said, softly. "It is a mistake to call them faints. I never was unconscious; and surely, Rosalind, he has a right to know. I have come to explain everything."

Roland Hamerton had been standing behind. He came close to Rosalind's side. "Madam," he said, "if you are not to stay here, wherever I have a house, wherever I can give you a shelter, it is yours; whatever I can do for you, from the bottom of my heart!"

Mrs. Trevanion opened her eyes, which had been closed. She shook her head very softly; and then she said almost in a whisper, "Rosalind, he is very good and honest and true. I should be glad if—And Amy, my darling! you must go and get dressed. You will catch cold. Go, my love, and then come back to me. I am ready, John. I want to make everything clear."

Rosalind held her hand fast. She stood like a sentinel facing them all, her left hand clasping Mrs. Trevanion's, the other free, as if in defence of her. And Roland stood close behind, ready to answer any call. He was of Madam's faction against all the world, the crowd (as it seemed to these young people), before whom she was about to make her defence. These two wanted no defence; neither did Mrs. Lennox, standing in front, wringing her hands, with her honest face full of trouble, following everything that each person said. "She is more fit to be in her bed than anywhere else," Mrs. Lennox was saying; "she is as white—as white as my handkerchief. Oh, John, you that are so reasonable, and that always was a friend to her—how can you be so cruel to her? She shall stay," cried Aunt Sophy, with a sudden outburst, "in my house—I suppose it is my house—as long as she will consent to stay."

Notwithstanding this, of all the people present, there was no one who in his heart had stood by her so closely as John Trevanion. But circumstances had so determined it that he must be her judge now. He made a pause, and then pointed to the doorway in which the two young men stood with a mutual scowl at each other. "Explain that," he said, in sharp, staccato tones, "first of all."

"Yes, John, I will explain," Mrs, Trevanion said, with humility. "When I met my husband first—" She paused as if to take breath—"I was married, and I had a child. I feel no shame now," she went on, yet with a faint color rising over her paleness. "Shame is over for me; I must tell my story without evasion, as you say. It is this, John. I thought I was a deserted wife, and my boy had a right to his name. The same ship that brought Reginald Trevanion brought the news that I was deceived. I was left in a strange country without a friend—a woman who was no wife, with a child who had no father. I thought I was the most miserable of women; but now I know better. I know now—"

John's countenance changed at once. What he had feared or suspected was never known to any of them; but his aspect changed; he tried to interrupt her, and, coming back to her side, took her other hand. "Grace," he cried, "Grace! it is enough. I was a brute to think—Grace, my poor sister—"

"Thank you, John; but I have not done. Your father," she went on, unconsciously changing, addressing another audience, "saw me, and heard my story. And he was sorry for me—oh, he was more than sorry. He was young and so was I. He proposed to me after a while that if I would give up my boy—and we had no living, nothing to keep us from starvation—and marry him, he would take care of the child; it should want for nothing, but that I must never see it more. For a long time I could not make up my mind. But poverty is very sharp; and how to get bread I knew not. The child was pining, and so was I. And I was young. I suppose," she said in a low voice, drooping her head, "I still wished, still needed to be happy. That seems so natural when one is young. And your father loved me; and I him—and I him!"

She said these words very low, with a pause between. "There, you have all my story," with a glimmer of a smile on her face. "It is a tragedy, but simple enough, after all. I was never to see the child again; but my heart betrayed me, and I deceived your father. I went and looked at my boy out of windows, waited to see him pass—once met him on a railway journey when you were with me, Rosalind—which was all wrong, wrong—oh, wrong on both sides; to your father and to him. I don't excuse myself. Then, poor boy, he fell into trouble. How could he help it? His father's blood was in him, and mine too—a woman false to my vow. He was without friend or home. When he was in great need and alarm, he came—was it not natural?—to his mother. What could be more natural? He sent for me to meet him, to help him, to tell him what to do. What could I do but go—all being so wrong, so wrong? Jane knows everything. I begged my poor boy to go away; but he was ignorant, he did not know the danger. And then Russell, you know, who had never loved me—is she there, poor woman?—found us out. She carried this story to your father. You think, and she thinks," said Mrs. Trevanion, raising herself with great dignity in her chair, "that my husband suspected me of—of—I cannot tell what shameful suspicions. Reginald," she went on, with a smile half scornful, "had no such thought. He knew me better. He knew I went to meet my son, and that I was risking everything for my son. He had vowed to me that in that case I should be cut off from him and his. Oh, yes, I knew it all. My eyes were open all the time. And he did what he had said." She drew a long breath. There was a dispassionate sadness in her voice, as of winding up a history all past. "And what was I to do?" she resumed. "Cut off from all the rest, there was a chance that I might yet be of some use to him—my boy, whom I had neglected. Oh, John and Rosalind, I wronged you. I should have told you this before; but I had not the heart. And then, there was no time to lose, if I was to be of service to the boy."

Everything was perfectly still in the room; no one had stirred; they were afraid to lose a word. When she had thus ended she made a pause. Her voice had been very calm, deliberate, a little feeble, with pauses in it. When she spoke again it took another tone; it was full of entreaty, like a prayer. She withdrew her hand from Rosalind.

"Reginald!" she said, "Rex! have you nothing to say to me, my boy!"

The direction of all eyes was changed and turned upon the lad. He stood very red, very lowering, without moving from his post against the door. He did not look at her. After a moment he began to clear his voice. "I don't know," he said, "what there is to say." Then, after another pause: "I suppose I am expected to stick to my father's will. I suppose that's my duty."

"But for all that," she said, with a pleading which went to every heart; her eyes filled, which had been quite dry, her mouth quivered with a tender smile—"for all that, oh, my boy! it is not to take me in, to make a sacrifice; but for once speak to me, come to me; I am your mother, Rex."

Sophy had been behind the curtain all the time, wrapped in it, peering out with her restless, dancing eyes. She was still only a child. Her little bosom had begun to ache with sobs kept in, her face to work, her mind to be moved by impulses beyond her power. She had tried to mould herself upon Rex, until Rex, with the shadow of the other beside him, holding back, repelling, resisting, became contemptible in Sophy's keen eyes. It was perhaps this touch of the ridiculous that affected her sharp mind more than anything else; and the sound of her mother's voice, as it went on speaking, was more than nature could bear, and roused impulses she scarcely understood within her. She resisted as long as she could, winding herself up in the curtain; but at these last words Sophy's bonds were loosed; she shook herself out of the drapery and came slowly forward, with eyes glaring red out of her pale face.

"They say," she said suddenly, "that we shall lose all our money, mamma, if we go to you."

Mrs. Trevanion's fortitude and calm had given way. She was not prepared for this trial. She turned towards the new voice and held out her arms without a word. But Sophy stood frightened, reluctant, anxious, her keen eyes darting out of her head.

"And what could I do?" she cried. "I am only a little thing, I couldn't work. If you gave up your baby because of being poor, what should we do, Rex and I? We are younger, though you said you were young. We want to be well off, too. If we were to go to you, everything would be taken from us!" cried Sophy. "Mamma, what can we do?"

Mrs. Trevanion turned to her supporters on either side of her with a smile; her lips still trembled. "Sophy was always of a logical mind," she said, with a faint half-laugh. The light was flickering round her, blackness coming where all these eager faces were. "I—I have my answer. It is just enough. I have no—complaint."

There was a sudden outcry and commotion where all had been so still before. Jane came from behind the chair and swept away, with that command which knowledge gives, the little crowd which had closed in around. "Air! air is what she wants, and to be quiet! Go away, for God's sake, all but Miss Rosalind!"

John Trevanion hurried to open the window, and the faithful servant wheeled the chair close to it in which her mistress lay. Just then two other little actors came upon the scene. Amy had obeyed her mother literally. She had gone and dressed with that calm acceptance of all wonders which is natural to childhood; then sought her little brother at play in the nursery. "Come and see mamma," she said. Without any surprise, Johnny obeyed. He had his whip in his hand, which he flourished as he came into the open space which had been cleared round that chair.

"Where's mamma?" said Johnny. His eyes sought her among the people standing about. When his calm but curious gaze found out the fainting figure he shook his hand free from that of Amy, who led him. "That!" he said, contemptuously; "that's not mamma, that's the lady."

Against the absolute certainty of his tone there was nothing to be said.

CHAPTER LXIII

Rivers had stood listening all through this strange scene, he scarcely knew why. He was roused now to the inappropriateness of his presence here. What had he to do in the midst of a family tragedy with which he had no connection? His heart contracted with one sharp spasm of pain. He had no connection with the Trevanions. He looked round him, half contemptuous of himself, for some one of whom he could take leave before he closed the door of this portion of his life behind him, and left it forever. There was no one. All the different elements were drawn together in the one central interest with which the stranger had nothing to do. Rivers contemplated the group around Mrs. Trevanion's chair as if it had been a picture. The drama was over, and all had resolved itself into stillness, whether the silence of death, or a pause only and interruption of the continuity, he could not tell. He looked round him, unconsciously receiving every detail into his mind. This was what he had given a year of his life for, to leave this household with which he had so strongly identified himself without even a word of farewell and to see them no more. He lingered only for a moment, the lines of the picture biting themselves in upon his heart. When he felt it to be so perfect that no after-experience could make it dim he went away; Roland Hamerton followed him to the door. Hamerton, on his side, very much shaken by the agitating scene, to which his inexperience knew no parallel, was eager to speak to some one, to relieve his heart.

"Do you think she is dead?" he said under his breath.

"Death, in my experience, rarely comes so easily," Rivers replied. After a pause he added, "I am going away to-night. I suppose you remain?"

"If I can be of any use. You see I have known them all my life."

"There you have the advantage of me," said the other, sharply, with a sort of laugh. "I have given them only a year of mine. Good-bye, Hamerton. Our way—does not lie the same—"

"Good-bye," said Roland, taken by surprise, and stopping short, though he had not meant to do so. Then he called after him with a kindly impulse, "We shall be sure to hear of you. Good luck! Good-bye."

Good luck! The words seemed an insult; but they were not so meant. Rivers sped on, never looking back. At the gate he made up to Everard, walking with his head down and his hands in his pockets, in gloomy discomfiture. His appearance moved Rivers to a kind of inward laugh. There was no triumph, at least, in him.

"You have come away without knowing if your mother will live or die."

"What's the use of waiting on?" said young Everard. "She'll be all right. They are only faints; all women have them; they are nothing to be frightened about."

"I think they are a great deal to be frightened about—very likely she will never leave that house alive."

"Oh, stuff!" Everard said; and then he added, half apologetically, "You don't know her as I do."

"Perhaps better than you do," said Rivers; and then he added, as he had done to Hamerton, "Our ways lie in different directions. Good-bye. I am leaving Aix to-night."

Everard looked after him, surprised. He had no good wishes to speak, as Roland had. A sense of pleasure at having got rid of an antagonist was in his mind. For his mind was of the calibre which is not aware when there comes an end. All life to him was a ragged sort of thread, going on vaguely, without any logic in it. He was conscious that a great deal had happened and that the day had been full of excitement; but how it was to affect his life he did not know.

Thus the three rivals parted. They had not been judged on their merits, but the competition was over. He who was nearest to the prize felt, like the others, his heart and courage very low; for he had not succeeded in what he had attempted; he had done nothing to bring about the happy termination; and whether even that termination was to be happy or not, as yet no one could say.

CHAPTER LXIV

Madam was conveyed with the greatest care and tenderness to the best room in the house, Mrs. Lennox's own room, which it was a great satisfaction to that kind soul to give up to her, making the little sacrifice with joy.

"I have always thought what a nice room to be ill in—don't you think it is a nice room, Grace?—and to get better in, my dear. You can step into the fresh air at once as soon as you are strong enough, and there is plenty of room for us all to come and sit with you; and, please God, we'll soon have you well again and everything comfortable," cried Mrs. Lennox, her easy tears flowing softly, her easy words rolling out like them. Madam accepted everything with soft thanks and smiles, and a quiet ending seemed to fall quite naturally to the agitated day. Rosalind spent the night by her mother's bedside—the long, long night that seemed as if it never would be done. When at last it was over, the morning made everything more hopeful. A famous doctor, who happened to be in the neighborhood, came with a humbler brother from Aix and examined the patient, and said she had no disease—no disease—only no wish or intention of living. Rosalind's heart bounded at the first words, but fell again at the end of the sentence, which these men of science said very gravely. As for Mrs. Trevanion, she smiled at them all, and made no complaint. All the day she lay there, sometimes lapsing into that momentary death which she would not allow to be called a faint, then coming back again, smiling, talking by intervals. The children did not tire her, she said. Little Johnny, accustomed to the thought that "the lady" was mamma, accepted it as quite simple, and, returning to his usual occupations, drove a coach and four made of chairs in her room, to her perfect satisfaction and his. The cracking of his whip did not disturb her. Neither did Amy, who sat on her bed, and forgot her troubles, and sang a sort of ditty, of which the burden was "Mamma has come back." Sophy, wandering long about the door of the room, at last came in too, and standing at a distance, stared at her mother with those sharp, restless eyes of hers, like one who was afraid to be infected if she made too near an approach. And later in the afternoon Reginald came suddenly in, shamefaced and gloomy, and came up to the bed, and kissed her, almost without looking at her. At other times, Mrs. Trevanion was left alone with her brother-in-law and Rosalind, who understood her best, and talked to them with animation and what seemed to be pleasure.

"Rosalind will not see," she said with a smile, "that there comes a time when dying is the most natural—the most easy way of settling everything—the most pleasant for every one concerned." There was no solemnity in her voice, though now and then it broke, and there were pauses for strength. She was the only one of the three who was cheerful and at ease. "If I were so ill-advised as to live," she added with a faint laugh, "nothing could be changed. The past, you allow, has become impossible, Rosalind; I could not go away again. That answered for once, but not again."

"You would be with me, mother, or I with you; for I am free, you know—I am free now."

Mrs. Trevanion shook her head. "John," she said, "tell her; she is too young to understand of herself. Tell her that this is the only way to cut the knot—that it is the best way—the most pleasant—John, tell her."

He was standing by with his head bent upon his breast. He made a hasty sign with his hand. He could not have spoken to save his own life, or even hers. It was all intolerable, past bearing. He stood and listened, with sometimes an outcry—sometimes, alas, a dreadful consent in his heart to what she said, but he could not speak.

The conviction that now is the moment to die, that death is the most natural, noble, even agreeable way of solving a great problem, and making the path clear not only for the individual most closely concerned, but for all around, is not unusual in life. Both in the greater historical difficulties, and in those which belong to private story, it appears often that this would be the better way. But the conviction is not always sufficient to carry itself out. Sometimes it will so happen that he or she in whose person the difficulty lies will so prevail over flesh and blood, so exalt the logic of the situation, as to attain this easy solution of the problem. But not in all cases does it succeed. Madam proved to be one of those who fail. Though she had so clearly made out what was expedient, and so fully consented to it, the force of her fine organization was such that she was constrained to live, and could not die.

And, what was more wonderful still, from the moment when she entered Mrs. Lennox's room at Bonport, the problem seemed to dissolve itself and flee away in unsubstantial vapor-wreaths like a mist, as if it were no problem at all. One of the earliest posts brought a black-edged letter from England, announcing the death of Mr. Blake, the second executor of Reginald Trevanion's will, and John, with a start of half-incredulous wonder, found himself the only responsible authority in the matter. It had already been his determination to put it to the touch, to ascertain whether such a will would stand, even with the chilling doubt upon his mind that Mrs. Trevanion might not be able to explain the circumstances which involved her in suspicion. But now suddenly, miraculously, it became apparent to him that nothing need be done at all, no publicity given, no scandal made. For who was there to take upon him the odious office of reviving so odious an instrument? Who was to demand its observance? Who interfere with the matter if it dropped into contempt? The evil thing seemed to die and come to an end without any intervention. Its conditions had become a manifest impossibility—to be resisted to the death if need were; but there was no need: for had they not in a moment become no more than a dead letter? Might not this have been from the beginning, and all the misery spared? As John Trevanion looked back upon it, asking himself this question, that terrible moment in the past seemed to him like a feverish dream. No one of the actors in it had preserved his or her self-command. The horror had been so great that it had taken their faculties from them, and Madam's sudden action, of which the reasons were only now apparent, had cut the ground from under the feet of the others, and forestalled all reasonable attempts to bring something better out of it. She had not been without blame. Her pride, too, had been in fault; her womanish haste, the precipitate measures which had made any better solution impossible. But now all that was over. Why should she die, now that everything had become clear?

The circumstances got revealed, to some extent, in Aix, among the English visitors who remained, and even to the ordinary population in a curious version, the point of the rumor being that the mysterious English lady had died with the little somnambulist in her arms, who, it was hoped for the sake of sensation, had died too. This was the rumor that reached Everard's ears on the morning after, when he went to seek his mother in the back room she had inhabited at the hotel, and found no trace of her, but this legend to explain her absence. It had been hard to get at his heart, perhaps impossible by ordinary means; but this news struck him like a mortal blow. And his organization was not like hers. He fell prostrate under it, and it was weeks before he got better and could be removed. The hands into which this weakling fell were nerveless but gentle hands. Aunt Sophy had "taken to" him from the first, and he had always responded to her kindness. When he was able to go home she took "Grace's boy" to her own house, where the climate was milder than at Highcourt; and by dint of a quite uncritical and undiscriminating affection, and perfect contentment with him as he was, in the virtue of his convalescence, did more to make of Edmund Everard a tolerable member of an unexacting society than his mother could ever have done. There are some natures for whose treatment it is well that their parents should be fools. It seems cruel to apply such a word to the kind but silly soul who had so much true bounty and affection in her. She and he gave each other a great deal of consolation and mutual advantage in the course of the years.

Russell had been, like Everard, incapable of supposing that the victim might die under their hands; and when all seemed to point to that certainty, the shock of shame and remorse helped to change the entire tenor of her life. She who had left the village triumphantly announcing herself as indispensable to the family and the children, could not return there in circumstances so changed. She married Mrs. Lennox's Swiss servant in haste, and thereafter spent her life in angry repentance. She now keeps a Pension in Switzerland, where her quality of Englishwoman is supposed to attract English visitors, and lays up her gains bitterly amid "foreign ways," which she tells any new-comer she cannot abide.

And Rosalind did what probably Mr. Ruskin's Rosiere, tired of her seven suitors, would in most cases do—escaping from the illusions of her own imagination and from the passion which had frightened her, fell back upon the steady, faithful love which had executed no hard task for her, done no heroic deed, but only loved her persistently, pertinaciously, through all. She married Roland Hamerton some months after they all returned home. And thus this episode of family history came to an end. Probably she would have done the same without any strain of compulsion had these calamities and changes never been.

Margaret Oliphant – A Short Biography

Margaret Oliphant Wilson was born on April 4th, 1828 to Francis W. Wilson, a clerk, and Margaret Oliphant, at Wallyford, near Musselburgh, East Lothian.

She spent her childhood at Lasswade, near Dalkeith, Glasgow before moving to Liverpool.

Her youth was spent in establishing a writing style so much so that, in 1849, she had her first novel published: Passages in the Life of Mrs. Margaret Maitland based on the Scottish Free Church movement. It met with some success and was a good start to her career.

Two years later, in 1851, her third book Caleb Field was published. It was also now that she met the publisher William Blackwood in Edinburgh and was asked to contribute to his well-received Blackwood's Magazine. It was to be a lifelong endeavor. Over the course of the relationship she would have well over 100 articles published.

In May 1852, Margaret married her cousin, Frank Wilson Oliphant, at Birkenhead, and they settled at Harrington Square, Camden, London. He was an artist working primarily in stained glass. With the marriage she became Margaret Oliphant Wilson Oliphant.

Their marriage produced six children but three tragically died in infancy.

When her husband developed signs of the dreaded consumption (tuberculosis) they moved, on the advice of doctors, to warmer climes. In January 1859 it was to Florence, and then to Rome where, sadly, he died.

Margaret was naturally devastated but was also now left without support and only her income from her writing. She returned to England and took up the task of supporting her three remaining children by her literary activity.

By now she was being published both as an established novelist and regularly in Blackwood's Magazine, amongst several others. Her incredible and prolific work rate increased both her commercial reputation and the size of her reading audience.

Against this her domestic life continued to be tragic, full of sorrow and disappointment.

In January 1864 her only remaining daughter, Maggie, died and was buried in her father's grave in Rome. Her brother, who had emigrated to Canada, was shortly afterwards involved in financial ruin. Margaret generously offered a home to him and his children, adding another demand to her already heavy responsibilities.

In 1866 she settled at Windsor to be closer to her sons, who were being educated at near-by Eton School. That year, her second cousin, Annie Louisa Walker, came to live with her as a companion-housekeeper. Windsor was now to be her home for the rest of her life.

Her literary career for three decades was one of constant delivery and success. Whether she wrote historical works or across several genres in fiction: domestic realism, historical, romance or supernatural she was successful.

For more than thirty years she pursued a varied literary career but family life continued to bring problems.

The literary ambitions she wished for her sons were unfulfilled. Cyril Francis, the eldest, died in 1890, leaving a Life of Alfred de Musset, which was later incorporated in his mother's Foreign Classics for English Readers. The younger, Francis, who she nicknamed 'Cecco', collaborated with her in the Victorian Age of English Literature and won a position at the British Museum, but was rejected by Sir Andrew Clark, a famous physician. Cecco died in 1894.

With the last of her children now lost to her, she had but little further interest in life. Her health steadily and inexorably declined.

Margaret Oliphant Wilson Oliphant died at the age of 69 in Wimbledon on 20th June 1897. She is buried in Eton beside her sons.

At her death, Margaret was still working on Annals of a Publishing House, a record of Blackwood's Magazine with which she had enjoyed such a successful relationship.

Her Autobiography and Letters, which present a thoughtful picture of her domestic anxieties, was published in 1899. Only parts were written with a wider audience in mind: she had originally intended the Autobiography for her son, but he died before she could finish it.

Opinions on Oliphant's work are split, with some critics seeing her as a 'domestic novelist', while others recognize her work as influential and important to the Victorian literature canon. Critical reception from her contemporaries is also divided. John Skelton took the view that Oliphant wrote too much and too quickly. Writing a Blackwood's article called 'A Little Chat About Mrs. Oliphant', he asked, "Had Mrs. Oliphant concentrated her powers, what might she not have done? We might have had another Charlotte Brontë or another George Eliot." However not all of the contemporary reception was negative. The esteemed M. R. James admired Oliphant's supernatural fiction, concluding that "the religious ghost story, as it may be called, was never done better than by Mrs. Oliphant in 'The Open Door' and 'A Beleaguered City'. Mary Butts lavished praise on Oliphant's ghost story 'The Library Window', describing it as "one masterpiece of sober loveliness".

More modern critics of Oliphant's work include Virginia Woolf, who asked in 'Three Guineas' whether Oliphant's autobiography does not lead the reader "to deplore the fact that Mrs. Oliphant sold her brain, her very admirable brain, prostituted her culture and enslaved her intellectual liberty in order that she might earn her living and educate her children."

Whatever the merits of their cases Margaret Oliphant has been shamefully neglected in modern years. She is now becoming more widely recognised as a leading writer of her day.

Margaret Oliphant – A Concise Bibliography

A canon of more than 120 works, including novels, travel books, histories, and volumes of literary criticism.

Novels
Margaret Maitland (1849)
Merkland (1850)
Caleb Field (1851)
John Drayton (1851)
Adam Graeme (1852)
The Melvilles (1852)
Katie Stewart (1852)
Harry Muir (1853)
Ailieford (1853)
The Quiet Heart (1854)
Magdalen Hepburn (1854)
Zaidee (1855)
Lilliesleaf (1855)
Christian Melville (1855)
The Athelings (1857)
The Days of My Life (1857)
Orphans (1858)

The Laird of Norlaw (1858)
Agnes Hopetoun's Schools and Holidays (1859)
Lucy Crofton (1860)
The House on the Moor (1861)
The Last of the Mortimers (1862)
Heart and Cross (1863)
Salem Chapel (1863)
The Rector (1863)
Doctor's Family (1863)
The Perpetual Curate (1864)
Miss Marjoribanks (1866)
Phoebe Junior (1876)
A Son of the Soil (1865)
Agnes (1866)
Madonna Mary (1867)
Brownlows (1868)
The Minister's Wife (1869)
The Three Brothers (1870)
John: A Love Story (1870)
Squire Arden (1871)
At his Gates (1872)
Ombra (1872
May (1873)
Innocent (1873)
The Story of Valentine and His Brother (1875)
A Rose in June (1874)
For Love and Life (1874)
Whiteladies (1875)
An Odd Couple (1875)
The Curate in Charge (1876)
Carità (1877)
Young Musgrave (1877)
Mrs. Arthur (1877)
The Primrose Path (1878)
Within the Precincts (1879)
The Fugitives (1879)
A Beleaguered City (1879)
The Greatest Heiress in England (1880)
He That Will Not When He May (1880)
In Trust (1881)
Harry Joscelyn (1881)
Lady Jane (1882)
A Little Pilgrim in the Unseen (1882)
The Lady Lindores (1883)
Sir Tom (1883)
Hester (1883)
It Was a Lover and his Lass (1883)
The Lady's Walk (1883)

The Wizard's Son (1884)
Madam (1884)
The Prodigals and Their Inheritance (1885)
Oliver's Bride (1885)
A Country Gentleman and His Family (1886)
A House Divided Against Itself (1886)
Effie Ogilvie (1886)
A Poor Gentleman (1886)
The Son of His Father (1886)
Joyce (1888)
Cousin Mary (1888)
The Land of Darkness (1888)
Lady Car (1889)
Kirsteen (1890)
The Mystery of Mrs. Biencarrow (1890)
Sons and Daughters (1890)
The Railway Man and His Children (1891)
The Heir Presumptive and the Heir Apparent (1891)
The Marriage of Elinor (1891)
Janet (1891)
The Cuckoo in the Nest (1892)
Diana Trelawny (1892)
The Sorceress (1893)
A House in Bloomsbury (1894)
Sir Robert's Fortune (1894)
Who Was Lost and is Found (1894)
Lady William (1894)
Two Strangers (1895)
Old Mr. Tredgold (1895)
The Unjust Steward (1896)
The Ways of Life (1897)

Short stories
Neighbours on the Green (1889)
A Widow's Tale and Other Stories (1898)
That Little Cutty (1898)
The Open Door (1918)

Selected Articles
Mary Russel Mitford (Blackwood's Magazine, Vol. 75, 1854)
Evelin and Pepys (Blackwood's Magazine, Vol. 76, 1854)
The Holy Land (Blackwood's Magazine, Vol. 76, 1854)
Mr. Thackeray and his Novels (Blackwood's Magazine, Vol. 77, 1855)
Bulwer (Blackwood's Magazine, Vol. 77, 1855)
Charles Dickens (Blackwood's Magazine, Vol. 77, 1855)
Modern Novelists—Great and Small (Blackwood's Magazine, Vol. 77, 1855)

Modern Light Literature: Poetry (Blackwood's Magazine, Vol. 79, 1856)
Religion in Common Life (Blackwood's Magazine, Vol. 79, 1856)
Sydney Smith (Blackwood's Magazine, Vol. 79, 1856)
The Laws Concerning Women (Blackwood's Magazine, Vol. 79, 1856)
The Art of Caviling (Blackwood's Magazine, Vol. 80, 1856)
Béranger (Blackwood's Magazine, Vol. 83, 1858)
The Condition of Women (Blackwood's Magazine, Vol. 83, 1858)
The Missionary Explorer (Blackwood's Magazine, Vol. 83, 1858)
Religious Memoirs (Blackwood's Magazine, Vol. 83, 1858)
Social Science (Blackwood's Magazine, Vol. 88, 1860)
Scotland and her Accusers (Blackwood's Magazine, Vol. 90, 1861)
The Chronicles of Carlingford (Blackwood's Magazine 1862–1865)
Girolamo Savonarola (Blackwood's Magazine, Vol. 93, 1863)
The Life of Jesus (Blackwood's Magazine, Vol. 96, 1864)
Giacomo Leopardi (Blackwood's Magazine, Vol. 98, 1865)
The Great Unrepresented (Blackwood's Magazine, Vol. 100, 1866)
Mill on the Subjection of Women (The Edinburgh Review, Vol. 130, 1869)
The Opium-Eater (Blackwood's Magazine, Vol. 122, 1877)
Russian and Nihilism in the Novels of I. Tourgeniéf (Blackwood's Magazine, Vol. 127, 1880)
School and College (Blackwood's Magazine, Vol. 128, 1880)
The Grievances of Women (Fraser's Magazine, New Series, Vol. 21, 1880)
Mrs. Carlyle (The Contemporary Review, Vol. 43, May 1883)
The Ethics of Biography (The Contemporary Review, July 1883)
Victor Hugo (The Contemporary Review, Vol. 48, July/December 1885)
A Venetian Dynasty (The Contemporary Review, Vol. 50, August 1886)
Laurence Oliphant (Blackwood's Magazine, Vol. 145, 1889)
Tennyson (Blackwood's Magazine, Vol. 152, 1892)
Addison, the Humorist (Century Magazine, Vol. 48, 1894)
The Anti-Marriage League (Blackwood's Magazine, Vol. 159, 1896)

Biographies
Edward Irving (1862)
Francis of Assisi (1871)
Count de Montalembert (1872)
Dante (1877)
Cervantes (1880)
Life of Sheridan in the English Men of Letters series (1883)
John Tulloch (1888)
Laurence Oliphant (1892)

Historical & Critical Works
Historical Sketches of the Reign of George II (1869)
The Makers of Florence (1876)
A Literary History of England from 1760 to 1825 (1882)
The Makers of Venice (1887)
Royal Edinburgh (1890)

Jerusalem (1891)
The Makers of Modern Rome (1895)
William Blackwood and his Sons (1897)
The Sisters Brontë. In: Women Novelists of Queen Victoria's Reign (1897)

www.ingramcontent.com/pod-product-compliance
Lightning Source LLC
Chambersburg PA
CBHW052026020726
47501CB00004B/1272